THE CYCLE

Phoenix sinks into decay
Haughty dragon yearns to slay.
Lyorn growls and lowers horn
Tiassa dreams and plots are born.
Hawk looks down from lofty flight
Dzur stalks and blends with night.
Issola strikes from courtly bow
Tsalmoth maintains though none knows how.
Vallista rends and then rebuilds
Jhereg feeds on others' kills.
Quiet iorich won't forget
Sly chreotha weaves his net.
Yendi coils and strikes, unseen
Orca circles, hard and lean.
Frightened teckla hides in grass
Jhegaala shifts as moments pass.
Athyra rules minds' interplay
Phoenix rises from ashes gray.

THE BOOK OF ATHYRA

Contains the complete text of
Athyra and Orca

Steven Brust

2003
50TH
ANNIVERSARY

ACE BOOKS, NEW YORK

THE BOOK OF ATHYRA

An Ace Book / published by arrangement
with the author

PRINTING HISTORY
Ace trade paperback edition / February 2003

The Book of Athyra, copyright © 2003 by Steven Brust.
Athyra, copyright © 1993 by Steven Brust.
Orca, copyright © 1996 by Steven Brust.
Cover art by Ciruelo Cabral.
Cover design by Rita Frangie.

Visit our website at
www.penguinputnam.com
Check out the ACE Science Fiction & Fantasy newsletter!

Library of Congress Cataloging-in-Publication Data

Brust, Steven, 1955–
[Athyra]
The book of Athyra / Steven Brust.
p.   cm.
"Contains the complete text of Athyra and Orca."
ISBN 0-441-01010-5 (alk. paper)
1. Taltos, Vlad (Fictitious character)—Fiction.   I. Brust, Steven, 1955– Orca.   II. Title.

PS3552.R84 A94 2003
813".54—dc21
2002033263

ACE®
Ace Books are published by The Berkley Publishing Group,
a division of Penguin Putnam Inc., 375 Hudson Street,
New York, New York 10014.
ACE and the "A" design are trademarks
belonging to Penguin Putnam Inc.

PRINTED IN THE UNITED STATES OF AMERICA

10 9 8 7 6 5 4 3

Author's Note

One of the questions I'm most often asked is: "In what order would you recommend reading these books?" Unfortunately, I'm just exactly the wrong guy to ask. I made every effort to write them so they could be read in any order. I am aware that, in some measure at least, I have failed (I certainly wouldn't recommend starting with *Teckla*, for example), but the fact that I was trying makes me incapable of giving an answer.

Many people whose opinion I respect believe publication order is best; this volume reflects that belief. For those who want to read the books in chronological order, it would go like this: *Taltos, Yendi, Dragon, Jhereg, Teckla, Phoenix, Athyra, Orca, Issola.*

The choice, I daresay, is yours. In any case, I hope you enjoy them.

Steven Brust
Minneapolis
March 1999

Pronunciation Guide

Adrilankha	ah-dri-LAHN-kuh
Adron	Ā-drahn
Aliera	uh-LEER-uh
Athyra	uh-THĪ-ruh
Baritt	BĀR-it
Brust	brūst
Cawti	KAW-tee
Chreotha	kree-O-thuh
Dragaera	druh-GAR-uh
Drien	DREE-en
Dzur	tser
Iorich	ī-Ō-rich
Issola	î-SŌ-luh
Jhegaala	zhuh-GAH-luh
Jhereg	zhuh-REG
Kiera	KĪ-ruh
Kieron	KĪ-rahn
Kragar	KRAY-gahr
Leareth	LEER-eth
Loiosh	LOI-ōsh
Lyorn	LI-orn
Mario	MAH-ree-ō
Mellar	MEH-lar
Morrolan	muh-RŌL-uhn
Norathar	NŌ-ruh-thahr
Rocza	RAW-tsuh
Serioli	sar-ee-Ō-lee
Taltos	TAHL-tōsh
Teckla	TEH-kluh
Tiassa	tee-AH-suh
Tsalmoth	TSAHL-mōth
Verra	VEE-ruh
Valista	vuhl-ISS-tuh
Yendi	YEN-dee
Zerika	zuh-REE-kuh

ATHYRA

For Martin, and it's about time

Acknowledgments

A whole bunch of people read early stages of this book and helped repair it. They are:

Susan Allison
Emma Bull
Pamela Dean
Kara Dalkey
Fred Levy Haskell
Will Shetterly
Terri Windling

As always, I'd like to humbly thank Adrian Charles Morgan, without whose work I wouldn't have a world that was nearly so much fun to write about.

Special thanks to Betsy Pucci and Sheri Portigal for supplying the facts on which I based certain portions of this book. If there are errors, blame me, not them, and, in any case, don't try this stuff at home.

Prologue

Woman, girl, man, and boy sat together, like good companions, around a fire in the woods.

"Now that you're here," said the man, "explanations can wait until we've eaten."

"Very well," said the woman. "That smells very tasty."

"Thank you," said the man.

The boy said nothing.

The girl sniffed in disdain; the others paid no attention.

"What is it?" said the woman. "I don't recognize—"

"A bird. Should be done, soon."

"He killed it," said the girl, accusingly.

"Yes?" said the woman. "Shouldn't he have?"

"Killing is all he knows how to do."

The man didn't answer; he just turned the bird on the spit.

The boy said nothing.

"Can't you do something?" said the girl.

"You mean, teach him a skill?" said the woman. No one laughed.

"We were walking through the woods," said the girl. "Not that *I* wanted to be here—"

"You didn't?" said the woman, glancing sharply at the man. He ignored them. "He forced you to accompany him?" she said.

"Well, he didn't *force* me to, but I had to."

"Hmmm."

"And all of a sudden, I became afraid, and—"

"Afraid of what?"

"Of—well—of that place. I wanted to go a different way. But he wouldn't."

The woman glanced at the roasting bird, and nodded, recognizing it. "That's what they do," she said. "That's how they find prey, and how they frighten off predators. It's some sort of psychic ability to—"

"I don't care," said the girl.

"Time to eat," said the man.

"I started arguing with him, but he ignored me. He took out his knife and threw it into these bushes—"

"Yes," said the man. "And here it is."

"You could," said the woman, looking at him suddenly, "have just walked around it. They won't attack anything our size."

"Eat now," said the man. "We can resume the insults later."

The boy said nothing.

The woman said, "If you like. But I'm curious—"

The man shrugged. "I dislike things that play games with my mind," he said. "Besides, they're good to eat."

The boy, whose name was Savn, had remained silent the entire time.

But that was only to be expected, under the circumstances.

1

I will not marry a dung-foot peasant,
I will not marry a dung-foot peasant,
Life with him would not be pleasant.
Hi-dee hi-dee ho-la!
  Step on out and do not tarry,
  Step on back and do not tarry,
  Tell me tell me who you'll marry.
  Hi-dee hi-dee ho-la!

SAVN WAS THE FIRST one to see him, and, come to that, the first to see the Harbingers, as well. The Harbingers behaved as Harbingers do: they went unrecognized until after the fact. When Savn saw them, his only remark was to his little sister, Polinice. He said, "Summer is almost over; the jhereg are already mating."

"What jhereg, Savn?" she said.

"Ahead there, on top of Tem's house."

"Oh. I see them. Maybe they're life-mates. Jhereg do that, you know."

"Like Easterners," said Savn, for no other reason than to show off his knowledge, because Polyi was now in her eighties and starting to think that maybe her brother didn't know everything, an attitude he hadn't yet come to terms with. Polyi didn't answer, and Savn took a last look at the jhereg, sitting on top of the house. The female was larger and becoming dark brown as summer gave way to autumn; the male was smaller and lighter in color. Savn guessed that in the spring the male would be green or grey, while the female would simply turn a lighter brown. He watched them for a moment as they sat there waiting for something to die. They left the roof at that moment, circled Tem's house once, and flew off to the southeast.

Savn and Polyi, all unaware that Fate had sent an Omen circling above their heads, continued on to Tem's house and shared a large salad with

Tem's own dressing, which somehow managed to make linseed oil tasty. Salad, along with bread and thin, salty soup, was almost the only food Tem was serving, now that the flax was being harvested, so it was just as well they liked it. It tasted rather better than the drying flax smelled, but Savn was no longer aware of the smell in any case. There was also cheese, but Tem hadn't really mastered cheeses yet, not the way old Shoe had. Tem was still young as Housemasters go; he'd barely reached his five hundredth year.

Polyi found a place where she could watch the room, and took a glass of soft wine mixed with water, while Savn had an ale. Polyi wasn't supposed to have wine, but Tem never told on her, and Savn certainly wouldn't. She looked around the room, and Savn caught her eyes returning to one place a few times, so he said, "He's too young for you, that one is."

She didn't blush; another indication that she was growing up. She just said, "Who asked you?"

Savn shrugged and let it go. It seemed like every girl in town was taken with Ori, which gave the lie to the notion that girls like boys who are strong. Ori was very fair, and as pretty as a girl, but what made him most attractive was that he never noticed the attention he got, making Savn think of Master Wag's story about the norska and the wolf.

Savn looked around the house to see if Firi was there, and was both disappointed and relieved not to see her; disappointed because she was certainly the prettiest girl in town, and relieved because whenever he even thought about speaking to her he felt he had no place to put his hands.

It was only during harvest that Savn was allowed to purchase a noon meal, because he had to work from early in the morning until it was time for him to go to Master Wag, and his parents had decided that he needed and deserved the sustenance. And because there was no good way to allow Savn to buy a lunch and deny one to his sister, who would be working at the harvest all day, they allowed her to accompany him to Tem's house on the condition that she return at once. After they had eaten, Polyi returned home while Savn continued on to Master Wag's. As he was walking away, he glanced up at the roof of Tem's house, but the jhereg had not returned.

The day at Master Wag's passed quickly and busily, with mixing herbs, receiving lessons, and keeping the Master's place tidy. The Master, who was stoop-shouldered and balding, and had eyes like a bird of prey, told Savn, for the fourth time, the story of the Badger in the Quagmire, and how he swapped places with the Clever Chreotha. Savn thought he might be ready to tell that one himself, but he didn't tell Master Wag this, because he might be wrong, and the Master had a way of mocking Savn for mistakes of overconfidence that left him red-faced for hours.

So he just listened, and absorbed, and washed the Master's clothes with water drawn from the Master's well, and cleaned out the empty ceramic pots, and helped fill them with ground or whole herbs, and looked at drawings of the lung and the heart, and stayed out of the way when a visitor came to the Master for physicking.

On the bad days, Savn found himself checking the time every half hour. On the good days, he was always surprised when the Master said, "Enough for now. Go on home." This was one of the good days. Savn took his leave, and set off. The afternoon was still bright beneath the orange-red sky.

The next thing to happen, which was really the first for our purposes, occurred as Savn was returning home. The Master lived under the shadow of Smallcliff along the Upper Brownclay River, which was half a league from the village, and of course that was where he gave Savn lessons; he was the Master, Savn only an apprentice.

About halfway between Smallcliff and the village was a place where a couple of trails came together in front of the Curving Stone. Just past this was a flattened road leading down to Lord Smallcliff's manor house, and it was just there that Savn saw the stranger, who was bent over, scraping at the road with some sort of tool.

The stranger looked up quickly, perhaps when he heard Savn's footsteps, and cursed under his breath and looked up at the sky, scowling, before looking more fully at the lad. Only when the stranger straightened his back did Savn realize that he was an Easterner. They stared at each other for the space of a few heartbeats. Savn had never met an Easterner before. The Easterner was slightly smaller than Savn, but had that firm, settled look that comes with age; it was very odd. Savn didn't know what to say. For that matter, he didn't know if they spoke the same language.

"Good evening," said the Easterner at last, speaking like a native, although a native of a place considerably south of Smallcliff.

Savn gave him a good evening, too, and, not knowing what to do next, waited. It was odd, looking at someone who would grow old and die while you were still young. *He's probably younger than I am right now,* thought Savn, startled. The Easterner was wearing mostly green and was dressed for traveling, with a light raincape over his shoulder and a pack on the road next to him. There was a very fragile-looking sword at his hip, and in his hand was the instrument he'd been digging with—a long, straight dagger. Savn was staring at it when he noticed that one of the Easterner's hands had only four fingers. He wondered if this was normal for them. At that moment, the stranger said, "I hadn't expected anyone to be coming along this road."

"Not many do," said Savn, speaking to him as if he were human; that is, an equal. "My Master lives along this road, and Lord Smallcliff's manor is down that one."

The stranger nodded. His eyes and hair were dark brown, almost black, as was the thick hair that grew above his lip, and if he were human one would have said he was quite husky and very short, but this condition might, thought Savn, be normal among Easterners. He was slightly bow-legged, and he stood with his head a little forward from his shoulders, as if it hadn't been put on quite right and was liable to fall off at any moment. Also, there was something odd about his voice that the young man couldn't quite figure out.

Savn cleared his throat and said, "Did I, um, interrupt something?"

The other smiled, but it wasn't clear what sort of thought or emotion might have prompted that smile. "Are you familiar with witchcraft?" he said.

"Not very."

"It doesn't matter."

"I mean, I know that you, um, that it is practiced by—is that what you were doing?"

The stranger still wore his smile. "My name is Vlad," he said.

"I'm Savn."

He gave Savn a bow as to an equal. It didn't occur to Savn until later that he ought to have been offended by this. Then the one called Vlad said, "You are the first person I've met in this town. What is it called?"

"Smallcliff."

"Then there's a small cliff nearby?"

Savn nodded. "That way," he said, pointing back the way he'd come.

"That would make it a good name, then."

"You are from the south?"

"Yes. Does my speech give me away?"

Savn nodded. "Where in the south?"

"Oh, a number of places."

"Is it, um, polite to ask what your spell was intended to do? I don't know anything about witchcraft."

Vlad gave him a smile that was not unkind. "It's polite," he said, "as long as you don't insist that I answer."

"Oh." He wondered if he should consider this a refusal, and decided it would be safer to do so. It was hard to know what the Easterner's facial expressions meant, which was the first time Savn had realized how much he depended on these expressions to understand what people were saying. He said, "Are you going to be around here long?"

"I don't know. Perhaps. It depends on how it feels. I don't usually stay anywhere very long. But while we're on the subject, can you recommend an inn?"

Savn blinked at him. "I don't understand."

"A hostel?"

Savn shook his head, confused. "We're mostly pretty friendly here—"

"A place to spend the night?"

"Oh. Tem lets rooms to travelers."

"Good. Where?"

Savn hesitated, then said, "I'm going that way myself, if you would like to accompany me."

Vlad hesitated in his turn, then said, "Are you certain it would be no trouble?"

"None at all. I will be passing Tem's house in any case."

"Excellent. Then forward, Undauntra, lest fear snag our heels."

"What?"

"*The Tower and the Tree*, Act Two, Scene Four. Never mind. Lead the way."

As they set off along the Manor Road, Vlad said, "Where did you say you are off too?"

"I'm just coming home from my day with Master Wag. I'm his apprentice."

"Forgive my ignorance, but who is Master Wag?"

"He's our physicker," said Savn proudly. "There are only three in the whole country."

"A good thing to have. Does he serve Baron Smallcliff, too?"

"What? Oh, no," said Savn, shocked. It had never occurred to him that the Baron could fall ill or be injured. Although, now that Savn thought of it, it was certainly possible. He said, "His Lordship, well, I don't know what he does, but Master Wag is ours."

The Easterner nodded, as if this confirmed something he knew or had guessed.

"What do you do there?"

"Well, many things. Today I helped Master Wag in the preparation of a splint for Dame Sullen's arm, and reviewed the Nine Bracings of Limbs at the same time."

"Sounds interesting."

"And, of course, I learn to tell stories."

"Stories?"

"Of course."

"I don't understand."

Savn frowned, then said, "Don't all physickers tell stories?"

"Not where I'm from."

"The south?"

"A number of places."

"Oh. Well, you tell stories so the patient has something to keep his mind occupied while you physick him, do you see?"

"That makes sense. I've told a few stories myself."

"Have you? I love stories. Perhaps you could—"

"No, I don't think so. It was a special circumstance. Some fool kept paying me to tell him about my life; I never knew why. But the money was good. And he was able to convince me no one would hear about it."

"Is that what you do? Tell stories?"

The Easterner laughed slightly. "Not really, no. Lately I've just been wandering."

"To something, or away from something?"

Vlad shot him a quick glance. "An astute question. How old are you? No, never mind. What's the food like at this place you're taking me to?"

"Mostly salad this time of year. It's the harvest, you know."

"Oh, of course. I hadn't thought of that."

Vlad looked around as they walked. "I'm surprised," he remarked a little later, "that this has never been cleared for farming."

"Too wet on this side of the hill," said Savn. "The flax needs dry soil."

"Flax? Is that all you grow around here?"

"Almost. There's a little maize for the stock, but it doesn't really grow well in this soil. It's mostly flax."

"That accounts for it."

They reached the top of the hill and started down. Savn said, "Accounts for what?"

"The smell."

"Smell?"

"It must be flax oil."

"Oh. Linseed oil. I guess I must be used to it."

"That must have been what they served the last place I ate, too, half a day east of here."

"That would be Whiterock. I've been there twice."

Vlad nodded. "I didn't really notice the taste in the stew, but it made the salad interesting."

Savn thought he detected a hint of irony in the other's tone but he wasn't certain. "Some types of flax are used for cooking, some we use to make linen."

"Linen?"

"Yes."

"You cook with the same stuff you make clothes out of?"

"No, not the same. It's different."

"They probably made a mistake, then," said Vlad. "That would account for the salad."

Savn glanced back at him, but still wasn't certain if he were joking. "It's easy to tell the difference," he said. "When you make the seedblocks and leave them in the coolhouse in barrels, the true, *true* salad flax will melt—"

"Never mind," said Vlad. "I'm certain you can tell."

A pair of jhereg flew from a tree and were lost in the woods before them. Savn wondered if they might be the same pair he had seen earlier.

They came to the last hill before Tem's house. Savn said, "You never answered my question."

"Question?"

"Are you wandering to something, or away from something?"

"It's been so long, I'm not certain anymore."

"Oh. May I ask you something?"

"Certainly. I might not answer."

"If you don't tell stories, what do you *do*?"

"You mean, everyone must do something?"

"Well, yes."

"I'm not too bad a hunter."

"Oh."

"And I have a few pieces of gold, which I show around when I have to."

"You just show them around?"

"That's right."

"What does that do?"

"Makes people want to take them away from me."

"Well, yes, but—"

"And when they try, I end up with whatever they're carrying, which is usually enough for my humble needs."

Savn looked at him, again trying to decide if he were joking, but the Easterner's mouth was all but hidden beneath the black hair that grew above his lip.

Savn tore his eyes away, lest he be thought rude. "That's it below, sir," he said, wondering if he ought to say "sir" to an Easterner.

"Call me Vlad."

"All right. I hope the house is to your liking."

"I'm certain it will be fine," he said. "Spend a few weeks in the jungles and it's amazing how little it takes to feel like luxury. May I give you something?"

Savn frowned, taken by a sudden suspicion he couldn't explain. "What do you mean?"

"It is the custom of my people to give a gift to the first person we meet in a new land. It is supposed to bring luck. I don't know that I believe it, but I've taken to following the old customs anyway."

"What—?"

"Here." He reached into his pouch, found something, and held it out.

"What is it?" said Savn.

"A polished stone I picked up in my wanderings."

Savn stared at it, torn between fear and excitement. "Is it magical?"

"It's just a stone."

"Oh," said Savn. "It's a very nice green."

"Yes. Please keep it."

"Well, thank you," said Savn, still staring at it. It had been polished until it gleamed. Savn wondered how one might polish a stone, and why one would bother. He took it and put it into his pocket. "Maybe I'll see you again."

"Maybe you will," said Vlad, and entered the house. Savn wished he could go in with him, just to see the look on Tem's face when an Easterner walked through the door, but it was already dark and his family would be waiting for him, and Paener always got grumpy when he didn't get home to eat on time.

As Savn walked home, which was more than another league, he wondered about the Easterner—what he was doing here, whence he had come, whither he would go, and whether he was telling the truth about how he lived. Savn had no trouble believing that he hunted—(although how could he find game? Easterners couldn't be sorcerers, could they?), but the other was curious, as well as exciting. Savn found himself doubting it, and by the time he reached the twinkling light visible through the oiled window of home, he had convinced himself that the Easterner had been making it up.

At dinner that night Savn was silent and distracted, although neither Paener nor Maener noticed, being too tired to make small talk. His sister kept up a stream of chatter, and if she was aware of Savn's failure to contribute, she didn't say anything about it. The only time he was spoken to, when Mae asked him what he had learned that day from Master Wag, he just shrugged and muttered that he had been setting bones, after which his sister went off on another commentary about how stupid all the girls she knew were, and how annoying it was that she had to associate with them.

After dinner he helped with some of the work—the little that could be done by Paener's feeble light-spell. There was wood to be broken up into kindling (Paener and Maener chopped the big stuff—they said Savn wasn't old enough yet), there was clearing leftover feed from the kethna pens so scavengers wouldn't be attracted, and there was cleaning the tools for the next day's harvest.

When he was finished, he went out behind the small barn, sat down on one of the cutting stumps, and listened to the copperdove sing her night song from somewhere behind him. The copperdove would be leaving soon, going south until spring, taking with her the sparrow and the white-back, the redbird and the daythief. But for the first time, Savn wondered where they went, and what it was like there. It must be too hot for them in the summer, or they'd remain there, but other than that, what was it like? Did any people live there? If so, what were *they* like? Was there a Savn who watched the birds and wondered what happened when they flew back north?

He had a sudden image of another Savn, a Savn naked to the waist and damp with sweat, staring back.

I could just go, he thought. *Not go back inside, not stop to get anything, just walk away. Find out where the copperdove goes, and who lives there, and what they're like. I could do it now.* But he knew he wouldn't. He'd stay here, and—

And what?

He suddenly thought of the jhereg he'd seen on Tem's roof. The flying reptiles were scavengers, just as, in another sense, were those of the House of the Jhereg. Savn had seen many of the animals, but none of the nobles of that House. What would it be like to encounter one?

Why am I suddenly thinking about these things?

And, *What is happening to me?* There was a sudden vertigo, so that he almost sat down, but he was afraid to move, for the instant was as wonderful as it was terrifying. He didn't want to breathe, yet he was keenly aware of doing so, of the air moving in and out of his lungs, and even filling his whole body, which was impossible. And in front of him was a great road with brick walls and a sky that was horribly black. The road went on forever, and he knew that up ahead somewhere were branches that could lead anywhere. And looming over them was the face of the Easterner he had just met, and somehow the Easterner was opening up some paths and closing others. His heart was filled with the joy of loss and the pain of opportunity.

With some part of his consciousness, he knew what was happening; some had called it Touching the Gods, and there were supposed to be Athyra mystics who spent their lives in this state. He had heard of such experiences from friends, but had never more than half-believed them. "It's like you're touching the whole world at once," said Coral. "It's like you can see all around yourself, and inside everything," said someone he couldn't remember. And it was all of these things, but that was only a small part of it.

What did it mean? Would it leave him changed? In what way? Who would he be when it was over?

And then it *was* over; gone as quickly as it had come. Around him the copperdove still sang, and the cricket harmonized. He took deep breaths and closed his eyes, trying to burn the experience into his memory so he'd be able to taste it again. What would Mae and Pae say? And Coral? Polyi wouldn't believe him, but that didn't matter. It didn't matter if anyone believed him. In fact, he wouldn't tell them; he wouldn't even tell Master Wag. This was his own, and he'd keep it that way, because he understood one thing—he could leave if he wanted to.

Although he'd never thought about it before, he understood it with every sense of his body; he had the choice of the life of a physicker in Smallcliff, or something unknown in the world outside. Which would he choose? And when?

He sat and wondered. Presently, the chill of early autumn made him shiver, and he went back inside.

Her name was Rocza, and sometimes she even answered to it.

As she flew upward, broke through the overcast, and began to breathe again, the sky turned blue—a full, livid, dancing blue, spotted with white and grey, as on the ground below were spots of other colors, and to her there was little to choose among them. The dots above were pushed about by the wind; those below by, no doubt, something much like the wind but perhaps more difficult to recognize.

She was not pushed by the wind, and neither did it carry her; rather, she slipped around it, and through it. It is said that sailors never mock the sea, yet she mocked the winds.

Her lover was calling to her from below, and it was that strange call, the call that in all the years she had never understood. It was not food, nor danger, nor mating, although it bore a similarity to all of these; it was another call entirely, a call that meant her lover wanted them to do something for the Provider. She didn't understand what bound her lover to the Provider, but bound he was, and he seemed to want it that way. It made no sense to her.

But she responded, because he had called, and because he always responded when she called. The concept of fair play did not enter her brain, yet something very much akin whispered through her thoughts as she spun, held her breath, and sliced back through the overcast, sneering at an updraft and a swirl that she did not need. Her lover waited, and his eyes gleamed in that secret way.

She saw the Provider before she scented him, but she wasn't aware of seeing, hearing, or smelling her lover; she simply knew where he was, and so they matched, and descended, and cupped the air together to land near the short, stubby, soft neck of the Provider, and await his wishes, to which they would give full attention and at least some consideration.

2

I will not marry a serving man,
I will not marry a serving man,
All that work I could not stand.
Hi-dee hi-dee ho-la!
Step on out . . .

THE NEXT DAY WAS Endweek, which Savn spent at home, making soap and using it up, as he wryly put it to himself, but he took a certain satisfaction in seeing that the windowsill and the kitchen jars sparkled in the blaze of the open stove, and the cast-iron pump over the sink gave off its dull gleam. As he cleaned, his thoughts kept returning to the experience of the night before; yet the more he thought of it, the more it slipped away from him. *Something* had certainly happened. Why didn't he feel different?

He gradually realized that he did—that, as he cleaned, he kept thinking, *This may be one of the last times I do this.* These thoughts both excited and frightened him, until he realized that he was becoming too distracted to do a good job, whereupon he did his best to put it entirely out of his mind and just concentrate on his work.

By the time he was finished, the entire cold-cellar had new ratkill and bugkill spells on it, the newer meal in the larder had been shuffled to the back, the new preserves in their pots had been stacked beneath the old, and everything was ready for the storebought they'd be returning with in the evening. His sister worked on the hearthroom, while Mae did the outside of the house and Pae cleaned the sleeping room and the loft.

His work was done by the fourteenth hour of the morning, and everyone else's within half an hour thereafter, so that shortly before noon they had a quick lunch of maize-bread and yellow pepper soup, after which they hitched Gleena and Ticky up to the wagon and set off for town. They always made the necessary stops in the same order, generally spiraling in toward Tem's house where they would have the one bought meal of the week, along with ale for Mae, Pae, and, lately, Savn, and beetwater for Polyi while they listened to the farmers argue about whether the slight dry spell would mean lower yields and poorer crops, or would, in fact, tend to make the flax hardier in the long run. Those of Savn's age would join in, listen, and occasionally make jokes calculated to make them appear clever to their elders or to those their own age of the desired sex, except for those who were apprenticed to trade, who would sit by themselves in a corner exchanging stories of what their Masters had put them through that week. Savn had his friends among this group.

The first two stops (the livery stable for the feed supplements, and the yarner for fresh bolts of linen) went as usual—they bought the feed supplements and didn't buy any linen, although Savn fingered a yarn-dyed pattern of sharply angled red and white lines against a dark green fabric, while Mae and Pae chatted with Threader about how His Lordship was staying in his manor house near Smallcliff, and Polyi looked bored. Savn knew without asking that the fabric would be too expensive to buy, and after a while they left, Mae complimenting Threader on the linen and saying they'd maybe buy something if His Lordship left them enough of the harvest.

They skipped the ceramics shop, which they often did, though as usual they drove by; Savn wasn't sure if it was from habit or just to wave at Pots, and he never thought to ask. By the time they pulled away from Hider's place, where they got a piece of leather for Gleena's girth-strap, which was wearing out, it was past the third hour after noon and they were in sight of both the dry goods store and Tem's house.

There was a large crowd outside Tem's.

Mae, who was driving, stopped the cart and frowned. "Should we see what it is?"

"They seem to be gathered around a cart," said Pae.

Mae stared for a moment longer, then clicked the team closer.

"There's Master Wag," said Polyi, glancing at Savn as if he would be able to provide an explanation.

They got a little closer, finally stopping some twenty feet down the narrow street from the crowd and the cart. Savn and Polyi stood up and craned their necks.

"It's a dead man," said Savn in an awed whisper.

"He's right," said Pae.

"Come along," said Mae. "We don't need to be here."

"But, Mae—" said Polyi.

"Hush now," said Pae. "Your mother is right. There's nothing we can do for the poor fellow, anyway."

Polyi said, "Don't you want to know—"

"We'll hear everything later, no doubt," said Mae. "More than we want to or need to, I'm sure. Now we need to pick up some nails."

As they began to move, Master Wag's eyes fell on them like a lance. "Wait a moment, Mae," said Savn. "Master Wag—"

"I see him," said his mother, frowning. "He wants you to go to him." She didn't sound happy.

Savn, for his part, felt both excited and nervous to suddenly discover himself the center of attention of everyone gathered in the street, which seemed to be nearly everyone who lived nearby.

Master Wag did not, however, leave him time to feel much of anything. His deeply lined face was even more grim than usual, and his protruding jaw was clenching at regular intervals, which Savn had learned meant that he was concentrating. The Master said, "It is time you learned how to examine the remains of a dead man. Come along."

Savn swallowed and followed him to the horse-cart, with a roan gelding still standing patiently nearby, as if unaware that anything was wrong. On the wagon's bed was a body, on its back as if lying down to take a rest, head toward the back. The knees were bent quite naturally, both palms were open and facing up, the head—

"I know him!" said Savn. "It's Reins!"

Master Wag grunted as if to say, "I know that already." Then he said, "Among the sadder duties which befall us is the necessity to determine how someone came to die. We must discover this to learn, first, if he died by some disease that could be spread to others, and second, if he was killed by some person or animal against whom we must alert the people. Now, tell me what you see."

Before Savn could answer, however, the Master turned to the crowd and said, "Stand back, all of you! We have work to do here. Either go about your business, or stay well back. We'll tell you what we find."

One of the more interesting things about Master Wag was how his grating manner would instantly transform when he was in the presence of a patient. The corpse evidently did not qualify as a patient, however, and the Master scowled at those assembled around the wagon until they had all backed off several feet. Savn took a deep breath, proud that Master

Wag had said, "We," and he had to fight down the urge to rub his hands together as if it were actually he who had "work to do." He hoped Firi was watching.

"Now, Savn," said the Master. "Tell me what you see."

"Well, I see Reins. I mean, his body."

"You aren't looking at him. Try again."

Savn became conscious once more that he was being watched, and he tried to ignore the feeling, with some success. He looked carefully at the way the hands lay, palms up, and the position of the feet and legs, sticking out at funny angles. No one would lie down like that on purpose. Both knees were slightly bent, and—

"You aren't looking at his face," said Master Wag. Savn gulped. He hadn't *wanted* to look at the face. The Master continued, "Look at the face first, always. What do you see?"

Savn made himself look. The eyes were lightly closed, and the mouth was set in a straight line. He said, "It just looks like Reins, Master."

"And what does that tell you?"

Savn tried to think, and at last he ventured, "That he died in his sleep?"

The Master grunted. "No, but that was a better guess than many you could have made. We don't know yet that he died in his sleep, although that is possible, but we know two important things. One is that he was not surprised by death, or else that he was so surprised he had no time to register shock, and, two, that he did not die in pain."

"Oh. Yes, I see."

"Good. What else?"

Savn looked again, and said, hesitantly, "There is blood by the back of his head."

"How much?"

"Very little."

"And how much do head wounds bleed?"

"A lot."

"So, what can you tell?"

"Uh, I don't know."

"Think! When will a head wound fail to bleed?"

"When . . . oh. He was dead before he hurt his head?"

"Exactly. Very good. And do you see blood anywhere else?"

"Ummm . . . no."

"Therefore?"

"He died, then fell backward, cutting open his head on the bottom of the cart, so very little blood escaped."

The Master grunted. "Not bad, but not quite right, either. Look at the bottom of the cart. Touch it." Savn did so. "Well?"

"It's wood."

"What kind of wood?"

Savn studied it and felt stupid. "I can't tell, Master. A fir tree of some kind."

"Is it hard or soft?"

"Oh, it's very soft."

"Therefore he must have struck it quite hard in order to cut his head open, yes?"

"Oh, that's true. But how?"

"How indeed? I have been informed that the horse came into town at a walk, with the body exactly as you see it. One explanation that would account for the facts would be if he were driving along, and he died suddenly, and, at the same time or shortly thereafter, the horse was startled, throwing the already dead body into the back, where it would fall just as you see it, and with enough force to break the skin over the skull, and perhaps the skull as well. If that were the case, what would you expect to see?"

Savn was actually beginning to enjoy this—to see it as a puzzle, rather than as the body of someone he had once known. He said, "A depression in the skull, and a matching one on the cart beneath his head."

"He would have had to hit very hard indeed to make a depression in the wood. But, yes, there should be one on the back of his head. And what else?"

"What else?"

"Yes. Think. Picture the scene as it may have happened."

Savn felt his eyes widen. "Oh!" He looked at the horse. "Yes," he said. "He has run hard."

"Excellent!" said the Master, smiling for the first time. "Now we can use our knowledge of Reins. What did he do?"

"Well, he used to be a driver, but since he left town I don't know."

"That is sufficient. Would Reins ever have driven a horse into a sweat?"

"Oh, no! Not unless he was desperate."

"Correct. So either he was in some great trouble, or he was not driving the horse. You will note that this fits well with our theory that death came to him suddenly and also frightened the horse. Now, there is not enough evidence to conclude that we are correct, but it is worthwhile to make our version a tentative assumption while we look for more information."

"I understand, Master."

"I see that you do. Excellent. Now touch the body."

"Touch it?"

"Yes."

"Master . . ."

"Do it!"

Savn swallowed, reached out and laid his hand lightly on the arm nearest him, then drew back. Master Wag snorted. "Touch the skin."

He touched Reins's hand with his forefinger, then pulled away as if burned. "It's cold!" he said.

"Yes, bodies cool when dead. It would have been remarkable if it were not cold."

"But then—"

"Touch it again."

Savn did so. It was easier the second time. He said, "It is very hard."

"Yes. This condition lasts several hours, then gradually fades away. In this heat we may say that he has been dead at least four or five hours, yet not more than half a day, unless he died from the Cold Fever, which would leave him in such a condition for much longer. If that had been the cause of death, however, his features would exhibit signs of the discomfort he felt before his death. Now, let us move him."

"Move him? How?"

"Let's see his back."

"All right." Savn found that bile rose in his throat as he took a grip on the body and turned it over.

"As we suspected," said the Master. "There is the small bloodstain on the wood, and no depression, and you see the blood on the back of his head."

"Yes, Master."

"The next step is to bring him back home, where we may examine him thoroughly. We must look for marks and abrasions on his body; we must test for sorcery, we must look at the contents of his stomach, his bowels, his kidneys, and his bladder; and test for diseases and poisons; and—" He stopped, looking at Savn closely, then smiled. "Never mind," he said. "I see that your Maener and Paener are still waiting for you. This will be sufficient for a lesson; we will give you some time to become used to the idea before it comes up again."

"Thank you, Master."

"Go on, go on. Tomorrow I will tell you what I learned. Or, rather, how I learned it. You will hear everything there is to hear tonight, no doubt, when you return to Tem's house, because the gossips will be full of the news. Oh, and clean your hands carefully and fully with dirt, and then water, for you have touched death, and death calls to his own."

This last remark was enough to bring back all the revulsion that Savn had first felt when laying hands on the corpse. He went down in the road and wiped his hands thoroughly and completely, including his forearms, and then went into Tem's house and begged water to wash them with.

When he emerged, he made his way slowly through the crowd that still stood around the wagon, but he was no longer the object of attention. He noticed Speaker standing a little bit away, frowning, and not far away was Lova, who Savn knew was Firi's friend, but he didn't see Firi. He returned to his own wagon while behind him Master Wag called for someone to drive him and the body back to his home.

"What is it?" asked Polyi as he climbed up next to her, among the supplies. "I mean, I know it's a body, but—"

"Hush," said Maener, and shook the reins.

Savn didn't say anything; he just watched the scene until they went around a corner and it was lost to sight. Polyi kept pestering him in spite of sharp words from Mae and Pae until they threatened to stop the wagon and thrash her, after which she went into a sulk.

"Never mind," said Pae. "We'll find out all about it soon enough, I'm sure, and you shouldn't ask your brother to talk about his art."

Polyi didn't answer. Savn, for his part, understood her curiosity; he was wondering himself what Master Wag would discover, and it annoyed him that everyone in town would probably know before he did.

The rest of the errands took nearly four hours, during which time they learned nothing new, but were told several times that "Reins's body come into town from Wayfield." By the time the errands were over, Savn and Polyi were not only going mad with curiosity, but were certain they were dying of hunger as well. The cart had vanished from the street, but judging by the wagons in front and the loud voices from within, everyone for miles in any direction had heard that Reins had been brought into town, dead, and they were all curious about it, and had accordingly come to Tem's house to talk, listen, speculate, eat, drink, or engage in all of these at once.

The divisions were there, as always: most of the people were grouped in families, taking up the front half of the room, and beyond them were some of the apprenticed girls, and the apprenticed boys, and the old people were along the back. The only difference was that Savn had rarely, if ever, seen the place so full, even when Avin the Bard had come through. They would have found no place to sit had they not been seen at once by

Haysmith, whose youngest daughter Pae had saved from wolves during the flood-year a generation ago. The two men never mentioned the incident because it would have been embarrassing to them both, but Haysmith was always looking out for Pae in order to perform small services for him. In this case, he caused a general shuffling on one of the benches, and room was made for Mae, Pae, and Polyi, where it looked as if there was no room to be found.

Savn stayed with them long enough to be included in the meal that Mae, with help from Haysmith's powerful lungs, ordered from Tem. Pae and Haysmith were speculating on whether some new disease had shown up, which launched them into a conversation about an epidemic that had cost a neighbor a son and a daughter many years before Savn had been born. When the food arrived, Savn took his ale, salad, and bread, and slipped away.

Across the room, he found his friend Coral, who was apprenticed to Master Wicker. Coral managed to make room for one more, and Savn sat down.

"I wondered when you'd arrive," said Coral. "Have you heard?"

"I haven't heard what Master Wag said about how he died."

"But you know who it was?"

"I was there while the Master was; he made it a lesson." Savn swallowed the saliva that had suddenly built up in his mouth. "It was Reins," he said, "who used to make deliveries from the Sharehouse."

"Right."

"I know he left town years ago, but I don't know where he went."

"He just went away somewhere. He came into some money or something."

"Oh, did he? I hadn't heard that."

"Well, it doesn't do him any good now."

"I guess not. What killed him?"

Coral shrugged. "No one knows. There wasn't a mark on him, they say."

"And the Master doesn't know, either? He was just going to look over the body when I had to go."

"No, he came in an hour ago and spoke with Tem, said he was as confused as anyone."

"Is he still here?" asked Savn, looking around.

"No, I guess he left right away. I didn't see him myself; I just got here a few minutes ago."

"Oh. Well, what about the b—what about Reins?"

"They've already taken him to the firepit," said Coral.

"Oh. I never heard who found him."

"From what I hear, no one; he was lying dead in the back of the cart, and the horse was just pulling the cart along the road all by itself, with no one driving at all."

Savn nodded. "And it stopped here?"

"I don't know if it stopped by itself or if Master Tem saw it coming down the road, or what."

"I wonder how he died," said Savn softly. "I wonder if we'll ever know."

"I don't know. But I'll tell you one thing—I'll give you clippings for candles that it isn't an accident that that Easterner with a sword walks into town the day before Reins shows up dead."

Savn stared. "Easterner?"

"What, you don't know about him?"

In fact, the appearance of the body had driven the strange wanderer right out of Savn's mind. He stuttered and said, "I guess I know who you mean."

"Well, there you are, then."

"You think the Easterner killed him?"

"I don't know if he killed him, but my Pae said he came from the east, and that's the same way Reins came from."

"He came from—" Savn stopped; he was about to say that he came from the south, but he changed his mind and said, "Of course he came from the east; he's an Easterner."

"Still—"

"What else do you know about him?"

"Precious little," said Coral. "Have you seen him?"

Savn hesitated, then said, "I've heard a few things."

Coral frowned at him, as if he'd noticed the hesitation, then said, "They say he came on a horse."

"A horse? I didn't see a horse. Or hear about one."

"That's what I heard. Maybe he hid it."

"Where would you hide a horse?"

"In the woods."

"Well, but *why* would you hide a horse?"

"How should I know. He's an Easterner; who knows how he thinks?"

"Well, just because he has a horse doesn't mean he had anything to do with—"

"What about the sword?"

"That's true, he does have a sword."

"There, you see?"

"But if Reins was stabbed to death, Master Wag would have seen. So would I, for that matter. There wasn't any blood at all, except a little where his head hit the bed of the wagon, and that didn't happen until he was already dead."

"You can't know that."

"Master Wag can tell."

Coral looked doubtful.

"And there was no wound, anyway," repeated Savn.

"Well, okay, so he didn't kill him with the sword. Doesn't it mean anything that he carries one?"

"Well, maybe, but if you're traveling, you'd want to—"

"And, like I said, he did come from the east, and that's what everyone is saying."

"Everyone is saying that the Easterner killed him?"

"Well, do *you* think it's a coincidence?"

"I don't know," said Savn.

"Heh. If it is, I'll—" Savn didn't find out what Coral was prepared to do in case of a coincidence, because he broke off in mid-sentence, staring over Savn's shoulder toward the door. Savn turned, and at that moment all conversation in the room abruptly stopped.

Standing in the doorway was the Easterner, apparently quite at ease, wrapped in a cloak that was as grey as death.

3

I will not marry a loudmouth Speaker,
I will not marry a loudmouth Speaker,
He'd get haughty and I'd get meeker.
Hi-dee hi-dee ho-la!
    Step on out . . .

HE STARED INSOLENTLY BACK at the room, his expression impossible to read, save that it seemed to Savn that there was perhaps a smile hidden by the black hair that grew above his lip and curled down around the corners of his mouth. After giving the room one long, thorough look, he stepped fully inside and slowly came up to the counter until he was facing Tem. He spoke in a voice that was not loud, yet carried very well. He said, "Do you have anything to drink here that doesn't taste like linseed oil?"

Tem looked at him, started to scowl, shifted nervously and glanced around the room. He cleared his throat, but didn't speak.

"I take it that means no?" said Vlad.

Someone near Savn whispered, very softly, "They should send for His Lordship." Savn wondered who "they" were.

Vlad leaned against the serving counter and folded his arms; Savn wondered if he were signaling a lack of hostility, or if the gesture meant something entirely different among Easterners. Vlad turned his head so that he was looking at Tem, and said, "Not far south of here is a cliff, overlooking a river. There were quite a few people at the river, bathing, swimming, washing clothes."

Tem clenched his jaw, then said, "What about it?"

"Nothing, really," said Vlad. "But if that's Smallcliff, it's pretty big."

"Smallcliff is to the north," said Tem. "We live *below* Smallcliff."

"Well, that would explain it, then," said Vlad. "But it is really a very pleasant view; one can see for miles. May I please have some water?"

Tem looked around at the forty or fifty people gathered in the house, and Savn wondered if he were waiting for someone to tell him what to do. At last he got a cup and poured fresh water into it from the jug below the counter.

"Thank you," said Vlad, and took a long draught.

"What are you doing here?" said Tem.

"Drinking water. If you want to know why, it's because everything else tastes like linseed oil." He drank again, then wiped his mouth on the back of his hand. Someone muttered something about, "If he doesn't like it here . . ." and someone else said something about "haughty as a lord."

Tem cleared his throat and opened his mouth, shut it again, then looked once more at his guests. Vlad, apparently oblivious to all of this, said, "While I was up there, I saw a corpse being brought along the road in a wagon. They came to a large, smoking hole in the ground, and people put the body into the hole and burned it. It seemed to be some kind of ceremony."

It seemed to Savn that everyone in the room somehow contrived to simultaneously gasp and fall silent. Tem scowled, and said, "What business is that of yours?"

"I got a good look at the body. The poor fellow looked familiar, though I'm not certain why."

Someone, evidently one of those who had brought Reins to the firepit, muttered, "I didn't see you there."

Vlad turned to him, smiled, and said, "Thank you very much."

Savn wanted to smile himself, but concealed his expression behind his hand when he saw that no one else seemed to think it was funny.

Tem said, "You knew him, did you?"

"I believe so. How did he happen to become dead?"

Tem leaned over the counter and said, "Maybe you could tell us."

Vlad looked at the Housemaster long and hard, then at the guests once more, and then suddenly he laughed, and Savn let out his breath, which he had been unaware of holding.

"So that's it," said Vlad. "I wondered why everyone was looking at me like I'd come walking into town with the three-day fever. You think I killed the fellow, and then just sort of decided to stay here and see what everyone said about it, and then maybe bring up the subject in case anyone missed it." He laughed again. "I don't really mind you thinking I'd murder someone, but I am not entirely pleased with what you seem to think of my intelligence.

"But, all right, what's the plan, my friends? Are you going to stone me to death? Beat me to death? Call your Baron to send in his soldiers?" He shook his head slowly. "What a peck of fools."

"Now, look," said Tem, whose face had become rather red. "No one said you did it; we're just wondering if you know—"

"I don't know," the Easterner said. Then added, "Yet."

"But you're going to?" said Tem.

"Very likely," he said. "I will, in any case, look into the matter."

Tem looked puzzled, as if the conversation had suddenly gone in a direction for which he couldn't account. "I don't understand," he said at last. "Why?"

The Easterner studied the backs of his hands. Savn looked at them, too, and decided that the missing finger was not natural, and he wondered how Vlad had lost it. "As I said," continued Vlad, "I think I knew him. I want to at least find out why he looks so familiar. May I please have some more water?" He dug a copper piece out of a pouch at his belt and put it on the counter, then nodded to the room at large and made his way through the curtain in the back of the room, presumably to return to the chamber where he was staying.

Everyone watched him; no one spoke. The sound of his footsteps echoed unnaturally loud, and Savn fancied that he could even hear the rustle of fabric as Vlad pushed aside the door-curtain, and a scraping sound from above as a bird perched on the roof of the house.

The conversation in the room was stilted. Savn's friends didn't say anything at all for a while. Savn looked around the room in time to see Firi leaving with a couple of her friends, which disappointed him. He thought about getting up to talk to her, but realized that it would look like he was chasing her. An older woman who was sitting behind Savn muttered something about how the Speaker should do something. A voice that Savn recognized as belonging to old Dymon echoed Savn's own thought that perhaps informing His Lordship that an Easterner had drunk a glass of water at Tem's house might be considered an overreaction. This started a heated argument about who Tem should and shouldn't let stay under his roof. The argument ended when Dymon hooted with laughter and walked out.

Savn noticed that the room was gradually emptying, and he heard several people say they were going to talk to either Speaker or Bless, neither of whom was present, and "see that something was done about this."

He was trying to figure out what "this" was when Mae and Pae rose, collected Polyi, and approached him. Mae said, "Come along, Savn, it's time for us to be going home."

"Is it all right if I stay here for a while? I want to keep talking to my friends."

His parents looked at each other, and perhaps couldn't think of how to phrase a refusal, so they grunted permission. Polyi must have received some sort of rejection from one of the boys, perhaps Ori, because she made no objection to being made to leave, but in fact hurried out to the wagon while Savn was still saying goodbye to his parents and being told to be certain he was home by midnight.

In less than five minutes, the room was empty except for Tem, Savn, Coral, a couple of their friends, and a few old women who practically lived at Tem's house.

"Well," said Coral. "Isn't *he* the cheeky one?"

"Who?"

"Who do you think? The Easterner."

"Oh. Cheeky?" said Savn.

"Did you see how he looked at us?" said Coral.

"Yeah," said Lan, a large fellow who was soon to be officially apprenticed to Piper. "Like we were all grass and he was deciding if he ought to mow us."

"More like we were weeds, and not worth the trouble," said Tuk, who was Lan's older brother and was in his tenth year as Hider's apprentice. They were proud of the fact that both of them had "filled the bucket" and been apprenticed to trade.

"That's what I thought," said Coral.

"I don't know," said Savn. "I was just thinking, I sure wouldn't like to walk into a place and have everybody staring at me like that. It'd scare the blood out of my skin."

"Well, it didn't seem to disturb *him* any," said Lan.

"No," said Savn. "It didn't."

Tuk said, "We shouldn't talk about him. They say Easterners can hear anything you say about them."

"Do you believe that?" said Savn.

"It's what I've heard."

Lan nodded. "And they can turn your food bad when they want, even after you've eaten it."

"Why would he want to do that?"

"Why would he want to kill Reins?" said Coral.

"I don't think he did," said Savn.

"Why not?" said Tuk.

"Because he couldn't have," said Savn. "There weren't any marks on him."

"Maybe he's a wizard," said Lan.

"Easterners aren't wizards."

Coral frowned. "You can say what you want, I think he killed him."

"But why would he?" said Savn.

"How should I—" Coral broke off, looking around the room. "What was that?"

"It was on the roof, I think. Birds, probably."

"Yeah? Pretty big ones, then."

As if by unspoken agreement they ran to the window. Coral got there first, stuck his head out, and jerked it back in again just as fast.

"What is it?" said the others.

"A jhereg," said Coral, his eyes wide. "A big one."

"What was it doing?" said Savn.

"Just standing on the edge of the roof looking down at me."

"Huh?" said Savn. "Let me see."

"Welcome."

"Don't let its tongue touch you," said Tuk. "It's poisonous."

Savn looked out hesitantly, while Coral said, "Stand under it, but don't let it lick you."

"The gods!" said Savn, pulling his head in. "It *is* big. A female, I think. Who else wants to see?"

The others declined the honor, in spite of much urging by Savn and Coral, who, having already proven themselves, felt they wouldn't have to again. "Huh-uh," said Tuk. "They bite."

"And they spit poison," added Lan.

"They do not," said Savn. "They bite, but they don't spit, and they can't hurt you just by licking you." He was beginning to feel a bit proprietary toward them, having seen so many recently.

Meanwhile, Tem had noticed the disturbance. He came up behind them and said, "What's going on over here?"

"A jhereg," said Coral. "A big one."

"A jhereg? Where?"

"On your roof," said Savn.

"Right above the window," said Coral.

Tem glanced out, then pulled his head back in slowly, filling the boys with equal measures of admiration and envy. "You're right," he said. "It's a bad omen."

"It is?" said Coral.

Tem nodded. He seemed about to speak further, but at that moment, preceded by a heavy thumping of boots, Vlad appeared once more.

"Good evening," he said. Savn decided that what was remarkable about his voice was that it was so normal, and it ought not to be. It should be either deep and husky to match his build, or high and fluty to match his size, yet he sounded completely human.

He sat down near where Savn and his friends had been seated and said, "I'd like a glass of wine, please."

Tem clenched his teeth like Master Wag, then said, "What sort of wine?"

"Any color, any district, any characteristics, just so long as it is wet."

The old women, who had been studiously ignoring the antics of Savn and his friends, arose as one and, with imperious glares first at the Easterner, then at Tem, stalked out. Vlad continued, "I like it better here with fewer people. The wine, if you please?"

Tem fetched him a cup of wine, which Vlad paid for. He drank some, then set the mug down and stared at it, turning it in a slow circle on the table. He appeared oblivious to the fact that Savn and his friends were staring at him.

After a short time, Coral, followed by the others, made his way back to the table. It seemed to Savn that Coral was walking gingerly, as if afraid to disturb the Easterner. When they were all seated, Vlad looked at them with an expression that was a mockery of innocence. He said, "So tell me, gentlemen, of this land. What is it like?"

The four boys looked at each other. How could one answer such a question?

Vlad said, "I mean, do bodies always show up out of nowhere, or is this a special occasion?"

Coral twitched as if stung; Savn almost smiled but caught himself in time. Tuk and Lan muttered something inaudible; then, with a look at Coral and Savn, they got up and left. Coral hesitated, stood up, looked at Savn, started to say something, then followed his friends out the door.

Vlad shook his head. "I seem to be driving away business today. I really don't mean to. I hope Goodman Tem isn't unhappy with me."

"Are you a wizard?" said Savn.

Vlad laughed. "What do you know about wizards?"

"Well, they live forever, and you can't hurt them because they keep their souls in magic boxes without any way inside, and they can make you do things you don't want to do, and—"

Vlad laughed again. "Well, then I'm certainly not a wizard."

Savn started to ask what was funny; then he caught sight of Vlad's maimed hand, and it occurred to him that a wizard wouldn't have allowed that to happen.

After an uncomfortable silence, Savn said, "Why did you say that?"

"Say what?"

"About . . . bodies."

"Oh. I wanted to know."

"It was cruel."

"Was it? In fact, I meant the question. It surprises me to walk into a place like this and find that a body has followed me in. It makes me uncomfortable. It makes me curious."

"There have been others who noticed it, too."

"I'm not surprised. And whispers about me, no doubt."

"Well, yes."

"What exactly killed him?"

"No one knows."

"Oh?"

"There was no mark on him, at any rate, and my friends told me that Master Wag was puzzled."

"Is Master Wag good at this sort of thing?"

"Oh, yes. He could tell if he died from disease, or if someone beat him, or if someone cast a spell on him, or anything. And he just doesn't know yet."

"Hmmm. It's a shame."

Savn nodded. "Poor Reins. He was a nice man."

"Reins?"

"That was his name."

"An odd name."

"It wasn't his birth name; he was just called that because he drove."

"Drove? A coach?"

"No, no; he made deliveries and such."

"Really. That starts to bring something back."

"Bring something back?"

"As I said, I think I recognize him. I wonder if I could be near . . . who is lord of these lands?"

"His Lordship, the Baron."

"Has he a name?"

"Baron Smallcliff."

"And you don't know his given name?"

"I've heard it, but I can't think of it at the moment."

"How about his father's name? Or rather, the name of whoever the old Baron was?"

Savn shook his head.

Vlad said, "Does the name 'Loraan' sound familiar?"

"That's it!"

Vlad chuckled softly. "That is almost amusing."

"What is?"

"Nothing, nothing. And was Reins the man who used to make deliveries to Loraan?"

"Well, Reins drove everywhere. He made deliveries for, well, for just about everyone."

"But did his duties take him to the Baron's keep?"

"Well, I guess they must have."

Vlad nodded. "I thought so."

"Hmmm?"

"I used to know him. Only very briefly I'm afraid, but still—"

Savn shook his head. "I've never seen you around here before."

"It wasn't quite around here; it was at Loraan's keep rather than his manor house. The keep, if I recall the landscape correctly, must be on the other side of the Brownclay."

"Yes, that's right."

"And I didn't spend much time there, either." Vlad smiled as he said this, as if enjoying a private joke. Then he said, "Who is Baron now?"

"Who? Why, the Baron is the Baron, same as always."

"But after the old Baron died, did his son inherit?"

"Oh. I guess so. That was before I was born."

The Easterner's eyes widened, which seemed to mean the same thing in an Easterner that it did in a human. "Didn't the old Baron die just a few years ago?"

"Oh, no. He's been there for years and years."

"You mean Loraan is the Baron *now*?"

"Of course. Who else? I thought that's what you meant."

"My, my, my." Vlad tapped the edge of his wine cup against the table. After a moment he said, "If he died, are you certain you'd know?"

"Huh? Of course I'd know. I mean, people see him, don't they? Even if he doesn't appear around here often, there's still deliveries, and messengers, and—"

"I see. Well, this is all very interesting."

"What is?"

"I had thought him dead some years ago."

"He isn't dead at all," said Savn. "In fact, he just came to stay at his manor house, a league or so from town, near the place I first saw you."

"Indeed?"

"Yes."

"And that isn't his son?"

"He isn't married," said Savn.

"How unfortunate for him," said Vlad. "Have you ever actually seen him?"

"Certainly. Twice, in fact. He came through here with his retainers, in a big coach, with silver everywhere, and six horses, and a big Athyra embossed in—"

"Were either of these times recent?"

Savn started to speak, stopped, and considered. "What do you mean 'recent'?"

Vlad laughed. "Well taken. Within, say, the last five years?"

"Oh. No."

The Easterner took another sip of his wine, set the cup down, closed his eyes, and, after a long moment, said, "There is a high cliff over the Lower Brownclay. In fact, there is a valley that was probably cut by the river."

"Yes, there is."

"Are there caves, Savn?"

He blinked. "Many, all along the walls of the cliff. How did you know?"

"I knew about the valley because I saw it, earlier today, and the river. As for the caves, I didn't know; I guessed. But now that I do know, I would venture a further guess that there is water to be found in those caves."

"There's water in at least one of them; I've heard it trickling."

Vlad nodded. "It makes sense."

"*What* makes sense, Vlad?"

"Loraan was—excuse me—is a wizard, and one who has studied necromancy. It would make sense that he lived near a place where Dark Water flows."

"Dark Water? What is that?"

"Water that has never seen the light of day."

"Oh. But what does that have to do with—what was his name?"

"Loraan. Baron Smallcliff. Such water is useful in the practice of necromancy. When stagnant and contained, it can be used to weaken and repel the undead, but when flowing free they can use it to prolong their life. It's a bittersweet tapestry of life itself," he added, in what Savn thought was an ironic tone of voice.

"I don't understand."

"Never mind. Would it matter to you if you were to discover that your lord is undead?"

"*What?*"

"I'll take that as a yes. Good. That may matter, later."

"Vlad, I don't understand—"

"Don't worry about it; that isn't the important thing."

"You seem to be talking in riddles."

"No, just thinking aloud. The important thing isn't how he survived; the important thing is what he knows. Aye, what he knows, and what he's doing about it."

Savn struggled to make sense of this, and at last said, "What he knows about what?"

Vlad shook his head. "There are such things as coincidence, but I don't believe one can go that far." Savn started to say something, but Vlad raised his hand. "Think of it this way, my friend: many years ago, a man helped me to pull a nasty joke on your Baron. Now, on the very day I come walking through his fief, the man who helped me turns up mysteriously dead right in front of me. And the victim of this little prank moves to his manor house, which happens to be just outside the village I'm passing through. Would you believe that this could happen by accident?"

The implications of everything Vlad was saying were too many and far-reaching, but Savn was able to understand enough to say, "No."

"I wouldn't, either. And I don't."

"But what does it mean?"

"I'm not certain," Vlad said. "Perhaps it was foolish of me to come this way, but I didn't realize exactly where I was, and, in any case, I thought Loraan was . . . I thought it would be safe. Speaking of safe, I guess what it means is that I'm not, very."

Savn said, "You're leaving, then?" He was surprised to discover how disappointed he was at the thought.

"Leaving? No. It's probably too late for that. And besides, this fellow,

Reins, helped me, and if that had anything to do with his death, that
means I have matters to attend to."

Savn struggled with this, and at last said, "What matters?"

But Vlad had fallen silent again; he stared off into space, as if taken by
a sudden thought. He sat that way for nearly a minute, and from time to
time his lips seemed to move. At last he grunted and nodded faintly.

Savn repeated his question. "What matters will you have to attend to?"

"Eh?" said Vlad. "Oh. Nothing important."

Savn waited. Vlad leaned back in his chair, his eyes open but focused
on the ceiling. Twice the corner of his mouth twitched as if he were smiling; once he shuddered as if something frightened him. Savn wondered
what he was thinking about. He was about to ask, when Vlad's head
suddenly snapped down and he was looking directly at Savn.

"The other day, you started to ask me about witchcraft."

"Well, yes," said Savn. "Why—"

"How would you like to learn?"

"Learn? You mean, how to, uh—"

"We call it casting spells, just like sorcerers do. Are you interested?"

"I'd never thought about it before."

"Well, think about it."

"Why would you want to teach me?"

"There are reasons."

"I don't know."

"Frankly, I'm surprised at your hesitation. It would be useful to me if
someone knew certain spells. It doesn't have to be you; I just thought
you'd want to. I could find someone else. Perhaps one of those young
men—"

"All right."

Vlad didn't smile; he just nodded slightly and said, "Good."

"When should we begin?"

"Now would be fine," said the Easterner, and rose to his feet. "Come
with me."

*She flew above and ahead of her mate, in long, wide, overlapping circles
just below the overcast. He was content to follow, because her eyesight
was keener.*

*In fact, she knew exactly what she was looking for, and could have
gone directly there, but it was a fine, warm day for this late in the year,
and she was in no hurry to carry out the Provider's wishes. There was*

time for that; there had been no sense of urgency in the dim echo she had picked up, so why not enjoy the day?

Above her, a lazy falcon broke through the overcast, saw her, and haughtily ignored her. She didn't mind; they had nothing to argue about until the falcon made a strike; then they could play the old game of You're-quicker-going-down-but-I'm-faster-going-up. She'd played that game several times, and usually won. She had lost once to a cagey old goshawk, and she still carried the scar above her right wing, but it no longer bothered her.

She came into sight of a large structure of man, and her mate, who saw it at the same time, joined her, and they circled it once together. She thought that, in perhaps a few days, she'd be ready to mate again, but it was so hard to find a nest while traveling all the time.

Her mate sent her messages of impatience. She gave the psychic equivalent of a sigh and circled down to attend to business.

4

I will not marry a magic seer,
I will not marry a magic seer,
He'd know how to keep me here.
Hi-dee hi-dee ho-la!
Step on out . . .

SAVN HAD THOUGHT THEY would be going into Vlad's room, but instead the Easterner led them out onto the street. There was still some light, but it was gradually fading, the overcast becoming more red than orange, and accenting the scarlet highlights on the bricks of Shoe's old house across the way. There were a few people walking past, but they seemed intent on business of their own; the excitement of a few short hours before had evaporated like a puddle of water on a dry day. And those who were out seemed, as far as Savn could tell, intent on ignoring the Easterner.

Savn wondered why he wasn't more excited about the idea of learning Eastern magic, and came to the conclusion that it was because he didn't really believe it would happen. *Well, then,* he asked himself, *why not? Because,* came the answer, *I don't know this Easterner, and I don't understand why he would wish to teach me anything.*

"Where are we going?" he said aloud.

"To a place of power."

"What's that?"

"A location where it is easier to stand outside and inside of yourself and the other."

Savn tried to figure out which question to ask first. At last he said, "The other?"

"The person or thing you wish to change. Witchcraft—magic—is a way of changing things. To change you must understand, and the best way to understand is to attempt change."

"I don't—"

"The illusion of understanding is a product of distance and perspective. True understanding requires involvement."

"Oh," said Savn, putting it away for a later time to either think about or not.

They were walking slowly toward the few remaining buildings on the west side of the village; Savn consciously held back the urge to run. Now they were entirely alone, save for voices from the livery stable, where Feeder was saying, "So I told him I'd never seen a kethna with a wooden leg, and how did it happen that . . ." Savn wondered who he was talking to. Soon they were walking along the Manor Road west of town. Savn said, "What makes a place of power?"

"Any number of things. Sometimes it has to do with the terrain, sometimes with things that have happened there or people who have lived there; sometimes you don't know why it is, you just feel it."

"So we're going to keep walking until you feel it?" Savn discovered that he didn't really like the idea of walking all night until they came to a place that "felt right" to the Easterner.

"Unless you know a place that is likely to be a place of power."

"How would I know that?"

"Do you know of any place where people were sacrificed?"

Savn shuddered. "No, there isn't anything like that."

"Good. I'm not certain we want to face that in any event. Well, is there any powerful sorcerer who lives nearby?"

"No. Well, you said that Lord Smallcliff is."

"Oh, yes, I did, didn't I? But it would be difficult to reach the place where he works, which I assume to be on the other side of the river, at his keep."

"Not at his manor?"

"Probably not. Of course, that's only a guess; but we can hardly go to his manor either, can we?"

"I guess not. But someplace he worked would be a place of power?"

"Almost certainly."

"Well, but what about the water he used?"

"The water? Oh, yes, the Dark Water. What about it?"

"Well, if he found water in the caves—"

"The caves? Of course, the caves! Where are they?"

"Not far. It's about half a league to Bigcliff, and then halfway down the slip and along the path."

"Can you find it in this light?"

"Of course."

"Then lead the way."

Savn at once abandoned the road in order to cut directly toward the hills above Bigcliff, finding his way by memory and feel in the growing darkness. "Be careful along here," he said as they negotiated the slip that cut through the hill. "The gravel is loose, and if you fall you can hurt yourself."

"Yes."

They came to the narrow but level path toward the caves, and the going became easier. Savn said, "Remember when you told me about how you encourage bandits to attack you?"

"Yes."

"Were you, uh, were you jesting with me?"

"Not entirely," said Vlad. "In point of fact, I've only done that once or twice, so I suppose I was exaggerating a bit."

"Oh."

"What makes you ask?"

"I was just wondering if that was why you carry a sword."

"I carry a sword in case someone tries to hurt me."

"Yes, but I mean, was that the idea? Is that why you do it, so these bandits—"

"No, I carried it long before that."

"But then why—"

"As I said, in case someone tries to hurt me."

"Did that ever happen? I mean, before?"

"Someone trying to hurt me? Yes."

"What did you do?"

"Sometimes I fought. Sometimes I ran."

"Have you ever . . . I mean—"

"I'm still alive; that ought to tell you something."

"Oh. Is that how—I mean, your hand . . ."

Vlad glanced down at his left hand, as if he'd forgotten he had one. "Oh, yes. If someone is swinging a sword at you, and you are unarmed, it is possible to deflect the blade with your hand by keeping your palm exactly parallel with the flat of the blade. Your timing has to be perfect. Also, you ought to remember to keep your pinkie out of the way."

Savn winced in sympathy and decided not to ask for more details. A little later, he ventured, "Isn't the sword annoying to carry?"

"No. In any case, I used to carry a great deal more."

"More what?"

"More steel."

"Why?"

"I was living in a more dangerous place."

"Where was that?"

"Adrilankha."

"You've been there?"

"Yes, indeed. I've lived most of my life there."

"I'd like to see Adrilankha."

"I hope you do."

"What's it like?"

"It's what you make of it. It is a thousand cities. It is a place where there are more noblemen than Teckla, it seems. It is a place of ease, luxury, and sudden violence, depending on where you are and who you are. It is a place of wishes fulfilled, and of permanent longing. It is like everywhere else, I think."

They began climbing up toward the caves. "Did you like it there?"

"Yes."

"Why did you leave?"

"Some people wanted to kill me."

Savn stopped, turned, and tried to look at Vlad's face to see if he was joking, but it was too dark to be certain. It was, in fact, almost too dark to walk safely. Vlad stopped behind him, waiting. There was a flapping sound overhead. Savn couldn't tell what sort of bird it was, but it sounded big. "We should get to the caves," he said after a moment.

"Lead on."

Savn did so. They came up the rise toward the first one, which was shallow and led nowhere interesting, so he ignored it. He said, "Have you really killed people?"

"Yes."

"Was there really someone in Adrilankha who wanted to kill you?"

"Yes."

"That must be scary."

"Only if they find me."

"Are they still looking for you?"

"Oh, yes."

"Do you think they'll find you?"

"I hope not."

"What did you do?"

"I left."

"No, I mean, why do they want to kill you?"

"I annoyed some business associates."

"What kind of business were you in?"

"One thing and another."

"Oh."

"I hear water from below."

"The river flats. That's where the people from Brownclay and Bigcliff go to bathe and wash clothes."

"Ah, yes. I was there earlier; I hadn't realized we were in the same place. This must be Bigcliff, then."

"Yes."

"You say you know a cave that has water in it?"

"One of the deep ones. That's where I'm taking us."

"Very good. It sounds like just what we're looking for."

"What will we do there?"

"You'll see."

"Okay. This is it. It goes way back, and down, and the further down you go, the wetter the walls get, and I remember once we heard water trickling below us, though we didn't actually find it."

"Excellent. Let's see what it looks like."

The immediate area filled with a soft, yellow light, displaying the weed-covered rocks. Savn said, "Was that witchcraft?"

"No, sorcery."

"Oh. My Paener could have done that, then."

"Yes. Let's go in."

The entrance to the cave was narrow and low, so that it would have been difficult to find even in the daylight if Savn had not known where it was. He pointed it out to Vlad, who bent over and caused his sorcerous light to fill the entrance. This was followed by the sounds of small animals, disturbed from their rest, who scurried off to find hiding places.

"Best not to know what they are," said Vlad.

"I agree," said Savn, and led the way into the cave.

At once it opened up, and in the sourceless, hazy light it appeared rather bigger than Savn remembered. He was very aware of the sound of their soft boots, and even the sound of his own breathing.

"Can you make light with witchcraft?"

"I don't know," said Vlad. "I've never tried. It's easier to bring torches. Which way?"

"Are you sure you want to go deeper, Vlad?"

"Yes."

"This way, then."

The pale light moved with them, growing brighter in small spaces, then more dim as they entered larger ones.

After a while, Savn said, "Do you want to go all the way down to the water?"

"If we can. It is certain to be a place of power."

"Why?"

"Because Lord Smallcliff used it. Even if it weren't before, it would be when he was done. He's like that."

"This is as far as I've ever gone."

"Bide, then."

Savn waited, listening to the flapping of bat wings, while Vlad's eyes narrowed, then widened slightly as he shook his head, and at last he moved his lips as if uttering an incantation. "All right," he said at last. "It's safe. If we climb over this ledge, crawl that way about forty feet, and drop down, we'll fall about five feet and land on a flat surface."

"How do you know?"

"That's what you've come here to learn, isn't it?"

"Was that witchcraft?"

"Yes and no. Without the Art, I couldn't have done it."

"And you're certain—"

"Yes."

Savn hesitated a moment, but Vlad, without waiting, went over the indicated ledge, actually a narrow slit in the rock wall which was barely large enough for them, and began creeping along it. Savn became aware that he'd been hearing the gurgling of water for some few minutes. He followed the Easterner; then, at the same place Vlad did, he hung over the edge and let go, landing easily. The sound of trickling water was louder as he landed. The yellow light grew until it faintly illuminated a large cavern, with a dark, narrow stream, perhaps four feet wide, making its leisurely way back into the hill.

"Is this the place?" said Savn, hearing his words come back to him. "Or should we go further in?"

"What do you think?" said Vlad.

"I don't know."

"Can you feel anything?"

"What do you mean?"

"Open yourself up to sensation. Do you feel power?"

Savn closed his eyes, and tried to feel something happening. There was a slight chill on his skin, and a soft whisper of wind against his ears, but that was all. "No," he said. "But I don't really know what I'm supposed to be feeling."

"Let's try it here, then. Sit down on that rock. Take my cloak and fold it up behind your head so you can lean back."

Savn did these things. "Now what?"

"Relax."

He tried to settle back into the unusual position, with only some success.

"Can you feel your scalp? The top of your head? No, I don't mean touch it. Put your hands back in your lap. Now, can you feel the top of your head? Think of your scalp relaxing. Imagine each hair on your head relaxing. Your temples, your ears, your forehead, your eyes, your cheeks, your jaw. One at a time, try to relax each of these muscles. Now the back of your neck. Feel your head sink into the cloak, pretend you are falling into the wall behind you. . . ."

Sometime later, Vlad said, "How do you feel?"

Savn realized that a great deal of time had passed, but he didn't know how much, nor what had occurred during that time. "I feel good," he said, surprised to discover it. "Like I'm, I don't know, alive."

"Good. You took to it well."

"You mean I'm a witch now?"

"No, that was only the first step, to prepare your mind for the journey."

"It feels great."

"I know."

"What do we do next?"

"Next, we get you home. It's late."

"Is it?" Savn reached for the time and blanched. "The gods! I had no idea—"

"Don't worry about it."

"Mae and Pae—"

"I'll speak to them."

"But they—" He bit off his words. He'd been about to say they wouldn't listen to an Easterner, then realized there was no polite way to say it. In any case, Vlad would find out for himself soon enough.

The Easterner did not appear to notice. He made a sign for Savn to approach, and when he was there, he clenched his fist, screwed his face up, and Savn found himself once more in Smallcliff, on the north side of town, barely able to make out his surroundings in the faint yellow radiance that Vlad continued to produce.

"You teleported us!" he cried.

"I know you live out somewhere in this direction, and this is the only place I knew well enough to—"

"But you teleported us!"

"Well, yes. You said you were late. I hope you don't mind."

"No, no, but I don't know anyone who is good enough to do that."

"It isn't all that difficult."

"You're a sorcerer."

"Well, yes, among other things."

Savn stared at him, his eyes wide, until he realized that he was being rude. Vlad just smiled back at him, then said, "Come. I don't know where you live, so we're going to have to walk the rest of the way."

Stunned, Savn set off along the deserted road. He said, "How do you teleport? I've heard of it—"

"It isn't that hard; you just have to be certain you know exactly where you're going. The tricky part is not getting sick afterwards, and for that there is witchcraft."

"But how do you know where you'll end up?"

"You have to remember it very well—perfectly, in fact. It's the remembering that allows the journey to take place."

"What if you can't remember it that well?"

"Then you're in trouble."

"But—"

"Sometimes you can prepare a place to teleport to. It limits you, but it's good if you're in a hurry."

"Can you teach me all this?"

"Maybe. We'll see. Where is your house?"

"On the other side of this hill, but we should take the road around, because the flax here hasn't been harvested yet."

"Very well."

Vlad seemed to have no trouble finding the road up to the house, though whether this was because Easterners had better night vision, or because of his magical powers, or for some other reason entirely, Savn didn't know and couldn't decide on a good way to ask, so he ended by saying nothing, and they spoke no more until they stood before the one-room house, with its single door held on with straps, and two windows covered with oiled paper. There was a pale yellow light from the lamps and the stove.

"Nice place," said Vlad.

"Thank you," said Savn, who had been thinking how small and plain it must look to someone who had lived in Adrilankha.

They had, evidently, been seen, because just before they reached the door it flew open so hard that Savn thought it would tear off its leather hinges, and there were Mae and Pae, silhouetted in the soft glow of the stove. They stood almost motionless, and while Savn couldn't see the expressions on their faces, his imagination had no trouble supplying Mae's wide-eyed anger and Pae's annoyed confusion.

As they stepped forward, Mae said, "Who are you?" which puzzled Savn for a moment, until he realized to whom she was speaking.

"Vlad. You saw me earlier today, at Tem's house."

"*You.* What have you been doing with my son?"

"Teaching him," said Vlad.

"Teaching him?" said Pae. "And what is it you think you'll be teaching my boy?"

Vlad answered in a soft, gentle voice, much different than Savn had ever heard him use before. "I've been teaching him to hear the voices of the stones," he said, "and to see prophecy in the movement of the clouds. To catch the wind in his hand and to bring forth gems from the dunes of the desert. To freeze air and to burn water. To live, to breathe, to walk, to sample the joy on each road, and the sorrow at each turning. I'm sorry if I've kept him out too late. I shall be more careful in the future. No doubt I will see you again. I bid you all a good evening."

Mae and Pae stood there against the light, watching the Easterner's back as his grey cloak faded into the night. Then Pae said, "In all my life, I never—"

"Hush now," said Mae. "Let's get this one to bed."

Savn wasn't sure what Vlad had done, but they didn't say a word more about the hour, or about what he'd been doing. He went over to his corner under the loft, spread his furs out, and climbed in underneath them without saying another word.

That night, he dreamed of the cave, which, upon waking, he did not find surprising. In the dream, the cave was filled with smoke, which, at least as he remembered it, kept changing color, and a jhereg kept flying out of it and speaking in Vlad's voice, saying, "Wait here," and, "You will feel well-rested, alert, and strong," and other things which he didn't remember.

The dream must have had some effect, however, for when he did wake up he felt refreshed and ready. As he prepared for the day he realized with some annoyance that he would have to spend several hours harvesting, and then several more with Master Wag, before he had the chance to find Vlad again and, he hoped, continue where they had left off.

He forgot his annoyance, however, after the morning harvest, when he arrived at the Master's, because the Master was in one of his touchy moods, and Savn had to concentrate on not giving him an excuse for a tongue-lashing. He spent most of the day listening to an oft-repeated rant to the effect that no one dies without a reason, so Reins couldn't have, either. Apparently Master Wag had been unable to find this reason, and was consequently upset with himself, Savn, Reins, and the entire world. The only time he seemed pleasant was while scratching Curry's left arm with the thorn of the blister plant to treat his fever, and even then Savn knew he was in a foul temper, because he simply did it, without giving Savn the lecture that usually accompanied treatment.

After the fifth rant on the subject of causeless death, Savn ventured, "Could it have been sorcery?"

"Of course it could have been sorcery, idiot. But sorcery *does* something, and whatever it did would leave traces."

"Oh. What about witchcraft?"

"Eh?"

"Could a witch—"

"What do you know about witchcraft?"

"Nothing," said Savn honestly. "That's why I don't know if—"

"If a witch can do anything at all beyond fooling the gullible, which I doubt, then whatever he did would leave traces, too."

"Oh."

Master Wag started to say more, then scowled and retreated into the cellar, where he kept his herbs, splints, knives, and other supplies, and where, presumably, he kept the pieces of Rein's skin, bone, and hair that he had preserved in order to determine what had happened. Savn felt queasy considering this.

He looked around for something to do in order to take his mind off it, but he'd already cleaned everything in sight, and memorized the Tale of the Man Who Ate Fire so well that the Master had been unable to do anything but grunt upon hearing Savn's recitation.

He sat down next to the window, realized it was too cold, discovered that he still had at least another hour before he could go home, and put some more wood onto the fire. It crackled pleasantly. He walked around the room, looking over the Master's collection of books, including *On the Number of the Parts of the Body, Knitting of Bones, The Sorcerer's Art and the Healing of the Self, The Remembered Tales of Calduh,* and the others which the Master had consulted from time to time in healing patients or instructing Savn. One book that he had never seen the Master consult was called *The Book of the Seven Wizards,* a thick, leather-bound volume with the title in gold lettering on the spine. He took it down, went over by the fire, and let it fall open.

It had been written in a neat, even hand, as if the scribe, probably a Lyorn, had attempted to remove all traces of his own personality. The pages were rather thicker than the leaves of many books, and in good condition. It occurred to Savn that Master Wag probably knew a spell to preserve books, so this one could be of any age. At the top of the page, he read: "On the Nature of Secrets."

He wondered if it were some sort of sign that it had fallen open in that spot—if, in fact, there were some sort of secret to be discovered. Probably not, he decided.

The book told him:

> *Be aware of power in hidden places, and be aware of that which is apparent, for secrets may lie open to view and yet be concealed. All of the Seven Wizards know of secrets, and each, in his own way, speaks of them, calls to them, and reveals them to those who search diligently and honestly.*

Diligently and honestly? he thought. Well, that could be said of everything. What about thoroughly? He turned his eyes back to the book and read:

> *She Who Is Small finds the secrets of the present in the past; that when the past is known, it is the power of the mage to find Truth in Mystery; that thus is the latter transformed into the former.*

It seemed to Savn that he knew very little of the past, and that there must be many secrets indeed that he could discover if he turned to history. He wondered how Master Wag would feel if he asked for a history book. Not today, in any case.

He turned back to the book and read:

She Who Is Tall says that the secret is in the song, and opens only to one who dares to sing. It is said that when she sings, the secret is plain to all who listen, but that it is hidden again when the song is past, and few are those who are blessed to hear the echoes of Truth in the Silence that follows.

Well, he liked music well enough, and he liked singing, but there was probably some sort of mystical and powerful meaning in the passage, which he didn't understand. He shrugged.

The next paragraph read:

She Whose Hair Is Red wraps the secret ever tighter in skeins of words, so that it vanishes as if it never were, and in these layers of words the secret emerges, shining, so that it is hidden to those who look, yet revealed to those who take joy in the unfolding patterns and sounds of words.

There was certainly some mystical and powerful significance to this, and he certainly didn't understand it. He tried to visualize something being wrapped up in words, but all he got was an image of the black lettering from the book, removed from the page, attaching itself to some undefined thing and smothering it.

He read:

He Whose Eyes Are Green knows where the secret lies, for his eyes pierce every shadowy place; yet he no sooner finds the secret than he buries it anew. But it is said that in the burying the secret has changed, while that which was hidden walks the land ever after, waiting but for one to recognize it, and offer it refuge.

That didn't make any sense at all. If he knew where the secrets were, why did he want to hide them? And who were these wizards, anyway?

The book went on:

He Whose Hair Is Dark laughs at secrets, for his pleasure is in the search, not the discovery—and the paths he follows in this search stem from whim, not from plan. Some say that in this way he reveals as many as another.

That almost made sense. Savn could imagine how it might be more fun to look for something than to actually find it. He wondered if there was something he was looking for, or something he *should* look for. The secret to Reins's death? But he could hardly expect to find that if Master Wag couldn't.

He continued reading:

> *Of the Gentle One it is said that she sets down the order and method of all things, and that, in this way, all hidden things may be found. To her, each detail is a signpost, and when each is placed in its own position, the outline of the secret will be laid bare for any who will look.*

Well, that was certainly possible, thought Savn. But what do you do when you don't know anything?

There was one more passage on the page:

> *The Master of Rhyme still searches for the Way of the Wizards, for to him, this is the greatest Secret of all. Yet, as he searches, he lets fall Truths for all of those who come after, and in this he sees no miracle, for what is plain to one is a Secret to the next. He is often praised for this, but it is meaningless to him, for who among Men will rejoice in finding Truth that he has never thought hidden?*

Savn frowned. That, too, almost made sense. It was as if you could see something, and maybe someone else couldn't, but to you it wasn't anything to get excited about, because it was right there all the time.

It occurred to him to wonder if there were things right in front of him that *he* couldn't see. He was pondering this when Master Wag returned and said, "What are you reading?"

Savn showed him the book. The Master snorted. "There's nothing in there you need, at least not yet. Why don't you go home?"

Savn didn't need to be given this suggestion twice. He put the book on the shelf, said farewell, and dashed out the door before the Master could change his mind.

He raced to Tem's house, expecting to see Vlad either lounging outside or in the common room, but the Easterner was not in evidence. As he stood there, wondering whether he dared to ask Tem which room Vlad was in, his sister walked through the door, accompanied by two of her friends, which caused him, for reasons he couldn't quite specify, to abandon this plan.

She came up to him at once and pulled him into a corner. "What happened to you last night?"

"What do you mean?"

"You were gone forever. Mae and Pae were going crazy. I finally went to bed, and when I got up this morning and asked if you'd shown up, they looked at me like they didn't know what I was talking about and said that you were already up and out."

"Well, I was."

"That's not the point, chag-brain."

"Don't call me chag-brain."

"Where *were* you?"

"Exploring the caves."

"At *night*?"

"Sure. Why not?"

"But why were you so late?"

"I lost track of time."

She frowned at him, clearly unsatisfied with the answer, but uncertain how to find out more. "Well, then," she said, "don't you think Mae and Pae were acting a little strange, the way they were so worried at first, and then—"

"Oh, you know how they get. Look, I'll talk to you later, all right? I have to go."

"Go where? Savn, stop it. Don't you dare go running off like that! Savn . . ."

Her voice followed him out the door, but he paid no attention. The only place he could think of to find Vlad was back at the caves, so he set off for them at once. He followed the Manor road for the first mile, then cut across to the slip. As he was about to start down it, however, he saw, some distance away, a grey-clad figure standing on the cliff itself. He broke into a run, and at about the same moment he became convinced that it was indeed Vlad, the Easterner turned and waved to him, as if he'd known he was there.

When he reached him, he said nothing, only stopped to recover his breath. Vlad stood, staring out at the river flats so far below them, dotted with people bathing, washing clothes, or just talking. Savn tried to view the scene as if it were new; the river rushing in from the right, turning sharply around the Black Rocks, foaming white, then suddenly widening into the flats, brown against tan, then narrowing gradually once more as it cut down into the plains and began turning south, toward the sea, many impossible hundreds of miles away.

"It's beautiful, isn't it?" said Savn.

"Is it?" said Vlad, without turning his head.

"Don't you think so?"

"Maybe. Nature usually doesn't excite me very much. I'm impressed by what man makes of his world, not what we started with."

"Oh." Savn considered. "I guess I'm just the opposite."

"Yes."

"Does it matter?"

Vlad looked at him, and something like amusement glittered for a moment in his eyes. Then he turned back to watching the river. "Yes and no," he said. "A couple of years ago I met a philosopher who told me that those like me build, while those like you take more pleasure in life."

"Aren't there those who like both?"

"Yes. According to this lady, they become artists."

"Oh. Do you enjoy life?"

"Me? Yes, but I'm naturally lucky."

"Oh." Savn thought back to what the Easterner told him the night before. "You must be, to still be alive with people trying to kill you."

"Oh, no. That isn't luck. I'm alive because I'm good enough to survive."

"Then what do you mean?"

"I'm lucky that, living the way I do, with people trying to kill me, I can still take pleasure in life. Not everyone can, and I think if you can't, there isn't much you can do about it."

"Oh. I've never met a philosopher."

"I hope you do some day; they're always worth talking to."

"Pae says such things are a waste of time."

"Your Pae, I'm sorry to say, is wrong."

"Why?"

"Because everything is worth examining, and if you don't examine your view of the world, you are still subject to it, and you find yourself doing things that—never mind."

"I think I understand."

"Do you? Good." After a moment he said, as if to himself, "I learned a lot from that lady. I was sorry I had to kill her."

Savn looked at him, but the Easterner didn't seem to be joking. They continued watching the River Flats and said nothing more for a while.

5

THEY WERE CLOSE ENOUGH so that Savn could identify some of the people below, more by how they dressed and moved than by their features. There were a few whose names he knew, but he knew none of the people well, and for the first time he wondered why that was. Smallcliff was closer to Bigcliff than to either Whiterock or Notthereyet, but those were the places he had visited, and from a little traveling and from his work with Master Wag, he knew a few people who lived in each of those villages; but the dwellers below were strangers, even those he could identify and had spoken with.

Mae and Pae hardly ever mentioned them at all, except for an occasional reference Pae made to its being filthy to bathe in the same place that you wash your clothes. Yet when those from below came to visit Master Wag, they seemed pleasant enough, and Savn didn't see any difference.

Odd, though, that he'd never thought about it before. Next to him, Vlad was watching them with single-minded concentration that reminded Savn of something he'd seen once, long ago, but couldn't quite remember. He felt something akin to fear as he made the comparison, however.

"Vlad?" said Savn at last.

"Yes?"

"Those people are . . . never mind."

"They are what?"

Savn haltingly tried to tell the Easterner what he'd been thinking about them, but he couldn't seem to find the right words, so eventually he shrugged and fell silent.

Vlad said, "Are they also vassals of Baron Smallcliff?"

"Yes. He's also the Baron of Bigcliff."

Vlad nodded. "What else?"

"I don't know. I know that someone else is lord over in Whiterock, though. A Dzurlord. We hear stories about him."

"Oh? What kind of stories?"

"Not very nice ones. You have to work his fields two days of the week, even in the bad years when it takes everything to keep your own going, and he doesn't care how hard that makes it for you, or even if you starve, and sometimes he does things that, well, I don't really know about because they say I'm too young to know about them, but they're pretty awful. His tax collectors can beat you whenever they want, and you can't do anything about it. And his soldiers will kill you if you get in their way, and when the Speaker tried to complain to the Empire they had him killed, and things like that."

"Things like that don't happen here?"

"Well, the tax collectors can be pretty mean sometimes, but not that bad. We're lucky here."

"I suppose so."

They fell silent again. Vlad continued staring down at the River Flats. Eventually Savn said, "Vlad, if you aren't enjoying nature, what *are* you doing?"

"Watching the people."

"They're odd," said Savn.

"So you said. But you didn't tell me in what way they're odd."

Savn opened his mouth and shut it. He didn't want to pass on what Mae and Pae said about them, because he was sure Vlad would just think he was being small-minded. He finally said, "They talk funny."

Vlad glanced at him. "Funny? How?"

"Well, there used to be a tribe of Serioli who lived down there. They only moved away a few hundred years ago, and until then they lived right next to the people from Bigcliff, and they'd talk all the time, and—"

"And the people from Bigcliff use Serioli words?"

"Not when they talk to us. But it's, that, well, they put their words together different than we do."

"Can you understand them?"

"Oh, sure. But it sounds strange."

"Hmmm," said Vlad.

"What are you watching them for?"

"I'm not certain. A way to do something I have to do."

"Why do you always talk that way?"

Vlad spared him a quick glance, which Savn could not read, then said, "It comes from spending time in the company of philosophers and Athyra."

"Oh."

"And having secrets."

"Oh."

A strange feeling came over Savn, as if he and Vlad had achieved some sort of understanding—it seemed that if he asked the Easterner a question, he might get an answer. However, he realized, he wasn't certain what, of all the things he wondered about, he ought to ask. Finally he said, "Have you really spent a great deal of time around Athyra nobles?"

"Not exactly, but I knew a Hawklord once who was very similar. And a drummer, for that matter."

"Oh. Did you kill them, too?"

Vlad's head snapped up; then he chuckled slightly. "No," he said, then added, "On the other hand, it came pretty close with both of them."

"Why were they like Athyra?"

"What do you know of the House?"

"Well, His Lordship is one."

"Yes. That's what brought it to mind. You see, it is a matter of the philosophical and the practical; the mystical and the mundane."

"I don't understand."

"I know that," said Vlad, still staring out at the River Flats.

"Would you explain?"

"I'm not certain I can," said Vlad. He glanced at Savn, then back out over the cliff. "There are many who are contemptuous of the intellectual process. But those who aren't afraid of it sometimes discover that the further you go from the ordinary, day-to-day world, the more understanding you can achieve of it; and the more you understand of the world, the more you can act, instead of being acted upon. That," he added, almost as an afterthought, "is exactly what witchcraft is about."

"But you said before you ought to get involved, and now you're saying you should stand apart."

"Got me," said Vlad, smiling.

Savn waited for him to continue. After a moment Vlad seated himself on the cliff.

"Not stand apart in actions," he said. "I mean, don't be afraid to form general conclusions, to try to find the laws that operate in the actions of history, and to—"

"I don't understand."

Vlad sighed. "You should try not to get me started."

"But, about the Athyra . . ."

"Yes. There are two types of Athyra. Some are mystics, who attempt to explore the nature of the world by looking within themselves, and some are explorers, who look upon the world as a problem to be solved, and thus reduce other people to either distractions or pieces of a puzzle, and treat them accordingly."

Savn considered this, and said, "The explorers sound dangerous."

"They are. Not nearly as dangerous as the mystics, however."

"Why is that?"

"Because explorers at least believe that others are real, if unimportant. To a mystic, that which dwells inside is the only reality."

"I see."

"Baron Smallcliff is a mystic."

"Oh."

Vlad stood abruptly, and Savn had an instant's fear that he was going to throw himself off the cliff. Instead he took a breath and said, "He's the worst kind of mystic. He can only see people as . . ." His voice trailed off. He looked at Savn, then looked away. For a moment, Savn thought he had detected such anger hidden in the Easterner that it would make one of Speaker's rages seem like the pouting of a child.

In an effort to distract Vlad, Savn said, "What are you?"

It seemed to work, for Vlad chuckled slightly. "You mean am I a mystic or an explorer? I have been searching for the answer to that question for several years now. I haven't found it, but I know that other people are real, and that is something."

"I guess."

"There was a time I didn't know that."

Savn wasn't certain how to respond to this, so he said nothing.

After a moment, Vlad added, "And I listen to philosophers."

"When you don't kill them," said Savn.

This time the Easterner laughed. "Even when I do, I still listen to them."

"I understand," said Savn.

Vlad looked at him suddenly. "Yes, I think that you do."

"You sound surprised."

"Sorry," said Vlad. "You are, I don't know, better educated than most of us from the city would have thought."

"Oh. Well, I learned my ciphers and history and everything because I filled the bucket when I was twenty, so they—"

"Filled the bucket?"

"Don't they have that in the city?"

"I don't know. I've never heard of it, at any rate."

"Oh. Well, I hardly remember doing it. I mean, I was pretty young at the time. But they give you a bucket—"

"Who is 'they'?"

"Mae and Pae and Speaker and Bless."

"I see. Go on."

"They give you a bucket, and tell you to go out into the woods, and when you come back, they see what's in the bucket and decide whether you should be trained for apprenticeship."

"And you had filled yours?"

"Oh, that's just a term that means they said yes. I mean, if you come back with water, then Bless will try you out as a priest, and if you come back with sticks, then, well, I don't really know how they tell, but they decide, and when I came back they decided I should be apprenticed to Master Wag."

"Oh. What did you come back with?"

"An injured daythief."

"Oh. That would account for it, I suppose. Still, I can't help wondering how much of that is chance."

"What do you mean?"

"How often a child picks up the first thing he sees, and ends up being a cobbler when he'd be better off as a weaver."

"That doesn't happen," Savn explained.

Vlad looked at him. "It doesn't?"

"No," said Savn, feeling vaguely annoyed.

"How do you know?"

"Because . . . it just doesn't."

"Because that's what you've always been told?"

Savn felt himself flushing, although he wasn't certain why. "No, because that's what the test is for."

Vlad continued studying him. "Do you always just accept everything you've been told, without questioning it?"

"That's a rude question," said Savn without thinking about it.

Vlad seemed startled. "You're right," he said. "I'm sorry."

"Some things," said Savn, "you just know."

Vlad frowned, and took a step away from the cliff. He clasped his hands behind his back and cocked his head slightly. "Do you?" he asked. "When you 'just know' something, Savn, that means it's so locked into your head that you operate as if it were true, even when you find out it isn't." He knelt down so that he was facing Savn directly. "That isn't necessarily a good idea."

"I don't understand."

"You're so convinced that your Baron Smallcliff is invincible and perfect that you'd stand there and let him kill you rather than raising a finger to defend yourself."

"That's different."

"Is it?"

"You're changing the subject. There are things that you know way deep down. You know they're true, just because they have to be."

"Do they?"

"Well, yes. I mean, how do you know that we're really here? You just know."

"I know some philosophers who would disagree with you," said Vlad.

"The ones you killed?"

Vlad laughed. "Well taken," he said. He stood and walked over to the cliff again, and stared out once more. Savn wondered what he was trying to find. "But sometimes," continued the Easterner, "when it's time to do something, it matters whether you know why you're doing it."

"What do you mean?"

Vlad frowned, which seemed to be his usual expression when he was trying to think of how to say something. "Sometimes you might get so mad that you hit someone, or so frightened you run, but you don't really know why. Sometimes you know why you should do something, but it's all in your head. You don't really feel it, so you have trouble making yourself do it."

Savn nodded. "I know what you mean. It's like when I've been out late and Maener asks what I've been doing and I know I should tell her, but I don't."

"Right. It isn't always easy to act on what's in your head instead of what's in your heart. And it isn't always right to. The whole trick to knowing what to do is deciding when to make yourself listen to your head, and when it's okay to just follow your feelings."

"So, how do you do it?"

Vlad shook his head. "I've been trying to figure that one out myself for the last few years, and I haven't managed. But I can tell you that it works best when you understand why you feel a certain way, and to do that, sometimes you have to take things you know and question them. That's one of the good things Athyra and philosophers do."

"I see what you're getting at," said Savn slowly.

Vlad looked at him once more. "Yes? And?"

"Some things you just know."

Vlad seemed about to say something, but evidently decided to let the matter drop. They fell silent, and Vlad went back to scanning the area below them.

After a while the Easterner said, "Who's that lady wearing the green hat, talking to everyone in sight?"

"I don't know her name, but she's their priestess."

"Of?"

"What do you mean, 'of'? Oh, I see. Of Trout."

"Hmmm. No help there."

"No help for what?"

"Never mind. Do you, also, worship Trout?"

"Worship?"

"I mean, who do you pray to?"

"Pray?"

"Who is your god?"

"Bless seems to be on good terms with Naro, the Lady Who Sleeps, so that's who he usually asks things of."

Vlad nodded, then pointed once more. "Who is that fellow walking down toward the water?"

"I don't remember his name. He makes soap and sells it."

"Where does he sell it?"

"Just there, along the river. Most of them make their own, I think, the same as we do, so he doesn't get much business except from those who are washing clothes and didn't bring enough."

"There's nowhere else he sells it?"

"No, not that I'm aware of. Why?"

"It doesn't matter."

"We don't wash at the river; we have wells."

"You wash in your wells?"

"No, no, we—"

"I was kidding."

"Oh. We go to the river to swim sometimes, but only upstream of them. You can't swim in the Upper Brownclay; it's too cold and fast."

"Who's that, just going beneath the scatterbush?"

"There? That's Fird. He came in to see Master Wag once with some sort of awful rash on his hand, and Master Wag rubbed it with rose leaves and it went away."

"What is he doing?"

"Selling fruit."

"Fruit? You have fruit around here?"

"Fird brings it in from upriver. We don't have very much. It's expensive. We get mangoes, though, and ti'iks, and oranges, and—"

"Doesn't Tem sell them?"

"He can't afford it. Fird is the only one."

"I'll have to meet him."

"He's by the river just about every day. We could go down if you want to."

"Not just yet. Where else does he sell this fruit?"

"Just here. And at the castle, I think."

"Really? He serves Smallcliff?"

"No, just those who serve His Lordship."

"That's interesting."

"Is it? At first that's all he did—bring in fruits and vegetables to feed His Lordship's staff, but then he found that if he went down to the river everyone wanted to buy something, so now, I think, he has more customers on the beach than in the servants, although I don't know if that matters—"

"His name, you say, is Fird?"

"Yes."

"Very well."

Vlad watched a little longer, then grunted and turned away from the cliff.

"Are we going to the caves again?" said Savn.

"No, I was thinking of going back to Tem's, for a glass of wine."

"Oh."

As they walked back along the slip, it seemed to Savn that the feeling had passed—that something which had been open within the strange man who walked next to him had shut again. *Well,* he thought. *Now that it's too late, I wonder what I should have asked him.*

As they reached the top of the hill and found the road once more, he said, "Uh, Vlad?"

"Yes?"

"Did you, um, *do* something to Mae and Pae last night?"

Vlad frowned. "Do something? You mean, cast a spell of some sort? What makes you think so? Are they acting strange?"

"No, it's just that I don't understand why they weren't angry with me for staying out so late."

"Oh. I took responsibility for it, that's all."

"I see," said Savn. He wasn't convinced, but then, he had trouble believing that the Easterner had really put a spell on them to begin with. Because he didn't want to leave that question hanging between them, he said, "What are your parents like?"

"They're dead," said Vlad.

"Oh. I'm sorry." He thought for a moment of what it would be like to be without Mae and Pae, then decided not to dwell on the thought. He said, "Are they the ones who taught you?"

"No, my grandfather did that."

"Is he—?"

"No, he's still with us. Or, at any rate, he was a few years ago. He's an old man, but witches, like sorcerers, tend to live a long time."

They came to the widening of the road that wagons used when they had to turn around, which was located just west of where the road began its twisting way into town. The forest still rose high on either side of them.

Savn said, "Were you going to show me some more witchcraft today?"

Vlad seemed to shrug without actually moving his shoulders. "What would you like to learn?"

"Well, I mean, I don't know. I'd like to learn to do something interesting."

"That's one approach."

They walked back along the road, passing the place where Savn had first seen Vlad, and started up the gentle slope that lead to the last hill before town.

"What do you mean?" said Savn.

"The Art can be approached from several directions. One is learning to do interesting things, another is the search for knowledge, yet another, the search for understanding, or wisdom, if you prefer, although it isn't really the same—"

"That's what you were talking about before, isn't it? I mean, about witchcraft, and understanding."

"Yes."

"But isn't knowledge the same as understanding?"

"No."

Savn waited for the Easterner to explain, but he didn't. Instead he added, "And yet another way is the search for power."

"Which way did you go?"

"Like you. I wanted to learn to do interesting things. I sort of had to."

"Why?"

"It's a long story."

"Oh. Well, what about me?"

"You should think about which direction you want to take."

"I know already."

"Oh? Tell me."

"Like I said, I want to do interesting things."

"Hmmm."

"Like you."

"Why is that?"

"To impress girls."

Vlad looked at him, and Savn had the feeling that the Easterner was, somehow, seeing him for the first time. After a moment, a smile came to Vlad's mouth and he said softly, "Well, why not? Let's step off the road a ways. Forests and jungles always feel right for this sort of thing."

"What about a place of power?"

Vlad chuckled. "Unnecessary—for this stage."

"All right. I suppose I'll understand eventually."

"Yes, chances are you will, but we won't worry about that for now."

"Here?"

"A little further, I think. I don't want to be distracted by the sounds of horses and wagons."

Savn followed him around thick trees, over low shrubs, and under hanging boughs until he seemed to find what he was looking for, whereupon he grunted, settled down against the wide base of a sugar maple, and said, "Get comfortable."

"I'm comfortable," said Savn, seating himself. Then, realizing that he wasn't, really, adjusted himself as best he could. He began to feel excitement, but he shook his shoulders back and waited, trying to remember the relaxed state he'd been in before. Vlad looked at him carefully, smiling just a little beneath the hair that grew about his lip.

"What is it?" asked Savn.

"Nothing, nothing. What do you know of psychic communication?"

"Well, I know people who can do it, a little. And I know that sorcerers can do it."

"Have you ever tried?"

"*Me*? Well, no."

"Why not?"

"Well, I, uh, I have no reason to think I can."

"Everyone can. You just have to be shown how."

"You mean, read minds?"

"Not exactly. It's more like speaking without making a sound. It is possible to read minds, but that is far, far more difficult, and even then you might be caught at it." Vlad paused, and seemed to be remembering something, to judge by the distant look in his eyes and the half-smile on his face. "Many people become annoyed if you attempt to penetrate their thoughts."

"I would think so," said Savn.

Vlad nodded, then reached for a chain that hung around his neck, hesitated, licked his lips, and removed it. On the end was a simple setting which held what appeared to be a piece of black rock.

"What is—?"

"Don't ask," said Vlad. At the same time, there was a sudden flapping sound overhead, as if two or three very large birds had been disturbed. Savn jumped, startled, but Vlad shook his head, as if to say that it was nothing to worry about.

"Remember how we relaxed before?" he said. "Well, we're going to do it again, only this time the experience will be rather different."

"In what way?"

"You'll see. There will be a disorientation in time, but that is nothing to worry about."

"All right."

Once more he closed his eyes and allowed Vlad's voice to lead him through each muscle in his body, letting the tension leave, letting it flow down, down, into the ground below him, until he felt the now-familiar sensation of floating, as if he were no longer part of his body—as if he stood apart from it, distant and unconcerned. Then Vlad said, "You are feeling very warm, and light—as if you are nothing but a bubble of air, and you can go anywhere. Yes. Think of yourself as an air bubble that moves where you will. You are surrounded by nothing, and you are empty. Feel that you can move however you please. You are relaxed and confident."

Yes, Savn agreed. *I will feel that way. I choose to, and so I do. Isn't that remarkable?*

"Now," said Vlad, "picture yourself, a bubble of nothingness, floating down through the ground, down through layers of stone, meshing with it, and, with each layer, you will fall more deeply asleep."

Yes, I will picture that; I will do that, he thought, and it seemed as if his body were far away.

"Now very slowly, open your eyes, and look at me, but do not rise up. Look at me, and imagine that I am there with you—we are together, two bubbles of air beneath the earth. With the eyes of your body, you see me holding a small piece of fabric. Now you imagine yourself a wind, and you brush against the fabric. There, you see how it flutters? Touch it again, and again. Don't push; will it to happen. Do you feel the texture of the cloth, smooth, slightly cold, the veins of weave distinct beneath the fingertips of your mind? Once more, a little push. Yes, that was you, you felt it.

"Now we, as two bubbles of air, will touch. Do you now hear my words, as if they were echoed, once spoken aloud, once whispered softly? One coming just ahead of the other, as if you were aware of the time it takes for the sound to pass your ears, because you are now aware of that time, and you choose to ignore it, so these sounds, both my voice, both identical, come together; they are strong, reinforcing each other. And now *you hear only the whisper, and without making a sound, whisper back to me with only your thoughts—you form words, and you give them to me, as if you were placing a feather in my hand, but your mouth and tongue do not move. Tell me, in this way, that you can hear me.*"

"I can hear you," Savn said, feeling awe, but a distant, vague sort of awe, the reverse of a dream, as if it were normal and nothing special, but he knew, somewhere, that it would be remarkable when he awoke.

"*And I can hear you,*" said Vlad. "*You will remember that feeling, of touching my mind with yours, and you will always be able to call it back.*"

"Yes," said Savn. "I will remember it."

"*Now, you begin to rise back through the ground, and with each layer, you begin to awake. You are coming back, closer and closer; you feel your limbs again, and know them as part of you, and* you hear my real voice in your real ears, and with this sound, you awake, remembering everything that has happened, feeling rested, alert, and confident."

Savn blinked, and felt as if he were opening his eyes, although they had been open. He said, "I feel . . . funny. How much time has passed?"

"About half an hour."

"Half an hour?" Savn took a moment to see if this was true, then said, "Did I really move that piece of cloth?"

"You moved it," said Vlad.

Savn shook his head, but found no words to say.

"How do you feel?" said Vlad.

"Fine. A little tired, I guess."

"It'll pass. You'll have some trouble sleeping tonight. I'd suggest a great deal of physical exertion."

"All right. I'll run all the way home."

"Good idea."

They stood up. Vlad picked up his pendant and put it around his neck again. They walked slowly back to the road and started in toward town again. Savn couldn't find anything to say, and he was too lost in wonder and confusion to try very hard. He shook his head. Even now, he seemed more aware of the breeze against his throat, of the sharp outline of the trees against the twilit sky, and the sounds of the birds coming from all around him. They had always been there—why had he chosen not to hear them, and why was he hearing them now?

Such were his thoughts until he realized that they were walking through the town, and, in fact, had arrived in front of Tem's house. They stopped, and he said, "When will I see you again?"

"I'm not certain, my friend. Perhaps tomorrow."

"All right."

He did, indeed, run all the way home, relishing the way the air flowed through his lungs, the pounding of his feet along the road, the darkening sky, and the breeze, just getting chilly, biting at his face.

He made it on time for the evening meal, which prevented Mae and Pae from questioning him. Polyi, as usual, chattered throughout the meal, but Savn, who wasn't really listening, caught a few pointed remarks about himself. Fortunately, Mae and Pae didn't pick up on them.

That night, Savn fell asleep at once and while he slept, he dreamed that he stood in the street in front of Tem's house, while Lova stood in the middle of a faceless crowd and looked at him adoringly as he made the ground open and close, and made fire fall from the sky. When he awoke, he remembered the dream, and remarked to himself, "That's odd. I hadn't even known I liked her."

What now?

She flew down toward the little structure where the Provider dwelt, knowing that her mate was already there. And, even as she cupped the air to light on the roof, and was reaching with her feet for a grip on the soft wood, he took to the air once more, passing directly in front of her.

She hissed, and followed.

A soft one? Her mate was thinking about a soft one. But how to tell one from the others?

She tried to understand what her mate was asking of her. She understood something about fruit, or the smells of fruit, but when she tried to find out what sort of fruit, her mate became agitated.

At last, she understood what her mate wanted, and thought, if it must be, it must be. And at least it was flying.

Now up, out, upon the currents, treading them, through the overcast, careful not to breathe. Then up higher, higher, and, for the sheer pleasure of it, diving, falling like a stone past the cliff, to catch the air and drift, and glide.

Something like a laugh came from her thoughts, and echoed from her mate.

He found the one they were to watch, and she followed the path he indicated. Yes, that was the one. So be it. A long, dull time would follow, she thought.

She hoped she would be able to stay awake.

6

I will not marry a cursing wizard,
I will not marry a cursing wizard,
I'd ask for snow and get a blizzard.
Hi-dee hi-dee ho-la!
    Step on out . . .

AFTER BREAKING HIS FAST, Savn went outside. He looked at the stubble that covered almost every field in sight, his view interrupted only by the bins and the outbuildings. The soil looked lumpy and harsh, and somehow more brown than it had in the spring, though he had been told that was just his imagination.

It seemed such a short time ago that he had come out here and seen the little flowers everywhere, most of them blue, a few areas of pink or white. But now it looked almost like a wasteland, save for the long, narrow strip that ran next to the road, where the densely packed flax stood as high as his waist. It was here that he and his sister would be working today. Mae and Pae had already finished the chores and were out among the flax plants, working from the west, and Polyi was holding the small reaper and waiting for him.

It was a fresh, cool day, and the air felt dry and clean. It was a good day to work; he hated the early part of the harvest most, because everything seemed twice as hard when it was hot. Rain was almost as bad, but it didn't feel like rain today, and there was no greying of the orange-red sky, so perhaps they'd continue to be lucky with the weather.

He took a couple of the long cloth bags from under the porch, shook them and turned them inside out, then nodded to his sister.

"We're almost done," she said.

"I know. Today, or maybe tomorrow."

Polyi, hands on her hips and scythe leaning against her side, twisted in place a couple of times, as if to loosen muscles that were already tired. Savn rolled his shoulders and put his lyorn-skin gloves on. His hands would be hot and sweaty in half an hour, but blisters, as he well knew, would be worse.

He said, "Let's get to it." They headed out to the last field.

Savn collected the plants into sacks while his sister went ahead of him with the reaper. They fell into the rhythm easily—which was important. If they didn't, Savn would have had to pick the plants up off the ground, which was hard on his back and took much longer. But by now they knew each other, so that as Polyi swung the tool for each cut, the plant would fall neatly into Savn's gloved hand, and then he would take a half-step backward in order to miss the back sweep. He didn't have to watch either his hands or the plants—only his sister, to be certain that if for any reason the rhythm changed he would be able to avoid the sharp blade. He knew well what could happen if he looked away at the wrong time— he had helped Master Wag patch up three people this harvest.

It was boring drudge-work, but also easy and satisfying now that they had the system worked out, and he could hear the steady *shhhick, shhhick* as Mae and Pae worked from the other end. Soon—probably tomorrow, he decided, they would meet, and that would be the end of the harvest for this year. Then Mae and Pae would prepare the ground for the winter, and next year they would start all over again, and the next year, and the next, until the day Savn would begin earning money as a physicker himself, either in Smallcliff or elsewhere. Then there would be a few lean years before he could afford to send enough money back to pay for the work he could not do, but after that Mae and Pae would be able to hire someone, and after that he could begin saving, until he had so much money that he'd be able to travel, and—

When did I decide I wanted to travel? he asked himself.

Well, he wasn't sure he did want to, come to that, but he remembered when he had begun thinking about it—it was while he was standing outside his house, and the night had seemed to speak to him of distant places. He remembered his own question of Vlad, which had seemed to impress the Easterner: are you running to something or away from something? If he, Savn, were to leave, would he be leaving his family, or searching for more? Would he be deserting his home, or would he be setting out to find adventure and fortune? Had the Easterner inspired all of these thoughts? Was the Easterner somehow responsible for the experience he'd had on that strange, wonderful evening? *I don't care what they say, I'll bet he didn't kill Reins.*

They finished the row and began on the next, and so the morning passed. When it was nearly noon, their rhythm was broken by Pae, who whistled through his fingers to signal that Savn and Polyi were finished for the day.

As they walked back to the house, Polyi said, "Do you think they'll finish without us?"

Savn looked back at what remained to be done and said, "I hope it doesn't rain tomorrow."

Polyi nodded. "Me, too. Shall we go to Tem's house today?"

"Sure."

"You didn't wait for me yesterday, you know."

"I didn't? That's right, I didn't. I guess I was thinking about other things."

"Such as what?"

"I don't know. Things. Anyway, today we'll go there."

Savn bathed, and as he'd promised, waited for his sister, and the two of them set off for Tem's house. They spoke little as they walked, although it seemed to Savn that a couple of times Polyi started to say or ask something, then thought better of it. Eventually she started singing "Dung-Foot Peasant," and, after a verse or two, Savn joined in, changing pronouns as appropriate. He hadn't heard it in some time, and laughed at a few of the verses that had been added since he was his sister's age. He also sang her a few verses that had apparently been forgotten, and he was pleased that she liked them.

When they reached Tem's house, Vlad was not in evidence, but there was the usual noon crowd, and Savn noticed that he was receiving some odd looks from many of them. Polyi noticed it, too.

"Do you see that?" she said. "The way they look at you? They're wondering why you've been spending so much time with that Easterner."

Savn quickly looked around, but no one was looking at him just at the moment. "Are they really?" he said.

"Yes."

"Hmmm." He shrugged. "Let them wonder, then."

"Well, what *are* you doing?"

"I'm learning things."

"Like what?"

"Like, um, like how to catch gems in the wind—no, I mean, catch water in, uh—oh, never mind. I'm learning stuff."

Polyi frowned, but couldn't seem to think of anything to say, which was perfectly all right with Savn. He quickly finished his salad, said good-bye to his sister, and headed off to Master Wag.

On the way, it occurred to him that the sharpness of sensation that he'd felt the evening before was gone. He wondered if it was something that would return as he became more adept in this strange art he had begun to study.

The Master was in better spirits today, puttering around his small house (which had seemed much larger a year before, when Savn had begun studying with him) scattering bits of history with explanations of both the general and the particular. Savn wondered if he had solved the problem of Reins's death, but decided that, if so, the Master would speak of it in his own time, and if not, he had best not bring the subject up.

And in fact, Master Wag made no mention of it during the entire day, most of which Savn spent cleaning up the Master's house and listening to the Master's stories and lectures—a pastime Savn rather enjoyed, even though once Master Wag began to speak he soon lost track of his audience and went far beyond Savn's knowledge and understanding.

He's quite a bit like Vlad, he thought, then wondered why the notion disturbed him.

Toward the end of the day, the Master had him recite the questions, conclusions, and appropriate cures for various sorts of stomach ailments, and seemed quite pleased with Savn's answers, although, actually, Savn left out stabbing pains in the side, and the questions that would lead to a dose of pomegranate seeds to ease an attack of kidney stones.

Master Wag was standing in front of Savn, who was seated on the stool with his back to the hearth; there was a low fire which was just on the edge of being too warm. As the Master finished his explanation, he said, "So, what have you been thinking about, Savn?"

"Master?"

"You've had something on your mind all day. What is it?"

Savn frowned. He hadn't, in point of fact, realized that he *had* been thinking about something. "I don't know," he said.

"Is it our friend Reins?" the Master prompted.

"Maybe."

"Well, it's nothing for you to worry about, in any case. I still don't know what he died of, but I haven't quit looking, either."

Savn didn't say anything.

Master Wag stared at him with his intense gaze, as if he were looking around inside of Savn's skull. "What is it?" he said.

"How do you know what to believe?" said Savn, who was surprised to bear himself ask the question.

Master Wag sat down opposite Savn and leaned back. "That is quite a question," he said. "Care to tell me what it springs from?"

Savn found that, on the one hand, he couldn't dissemble when the Master was staring at him so, but on the other hand, he wasn't certain of the answer. At last he said, "I've been wondering. Some people say one thing, others say another—"

"Who's been saying what, about what?"

"Well, my friends think that the Easterner had something to do with Reins's death, and he says—"

"Rubbish," said Master Wag, but in a tone that was not unkind. "Your friends know nothing, and the Easterner is not to be believed.

"On the other hand," Wag continued, "that doesn't answer your question. The way to tell what is true is simply to keep your eyes and ears open, and to use your head. That's all there is to it."

Savn nodded, although he felt as if his question hadn't really been answered. But then, was Master Wag really the person to answer the question at all? He knew about helping people who were ill, but what need did he have to wonder about what truth was? He could ask Bless, but Bless would only tell him to trust the gods, and Speaker would tell him to trust what Speaker himself said.

But then, he wondered, what need did he, Savn, have to think about any of this, either? To this there was no answer, but it didn't help. He discovered that he wanted very badly to talk to Vlad again, although he wondered if trusting the Easterner too much would be a mistake.

He said, "Thank you, Master. Is there anything else?"

"No, no. Run on home now. And don't worry so much."

"I won't, Master."

He stepped out into the warm autumn afternoon and immediately began running back toward town, wishing he could teleport. *That would be best,* he thought. *All this time I spend getting from place to place, I could just be there.* He wondered if he could convince Vlad to show him how that was done. Probably not, he decided. Most likely it was too difficult, in any case.

Soon enough he was there, and, almost to his surprise, he found Vlad right away, sitting in Tem's house drinking wine and watching the door, as if he was waiting for Savn, and the smile he gave seemed to confirm this. There were three or four familiar faces as well, but no one Savn felt the need to speak to.

He sat down with the Easterner and gave him a good day, which Vlad returned, and offered to buy him a glass of ale. Savn accepted. Vlad signaled Tem, and Savn couldn't help but notice the glance the Housemaster gave him as he set the ale down. He wondered if he should be annoyed, and concluded that he didn't really care.

When Tem had returned to his place behind the counter, Savn said, "I've been thinking about our lesson all day. Can you show me some more?"

"Certainly," said Vlad. "But are you sure you want to be seen with me so much?"

"Why not?"

"Didn't you notice the looks you've been getting?"

"I guess I have," said Savn. "I noticed it earlier today, too, when I was here with my sister. But why?"

"Because you're with me."

"Why do they care about that?"

"Either because I'm an Easterner or because they still think I had something to do with the death of Reins."

"Oh. But you didn't, did you?"

"I've been wondering about that," said Vlad.

Savn stared at him. "What do you mean?"

"Well, I didn't kill him," said Vlad. "But that doesn't mean I had nothing to do with his death."

"I don't understand."

"As I said before, I doubt it's coincidence."

"I wish," said Savn slowly, "Master Wag could have learned what killed him."

"Your Master has failed?"

Savn considered the Master's words about not having given up, and he said, "Yes. He doesn't know."

"Then I do."

Savn felt his eyes growing wide. "What?"

"I know what killed him."

"How could you?"

"Because Master Wag failed. That is all the information I need."

"But, well, what was it?"

"Sorcery."

Savn shook his head. "Master Wag said that sorcery leaves traces."

"Certainly, if used in a simple, straightforward way, such as causing the heart to stop, or inducing a hemorrhage, or in a way that leaves a visible wound."

"But, then, what happened to him?"

"Do you know what necromancy is?"

"Well, not exactly."

"Necromancy, in its most basic form, is simply the magic of death—those particular forces that are released when a living thing passes from existence. There are those who study ways to cheat death, ways to extend or simulate life, attempting to erase the difference between life and death. And some study the soul, that which exists after the death of the body, and where it goes, which leads to the study of other worlds, of places that cannot normally be reached and those beings who live there, such as gods and demons, and the forces that operate between worlds, places where life meets unlife, where reality is whim, and Truth dances to the drum of desire, where—"

"I don't understand."

"Oh, sorry. I was rambling. The point is, a skilled necromancer would be able to simply send a soul into limbo, without doing anything that would actually kill the person."

"And the person would just die?"

"Usually."

"Usually? What happens the rest of the time?"

"I don't want to talk about it. It doesn't matter in this case, anyway. A necromancer could achieve the effect you saw in Reins."

"What about the horse?"

"What about it?"

"Well, it bolted, as if it were afraid of something."

"That doesn't surprise me. Animals are often very sensitive to magic. Especially the dumber beasts." There was something odd in the way he said that, as if he were sharing a joke with himself.

Savn thought all of this over, and said, "But who—?"

"Loraan, of course. I mean, Baron Smallcliff. He is a necromancer. Moreover, he is undead himself, which proves that he is a skilled necromancer, if I hadn't known it before."

"Undead? You want me to believe His Lordship is a vampire?"

"A vampire? Hmmm. Maybe. Do you know of any cases of mysterious death, blood drained, all that?"

"No. If something like that happened around here, I'd have heard of it."

"So perhaps he is not a vampire. Although that proves nothing. Sethra is a vampire, but she still eats and drinks, and requires very little blood."

"Who?"

"An old friend."

"I think I've heard of her," said Savn. "Although I can't remember from where."

"Doubtless just someone with the same name."

"I suppose. But do you really know a vampire?"

"An odd one. Never mind. Still, I wonder what he is—"

"What other sorts of undead are there?"

"I'm not an expert on the subject. Perhaps dear Lord Smallcliff will let me use his library to look it up."

"But then you could just ask him."

"I wasn't serious," said Vlad.

"Oh. I can't believe His Lordship is undead."

"Why not?"

"Well, because, uh, I just can't."

"I understand," said Vlad. "All your life there are people you just assume you can trust, yet you don't really know them. Then, out of nowhere, someone walks up to you and asks you to believe that one of them is some kind of monster. I wouldn't believe it either. At least, not without a lot more proof than you've seen."

Savn stared at him, not certain what to say. He seemed to be talking to himself, and, once more, Savn felt the undercurrent of hatred in the Easterner's voice.

"That's how they do it, that's how they get away with everything, because it's so much easier just to go along with what you're told than to look at—" He caught himself, as if aware that he had left his listener far behind.

For a moment he seemed to be thinking about trying to explain; then he shrugged. "Believe it or not, as you will. What I want to know is what the son of—uh, what the fellow has planned. The coincidence, as I said, is too great. He can't just kill me the way he killed Reins, so—"

"Huh? He wants to kill you?"

"He does indeed. But I'm protected rather better than Reins was."

"Oh. But why would he want to kill you at all?"

"He has reasons."

Savn thought about this. "So, what is he going to do?" he asked.

"I wish," said Vlad, "that I had some means of figuring that out.

There's probably no point in running once things have gone this far. Besides, I owe him, for Reins."

"You owe him? You said something about that before. What do you mean?"

Vlad shrugged. "I was mostly talking to myself. But I just wish I knew what he was planning."

"Can't witchcraft tell you?"

"It's not very useful for seeing the future."

"That's too bad."

"Maybe."

"So what *are* you going to do?"

"Try to find out," said Vlad. "I have other ways. Sometimes they even work."

He stared off into the distance, as if he were communing with things unseen.

7

I will not marry a poor musician,
I will not marry a poor musician,
He'd be playing and I'd be wishin'.
Hi-dee hi-dee ho-la!
    Step on out . . .

Vlad toyed with his salad but ate little, either because he didn't like the taste or because he was thinking of other things. Savn ate his own salad with, if no great delight, at least considerable appetite.

Savn felt Vlad watching him, which made him slightly nervous as he squeezed an expensive piece of lemon over the cheese and vegetables, put another handful of salad into his mouth, and wiped his hand on his shirt. The Easterner sighed. "I know a place," he said, "where one could eat every day for half a year and never taste the same dish twice. Where the servers are discreet and efficient; you never noticed them, but there is always a full plate in front of you and wine in your glass. Where the room is quiet and serene and tasteful, calling the diner's attention to the delight of the tongue. Where the appetizer is fresh, enticing and excites the senses like the first touches of love. Where the fruit is sweet and plump, or tart and crisp, and complements the cheese as the salad complements the bread—with reverence and solemn joy. Where there is a choice of wine to suit the most diverse taste, yet each has been selected with care, and tenderness. Where each meat is treated with the honor it deserves, and is allowed to unfold its own flavor in the natural juices the gods gave it, with touches of savory, ginger, or tarragon added to direct the attention of the palate to the hidden joys which are unique to that particular cut. Do you know what I am saying? A place where the mushroom and the onion dance with the wine and the peppers in sauces that fire the palate, and the sweet at the end of the meal is the encore to a symphony of the heart. Where—"

"You don't much like the food here, do you?" said Savn.

"—there is quiet and ease, with only that conversation that flows like the wine from the bottle, easy and natural, and all else, save the sounds of dining, is the silence that food requires for—"

"There isn't any music? I thought the best taverns had music."

Vlad sighed and returned from his reverie. "No, there is no music. I don't like music when I eat. Although," he added, "I must admit that, here, music would be a welcome distraction."

"Well, you are likely to get your wish. There will probably be someone arriving today or tomorrow. There hasn't been a minstrel in several days, and there are usually one or two a week. Besides, harvest is almost over, and they always show up around the end of harvest."

"Indeed?" said Vlad, sounding suddenly interested. "A minstrel? Good."

"Why?"

"I like minstrels," said Vlad.

"You mean you like to listen to them, or they are the sort of people you like?"

"Both, actually."

"You've known minstrels, then?"

"Several."

"I didn't know they had them in the big cities."

"Just about anything you can find outside the city you can find in it as well."

"Really?"

"Yes." Vlad looked thoughtful for a moment, then added, "Although there are exceptions."

Savn returned to his salad, while waiting for Vlad to continue. When the Easterner did not do so, Savn swallowed and said, "What are the exceptions?"

"What? Oh. Peace and quiet, for example," said Vlad. "You don't know how pleasant these things are unless you've gone most of your life without them. Do you know, when I left the city I had trouble sleeping for quite a while, just because I wasn't used to the silence."

"That seems odd."

"Yes, it seems odd to me, too."

"When did you leave?"

"Shortly after the Uprising."

"What uprising?"

Vlad granted him another indecipherable look, this one a quick frown. He said, "There was some trouble in the city with the Easterners and the Teckla."

"Oh," said Savn. "Yes. I heard something about that. Didn't some traitors kill Her Majesty's personal guards and try to kidnap her?"

"Not exactly," said Vlad.

"Wait a minute," said Savn. "Were *you* involved in that? Is that why you had to—"

"No," said Vlad. "I was involved, I suppose, but only in trying to stay out of the way."

"Well, what did happen?"

Vlad shook his head. "For the most part, I don't know. There was almost a war, and there was conscription, and there was blood, and then it was over."

"What's conscription?"

"When they put you in the army or the navy and send you off to fight."

"Oh. I should like that, I think."

Vlad gave him another quick glance, then almost smiled, and said, "I wouldn't know, myself. I've never been in the army."

"Well, but you've killed people. It's the same thing, isn't it?"

Vlad laughed briefly. "Good question. There are soldiers who would disagree with you. I tend to think you're right, though. Who's to say?"

"I used to dream about being a soldier," said Savn.

"Did you? That seems odd. On the one hand a soldier, on the other a physicker."

"Well, but . . . I see what you mean. But when I wanted to be a soldier it was, I don't know, different."

"I know," said Vlad. "When one dreams of being a soldier, one imagines killing the enemy but not seeing the enemy bleed. Or seeing friends bleed, for that matter."

Savn nodded slowly. "I was young and—" He shrugged and smiled a little. "I thought the uniforms looked so nice."

"And the idea," said Vlad, "of getting away from here?"

"Maybe, though I never thought about it that way. Have you ever known a soldier?"

"I've known warriors," said Vlad.

"What's the difference?"

"Another good question. I'm not sure, but that's how they described themselves."

"What were they like?"

"Arrogant, but not unpleasantly so."

"Did they frighten you?"

Vlad laughed. "At one time or another, nearly everyone I've ever known has frightened me."

"Even your friends?"

"Especially my friends. But then, I've had some unusual friends."

"Yes, and one of them is a vampire."

"Indeed."

"That would frighten me," said Savn thoughtfully. "There's something about the idea of someone who should be dead that—You still say His Lordship is undead?"

"Yes."

"Do you really mean it?"

"Yes."

Savn shook his head. "I still don't believe it."

"I know."

"How do you talk to someone who's undead? I mean, isn't it creepy?"

Vlad shrugged. "You get used to—" He stopped, his eyes straying toward the door. "Ah. You must be prescient. The minstrel, I suppose."

Savn turned, and, indeed, a lady was just coming in the door to the smiles of Tem and the few patrons of his house. She wore a travel-worn white blouse and pants, with a green vest and a light green cloak. She carried a pack slung at her hip, and hanging at her back were a long-necked kordu and a shiny black horn- or pipe-like instrument that Savn didn't recognize. Savn thought she was very pretty.

"An Issola," remarked Vlad.

"Green and white," agreed Savn. He was always excited when a minstrel arrived, but especially so when it was a noble, because they always had a wider variety of instruments and songs, and could tell stories of what happened in the courts of the highborn.

By whatever magic caused news to spread, people were beginning to drift into Tem's house already, before the minstrel had finished speaking with Tem, presumably making arrangements for a room and meals in exchange for songs and stories, news and gossip.

Vlad said, "I'm going to have to speak with her, but that can wait."

"Oh? Why?"

"Minstrels know things."

"But will she speak to you?"

"Why not? Oh. Because I'm an Easterner? I suspect that won't be a problem."

Savn started to ask why, but changed his mind. He was, he decided, beginning to be able to anticipate when he was reaching a subject the Easterner wouldn't want to discuss. The minstrel finished her discussion with Tem, and, with a surprisingly shy-looking smile directed at everyone present, she went back toward the chambers that Tem let out to travelers.

Tem cleared his throat and said, "She'll be back and play for us in a few minutes, after she's refreshed herself." This seemed to be a pleasing prospect to everyone. More and more people drifted into the house.

As they did, Savn couldn't help but notice that many, perhaps most of them, looked at him sitting with the Easterner, then quickly looked away. He caught a glimpse of what might have been disgust in Firi's expression, and dark-haired Lova, who was sitting next to Firi, seemed faintly puzzled. Lan and Tuk were sitting together with some of their friends, and, though Tuk only looked at the table in front of him, Lan seemed, for a moment, to be looking at Savn unpleasantly.

For the first time, he began to seriously question whether he ought to be seen with Vlad so much. Vlad looked at him with a slightly amused expression, and Savn wondered if his thoughts were being read. But Vlad said nothing, and presently the minstrel returned.

She had changed to a loose, clean, white blouse with green embroidery, and her leggings were a light, fresh green. Her hair was brown, with a subdued but unmistakable noble's point, and her eyes, very dark, stood out sharply in contrast to her complexion and clothing. She carried both of her instruments, and set them at a table in the corner that was hastily cleared for her. Her teeth were white when she smiled.

"Greetings, my friends," she said in a melodic, carrying voice. "My name is Sara. I play the reed-pipe and the kordu, and I sing, and I even know a few stories. If there were a drink in front of me, I might play something."

The drink was provided quickly. She smiled her thanks and sipped from whatever she'd been given, nodded approval, and poured some of the liquid over the mouthpiece of the long black flute.

"What's she doing?" whispered Savn.

Vlad shrugged. "It must be good for it. She wouldn't wreck her own reed."

"I've never seen one of those before."

"Neither have I."

"I wonder what it sounds like."

This question was answered almost at once, when a low, rich dark sound emerged and at once spread as if to fill every corner of the room. She went up and down the scale once or twice and the instrument went both higher and lower than Savn would have guessed. Then she began to play an eerie, arhythmic tune that Savn had never heard; he settled back to enjoy the music. Vlad's face was expressionless as he studied the minstrel.

She sat on a table, one foot resting on a chair, tapping slowly and steadily, though Savn could not find a rhythm that she might be tapping to. When the tune ended, she played another, this one more normal, and, while Savn couldn't remember its name, it was very familiar and seemed to please Tem's guests.

After playing the pipe for a while, she picked up the other instrument, quickly tuned it, and with an expression of sweet innocence, began singing a scandalously bawdy song called "I'll Never Trust a Shepherd, I'll Never Trust a Thief," that, without ever saying anything directly, implied things about her character and pleasures that Savn found unlikely. Everyone pounded on the tables, laughed, and bought Sara more drinks.

After that, she could do no wrong, and when she began singing an old, sweet ballad about Chalara and Auiri, everyone sighed and settled back to become lost in music and sentimentality. In all, she performed for about two hours. Savn liked her singing voice; she chose good songs; and there were stories he had never heard before, as well as some that were as familiar to him as his sister's face.

Eventually Sara stood and bowed to the room at large, making it seem as if she were bowing to every man or woman present. Savn found himself whistling and slapping the table with everyone else. She said, "You are all charming and very kind. With your permission, I will have something to eat, and then, if you wish, I will play again in the evening and tell you what news I have."

Everyone in the house did, indeed, so wish. Sara bowed again to acknowledge the compliment, and carefully set her instruments down.

For the first time since the minstrel had begun, Savn remembered the Easterner sitting next to him, and said, "Did you enjoy the music?"

"Hmmm? Oh, yes, it was fine," said Vlad. He was looking quite fixedly at the minstrel, and his thoughts seemed to be elsewhere. Savn decided against asking what he was thinking about; he sipped his watered wine and looked around the room. Once more he noticed people at other tables surreptitiously glancing at him, at Vlad, or at both of them.

Savn drank slowly and let his mind drift, until, after perhaps a quarter of an hour, Vlad suddenly stood up.

"Are you leaving?" asked Savn.

"No, I wish to speak with this minstrel."

"Oh."

Vlad walked over to her. Savn stood up and followed.

"Good evening, my lady," began Vlad.

The minstrel frowned at him briefly, but said, "And a good evening to you as well."

"My name is Vlad. May I join you for a moment?" As he spoke, he seemed to show her something in his hand. Savn looked at her face in time to see her eyes widen very briefly.

Then she recovered and said, "By all means. Please sit down. It is a pleasure indeed to meet you, Vlad. Who is your friend?"

"My—" Vlad turned, and Savn realized that the Easterner hadn't known he'd been followed. For an instant he seemed annoyed, but he only shrugged and said, "His name is Savn."

"How do you do, Savn?"

Savn found his voice and made a courtesy. "Very well, m'lady."

"Would you both do me the honor of sitting with me?"

They sat. Vlad said, "Please accept my compliments on your performance."

"Thank you," she said. And, to Savn, "You seemed to be enjoying the music a great deal."

"Oh, I was," said Savn, while he wondered if the Issola's remarks contained a hint that she had noticed how little attention Vlad had actually been paying to the music. If so, Vlad gave no sign of it.

"First things first," said Vlad. He handed her a small piece of paper, folded so that Savn couldn't read it.

The Issola opened it up, glanced at it, put it into her pouch, and smiled. "Very well, my lord," she said. "Now, what can I do for you?"

'My lord'? thought Savn, startled. *How can an Easterner be 'my lord'?*

"I have a few questions for you. Perhaps you can answer them, perhaps not."

"I will certainly try," said the minstrel.

"Do you know Baron Smallcliff?"

"Indeed, yes. I gave him a performance yesterday."

"Excellent." He paused, thinking, then glanced at Savn. "I wonder," he said, "if you would be so good as to return to the table, Savn. I'd really rather make this private, if you don't mind."

"I don't mind," lied Savn. He stood and gave the minstrel another courtesy. "It has been an honor to meet you, my lady," he said.

"And a pleasure to meet you, Savn," said the minstrel.

As Savn walked back to the table he felt that everyone was either staring at him or pointedly not staring at him. He glanced at his friends, and this time there was no mistake; Coral, who was speaking to the others, was at the same time directing a look of unconcealed hatred at Savn.

The feeling of being the center of hostile attention suddenly became so strong that before Savn could reach his seat, he found that he had turned and begun walking toward the door.

And by the time he reached it, he was running.

How LONG HE RAN or where he went he did not know, but at last he found that he was lying on the soft grass of a hill, staring up at the dead night sky, breathing in the smell of autumn leaves.

He tried to account for his friends' behavior, but he couldn't. He tried to understand his own reaction, his panicked flight, but his mind shied away from the subject.

He thought about going back to Tem's house and asking his friends to tell him what the problem was. But what if they did? What if, as they were almost certain to do, they berated him for associating with the Easterner? What would he say?

And, for that matter, why *was* he spending so much time with the Easterner?

He stood up and looked around. He was west of town, not far from Master Wag's, and quite near the road. The way home would take him past Tem's house. He thought of taking a long way round, but chided himself for cowardice.

He climbed up to the road and turned toward town. It was late; Mae and Pae would be starting to worry about him soon. He broke into a jog. He passed Tem's house. It was quiet, and he thought about going in, but quickly rejected the idea; he had no intention of confronting his friends tonight—not until he knew what to say to them.

His lengthening shadow, cast by the lamp from Tem's, preceded him down the road out of the cluster of buildings he thought of as "town." As it disappeared, he nearly ran into an indistinct shape that appeared in front of him. He stopped, and the shape resolved itself into several, he thought three or four, individual areas of darkness darker than the night around them. It took the length of two breaths for Savn to realize that they were people.

The panic that had gripped him before was suddenly back, but he resolved not to give in to it. If it was only his imagination at work, he'd look ridiculous if he ran away. And if it wasn't, running probably wouldn't help.

"Hi," he said. "I can't see who you are."

There was the sound of soft laughter, and he knew, with stomach-dropping certainty, that his fear was not misplaced.

"Who are you?" he said, trying to think of something to say that might get him out of this.

"We're your friends," said a voice he recognized as Coral's. "We're your friends, and we want to know why you don't introduce us to your new buddy?"

Savn found that he had some difficulty swallowing. "You want to meet him? Sure. I mean, he's just a guy. You'd like him. Why don't we—"

"Shut up," said Coral, and, at the same time, someone pushed Savn.

He said, "Coral? Look—"

"Shut up," repeated Coral.

He was pushed again, this time so hard that he fell over. His fall was cause for more laughter. He wondered who else was there. He thought uncomfortably about how big Lan was.

He thought about trying to run, then, but one of the three was bound to catch him, and it would probably make it worse if he tried to run. He stood up slowly, trying to think of something to do, and not succeeding.

Coral called him a name and waited. Savn didn't do anything. He was sent sprawling once more, and once more he got up. He thought about charging them, but he couldn't make himself do it; some part of him kept hoping that they'd be satisfied just to push him around a bit, although he knew the hope was vain.

Then the boy next to Coral called him another name, and Savn recognized Lan's voice. He guessed the third to be Lan's brother Tuk, and this was confirmed in a moment.

Savn stood and waited, feeling as if none of this could really be happening. Someone pushed him yet again; then someone else pushed him, and this continued for a dizzying time until he fell to the ground again. He wondered what would happen if he just lay there, and decided they'd probably kick him. He stood up slowly, wondering in a distant way if they could see him well enough to hit him.

Then someone punched him in the stomach, knocking the wind out of him and doubling him over. *Answers that question*, he thought, beginning to feel as if he were somewhere else.

"Here, let me," said Lan, and Savn waited.

Her mate was trying to tell her there was a problem, and she didn't understand what he meant. Well, she understood the part about there being a problem, but not what it was. She tried to tell her mate this, and he, in turn, got confused.

They wheeled about in the sky.

After a time, he managed to convey what he wanted, if not why he, or, rather, the Provider, wanted it done. She didn't have any real objection, but she didn't understand how they were to tell one of them from the others.

Her mate seemed to think that this didn't matter, that things would work out anyway. This was somewhat puzzling, but she trusted him.

He led her through the sky, below the overcast.

On the ground, a grey wildcat prowled the night, leaving her nest briefly unattended. She called her mate's attention to this, but he insisted that this other matter, whatever it was, should be attended to first.

They came to a place, and through the darkness, she became aware of a group of animals, much like the Provider himself, huddled together as if in a herd.

They circled, and, after a time, it began to look as if one was being singled out by the others, either to be driven off, or to be mated with, or for some other reason. Was that the one? she wondered. No, all of the others.

Very well, then. Now?

Now.

They flew down together. She felt her wings cup the air, and she was suddenly very close to one of them, his face white and ugly in front of her—

And, her mate insisted in her mind, they were not to bite. How could she not bite? How?

Very well, she would do her best for him.

She hissed and veered away, looking for another, but the others were already running away. Would her mate allow pursuit? Yes, he would allow pursuit. A little, at any rate. She set off after them.

When her mate thought they had frightened them enough, she pulled up, swirled around her lover, held her breath, and they climbed above the overcast once more, taken again by the sudden beauty of the countless stars. They danced there for a while, laughing together, then turned to where the Provider waited for them with, her mate told her, his thanks.

Just his thanks? Wasn't there something tasty to go along with his thanks?

Of course. Wasn't there always?

8

I will not marry a guzzling drinker,
I will not marry a guzzling drinker,
He'd be no lover and no thinker.
Hi-dee hi-dee ho-la!
    Step on out . . .

SAVN STEPPED INTO THE house, shutting the chill out behind him. The fire on the hearth had died down to coals, but the stove was still giving off heat. It seemed very safe; but he didn't feel any sense of relief. This was strange, and it occurred to him that he hadn't felt frightened—that he hadn't felt much of anything.

"Where have you been?" said Mae, in a dim, distracted sort of way, as if she expected a reasonable answer, and would be satisfied with almost anything.

Even while Savn was wondering what to say, he heard his own voice explaining, "A minstrel showed up at Tem's house, so I stopped and listened to her."

"Oh, that's nice," Mae said. "Perhaps tomorrow, after the harvest is done, we'll all go together. Was she good?"

"Yes, Mae," said Savn, wondering how he was managing to answer.

"Well, go to bed now. Your sister's already asleep, and we have a big day tomorrow."

"I will, Mae."

Pae listened to this mild interrogation with abstracted interest, and made no comment.

There is much that I do not understand, thought Savn, looking at Mae and Pae. *Everything has changed somehow, and nothing makes sense any-*

more. Why don't I care? What is happening to them? What is happening to me?

Savn found his place next to Polyi, who was already asleep. He got into his nightclothes and crawled in among the furs, warmed by the low fire in the stove. It was starting to get chilly at night. Funny he hadn't noticed it earlier this evening. Or maybe not; he'd been occupied with—with other things.

He lay back and stared at the ceiling, his thoughts running in circles like mating tsalmoth.

Tomorrow morning would see the end of the harvest.

Then would come the Festival.

Then would come . . . what?

He didn't want to stay in Smallcliff anymore, but the idea of leaving was dim, impossible, unreal—as unreal as the experience outside the house, as unreal as those things he'd learned from the Easterner, as unreal as what had happened that night. He was caught between leaving and staying, but the choice was somewhere off in the distance.

The idea of the morning was also dim, impossible, and unreal. And the day that was ending could not have happened. Maybe it was a dream. He'd have to tell Coral about it. . . .

Coral . . . the jhereg . . . the same ones? Vlad . . .

What do you do when nothing makes sense? Stare at the ceiling and watch it dissolve into wavy lines, and wonder if your future is engraved therein.

Savn slept, and if he dreamed, he had no memory of it. The next thing he knew it had become morning, and with the morning came the familiar sounds of everyone stirring around and the smell of the tea that Pae, always the first one up, brewed fresh for the family every morning. Savn's arms were stiff and sore; he had fallen asleep with them locked behind his head. He made fists and shook his arms, then stared at his hands as if they were not part of him. He remembered that Vlad had looked in the same way at his maimed hand.

Everything had an odd, ethereal feel, as if time had become disconnected. Savn stood outside the house and realized that he didn't remember breaking his fast, yet he felt the warmth of the bread in his stomach. Later he stood behind Polyi, holding a sack, and didn't remember getting there, nor how the sack had become so full.

Pae was in the bins, already beginning to seed and strip the plants, preparing to send them off to town, while Mae was counting and weighing the sacks in order to make the account, so Savn and Polyi were alone in the field. Occasionally Polyi would say something, and Savn would realize a little later that he had answered, but he had no memory of the conversation.

They finished the harvest, and he hardly noticed. Polyi cut the last plant, Savn put it in the half-full sack, tied it, and hauled it in to Pae. There had been no need for such caution; it hadn't rained. But then, if they'd neglected to store everything in the bin, it probably would have. Was that really true? Was anything really true?

Savn set the sack next to the full ones. He felt Polyi standing behind him. Pae looked at the sack, and gave Savn a smile which he felt himself responding to.

"That's it," said Polyi.

"Well," said Pae, standing, his knees cracking. He wiped his hands on his leggings, and said, "Fetch the bottle, then. You know where it is."

He's an old man, thought Savn suddenly. But that thought, too, was distant.

"Mae's getting it already," said Polyi. "Are we going to drink it here?" She looked around the bin, full of sacks. The smell of linseed oil seemed to hang in the air.

"Why not?" said Pae. "Well, perhaps we can step out into the air."

It's odd, thought Savn, *that none of them think I'm acting strange. Even Polyi didn't notice while we were working. Maybe I'm not acting strange at all. Maybe I just feel funny, and no one can tell.*

Mae came in with the bottle and four of the special mugs, set on the silver tray. She unwrapped the top, pulled the wax from the bottle's mouth, and handed it to Pae to pour. Savn was keenly aware of the faded black lettering against the green label, and found himself wondering who had written that label—Was it done where the wine was made? Who made the bottle? Did he live in a big city somewhere? Did he ever wonder who would buy the bottle, and what would go in it, and who would drink from it?

For that matter, Savn thought, *where does all of this flax go? That last plant we cut down, what will happen to it? Will the fiber be thrown away, or turned into linen? What will the linen be used for? Sheets? Perhaps a gown for a lady? Who will wear it? The seeds will be turned into oil blocks, and then it will be put in the coolhouse, and then packed into barrels and sent somewhere. Who will use that bit of oil? And for what? Probably it will be made into linseed meal to feed the livestock. Or maybe given to His Lordship to sell.*

His Lordship . . .

Could he really be undead?

Savn shuddered, and became aware that he was now back in the house, standing in a huddle with Mae, Pae, and Polyi, and that the ritual wine-drinking had ended, and he felt a dim sadness that he hadn't been aware of it—he only knew he had participated from the sting on his tongue, the cool ceramic in his hand, and the faint ring of half-remembered words in his ear. He recalled the end of harvest from all the other years, and the memories blended together as tears threatened to come to his eyes, but even this sadness was far removed from where he drifted, in the center of his emotions but not part of them.

"I can't believe it's over," he said.

"Hunh," said Mae, who was drinking while sitting on the cushions below the loft. "It's over for you, perhaps, but we still have to—"

"None of that, Mae," said Savn's father. "The hard part is over, and the children can enjoy themselves today."

Savn wondered if they'd still be "the children" when they had survived a millennium and had children of their own. Probably. He made a note to himself, for the hundredth time, not to refer to his own children that way after they reached their sixtieth year. Well, seventieth, maybe. On reflection, he *had* been pretty young at seventy.

After eating, for which they allowed a good, long time, and after the dishes had been cleaned, Savn and Polyi took a slow walk around what had been the garden, jumping from stone to stone and playing sticks and bricks. Polyi chatted about how sore she was, and how she hadn't even noticed at the time, and about how it was such a shame that by the time harvest was over it was too late to swim, and did he remember the sweater she'd been working on all summer, and did he think the color was right for her. Savn said that this was the first harvest he remembered where he *wasn't* sore afterwards, and attributed it to the way he'd spent most of the summer rearranging Master Wag's house, and that he, too, would enjoy swimming, and did Polyi know a girl named Lova and what did she think of her.

It was, in all, one of the most pleasant mornings Savn had had since summer, and he felt sad that he wasn't really there to enjoy it.

He heard Polyi suggesting that they go to Tem's house early; she had heard that a minstrel had arrived last night. Savn heard himself agreeing. *Tem's house? Yes, there will be a minstrel. And Vlad will be there, and perhaps Coral and Tuk and Lan. Why aren't I afraid?*

Mae and Pae didn't mind their leaving early.

What had Pae said? Something about having done well this year. Savn put the big kettle over the fire to prepare bath water for himself and Polyi, then stood in the door, looking out over the stubble of the harvested fields, and a little later he realized that he was now wearing clean clothes, and his hair smelled of soap. Polyi was saying that she was ready to go, and asking if Savn was.

He shook his head, as if he could clear it of whatever strange mood had fallen upon him, then nodded to Polyi. She looked slightly puzzled, then seemed to forget about it as they set off for town.

The morning was still bright around them, the air cool with the promise of autumn. The red, yellow, and gold of the leaves, already starting to fall, exploded all about them as they walked. Polyi sang "Dung-Foot Peasant," and didn't seem to notice that Savn wasn't joining in.

They passed the place where, as near as he could guess, he had been attacked the night before by his best friends. *Why aren't I afraid?*

As they came into town, Savn noticed Bless on the other side of the street, along with his apprentice, Ori. Ori was looking at them, but then he looked away and said something to Bless, who glanced at them quickly, took Ori by the shoulder, and turned him in the other direction while saying something in his ear. *Why don't I care?*

Polyi had not noticed them, which seemed odd, too; Polyi, like all the other girls in town, always noticed Ori. *Maybe it's a disease, and I've given it to Mae and Pae and Polyi. I could ask Master Wag. Only I won't. Perhaps I should ask Bless, but I don't think he wants to talk to me.*

Tem's house was empty except for Tem and Vlad, the one behind his counter, the other at the far end of the room. The minstrel was not in sight. Savn looked at the Easterner, and found that he had begun to tremble.

"What is it, Savn?" said Polyi.

So, she's noticing something, he thought. "Nothing. I don't feel well."

"Here, sit down."

"Yes."

Vlad was not looking at him.

He realized, and wondered why it had taken him so long, that the Easterner had, somehow, been responsible for the two jhereg who had chased Coral, Lan, and Tuk away last night. Yes. It had really happened. They were going to beat him—had actually hit him—and then there was the flapping, and the small, horrible shapes, wings dark in the darkness. It had been real. It had all been real. And, somehow, the Easterner had done it. Polyi went to fetch ale for him and watered wine for herself while Savn sat and trembled.

To have such power . . .

He glanced at Vlad, but the Easterner was sitting back in his chair, staring at the ceiling as if deep in thought. Savn's intention had been to ignore Vlad; and if Vlad had even looked at him, he would have been able to do it. But it was as if Vlad, by ignoring him, was saying, "I understand that you don't want to be seen with me, and it's all right." And that was something Savn would hate.

Polyi came back and set a glass down in front of him. He stood up and said, "I'll be back in a minute," and walked over to Vlad's table. The Easterner glanced up at him, then looked away as if he didn't recognize him.

Savn hesitated, then sat down.

Vlad looked at him again. "Good morning," he said. "I didn't expect you so soon."

"Harvest is done," said Savn. "We finished early."

"Congratulations. I suppose there will be a festival before too long."

"Yes."

"You'll enjoy that, I think."

"Yes."

Vlad looked at him closely, his eyes narrow. "What is it?" he said.

"Nothing."

"Crap. What's wrong?"

"I don't know. I feel funny."

"Funny, how?"

"Disconnected."

"Mmm. How long have you had this feeling?"

Savn suddenly wanted to laugh, because Vlad was sounding like Master Wag. He did not laugh, however. He said, "I guess since this morning. No, last night, I suppose."

Vlad nodded, slowly, still watching Savn's face. "It'll pass," he said. "I know the feeling. Believe me, I know the feeling."

Savn whispered, "Why did you do it?"

"I beg your pardon?"

He cleared his throat. "Why did they do it?"

"Do what?" said Vlad.

Savn tried to find some indication in the Easterner's face that he knew what Savn was talking about, but Vlad seemed to be frankly inquiring.

"My friends tried to beat me last night."

"Oh," said Vlad. "I'm sorry."

"But why?"

"I don't know," said Vlad. "Fear, perhaps."

"Of me?"

"Of me."

"Oh." Savn could feel Vlad's eyes on him. He looked back, then said, "What did you do?"

"I?" said Vlad. "Nothing."

"But I would have been beaten if—"

"If something happened that prevented a beating, consider yourself lucky and don't ask any questions."

Savn watched him for a while. "You've been beaten before, haven't you? I mean, when you were younger."

"Oh, yes."

"Because you were an Easterner?"

"Mostly."

Savn felt himself smiling a little. "Well, you survived; I suppose I will too."

"Very likely," said Vlad. "Only . . ."

"Yes?"

"Nothing."

"Did you have a friend who helped you?"

The familiar enigmatic smile came and went. "Yes, I did."

"Did he ever explain why he helped you?"

"No," said Vlad slowly, as if the thought had never occurred to him. "No, she never did."

"Did you ever wonder?"

"I still do."

"Maybe I always will, too, then."

"No," said Vlad. "I suspect one day you'll know."

Savn nodded, and decided that this was all the information he was likely to get. "How was your talk with the minstrel?"

"Satisfactory. I got some of what I was after; I'm hoping to get more."

"Then I don't doubt that you will," said Savn. "I'll see you later," he added, standing.

"Are you certain?"

"Oh, yes." Savn felt a small smile come to his lips and wondered if he was starting to copy Vlad's mannerisms. He said, "I still want to impress girls." He walked back to the table where he'd left his sister, and discovered that she was watching him.

"What were you talking to him about?"

"Just passing the time," said Savn, picking up his ale. As he sipped, he realized that whatever mood or spell had been on him had broken; he was himself again.

He finished his drink in silence, then announced, "It's time for me to go."

"Already?"

"Yes."

"All right. I'll wait here for the minstrel."

"Your friends will probably be joining you."

"Maybe," said Polyi, as if she couldn't have cared less.

Savn looked at her for a moment, then leaned over and kissed the top of her head.

"What was that for?" she said.

"Because," he said. "Not everyone has a sister." He stood up and headed for the door. Just before he walked out, he turned and looked at Vlad, who was watching him. Savn inclined his head toward Vlad, and set off to spend the day with Master Wag.

He stopped about twenty paces outside the door, just to take in the day—doing what Master Wag called "Enjoying the now of it all," though Savn thought that was a silly way of putting it.

The row of thin maples that marked the Manor Road wagged in the odd dance of mildly windswept trees, looking as if there were an entirely different breeze for each one. The sky had greyed, covering the overcast and hinting at the rain that Savn had been expecting each day of the harvest. Polite of it, he decided, to wait until they were done.

There was almost no one in sight, perhaps because of the threatening weather. Savn rather enjoyed being rained on, unless it was also cold and windy, but most people seemed not to like—

His meditations were interrupted by the odd sight of six or seven strangers walking around from behind Plaster's hut, just across the way from Tem's. They were all armed with long, heavy swords, and dressed in black, and Savn fancied he could see that above each breast was the Athyra crest of His Lordship.

What would seven of His Lordship's men-at-arms be doing here, now?

He didn't consciously answer his question, nor did he consciously decide to do anything about it, but he turned at once and went back to Tem's to find Vlad.

When he entered once more, Polyi, who was still seated near the door, said, "What is it, Savn?" which was the last clear thing he remembered; all the rest of it he reconstructed afterwards from what Polyi told him and the fragments of memory that remained.

He shook his head and walked over to Vlad's table, according to Polyi. Savn remembered how the Easterner was staring off with a distracted look on his face. Before Savn could say anything, however (Savn was never certain what he was going to say, in any case), Vlad rose abruptly to his feet; the table at which he had been sitting tipped over, landing on its side with a loud *thunk*. Vlad moved so quickly, Savn could hardly see him, which Savn later remembered as being the point at which he realized that Something Was Wrong.

There was a heavy step behind him, and he turned and saw one of the soldiers he'd noticed earlier, now holding his sword and charging through the door, directly at Savn.

No, he realized suddenly, at Vlad.

Savn never remembered deciding to get out of the way, but somehow he was against the counter, watching more soldiers enter the door. They stepped over the body of the first one—Savn had not seen what happened to him—and Savn realized the scream in his ears had come from his sister.

He looked back at Vlad, who was now standing on a table, holding a sword in his right hand, and swinging what looked like a gold chain in his left. The sight of the Easterner's shiny black boots on top of Tem's table imprinted itself on Savn's memory and brought back older memories, of a dancer who had come through town a long, long time ago.

There came a splash of red on the boots, and Savn's eyes traveled up Vlad's body until he was aware of an ugly slash along the Easterner's side. He didn't know how he'd gotten it. He also saw one of the soldiers writhing on the floor, and there was the glint of steel reflecting the lamps on Tem's walls.

Somewhere, far from Savn's conscious thoughts, he was aware of Tem and his guests all scampering out of the way through doors and windows, but this seemed unimportant; Savn, unable or unwilling to move, stared at the scene before him.

For just an instant, he was able to watch the swordplay, three soldiers against the Easterner, all four blades slicing, thrusting, and whirling as if they went through the movements of a beautiful, terrible dance, and when one slipped through and struck Vlad deeply in the upper thigh, that, too, was planned and necessary.

The illusion shattered when Vlad suddenly teetered and fell, amid tables and chairs. At the same time, one of the soldiers fell back and turned around. At first, Savn thought the man's hand had been injured, and then Savn realized that the man was clutching his throat, which had been horribly cut open. He watched the man fall, and felt ill.

And two familiar, winged shapes flew into the room and struck at the backs of the two soldiers who still stood, and two more soldiers came in from the back of the room.

Savn remembered thinking very clearly, *Well, if I had any doubts about the jhereg, this should settle them.*

There was an instant that was filled with swords flailing against the air, and then it all stopped, and the two jhereg flew back out the door.

One of the soldiers said, "Where did he go?"

Another said, "Get the healer!"

Another said, "It's too late for Tevitt."

Savn stared at the place where Vlad had been, and where now there were only reddish stains; then, without a thought for the injured soldiers or his terrified sister, he turned and fled out the door. He ran around to the back of Tem's house and hid behind the stables, trembling.

9

I will not marry a starving painter,
I will not marry a starving painter,
I'd get skinny and just grow fainter.
Hi-dee hi-dee ho-la!
Step on out . . .

SAVN HEARD THE HEAVY tramp of feet leaving Tem's house. He waited a little longer to be sure, then made his way back inside. Polyi sat where she had been, looking awestruck and slightly ill. There were no injured or dead in sight, but Tem was already cleaning the floor where blood had been spilled.

He sat down next to Polyi and noticed that his hand was shaking. He put it on his lap under the table. She said, "Aren't you late for going to Master Wag's?" as if nothing out of the ordinary had happened.

"I guess so," he said.

After a moment, she said, "Why did you run out?"

"I was too frightened to stay," he said.

"Oh. Me, too."

"Then why didn't you run out?"

"I was too frightened to move."

"Are you all right now?"

"I think so. I'm shaking."

"Me, too."

He noticed that several people had come in, attracted to the scene of the excitement by some magic he didn't understand. They were talking in low tones, and pointing to the overturned tables and chairs that Tem was in the process of straightening.

"You should go home," said Savn.

"I will," said Polyi. "Are you going to Master Wag's?"

"Yes, I—I'm not certain. I just want to sit here for a moment."

Polyi's eyes widened suddenly. "I can't wait to tell Slee about this." Before Savn could say anything, even if he'd thought of something to say, she was up and out of the door, running.

Savn considered what he wanted to do. Master Wag was expecting him, but Vlad was out there somewhere, hurt. But there was no way to find Vlad, even if he wanted to.

After a moment of thinking, he went up to Tem, who had finished cleaning the floor. He asked Tem for some food, which he put into a large sack that Tem supplied. Tem didn't seem curious about what Savn wanted these for, or maybe the Housemaster, too, was so stunned by what had happened that he wasn't thinking clearly. Savn got a large jug of water, sealed with a wax plug, and put it into the sack with the food, working it down to the bottom so it wouldn't crush everything else.

He slipped into the back and found an empty bedchamber, from which he removed a towel, a sheet, and a blanket. Vlad would be able to pay Tem back for these, if . . .

He went out the back way, and wondered where to begin looking. Vlad had certainly teleported, and done so faster than Savn had thought possible. How long had it taken? In fact, he didn't know; everything had happened so fast. But it was certainly much quicker than it had before.

What was it he had said? Something about if you were in a hurry . . . Yes, it was about setting up a place to teleport to, which could be any-where; there was no way to know—

He suddenly remembered his first sight of the Easterner, standing next to the Curving Stone, making lines on the ground with a dagger.

But he had said that was witchcraft.

But he was certainly capable of lying.

Savn began running down the Manor Road, convinced he knew where Vlad was. As he ran, he realized that he had no idea why he was going to all of this trouble, and he wondered, too, about the heavy sack in his hand, which was making running so tiring as it bumped against his hip. He shifted it to his other hand and slung it over his shoulder as he reached the top of the hill and started down the long, bending road that led to the Curving Stone.

Why am I doing this? he wondered, and the answer came as quickly as he'd formed the question.

If he ignored Vlad, he'd never learn anything more, and what he'd learned felt like a door that had opened just enough to let him see that on the other side was a place he desperately wanted to visit, maybe even to live. And he knew he would always berate himself for cowardice if he let himself be driven away from the Easterner.

He could try to sneak around, and still spend time with Vlad without being seen, but that didn't feel right either, and he suspected that he wasn't much good at sneaking around. And to be found out would be worse than being openly seen with him.

But if he continued associating with the Easterner, how would he continue to live here? There wouldn't always be friendly jhereg to—

He shook his head, shying away from wondering how it had happened that, just when he faced being beaten by his friends, out of nowhere there came . . . No. He didn't want to think about it, not yet.

And so, naturally, it was just then that he noticed a rustling in the trees overhead, and, yes, of course there were two jhereg, arrogantly sitting in the branches, almost as if they were watching him. He stopped abruptly and stared back at them.

They were the same size and color as the two he had seen—when was it? He'd been walking with Polyi, and then he'd gone to Master Wag's, which was the day Dame Sullen's arm had been broken, so that would be . . .

The same day Vlad had shown up.

They were the same two, of course; it was silly to try to deny it. The same two who had rescued him, and who had rescued Vlad, and who he'd been seeing, again and again, since Vlad had appeared. Maybe it had even been one of them that had been sitting on the roof of Tem's house, listening in on everything that was said.

He tore his gaze away and covered the remaining twenty or thirty feet to the Curving Stone, breathing hard, and looked for traces of blood on the ground. He found them right where he expected; large red splotches.

Where had the Easterner gone? He tried to find a trail of blood, but there didn't seem to be one.

He turned back to the jhereg, who were still watching him. If he spoke to them, could they understand him? Of course not. He frowned.

"Well?" he said aloud. "What do you want? Why are you following me?" He swallowed, hearing the echo of strain in his own voice. In the back of his head he heard Master Wag talking about hysteria. The jhereg stared back at him impassively. He shut his eyes, took a deep breath, and opened his eyes again. He spoke again, this time slowly and carefully. "I've brought food for him. Where is he?"

The smaller of the two jhereg spread its wings, then refolded them, looking hesitant. When folded and seen from the side, each wing formed an almost perfect triangle, as if nature had intended to give the beast a shield against the arrows of men. Yet seen from the front, it looked like there was a snake's head bobbing up and down between the walls of two houses that had been built too close together.

It spread its wings again, and this time left its perch. It dropped just a little until it caught the air, and then rose quickly and flew over Savn's head. Its mate followed it, and Savn turned to watch them fly.

They made a high circle, climbing until he thought they were going to vanish into the overcast; then they flew back down so quickly he thought they were about to attack him, but they landed some distance away. He could barely see them through the trees—about forty feet from the road.

Savn plunged into the thicket after them. Just below the tree in which they rested he almost tripped over the Easterner's sword; no doubt Vlad had dropped it as he'd stumbled along. He picked it up by the hilt, noticing that the blade was still stained with blood. He wondered what it was like to hit someone with it. His musings were interrupted by a hiss from one of the jhereg. He jumped, startled. They were, apparently, impatient for him to find Vlad.

Very well, then. He looked further ahead, and at once saw a dark object, not far away at all, that looked like it didn't belong. A few steps closer and he realized that it was the bottom of Vlad's boot, toe pointed toward the sky.

Savn knew, even before he reached Vlad, that the Easterner was alive, because his breathing was obvious—quick and shallow. Breathing like that meant something, he knew, but he couldn't remember what. Or maybe there were several things it could mean. Was it blood loss? It wasn't a concussion, he was sure of that. It occurred to Savn that one of Vlad's lungs might have been punctured, in which case he'd be unable to do anything except watch the Easterner die.

Savn came up next to him, knelt down, and studied his face, seeing at once that his skin had an odd grey tint and that his lips were blue, and, in fact, so were his eyelids and ear lobes. The colors meant something; he was sure of it. Savn shook his head and thought, *He's dying.*

And so he seemed to be. Not only did his lung appear punctured, but it looked like his neck had been broken—the veins and the windpipe stuck out horribly from the throat, and at a funny angle, down toward the Easterner's left side.

He was muttering as well, but only incoherent sounds, grunts and squeaks, as if his ability to make words were gone. His arms and torso were moving weakly, and without any apparent purpose. A terrible sorrow filled Savn—he was convinced that Master Wag would be able to heal him, punctured lung and broken neck or not, but Savn himself just didn't know enough. If Master Wag were here, he'd . . .

Savn frowned. If Vlad's neck was broken, could he move about like that? Savn tried to think of what the Master had said about such injuries, but he couldn't remember hearing about them. The Master had spoken about the neck as the stream that fed the mind, and that if the spine were severed, the brain would starve from want of thoughts. Maybe this was what he meant; this was what a body did when there were no thoughts to guide its actions. It was horrible.

And then, as if to underline the ghastly sight, Vlad's delirious babbling ceased long enough for Savn to hear an awful sucking, bubbling sound that came from somewhere on his body.

As Vlad began mumbling again, Savn wondered what could cause the sucking noise. If the lungs had been pierced, that might account for a wheezing, but would the escaping air sound like that? Probably, he decided. But still . . .

There was a dagger at Vlad's belt. He removed it and one of the jhereg hissed at him.

"Shut up," said Savn abstractedly. He cut open Vlad's jerkin down the middle and pulled it aside, exposing a chest full of dark, curly hairs. Was that normal for Easterners? He didn't stop to give it further thought, because he saw the wound at once—about halfway down on Vlad's right side. There wasn't all that much blood—Savn almost wished there were more, so that he wouldn't have to look at the pink tissue that was lying open—but what there was of the escaping blood bubbled and frothed.

Vlad's breath was still coming rapidly, and was very shallow. Oddly, though, only one side of his chest—the left side, away from the wound—was rising and falling. And what bothered Savn most about the queer chest movement was that he'd seen or heard of such a thing before.

Where? When?

He looked at Vlad's face once more; it was grey, but seemed no more so than it had a moment before. He looked again at Vlad's chest, watching the left side rising and falling rapidly, while the right side hardly moved. It was familiar, and it wasn't. He closed his eyes, and tried to recall Master Wag's words.

"I found it because I was looking for it. It isn't the sort of thing you can see easily. . . ."

That couldn't be it, because it *was* easy to see.

"I was looking for it because I found the broken rib. And I found the broken rib because it was hit in the side."

Wait, though. "It"?

". . . the sort of thing you can see easily in a pig." Yes! Cowler's stud-hog, butted by their goat. Cowler had spent ten minutes on his knees begging Master Wag to look at it, because Birther was off somewhere, and Master Wag had finally agreed only because he thought Savn might be able to learn something useful. "We're a lot like pigs, inside, Savn," he'd said, and refused to make any jest on the subject. Yes.

Vlad was still mumbling. Savn tried to ignore him and remember what the Master had said. It hadn't been *that* long ago. ". . . knocked a hole in the Cave of the Heart, so the lung collapsed . . . no, not the heart, the *Cave* of the Heart, where the heart and the lungs live. Same thing can happen to a man, you know. You'll learn about that some day. Now, go fetch a bottle with a plug, and you'll learn what I can do with a couple of reeds. Good thing this was a hog; they have the same sort of lungs we have, which I told you half an hour ago, though you probably weren't listening, as usual. You'll learn about that, too, someday. Run along now, before this smelly beast up and dies and makes a fool of me."

The procedure came back to him, and with the memory came the fading of hope. He had the water, which he'd brought for Vlad to drink and to repel the Imps of Fever from the wound, and there was even a wax plug in it, but he had no reed, nor anything that could be used as one; none of the plants that grew around here were both hollow and wide enough to work, and it would take hours to reach the river and return. Vlad didn't look like he would live for hours.

He glanced at the sword which he'd dropped next to Vlad. If it was hollow, it would be perfect; long and flexible . . .

He stared at the empty sheath at Vlad's hip. How well-made was it? Savn had drunk from leather flagons; leather could certainly be made watertight.

He had to hurry, but there was still time for thought. He'd waste less time if he figured out what he had to do, every step, before he did anything else. Finding the sheath was enough to give him hope; he began to think that everything he needed was here if he could just find it; what he had to do was get it right the first time. How could he make the puncture? No, he didn't have to; the sword that had cut Vlad had made a fine puncture; all he had to do was seal it up while he was working on it, and then again afterwards. How?

Well, for the first step, his hand would do well enough, but how about later? The sheet he'd taken from Tem's house certainly wasn't airtight; could it be made so? Was something that was watertight also airtight? It had to be; how could air get through if water couldn't? Well then, if he could find a candle, he could melt wax onto the cloth from the sheet.

He took Vlad's belt off, found his belt pouch, dumped it out, and looked at the contents. There was a piece of flint (why would a sorcerer need flint?), a few odd-looking sewing-needles (but no thread), a few scraps of paper, a purse with several gold coins in it as well as some silver, a bit of wire, a few small clay vials of the kind that Master Wag kept potions in, but no candles. Well, that made sense, why would a sorcerer need a candle? Then he frowned . . . the wax plug on the water bottle? He'd have to melt it, but it might work. So he'd need a fire. Okay, there was plenty of wood around, and he could set the cloth near the fire, and then cut shavings from the plug and set them on top of the cloth where they could melt and make an airtight seal to put over the wound; it wouldn't have to be very big; the wound itself was less than an inch wide.

He should cut the strips first, before doing anything else, so he could have them ready. And he'd have to cut the bottom of the sheath. . . . What about the second tube? Oh, yes, there was the sheath for Vlad's dagger. That was also leather. Would they both fit in the jug?

He felt an instant's panic at the thought that he'd dropped the food sack somewhere, but it was sitting next to him, where he'd set it down while he looked at Vlad. He took out the water jug he'd gotten from Tem. Yes, the mouth was good and wide. It would be hard to jam the leather sheaths through the wax plug though, and he'd have to be careful not to push the plug out, or rather in. Well, he had the dagger, he could cut holes in it.

How much water should be in it? He wished someone would make a jug one could see through. Well, about half-full would be easiest, because then he could be certain that the long sheath was in the water and the short sheath was out of it—or was it supposed to be the other way around? No, that was right: "wound to water, air to air," Master Wag had said. "Why?" Savn had asked. "Because it works," the Master had replied.

Savn went through the entire procedure in his mind, and when he was sure he had it right, he cleared a three-foot circle of ground, gathered a few twigs and leaves and struck a small fire with his own flint an arm's length from Vlad. He got it going, added a couple of branches, and found a few rocks to set next to it. While they were getting warm, he cut several strips from the bedsheet he'd taken from Tem's house and set them on the stones.

The jhereg hovered around, looking interested; Savn tried not to think about them. Vlad seemed greyer. His arms and legs were still moving about without purpose, and he'd shifted his position slightly. The odd angle of his throat seemed to be worse, too. His speech was still unrecognizable. Savn remembered that Master Wag had said something about the heart being crushed if the Cave of the Heart became too small. Savn started working faster.

The dagger was sharp enough to cut through the leather of the sheaths with little difficulty. Savn made the cuts at an angle, so there was almost a point on them.

He took another look at Vlad. The process—whatever it was—was accelerating; he could almost see Vlad's skin getting greyer. "Don't die," he said aloud. "Don't you *dare* die. You hear me?"

He took the water jug and made two holes in the plug with the dagger, then widened them as much as he dared. "You just hold on there and breathe, and I'll fix you up, but if you die I'll kick you in the head." He measured the two sheaths against the bottle, and made marks on them with the dagger at the appropriate levels. "Breathe now, you Eastern son of a kethna. Just keep breathing."

The smaller of the jhereg watched him raptly. "Okay," he told it, "here's the first hard part." The sword sheath slid into the hole with surprising ease, and the sheath for the dagger just as easily. He held a piece of hot wood near it to melt the wax, then blew on the plug; there was now a water jug with two leather sheaths sticking out of it, looking like the remains of a flower arrangement that hadn't been very pretty in the first place.

"Hmmm," he told the jhereg. "That wasn't bad. Now for the first test." He blew into the open end of the sword sheath, and was rewarded by a bubbling sound from the bottle, and the feel of air against his left hand held over the other sheath.

"Airtight," he announced to the jhereg. "This might really work. I'm glad he has such well-made stuff."

He sat next to the Easterner and put a hand on his chest. Vlad didn't react to the touch, so maybe he was too far gone to notice what was about to happen. This part was scary, and Savn was afraid that if he hesitated at all, his courage would fail. "Here we go," he said to the jhereg, and opened up the wound with his fingers.

The puncture was small but ugly, between the fifth and the sixth ribs, still not bleeding much, but still bubbling and frothing, and making a bubbling sound that ought never to come from a body. The end of the sheath would fit over the puncture easily, but he'd have to get past the outer edge of the wound, which might be too big.

Savn started to bend the sword sheath, but the bottle almost tipped over. He cursed, let go of the wound, and bent the sword sheath with both hands, putting a kink into it. That would never do.

He felt himself trembling, and almost gave up the whole idea, but instead he gritted his teeth and played with the position and angle of the bottle until he could draw the long sheath smoothly all the way to the wound with no sharp bends in it.

Once again he opened the wound with the fingers of his left hand and tried to put the point of the sheath into it. It was a tight fit, and the skin actually tore slightly, but he was able to cover the puncture while wrapping the outer edge of the wound over the sheath. He held it in place as tightly as he could, wishing he had thought of a way to secure it without using his hand. Well, with any luck, Vlad's skin would provide the seal, and it wouldn't have to be there long.

It took a long couple of seconds to bend over to the bottle without changing the position of the sword sheath, but he managed, and, while he had the chance, exhaled.

Then he put his mouth over the dagger sheath, made sure of the grip of his left hand, and inhaled through the sheath.

The results were astonishing.

There was a bubbling sound in the bottle and Vlad gave a twitch; Savn was only barely able to keep the sword sheath in place over the wound. But he held tight, and when he dared to look at the Easterner, he could hardly believe the change. Both sides of his body were now expanding evenly, and his throat was no longer angled so oddly—Savn had thought that even if it worked, it wouldn't happen so quickly. Since it had, he was suddenly fearful that he'd overdone it somehow, though he didn't know if that was possible, or what the results would be.

He wished he'd paid more attention to Vlad's normal color, but his skin was certainly losing its ashen appearance, and his lips no longer looked blue. He had stopped waving his arms about, and his breathing was deeper and slower.

"That was quick," remarked Savn to the jhereg. The smaller one hissed, spread its wings, and was still, which Savn hoped meant that it was pleased.

The next step, however, was the hard one: sealing the wound without letting Vlad's lung collapse again.

His left hand still held the sheath against the wound in Vlad's side; he increased the pressure as much as he could, and took the dagger into his right hand. One of the jhereg hissed. "Shut up," he said distractedly. "I'm trying to help him."

Manipulating the knife to shave off bits of the wax plug while keeping a firm grip on the wound was perhaps the hardest thing Savn had ever done—he would have been unable to do it at all if he'd had to hurry. As it was, he was concentrating so totally that he hardly noticed when Vlad began speaking again, this time in words, but with no apparent thought behind them. Savn heard him speak but paid no attention.

When he had a shaving of wax on the flat of the knife, he set it on one of the cloth strips that was resting on the rock near the fire, then went back for another shaving before he could take the time to consider how difficult this really was. He dropped the next one, left it on the ground, and went back for another, which he managed to bring over to the cloth. Then a third.

That should do it.

The wax had melted, and what had been a cloth now ought to be an airtight patch. He picked it up by an end and waved it around enough to cool it off.

"Here it goes," he told the jhereg. The jhereg watched him mutely.

Savn held the patch next to the wound, and at as close to the same time as he could, withdrew the makeshift tube and slapped the cloth over it.

Vlad moaned once, but fortunately didn't begin thrashing. Savn watched his chest motions, but they never wavered. He held the patch in place and took some of the longer strips to wind them about Vlad's body.

One problem that he hadn't anticipated was how hard it would be to get the cloth under the Easterner's back while making sure the patch didn't slip from the wound, which would open up the Cavern of the Heart and he'd have to do everything all over again. In the end, he had to let go of the patch for an instant, but fortunately the wax seemed to hold it against Vlad's skin long enough for Savn to slip the cloth strip under him. He positioned it carefully, then tied it tight around the Easterner's stomach, making sure it held the patch in place. Then, just to be sure, he wrapped two more strips around Vlad, again making them as tight as he could.

He let out his breath as if he'd been holding it the entire time, and said, "I don't believe I did it." He stood up and staggered over to a nearby tree to rest his back. He noticed that his hands were shaking. That was stupid. Why should they shake now, when everything was all right? Well, it was a good thing they hadn't been shaking before.

The smaller jhereg hissed at him angrily. It seemed to be staring intently at Vlad's left leg, where blood had soaked through his leggings.

"Oh," said Savn wearily. "Yes. Well, he can't be bleeding much, or he'd be dead already." The jhereg resumed hissing at Savn. He sighed and went back to Vlad, made a slit down his legging and pulled it back to expose the wound, which was still bleeding, though not profusely. He splashed water over it so he could see it better, and because water was always good for keeping the Fever Imps from a wound.

The small jhereg was staring at Savn, as if waiting to hear the report of his examination. "The seam itself is but shallow," he said, imitating Master Wag's tones, "yet the scar will go from his knee to his ankle, and it will take a great deal of cloth to cover it. I hope I have enough," he added to himself. Then he noticed how bloody the water was, and resolved to find a stream and get clean water as soon as he could.

Vlad was still talking to himself. Savn made certain his breathing was all right and that his throat looked straight, then set about cutting the rest of the sheet into strips, wondering why his throat had been fixed at that funny angle, and what had caused it to return to normal. He would have to ask the Master about that.

Master Wag would, no doubt, consider that today had been well-spent in learning his future trade, but Savn had no intention of telling him about it.

He gave Vlad a last inspection. As far as he could tell, the Easterner would be fine; he'd even stopped mumbling. For a moment Savn just stared at the Easterner, amazed that someone who had been so close to dying a few short minutes before now appeared to be sleeping peacefully, as if nothing at all was wrong with him. He felt unreasonably annoyed, as if Vlad's apparent health were mocking all the work he'd done. Then he shook his head. "I'll never understand how people are put together," he muttered.

She perched in one of the thick lower branches of a friendly maple and watched her mate, waiting for the signal to kill, but it didn't come.

She was not unhappy with the battle she'd been in earlier, but when the Provider had been hurt, her mate had screamed as if he'd been the one who was injured. She wished she'd understood what the fight had been about, since no one had seemed interested in eating anyone, but she was used to this. She also wished her mate would decide once and for all whether this soft one below her was a friend or an enemy.

Her mate continued watching it, and she felt his moods—now suspicion, now amusement, now something not unlike affection—but never a firm decision. She whipped her tail with impatience, but he didn't notice, and just then she suddenly realized that the Provider was going to live. This surprised her, although she hadn't been aware of how she knew he was dying, either.

And at about this same time, her mate suddenly turned, took to the air, and landed beside her.

Very well, then, they'd let the soft one live. She hoped either it or the Provider would supply some food soon; she was hungry, and she hated hunting.

10

I will not marry a wealthy trader,
I will not marry a wealthy trader,
He'd keep me now and sell me later.
Hi-dee hi-dee ho-la!
*   Step on out . . .*

SAVN BECAME AWARE THAT the shadows had lengthened, and wondered if he'd fallen asleep, sitting with his back to the tree. Perhaps he had. Everything was very still. He checked Vlad's breathing, which was all right, then checked the bandage on his leg, which had soaked through. He removed it and inspected the wound. It was no longer bleeding, at any rate—or, rather, it hadn't been bleeding until he removed the bandage. He knew there was a way to take bandages off without starting the wound to bleeding again, but he couldn't remember what it was. It annoyed him that he could have managed something as tricky as getting Veld's lungs working again but couldn't remember how to treat a wound.

But he cleaned it once more, using the water sparingly, then wrapped it in what remained of Tem's fine cloth bedsheet. He noticed again how bloody the water looked, and wondered if it really mattered; it was, after all, Vlad's own blood; perhaps it was good for him.

He leaned against the tree again. He wondered if he ought to go to Master Wag's where he was expected, but he didn't want to leave Vlad alone; he preferred not to take any chances on someone or something, by accident or design, undoing all of his work.

As this thought formed, he realized that he felt rather fine; he had managed a very difficult procedure under far from ideal conditions, in spite of having only the vaguest idea of what the problem was, much less the solution. He looked at Vlad and smiled, then looked at the two jhereg, who were now seated next to each other on the ground, their wings folded.

"I feel like I can do anything," he told them.

The smaller one looked at him for a moment, then curled around and rested its head on its neck, looking at Vlad. What was the relationship between Vlad and the jhereg? It had something to do with witchcraft, he knew, but what was it exactly? Would he ever know? Would he ever be enough of a witch to do such things himself?

Why not?

If he could save a man's life with a jug of water and two pieces of leather, he ought to be able to perform spells, especially after everything he'd been shown. He remembered that odd state of mind, which felt like a dream, but where his thoughts were sharper than being awake—distant, but present. Why shouldn't he be able to get there himself? He remembered how Vlad had done it; he should be able to do it on his own.

He leaned back against the tree, pretending he was sinking into it. Slowly, methodically, he took himself through the procedure that Vlad had shown him, relaxing his head, neck, shoulder, arms, and every other part of his body. By the time he reached the soles of his feet, he felt curiously lethargic—he knew he could move if he wanted to, but he didn't want to; he was held motionless by his own will. It was an odd feeling, but not quite what he wanted.

Sink, he told himself. *Back into the tree, down into the ground. Feel heavy. I am a beam of light, and empty, and I will travel in and down. I am heavy, so I will fall. There are steps that lead into the tree, past its roots. I will take each, one at a time, and with each step, I will go deeper.* And, almost to his surprise, it worked—he felt light as air, heavy as stone; his vision was as intense as a dream, yet he could control it.

He was very aware of his own breathing, of the sounds of the small, scurrying animals around him, of the light through his eyelids. He wished to remove himself from all of these things that were part of his world, so: *Again, deeper. Deeper. Draw in and down.*

Savn imagined his body sinking further through the dirt and the clay and the stone, and with each layer, he became more distant from himself, from Vlad, from the world he knew. He was aware of controlling his descent, and so he gave up the control, and drifted.

Falling through the ground to the spaces beneath, alone, spinning in place, seeing without eyes, walking without legs, coming to an emptiness where emotion is pale and translucent, and sensations are the fog through which thoughts are observed. He regarded himself, reflected in narrow seclusion, and realized that, in fact, he was not alone, had never been alone. His sister, his mother, his father, Master Wag—they slowly spun around him, looking away; his own gaze retreated and advanced, went past them all, past his friends, past the Easterner.

He created a vast forest to walk through—a forest the like of which he'd never seen, where the trees rubbed shoulders and their tall, thick branches created a roof. At his feet was a large silver goblet. He picked it up and carried it with him for a while, enjoying the coolness he imagined against his fingers. Or did he imagine it?

There was a break in the forest, a clearing, and tall grasses grew there. He was barefoot now, and he loved the way the grass felt between his toes. In the center of the clearing was a pond of clear water. He dipped his goblet into it, and drank. It was very cold, yet he knew that he could dive in and it would be as warm as a spring afternoon. He thought of doing so, but now was not the time.

He walked on, and before him was a high stone wall. In the way of dreams, it had appeared before him with no warning, stretching out to the sides forever, and towering high above him. For a moment he quailed, as if it were a threat rather than an obstacle, but he thought, *This is my dream, I can do as I will.*

And so he took to the sky, like a jhereg, circling once, then up, past the wall and out over the chasm of the future, into which he could climb or jump, the choice arbitrary but full of significance.

Like a jhereg?

There was a jhereg there—no, two of them—flying about over and under him, saying, *Isn't it grand to fly to fly to fly? But now you must choose must choose must choose.*

It annoyed him, to be told what he had to do by jhereg, so he refused to choose, but instead continued once he was over the wall, continued aloft, light as the air, warmed by the winds of chance, until the burden of his own power threatened to pull him down.

"I need wings," he said to the emptiness below him.

"No," said a voice which he did not recognize. "You *are* wings. You do not fly, you are flight."

The surprise of hearing a voice where nothing could exist outside of his will was buffered by the words themselves—What did it mean to be flight? He was now wrapped in the dream fabric he had created, and in his confusion chasm and world disappeared, leaving him bodiless and nowhere, yet he scarcely noticed, for the sensation of flight never left, which, he realized suddenly, was the answer.

"I can go anywhere, then; do anything."

"Yes." The voice was quiet, and echoed oddly in what were not his ears, its age and sex impossible to determine, and irrelevant.

"But this is only my dream. When I am awake, I can't fly and there is only one path."

"This place will always be here."

"But it isn't real."

"Real? No. It is not. The trick is to find this place along the one path you think you have. Then, perhaps, you will find others."

"I don't understand."

"I know."

"This is where Vlad lives, isn't it?"

"Sometimes."

"Are you G'mon, the Lord of Dreams?"

The answer was accompanied by a laugh that reminded him of Polyi's. "No."

"Then who are you?"

"It does not matter."

Below him, around him, there were points of light. He knew without trying that he could focus on any of them, and learn of it, and it would be as important as he chose to make it. How, then, to choose among them?

"What does matter?" he said.

"You matter, and he matters."

"He? Vlad?"

"Yes."

"I need his help."

"Yes, you do. But he needs you more than you need him, you know."

"I saved his life."

"Yes. And he will need you again."

"For what?"

"Be kind," said the voice, trailing away in an impossible direction. He tried to follow, and rose up, up, up. The world he had built was gone, so he thought to build another as he rose. He was climbing now, and weaving in and out of thick strands that were the roots of the tree of the world. There was a strange sound, and it was a coolness on his face. The darkness had become light, yet he was unaware of the transition. Sensations grew, and seemed real: a stiffness in a shoulder, the fluttering of a bird, the smell of the trees and the brush.

He opened his eyes.

"You were far away," said Vlad.

Savn stared. The Easterner still lay on his back, but his eyes were open. In his hand was the wax plug from the bottle, and the two leather sheaths that were still thrust through it.

"You're awake," said Savn.

"Yes."

"How do you feel?"

"Pleased to be alive, as well as surprised."

"I—"

"No," said Vlad, "don't tell me." He looked at the odd device in his hand, inspecting the blood at the cut end of the sword sheath. "I think I'd rather not know how you did it."

"All right."

"But I owe you my life, and I won't forget that. Where did you go?"

"I was, uh, I guess I was exploring."

"How was your journey?"

"It was . . . I don't know. I'm not sure where I went."

"Tell me about it."

"Well, I was alone, only then everyone was there, and I made a forest and walked through it, and then there was a wall, and I flew over it, and there was a voice. . . ." He scowled. "I don't think I can describe it."

"That was sufficient," said Vlad. "You went to visit your dreams."

"Yes. I knew it was a dream, and I knew I was making it up."

"Did you like your dream?"

"Yes," said Savn, sitting up suddenly. "I did."

"That's a good sign, then. You should always like your own dreams."

Savn didn't know what to say. On the one hand, he wanted to talk about it, but on the other, it seemed too private. He waited for Vlad to ask him a question, but the Easterner just closed his eyes.

"I have some food," said Savn.

"Not now," said Vlad.

"Do you think you can move?"

"No."

"Oh. I'd like to get you somewhere safer."

"Then you know I'm in danger?"

"I saw the fight."

"Oh, yes. Sorry. It's a little hazy. How did I do?"

"How did you—"

"Never mind. Perhaps it will come back to me."

The two jhereg rose, took a couple of steps forward, and flew off. Savn tried to follow them with his eyes, but they soon became lost in the trees. A moment later, Vlad said, "There is no one around."

"Still," said Savn. "I'd like—"

"In a while. I'm feeling very weak, right now; I need to rest. You don't have to stay, however. I'll be fine."

Savn grunted. Vlad started to say something else, but instead he closed his eyes again. Savn ate bread and cheese, then took a chance and carried the water jug to the nearest stream and filled it, which took over an hour. When he returned, Vlad was still sleeping, but presently his eyes snapped open and he said, "Is someone pounding nails into my side?"

"No, you—"

"Just wondering."

"It hurts?"

Vlad didn't see fit to answer this question; he just closed his eyes tightly, then opened them again, then closed them once more and fell asleep. Savn felt his forehead, which he remembered to be the first place the Imps of Fever liked to attack, once a wound had allowed them into the body—he remembered how Master Wag had sat up with Lorr from Bigcliff for three days, bathing his head and chanting. But Vlad's forehead seemed, if anything, slightly cool. Perhaps Easterners had cooler blood than humans.

It occurred to Savn that wet applications and chanting couldn't hurt, in any case. He took some bloody scraps of the first bandage he'd made, dampened them, and put them on Vlad's forehead, while pronouncing as much as he could remember of the ward against Fever Imps. He also tried to make Vlad drink water, and had some success, though much more water dribbled down his face than went into his mouth. Savn continued the chanting and the applications for about half an hour, until he noticed that Vlad was awake and watching him.

"How do you feel?" said Savn, who, for some reason, felt self-conscious.

"Weak," said Vlad. "My side hurts like . . . It hurts."

"Can you eat?"

"No."

"You should eat."

"Soon."

"All right. Want some water?"

"Yes."

Savn gave him some water.

"I've been having some odd dreams," said Vlad. "I can't tell how many of them are real. Did I just have a fight with about six very large people with swords, wearing livery of the Athyra?"

"Seven, I think."

"And one of them got me?"

"Two or three."

"And I got a few of them?"

"Yes."

"So that much was real. I was afraid it might be. Did someone harness me to a horse and use me as a plow?"

"No."

"I suspected that was a dream. Were there three little tiny people standing around me arguing about who got what pieces of my body, and what to do with the rest?"

"No."

"Good. I wasn't sure about that one." He winced suddenly, his jaw muscles tightening and his eyes squinting. Whatever it was passed and he let out his breath. "My side really hurts," he said conversationally.

"I wish there was something I could do," said Savn. "I don't know much about stopping pain—"

"I do," said Vlad, "but witchcraft would kill me, and sorcery would make my brain explode. Never mind. It will pass. I hope. Did I talk during my dreams?"

"You were mumbling when I got to you, but I couldn't hear any of the words. Then, later . . ."

"Yes?" said Vlad, when Savn didn't continue.

"You said things."

"What sorts of things?"

Savn hesitated. "You said some names."

"What names?"

"Cawti, was one."

"Ah. What were the others?"

"I don't remember. I think you called 'Kiera.' "

"Interesting. What else did I say?"

"The only other thing that I could make out was 'wind it the other way.' "

"Hmmm. I imagine that was terribly important."

"Do you think you can move?"

"Why?"

"I don't know. It makes me nervous to leave you out here. We aren't far from the Manor Road, you know, and—"

"And they may be looking for me. Yes. Unfortunately, I really don't think I can move."

"Then I should get you some more blankets, and water, and food."

Vlad seemed to study Savn's face, as if looking there for the solution to some mystery. Then he closed his eyes.

"There's fresh water in the jug," said Savn. "And some food."

"I'll be fine," said Vlad.

"All right," said Savn, and turned back toward the Manor Road, which would take him back into town.

SAVN HEARD THE MOB before he saw them, which gave him the opportunity to slip off the road before they reached him. He was just coming up over the last hill before Tem's house, and there came an unintelligible assemblage of voices, followed by the tramp of many feet. Savn hid in the flatbushes that grew along the road and watched as the townspeople came over the hill and passed in front of them. There must have been twenty-five or thirty of them, and he recognized several faces. Most of them were carrying hoes and rakes, and he saw knives in a few hands. They seemed grim but excited.

Savn waited for a few minutes after they'd passed, then rushed down to Tem's house. It was, as he'd expected, empty except for Tem, who was wiping tables, and the minstrel Sara, who was sitting alone with her instruments and a cup. Tem looked up as Savn entered. "You missed them," he said.

"Missed who?" said Savn.

"Everyone. They've gone off to look for the Easterner."

Savn felt as if his heart dropped three inches in his chest. "Why?"

"Why? He killed some of His Lordship's men, that's why. His Lordship sent a messenger telling us that since it happened here, it was our responsibility to look for him."

"Oh. Then they don't know where he is?"

"No, they don't," said Tem. He looked hard at Savn. "Why? Do you?"

"Me?" said Savn. "How would I know? Did everyone in town go?"

"Everyone who was here except me and old Dymon. I stayed to spread the word to anyone who shows up late."

"Dymon didn't go with them?"

"No. He said it was none of our business, and tried to talk everyone out of it. I think he may have had a point, too. But no one else did. He called them a bunch of chowderheads and stormed off."

"Where are they looking?"

"Everywhere. And they're spreading the word, so your Mae and Pae will probably hear about it. You should get on home."

"I guess so," said Savn. He moved toward the door, then stopped and looked back. Tem was ignoring him; Tem didn't want to be part of the mob, either. Nor did old Dymon, whom Savn didn't know well. But what about the rest? What about Lova, and Coral, and Lem, and Tuk? Why was nearly everyone in town so certain that finding and maybe killing Vlad was the right thing to do? Or, put the other way, why was he, Savn, not sure? Had he been enchanted? He didn't *feel* enchanted.

He noticed that the minstrel Sara was looking at him. On impulse he went up to her table, and without preamble, said, "What about you?"

"I beg your pardon?"

"Why aren't you trying to find Vlad?"

The Issola looked at him. "I'm certain that I would be of no use to them," she said. "And I don't live here, so I don't believe it would be proper for me to interfere."

"Oh. But what about *him*?"

"I'm sorry, I haven't understood you."

"I mean, aren't you worried about what they'll do to him?"

"Well," she said. "One can't go around killing men-at-arms, can one?"

Savn shook his head, and, in so doing, noticed Tem going back toward the pantry, which reminded him why he had come in the first place.

"Excuse me," he told Sara. "I'd best be going."

"Perhaps I'll see you again," said the minstrel.

Savn bowed as well as he could, and continued past her and through the curtain to the guest rooms. He found the room Vlad had stayed in, identifiable by the leather pack on the floor, and picked up this pack, along with a neatly folded blanket that lay at the foot of the bed. He rolled them into a bundle, which he tied with his belt, looked out the window, and then slipped through it.

The afternoon was giving up the battle with evening as he made his way out to the Manor Road, only to be hailed by a call of "Savn!" before he had left the last buildings of town behind him.

He almost bolted, stopped, almost bolted again, then turned and peered into the darkness, realizing that he knew the voice. "Master?"

"You didn't come today. I was expecting you."

"No, Master. I—"

"You were off searching the green for this monster with whiskers, along with everyone else?"

"Uh, no, Master."

"No? Why not?"

"Why aren't you?" asked Savn.

Master Wag snorted, and came closer. "Is that how you talk to your Master?" He didn't wait for Savn to answer, however. He said, "I don't know this Easterner, and he didn't do anything to me, so why should I hunt him down? Now, what about you?"

Savn, not quite knowing why he did so, said, "I want to help him."

"Hmmph. I suspected as much. Why?"

"Well, because . . . I don't know. I saved his life, and if they find him—"

"You saved his life?"

"Yes, Master. He'd been injured."

"Tell me about it."

Savn, as coherently and quickly as he could, gave a brief summary of the fight, explained the odd wound, and described what he'd done about it.

"Hmmph. Not bad. Did you perform the rituals against infection?"

"Not very well, Master. I don't really know them, and I haven't any herbs."

"Hmmph. Then you can bet the demons have infested him by now."

"I think he's past the worst of the wound—"

"Not if he's burning up inside."

"But I can't move him, and he'll need blankets, so—"

"So, nothing. We can find the herbs we need as we go, if we go now, while there's still light."

"*We*, Master?"

"We'll also need torches."

"Torches?"

"It's dark in the caves, and I can't think of anywhere else he'll be safe. There are torches at Speaker's house, but I'd better get them myself, in case Speaker hasn't gone with the others—I don't think you could survive his questions. Wait here while I get them; then we'll go see what we can do for your friend."

11

I will not marry a filthy hermit,
I will not marry a filthy hermit,
Such a life I could not permit.
Hi-dee hi-dee ho-la!
Step on out . . .

MASTER WAG, TO SAVN'S surprise, led them through the woods by paths that he, Savn, had never known. He had always assumed, without really thinking about it, that no one over the age of ninety or so, except perhaps for trappers and hunters, knew anything about the woods. The idea that Master Wag knew, or at any rate remembered, the forest near town startled him.

They made good time, even with a few stops to gather knotweeds and blowflowers, and they found Vlad as daylight was failing. The two jhereg were still there, and hissed suspiciously at Master Wag, who jumped back and began waving his arms around, as if to shoo them away. They didn't move, but kept staring at him as if wondering what his peculiar gestures were intended to accomplish.

"It's all right," Savn said; then he repeated the words, this time speaking to the jhereg. He felt Master Wag looking at him, but the jhereg calmed down, moving closer to Vlad and watching carefully.

"When there is time," said the Master, "you must explain this to me." Then he knelt next to the Easterner. He moved his hand slowly, watching the jhereg. When they remained motionless, the Master touched Vlad's forehead and cheek, and frowned. "He seems feverish," he said, "but I don't know about Easterners—perhaps they have warmer blood than we do."

Savn touched Vlad's forehead and said, "He was cooler than this when I left."

"Well, then."

"What do we do?"

"We get him to a cave, and then we bring his fever down. First, wrap him in the blanket."

"All the blankets? Do we need to keep him warm?"

"No, no. It's just easier to carry him that way. We have to keep him cool, not warm."

"That's what I thought."

"Roll up the blanket first, just a little on each side so we can grip— No, the other way. Good. Now lift his head and I'll slide this—Good. Now lift up his waist. That's right. Now his feet. Good. You're younger than me; you take that end."

"Just a minute," said Savn, and picked up the sack containing the food and the water jug. He looked around for a moment, trying to figure out how to carry it, until Master Wag set it carefully on the Easterner's legs. Savn opened his mouth to object, but could find no reason to. He felt his face turn red and was glad there was so little light.

Savn picked up the blanket at Vlad's head, Master Wag picked it up at Vlad's feet. They had no trouble lifting him. "Master," said Savn, "it's getting dark—"

"I know the way. Let me get turned around . . . There. Now, be careful; we'll have to go slowly."

He led them deeper into the woods, but he must have struck some sort of path, because they didn't have to stop or even slow down. They began to go down a gentle slope, and there were not even twigs brushing against Savn's face, although Vlad seemed to get heavier with each step. Savn recalled the dreamwalking he had done, and wished this journey were as easy.

They came to the loose stone of the slopes above the caves and went down sideways, never quite losing their balance, but feeling the strain of maintaining it. Savn began to feel the effects of carrying the Easterner, light though he was. At about this time Vlad began to moan softly. Savn asked, "Vlad, are you awake?" but the Easterner said nothing that sounded like a response. A little later Savn said, "Master, maybe we should try this one?"

"I don't remember how to get back to the water. Do you?"

Savn blinked back his surprise. "Yes, I think so."

"All right. This way, then. Stop; this is far enough. I have to light a torch, or have you learned how to see in the dark?"

"How can we hold a torch and still carry Vlad?"

"I'll drill a hole in your head for it."

Savn considered himself answered. After carefully setting the Easterner on the floor of the cave, Master Wag brought one of the torches to light. He put it into his fist so it stuck out to the side, then indicated that Savn should pick Vlad up again.

They made their way back into the cave, Savn leading, until they could hear water dripping. "This is as far as we can go," said Savn. "To get to the stream we have to go over this ledge and down a very narrow—"

"I understand. Set him down and let's see how his fever is doing." Vlad moaned again, and muttered something that sounded like "Do it yourself."

Master Wag felt his forehead and said, "Start bathing his face with cool water, and find something to fan him with. I'm going to find the infection and see if we can exorcise it. Here, wipe this on his face, too. I have to find somewhere to put the torch—look!"

Savn looked in the direction Master Wag was pointing, but saw nothing except the two jhereg, who were sitting on the floor of the cave, wings folded, watching the proceedings. "What is it?" he said.

"They followed us!"

"Oh. Well, they've been doing that."

"Mmmmm," said the Master. "All right."

He found a place to wedge the torch in between a pair of rocks, lit another, and set that on the other side of the cave. His two shadows performed an odd dance as he returned to the motionless Easterner. Savn continued bathing Vlad's face and fanning him with the leather pouch taken from his room.

Master Wag peeled back Vlad's shirt, and carefully removed the bandage. "Not bad," he said.

"Master?"

"You could have done worse with this. But there are no signs of infection, which puzzles me. The fever—"

"Perhaps his leg," said Savn.

Master Wag looked at the bandages wrapped around the Easterner's thigh (which was hairy, like an animal's, though Savn had not noticed this before), and began removing them. "Keep fanning," he said.

Savn did so, and presently Master Wag said, "Yes, indeed."

The wound had changed in the few hours since Savn had bound it. It was red, swollen, and puffy, and there was a thick white fluid coming from it. Savn stared, more fascinated than disturbed.

"Bathe his face again and keep fanning him."

"What are you going to do?"

The Master didn't answer, but began to remove things from his pouch—a sprig of laith, a vial labeled "essence of dreamgrass," another vial with a light brown powder, mortar and pestle—and set them out around himself along with the knotweed and blowflower he'd collected on the way. Once more, watching the fluid efficiency of his hands while he worked, Savn was reminded of Vlad.

"Bathe his face," repeated the Master, and Savn started guiltily, and complied. As he was doing so, his hand touched Vlad's forehead; it had become even warmer in the time it had taken to get to the cave.

Savn began to fan him, but the Master said, "Wait, hold his head up so I can make him drink this."

"What is it?"

"Crushed root of prairiesong, knotweed, and water. Tip his head—there. Down now, and begin fanning him again. Above all, he must be kept cool."

Master Wag began touching and pressing the wound, and probing it with a thin, silvery tool that Savn could not recall having seen before, and, as he worked, the Master began to chant softly under his breath. Savn wanted to ask about the incantation, the tool, and the procedure, but he didn't dare interrupt the spell. The Master broke off long enough to nod toward a pile of herbs and say, "Mash them well and add a little water."

Vlad began speaking again, muttering phrases of which only a word or two was understandable. Master Wag looked up. "We do not pay attention to the ravings of those under our care," he said, then returned to his soft chanting.

Savn did not answer. He handed the mortar to the Master, who took it without breaking off and poured the contents over the wound. Then he handed the empty vessel back to Savn and said, "Clean it, crush a small handful of those, put in three drops of this, and add more water to it. When it is done, make him drink it."

Savn did so, holding Vlad's head up. Vlad was still speaking, which made it easier to get the liquid down his throat. The Easterner coughed and half-choked, but did manage to swallow it.

The Master stopped his chanting and probing. "Notice," he said, "how the edges of the wound are red. Are your hands clean? Then touch, here."

Savn did so, tentatively. The wound seemed even warmer than Vlad's forehead. "Sometimes," said Master Wag, "it is possible to find the cause, the vehicle on which the Imps rode into the body. This time we were able to."

"What?" said Savn.

"See, on the end of the probe?"

"What is it?"

"I believe it is a piece of his clothing, which was driven into the wound."

"Clothing?"

"We wear clothing, why cannot the Imps? When a piece of cloth enters the body, it is almost certain that the spirits are riding it to a new home. It is our task to expel them. Thus I poured onto the wound the purest water I could find, mixed with laith, which demons hate, and blowflower leaves which purify. And through his mouth we give him dreamgrass to help him sleep, and prairiesong which cools the soul."

"I see."

"Now I push—here—and we expel the Imps. You see how thick and grey is the solution? That is the grey of death. Necromancers are known to use it for evil purposes, so we catch it on a cloth, which we will then burn thoroughly. Here. Set it aside for now, until we have the chance to build a fire. Hand me a clean cloth."

Savn did these things. Master Wag's mention of necromancers made him think of His Lordship, but he put the thought out of his head, telling himself sternly to concentrate on the task at hand. As he was reaching for the clean cloth, both jhereg suddenly rose as one, stared down the cave, and hissed.

Savn looked but didn't see anything. "Who's there?" he said.

The answer seemed to come from a long distance away, and it was full of echoes. "Savn? Where are you?"

The Master looked at him, his eyebrows raised.

Savn got one of the torches and began walking down back through the cave, the jhereg, still hissing, at his heels. "No," he told them, "it's all right." He wasn't certain if they believed him; at any rate, they continued hissing.

He found Polyi about fifty feet away, apparently caught between several diverging paths. "What are you doing here?"

"Following you," she said.

"Why?"

"To see what—Eek!"

"It's all right," said Savn. "They won't hurt you." He hoped he was right.

"Are those the same—"

"Never mind that. Come with me. We're trying to heal the Easterner."

"I know. I saw you."

The jhereg watched Polyi suspiciously, but didn't seem inclined to attack her. Savn led the way back to where Master Wag was tending Vlad.

"It's my sister," he said.

The Master grunted, then said, "Get back to work."

Polyi didn't speak.

Savn knelt down and touched Vlad's forehead, which was still warm, as well as wet with perspiration.

"Bathe his head," said Master Wag. "And I will teach you the spells. We will recite them together, and we will wait."

"Savn—" said Polyi.

"Not now," said Savn.

LESS THAN AN HOUR later, Master Wag touched Vlad's forehead and said, "His fever has broken. We must let him sleep now."

"My throat is sore," said Savn.

"You must practice chanting," said Master Wag. "Sometimes you will spend hour after hour doing nothing but sitting and reciting the spells. Your Easterner friend is lucky."

Savn nodded. "How long will he sleep?"

"There's no way to know. Probably a long time. But when he wakes, he will require water and—"

"*Murmumph*," said Vlad. His eyes were open, and his expression was intelligent and aware. The two jhereg, forgotten by the side of the cave, began to hop around near his head. Polyi, who had not spoken for the entire time, just watched, her eyes wide and gleaming in the torchlight.

"I can't understand you," said Savn to Vlad.

The Easterner opened his mouth, closed it again, and said, "Who?"

"This is Master Wag. He treated your fever."

"Fever?" His voice was just above a whisper.

"Yes."

Vlad glanced quickly at the jhereg and at Polyi, then nodded to Savn. Master Wag said, "Would you like water? Food?"

"Yes," said Vlad. "And yes."

The Master nodded to Savn, who helped Vlad drink from the wineskin. "Do you have food?"

"Yes. I have some bread, and cheese, and spring onions, and beets, and a few seasonings."

"Help me sit up," said Vlad. Savn looked at Polyi. She hesitated, then helped Savn assist Vlad. It seemed to be quite an effort for the Easterner, but at last he was in a sitting position, his back very straight. He took slow, deep breaths. Something about the flickering of the torches made his face seem even more gaunt than usual. "More water," he said.

Savn helped him drink.

"Back down," said Vlad.

Savn and Polyi helped Vlad lower himself, and when he was flat once more, his breathing was labored. He shut his eyes, and in a few minutes his chest rose and fell normally. Savn became aware for the first time of the smell of Vlad's sweat—very much like the smell of a human who had been working hard or was ill.

About the time Savn had decided that Vlad had fallen asleep, the Easterner opened his eyes again and said, "Food?"

Polyi said, "Where—?"

"I'll get it," said Savn.

He found the sack and rummaged around in it until he found the food. As he tore off a piece of bread, he noticed that his hand was trembling. "What should I give him?" he asked the Master.

"The bread is fine, and perhaps some cheese."

"Put a spring onion on it," said Vlad, "and whatever herbs you have."

Savn did so, and then frowned. "Is it all right?" he asked Master Wag.

"Yes," said the Master. "You may season the cheese. You must not put another scallion on it."

Savn held Vlad's head. Vlad managed a couple of laborious bites before he shook his head and asked for water. Savn supplied it, and Vlad leaned back once more, and this time he did fall asleep. While he slept, Savn tried a bite. Not bad, he decided. He offered some to his sister, who declined with a quick shake of her head.

"He'll sleep for a while now," said Master Wag. "Let's start a fire."

"Is it safe to leave him here?"

"Probably. But if your sister wants to help you find wood, I can watch him."

"Would you like to help, Polyi?"

"All right," she said in a small voice.

They took one of the torches and made their way out to the woods. "Savn," said Polyi when they were alone. "What is—?"

"Why did you follow us?"

"I thought you'd know where he was."

"Well, you were right. Now what? Are you going to tell Speaker where we are?"

"I don't know."

They gathered sticks and fagots from the thinly wooded area above the caves. "Why are you helping him?" she said.

"Because he's my friend, and because everyone else is after him, and he didn't do anything."

"Didn't do anything? You saw Reins."

"What makes you think he killed Reins?"

"What makes you think he didn't? And what about all those men of His Lordship's?"

"They attacked him."

"Well, but what's he doing here, anyway? Who is he?"

Savn remembered some of the things Vlad had uttered while feverish, and didn't answer.

They brought the wood back into the cave. "Where shall we put the fire?" asked Savn.

"Over here," said the Master. "Even though his fever is broken, we don't want him getting too warm. Burn the cloth, keep the fire going, and I'll return tomorrow. You should sleep, too."

Savn nodded. The three of them built the fire together, after making certain there was enough of a draft to carry the smoke out of the cave.

"Tomorrow," said the Master.

"I'll still be here," said Savn.

"You will?" asked Polyi.

"Yes."

Master Wag left without another word, taking one of the torches to guide him out. Savn made a pillow out of Vlad's pack, another out of one of the blankets, and stretched out on the hard cave floor. "I'm tired," he said. "We'll talk more after I've slept." Actually, he doubted that he'd be able to fall asleep, but he didn't know what to tell his sister.

As it turned out, he was wrong; he fell asleep almost at once.

Savn woke up to a not-unpleasant, wet warmth in his ear, accompanied by a nibbling that was almost affectionate and tickled. He rolled away from it, but the hard floor of the cave woke him more fully, and as he realized what was licking his ear, he sat up abruptly with a half-stifled scream. The smaller of the jhereg scurried away, then turned to look at him, its wings folded in tightly and its snakelike head bobbing up and down. Savn had the feeling that he was being laughed at.

"What happened?" said Polyi.

"Nothing," said Savn, feeling himself blush and hoping Polyi couldn't see his face in the dim light. The fire had gone out and so had one of the torches. The other torch was burning strongly.

Savn glanced at Vlad, who was awake and staring at the ceiling, apparently oblivious to the comedy being performed around him.

"How do you feel?" asked Savn.

"Water." His voice seemed no stronger than it had before. Savn wondered how much time had passed, and was surprised to learn that it had been almost four hours.

"A moment," said Savn. He lit a new torch and replaced the one that had gone out, then stepped into a side cave and relieved himself. When he returned, he found the skin and made sure there was still water in it, then helped Vlad to drink. Vlad seemed to have some difficulty swallowing. When he had done so, he said, "Weak."

"Food?"

"Later."

"If you need to ease yourself, there is a place not far from here, but you'll have to get up and—"

"I'm all right for now," said Vlad.

"Over there?" said Polyi. "I'll be right back."

The jhereg who had nuzzled Savn did the same to Vlad, who attempted a smile. Savn, watching, had mixed feelings. A little later, Vlad announced that he was ready to eat, and Savn and Polyi helped him do so. The bread was going stale but was still edible. Vlad had another drink of water. Then, with Savn's help, he pulled himself over to the nearest wall so he could sit up and lean against it.

With no warning or explanation, both jhereg suddenly turned and began flying out of the cave. Vlad did not appear surprised. Savn wondered if they could see in the dark, like bats and dzur.

"What are we going to do?" asked Polyi.

"I don't know," said Savn. "It depends on Vlad."

"Do?" said the Easterner weakly. "About what?"

"Well, they must still be after you."

"Yes."

"Can you teleport out of here?"

"Not now."

"Why?"

Vlad searched Savn's face. "Too weak," he said at last.

"Oh."

"Must recover first," said Vlad.

"And then?"

Vlad looked slightly puzzled, as if Savn had asked him whether harvest came before or after planting. "Then I must kill Lord Smallcliff, of course," he said, and, as if producing such a long sentence had exhausted him, he fell back asleep.

She felt his unhappiness as if it were a cord that connected them, though she didn't express it to herself that way. But there was a feeling of painful unease that made its way into her consciousness, and it was connected to the Provider, to his injuries.

They spiraled up from the caves, stopping below the overcast, and they began their search out over the bare fields between the town and the woods.

She hated hunting.

She enjoyed flying, and she enjoyed searching the ground for food, but she didn't like chases, and she certainly didn't like fights. In one case, she was certain to get tired; in the other, she might get hurt. And—

There was a movement, small and furtive, almost directly below her. She told her lover, but made no sudden moves. They rose and described a slow, leisurely turn. Her straining eyes picked out a patch of brown that didn't quite blend with the surrounding grass and weeds. They continued past it once more, dividing up and selecting the best angles from which to attack. If one had to hunt, it was better together.

And sometimes, one had no choice.

12

I will not marry a fat old cook,
I will not marry a fat old cook,
For the larding pan I'd be forsook.
Hi-dee hi-dee ho-la!
Step on out . . .

AFTER THE SILENCE THAT followed Vlad's declaration, Polyi echoed Savn's own thoughts: "He can't mean it."

Savn stared at the sleeping Easterner, but the things he'd said while delirious wouldn't go away. "I don't think so either," said Savn at last. "But . . ."

"But what?" said Polyi when he didn't continue.

"But I don't know. Let's get the fire going."

"All right."

They managed to get the fire started, and after some discussion, decided there was enough wood to keep it going for a while without having to leave the cave again, which neither of them felt inclined to do.

"Mae and Pae must be pretty worried about us," said Polyi.

"Yeah," said Savn.

"Well, I think we should tell them where we are," said Polyi.

Savn shook his head. "They'll tell Speaker, sure as drought in summer."

Polyi stared at the sleeping Easterner, and Savn could practically feel her thinking, *So what?* And the worst of it was that he didn't know how to answer that thought.

A few minutes later there was the sound of flapping wings. Polyi jumped and stifled a shriek, and the two jhereg landed on the floor of the cave.

"It's all right," said Savn. "They're tame."

"Tame?" said Polyi, sounding on the verge of hysteria.

"Well, I mean, they're friends of his."

She stared at the Easterner wide-eyed, while the larger of the jhereg deposited what looked like a dead norska. They walked triumphantly over to Vlad and sat down near his head.

Polyi looked a question at Savn, who said, "I guess he wanted meat."

"But how—?"

"Let's find something we can use as a spit."

Polyi looked at him, questions dancing on her face, but she didn't ask any of them. They looked through the wood they'd collected and found something suitable, while the two jhereg seemed to be arguing with each other about whether the norska should be eaten right away. Savn settled the issue by taking it away from them and proceeding to skin it as best he could, which earned him an angry hiss from the larger jhereg.

"Sometimes," said Savn, "people say really funny things when they're feverish. Once Needles had the Dry Fever for almost two days, and she—"

"It doesn't matter," said Polyi. "He can't mean it."

"Yes. No one can kill His Lordship anyway, because of the box."

"That's right."

Savn set the bloody skin aside for the moment, wondering what to do with it so it wouldn't attract pests. They worked the makeshift spit through the norska.

"What should we set it on?" asked Polyi.

"I don't know. Two of the logs?"

"What if they catch fire?"

"Well, we don't have any big stones or anything."

"We could just sit on each side of the fire and hold it."

"I guess. How long will it take to cook?"

"I don't know."

"Can you tell when it's done?"

"Can you?"

"Maybe," said Savn, and motioned Polyi over to the other side of the fire. "Best to keep it as high as we can, so we don't burn it."

Blood and fat dripped on the fire, sending the flames higher and making the cave alarmingly bright, but after only two minutes Polyi announced, "My arm's getting tired."

"Mine too," Savn admitted. "I don't think this is going to work."

"Well, what should we do?"

They moved away from the fire and set the slightly warmed norska down on the floor of the cave. Savn glanced at Vlad, and observed that the Easterner was awake, and watching him intently.

"Why don't you see if you can find something," said Savn.

"Me?" said Polyi.

"You," said Savn.

She started to argue, then scowled and got up. "Take a torch with you," he said. She didn't answer.

Savn turned to Vlad and said, "They brought you some dinner; we're trying to figure out how to cook it."

He nodded. "Pour wine over it," he said. "My flask—"

"All right," said Savn, and continued, "You said some funny things while you were feverish."

Vlad's eyes narrowed. The torchlight illuminated the side of his face nearest Savn, and the shadow of his forehead made his eyes seem very dark. "Tell me," he said. His voice was forceful, in spite of its weakness.

"You used the word 'Morganti' several times."

"Did I? I'm not surprised." He paused to collect his strength. "You know what it means?"

"Yes. It's a weapon that kills, not only the body, but—"

"Yes. Well, that's probably what they'll use on me if they catch me."

"Who?"

Vlad didn't answer for a moment, and Savn thought he had fallen asleep again, because his eyes were closed. Then he opened them and said, "The people who are after me."

"That isn't what His Lordship's men used."

"No," said Vlad, frowning, "it isn't." He screwed his eyes tightly shut, then opened them again. He stared straight ahead, looking puzzled, then shook his head as if dismissing a line of thought. "What else did I say?"

"Lots of stuff. Most of it I couldn't understand. And there were names and things."

"And?"

"And you said, 'I won't kill for you anymore.' "

"Oh." Vlad seemed to consider this. "Anything else?"

"Just before you fell asleep, you said you were going to kill His Lordship."

"Did I? I must have been very tired."

"To think it?" said Savn. "Or to say it?"

Savn waited, but Vlad made no answer to this. Savn said, "Why do you hate him so much, anyway?"

Vlad's widened nostrils flared. When he spoke, his voice was almost normal. "He's a necromancer. He works with souls. When he needs one, he takes it, and does what he will. Do you understand what I'm saying? Does that mean anything to you? Would you like it if your life was snuffed out one day, with no warning, and for no crime, just because someone needed your soul, the way you might need a yard of cloth? What sort of person does that, Savn?"

Then he fell back, and he seemed to fall asleep at once.

A few minutes later Polyi returned. "I've found a couple of stones that might work," she said. "But you're going to have to help me roll them in."

"All right," said Savn.

"Did he wake up?"

"Yes."

"Did he tell you anything?"

"Yes. He really is going to kill His Lordship."

THE SMELL OF COOKING norska filled the cave, and Vlad still slept as Savn and Polyi continued their discussion. "I still say we should tell someone," said Polyi.

Savn shook his head. "Even if no one will believe us?"

"Even so."

The jhereg watched them, seemingly fascinated. Savn doubted they could understand the conversation, and hoped he was right.

"And even if His Lordship isn't in any danger?"

"How can you know that?"

"No one can kill him, because he hides his soul in a magic box."

"Well, we should still—"

"And even if they kill Vlad, if they find him?"

"He might be lying about that, you know," said Polyi.

"I don't think he is," said Savn.

Polyi started to speak, looked at the sleeping Easterner, and shut her mouth. Savn turned the spit once more. Fat dripped; the fire blazed up, then died down again. Savn's mouth was beginning to water and his stomach was growling.

"How long?" asked Polyi, who was evidently feeling the same way.

"I don't know. How do you tell when it's done?"

"Well, it's brown on the outside. Pae always cuts it open, though."

"Yeah, but what does he look for?"

"I guess if it looks like it's ready."

Savn scowled and found Vlad's dagger, and cut open the norska. Some of the flesh was white, but some of it seemed translucent. "Well?" he said.

"I don't know what norska should look like," said Polyi. "I've never eaten any."

"Well, I don't think it's done. Let's let it cook some more."

"I'm hungry," said Polyi.

"Me, too."

She stared at the fire and the roasting norska, and said, "Why does he hate His Lordship so much?"

"I don't know, exactly. But he thinks His Lordship killed Reins, and—"

"He couldn't have!" said Polyi.

"Why not?" said Savn.

"Well, because, he just *couldn't* have."

"I don't know. But Vlad thinks so, and I guess he liked Reins or something."

"Liked him? Were they, you know, lovers?"

"I don't know."

"They must have been," said Polyi. "I mean, you don't go killing somebody just because he killed someone you like, do you? If people did that, we'd have killed every soldier in the army by now."

"Well, I don't know if it's the same thing."

"Why not?"

"Because . . . I don't know. Maybe you're right."

"I'll bet they were lovers."

"So now you think maybe His Lordship really did kill him?"

"Well, no, I'm not saying that."

"Then what?"

"Well, just that maybe Vlad thinks so."

"He seemed pretty sure."

"So? He's an Easterner; maybe they're always like that."

"Maybe," said Savn, and fell silent.

This was, he realized, what anyone would call an adventure, and it felt like it. Yes, in a way it was terrifying, but it also had an odd, storylike quality to it—it wasn't quite real.

Savn had never seen people killed before his eyes, and yet here was this Easterner talking very seriously of killing His Lordship. None of it had a sense of being his own memories; it was as if these were things he heard of in a song. The cave was real, and the feeling that he had embarked on something that he'd be able to tell stories about for the rest of his life; but the death and danger were off in the distance, not actually present, like when he had been standing outside of his house.

He kept coming back to that experience, he decided, because it puzzled and intrigued him, and because it seemed to mark a starting point. It had seemed, at the time, to be the beginning of something, but he hadn't expected it to be the beginning of a time when he would be going through one thing after another that seemed unreal. In retrospect, though, it made a certain kind of sense.

He looked at Polyi. Was it real for her? She was wearing a frown of great concentration. He hoped that whatever her thoughts, they were not carrying her into a place she'd have trouble coming back from, because that would be truly, truly sad. For that matter, how was it going to affect *him* when it was over? Would he have nightmares for the rest of his life? Would he and Polyi wake up screaming for no reason that they could explain? He shuddered.

He caught Polyi glancing at him speculatively, and it occurred to him that she had seen him with the Easterner, and heard him agreeing that something that she might—no, *would* see as a great crime—was reasonable. He thought about trying to explain things to her, but realized that he really had no explanation; he was going to have to wait until she brought it up herself, if she ever did.

After a time, she said hesitantly, "Savn . . ."

"What is it, Polyi?"

"Will you tell me something?"

"Sure."

"Do you *like* Lova?"

"VLAD, WAKE UP," SAID Savn. "I think the food's ready."

"I'm awake," said the Easterner in a voice so low Savn could hardly hear it. "Let's see the norska."

Savn suddenly wondered how much of the conversation Vlad had overheard, and decided it had been stupid to talk about it right in front of him in any case. He took the spit off the stones and showed it to Vlad.

"It's done," announced the Easterner. "Help me sit up."

Savn and Polyi put the spit back on the stones, then helped him sit up.

"Now I want to stand."

Savn said, "Are you sure you should—"

"And help me to the latrine."

"Oh. All right."

They took his arms and helped him up, and guided him to the other cave, and held him up until he was done. Then they brought him back and helped him sit up against the wall of the cave. The jhereg scampered along with him all the way. He sat there for several moments, breathing deeply, then nodded. "Let's eat," he said.

While they'd been helping him, part of the norska had burned slightly, but the rest was fine.

They ate in silence at first. Savn thought it was one of the best things he'd ever eaten. He wasn't certain what Polyi thought, but she was eating with great enthusiasm.

"Do you know," said Savn suddenly, "it just occurred to me that if there are people looking for us, and if they are at all nearby, the smell will bring them right to us." He took another bite of roasted norska.

Vlad grunted and said, "Should my friends take that as a compliment on their choice of food?"

Savn took his time chewing and swallowing, then said, "Yes."

"Good. I think the cave is deep enough that no smells will escape."

"All right," said Savn.

Polyi was still eating and not talking. Savn tried to decide if she was looking sullen, but he couldn't tell.

"It's the wine that does it," said Vlad. His voice seemed slightly stronger; at any rate, he seemed to have no trouble talking. "Cooking over an open flame is its own art, and doesn't have much to do with oven cooking or stove cooking. I'm not really good at it. But I know that wine always helps."

Savn wondered if it was the wine that made the norska taste so good, or if it was really the circumstances—if it wasn't still the feeling that he was on some sort of adventure. He knew there was something wrong with thinking about it this way, but how could he help it? He was sitting in a cave with a man who spoke of killing His Lordship, and he was eating norska taken with magic—

"Vlad," he said suddenly.

"Mroi?" said Vlad. Then he swallowed and said, "Excuse me. What?"

"I had always heard that it was bad luck to hunt with magic, except for finding the game."

"I've heard that, too."

"Well, then," said Savn. "What about—"

"Oh, this? Well, it wasn't exactly magic. At least, not directly."

"I don't understand."

"Never mind. It isn't important."

Savn decided that he was probably never going to understand what Vlad thought important. The most trivial things seemed to provoke the biggest reactions, like when Savn had mentioned that His Lordship's men hadn't been using Morganti weapons. Savn shook his head, wondering.

All of a sudden Polyi said, "You can't kill His Lordship."

Vlad looked at her without speaking.

Savn said, "Polyi—"

"Well," she said to Vlad. "You can't."

"Of course not," said Vlad.

"But you mean to. I know it."

"Polyi—"

"Just out of curiosity," said Vlad, "why couldn't I kill him?"

"He's a wizard."

"So?"

Polyi frowned. "They say that he can never die, because his magic protects him. They say that there are rooms in his keep where he just walks in and comes out younger, and that he is only as old as he wants to be. They say—"

"And how much of this do you believe?"

"I don't know," said Polyi.

Savn said, "If it's true, though—"

"It's true that he's a sorcerer."

"Well, then?"

"No matter how subtle the wizard, a knife between the shoulder blades will seriously cramp his style."

Savn couldn't find an answer to that, so he didn't make one. He looked at Polyi, but she was just staring angrily at Vlad. There was a sense of unreality about the entire conversation—it was absurd that they could be talking about killing His Lordship as if discussing the price of linen. There had been a time, some five years before, when he, Coral, and Lan had drunk wine until they had become sick. The thing he remembered most clearly about the incident, other than walking around for the next week hoping Mae and Pae didn't find out about it, was sitting with his head bent over, focusing on nothing except the tabletop, slowly memorizing every mark on it. The memory came back to him with such a rush that it almost brought along the giddy, sickly, floating feeling he had had then.

At last he said, "But what if he is undead, like you say?"

"He is," said Vlad. "That makes it a little trickier, that's all."

"Then you admit you're going to do it," said Polyi, in the same tone of voice she used upon discovering the piece for her game under Savn's blankets.

"What if I am?" said Vlad. "Do you think I should just let him kill me?"

"Why don't you teleport away?" said Savn.

"Heh," said Polyi. "Teleport? If he could do that, he could have fixed his finger."

"Polyi—" said Savn.

"First of all," said Vlad, looking at Polyi, "I'm not a physicker. A physicker who knew sorcery could have healed my hand if I'd gotten to him quickly. Now it would be very difficult, and I haven't been in touch with anyone that good in some time.

"Second," he continued, looking now at Savn, "never attempt complicated sorcery—and teleportation is complicated—when you're weak in the body. It upsets the mind, and that can be fatal. I've done it, when I've had to, and I will again, if I have to. But I've been lucky, and I don't like to depend on luck.

"Third," he said, addressing them both, "I do, indeed, intend to kill Loraan—Baron Smallcliff. But I'm in no shape to do so now. He knows I want to kill him; he killed Reins in order to draw me in, so that when I tried to kill him he could kill me. I don't know everything that's going on yet, so I don't know how I'm going to kill him. If I did, I certainly wouldn't tell you. I wouldn't have told you this much if I hadn't betrayed myself already, and if I didn't owe it to you.

"But there it is," he said. "I've told you my plans, or as much of them as I have. If you want to betray me, I can't stop you."

He looked at them and waited. At last Savn said, "I don't know what to do."

"I think we should go home," said Polyi.

"Then what?" said Savn.

"I don't know."

Savn looked at the Easterner, who was watching them carefully, his expression blank. "She's right," said Savn. "We really should go home."

"Yes," said Vlad. "I'll be all right here."

"Are you sure?"

"Yes. And, whatever happens, no one is going to be able to take me by surprise."

Savn glanced at the jhereg and nodded.

Vlad settled back against the wall of the cave and closed his eyes. "I believe I will sleep now. Will you help me to lie down?"

When they were done eating, they gave the bones to the jhereg, who seemed well pleased with them. Savn wanted to say goodbye to Vlad, but the Easterner was sound asleep. He and Polyi left the cave together, blinking in the bright afternoon sun.

They started for home.

13

I will not marry a handsome soldier,
I will not marry a handsome soldier,
He would not want me when I'm older.
Hi-dee hi-dee ho-la!
Step on out . . .

BY UNSPOKEN AGREEMENT THEY took the long way, not passing through town; as a result they didn't see anyone. Savn wondered if there were still parties out looking for Vlad, and if Mae and Pae had joined them. Thinking of Mae and Pae filled him with a vague unease over and above his fear of whatever punishment they'd inflict on him for staying out all night. He thought about it, trying to figure out why, and eventually remembered how oddly they'd acted the night Vlad had come to their home, at which point Savn realized that he wasn't afraid of what Mae and Pae would say; he was afraid of what they wouldn't say.

It was as bad as Savn had feared, or worse. Mae looked up, nodded at them, and went back to stripping seeds. Pae, who was counting sacks, just gave them a brief smile and said, "Savn, isn't it time for you to be at Master Wag's?"

"Yes, Pae," said Savn, trying to keep his voice from trembling.

"Well, be on your way, then."

Savn watched Polyi, who was obviously trying to conceal how upset she was. She said, "Don't you want to know where we've been?"

"Well," said Mae, straightening up and stretching her back, "you're here, aren't you? You've been fine, haven't you?"

"Yes, but—"

Savn caught her eye and she fell silent.

"We'll be going, then," said Savn.

Mae and Pae nodded abstractedly and returned to their work. Savn and Polyi didn't speak until they reached the house, where Savn gallantly offered to let Polyi bathe first.

She ignored his offer and said, "What's wrong with them?"

"With who?"

"Cut it out," said Polyi. "You know what I mean."

Savn started to protest, then gave up and said, "I don't know. I think— No, I don't know."

"What do you think?"

"Never mind."

"Is it something Vlad did to them?"

Savn looked away and repeated, "I don't know."

"Maybe he—"

"I don't know."

"All right," she said, pouting. "Don't yell at me."

"Do you want to bathe first, or should I?"

"I don't care. Go ahead. No, I will."

"Let me, I have to get to Master Wag's."

"Then why did you ask?"

"I don't know. I'll hurry."

Savn bathed quickly, and leaving the house, cut across the fields away from the counting bin so he wouldn't have to face Mae and Pae again. He also skirted the town, although he was frightfully curious about whether they were still searching for Vlad.

When he arrived at Master Wag's, he was greeted with the words, "I didn't expect you to be here today. How's our patient?"

"He was well when I left him, about five hours ago."

"Had he eaten?"

"Yes."

"No fever?"

"None."

"Still weak?"

"Very."

"Did he empty his bowels?"

"No. Liquid only."

"Hmmm. Not good, but not yet bad, either."

"Are they still looking for him?"

The Master nodded. "Not with any great intensity, perhaps, but

Speaker insisted that they keep searching the area until they were certain he had left."

"That sounds like they think he did."

"Speaker probably does, but that doesn't much matter. They'll keep looking, I'm afraid, and eventually they'll find the caves."

"It may take a long time."

"Oh, yes. It would take days to just search the caves—they're immense, convoluted, and lead all the way back into the cliff. But still—"

"Yes. I hope they don't get to them soon."

"In any case, Savn, the Easterner shouldn't be alone for very long. He could relapse at any time."

"All right," said Savn. "I'll return at once."

"No, as long as you're here, you may as well relax for a while. We can discuss that procedure you performed. I want to show you just what you did, and why it worked, so you can be more certain next time."

Which is what they did for the next hour; the Master explained the problem and the cure, while Savn listened more intently than he ever had before. It was different, he realized, when you knew exactly why you were doing something, when you'd actually seen someone with the injury and were learning how to save him.

After that, the conversation drifted onto other matters of the healing arts, and even here Savn noticed a difference in the Master's attitude: he was less brusque and somehow more respectful of Savn—as if by saving the Easterner, Savn had proven himself to Master Wag.

At one point, the Master stopped in the middle of explaining the sort of thoughts that must be kept out of the head of a person in danger of fever, and said, "What is bothering you, Savn? You seem disturbed about something."

"I'm not certain, Master."

The Master looked at him closely. "Is it," he said, "that you aren't certain you should have saved the Easterner? Because, if that is the trouble, it shouldn't bother you. Saving lives is our trade—all lives. Even, sometimes, that of livestock. Yes, if it is a choice between saving the life of a human being and saving the life of an Easterner, that is one thing. But in this case, you found someone who was injured and you cured him. It is no betrayal of His Lordship for you to perform your calling."

"It isn't that, Master. I think it's Mae and Pae."

"What about them?"

"Well, they've been acting funny, that's all."

"Funny? What do you mean?"

"Well, they seem distracted, like they're far away."

"Explain what you mean, Savn. Be precise."

"It's hard to, Master. It's a feeling I have. But when Polyi and I were out all night, they didn't say a word to us about it."

"You're growing up, Savn. They recognize this, and feel you can be trusted more. That's all it is."

Savn shook his head. "I'm afraid Vlad put a spell on them."

The Master cocked his head. "A spell? What sort of spell, and why would he do something like that?"

"A witchcraft spell."

"Witchcraft!" said the Master. "Nonsense. If you believe all of the rubbish that—Hullo, is someone there?"

There did, indeed, seem to be someone clapping at the door. Savn got up and opened it, and was startled to find himself looking up at Fird, the fruit-seller from Bigcliff.

Savn stared, open-mouthed, his thoughts racing. For one thing, he had forgotten how tall Fird was. For another, Vlad had been asking about him just the other day, and . . . Savn realized he was being rude. He closed his mouth, opened it again, and said, "May I be of some service to you?"

"I be here looking," said Fird, in his low, careful voice, and with the odd grammatical formulations of Bigcliff, "for Master Wag."

"Who is it?" called the Master from inside.

"Please come in," said Savn, stepping out of Fird's way.

"My thanks to you for that," said Fird, ducking his head as he passed under the Master's doorway. Over his shoulder was a large sack, which Savn assumed contained the fruit he'd been selling.

The Master rose as he entered, and said, "What seems to be the matter, goodman?"

"A note is sent me to you, by for this Eastern devil. You know him?"

"Eastern devil?" said Master Wag and Savn with one voice. The Master gave Savn a look, then continued. "Do you mean the Easterner, Vlad?"

"The same as him, yes," said Fird.

"I know him. He sent you a note?"

"That were, or the mountains grew him."

Savn had to stop and figure this one out, but Master Wag said, "May I see it?"

"To you be done, then," said Fird, and handed a small piece of pale, almost white parchment to the Master. The Master, in turn, frowned, read it several times, and, with a look that asked permission of Fird, handed it to Savn.

At first, Savn mentally *tsked* at the Easterner's penmanship; then he wondered how Vlad had written it. It had probably been done in wood-ash using a dagger's point. It read: "Sorry I missed you I've been hurt ask Master Wag to bring you to me I'll pay gold."

Savn handed it back to Fird, while the Master asked, "How do you know him?"

"How? As one will know another. Gold he is offered to me, and then he is not where his promise is. I be curious, I be finding fruit in sack, I be finding note, I be reading, I be coming here. But you he is knowing, and this I be in wonder at."

"He's hurt, as he said," said the Master. "I helped him."

"So?" said Fird, shrugging. "He is hurt. I have mangoes and apples, which will cure like a physicker."

"Maybe," said the Master, sounding doubtful.

"Apples. Apple's the thing. Where with to—"

"Savn here will lead you to him."

"Master—"

"You think it's a trick?"

"Well—"

"If His Lordship, or Speaker, or anyone else knows enough to attempt this sort of trick, it doesn't much matter if we fall for it."

"Not to us, but—"

"Think about it, Savn. Think about how much they would have to know."

"Trick?" said Fird. "Is what this—"

"The Easterner," said Master Wag, "is hurt because some people tried to kill him. Savn is concerned that—"

"Ah. Well, is to careful, then, but I—"

"Yes, I know," said the Master. "Savn?"

"All right. Should we go now?" Both Fird and Master Wag nodded.

"I may join you later, to check on our patient, or else I'll see you tomorrow."

"Very well, Master," said Savn, and led the way out the door and down the road toward the Curving Stone.

He was saved from the necessity of deciphering Fird's speech by the fact that Fird didn't seem inclined to make conversation, and Savn, for his part, didn't know what to say. Just past the Curving Stone he led the way into the woods, through them, and out over Bigcliff. Fird looked down with interest at the beach where, though he probably didn't know it, Savn had first pointed him out to Vlad.

Savn still wondered what the Easterner wanted with the fruit-seller. As they approached the cave, Fird stopped, sniffed the air, and said his first words since they set out: "Norska is been roasted."

Savn smelled it too, and repressed a chuckle. So much for the smell not getting out. "This way," he said, and led Fird into the cave. "Can you make a light?"

Fird grunted, and a soft red glow filled the cavern. They went through the first, large chamber, and Savn led the way unerringly into the correct passage, and another large chamber. Here, even though Savn half expected it, he was startled by the flapping of wings as the jhereg appeared before him. Fird jumped, and his sorcerous light wavered for a moment as Savn said, "It's all right, they won't hurt us." Fird didn't appear convinced, but watched the jhereg closely and kept a short knife in his hand.

The jhereg flew around the opening for a moment, then disappeared.

"Is Easterner magic to tame carrion-eaters?" asked Fird.

"I guess," said Savn.

Fird's mouth twitched. "Then is onward."

They continued, Fird ducking to traverse corridors that Savn was able to walk through upright, until they saw the flickering glow of the torches.

Savn called out, "Vlad? It's Savn. Fird, the fruit-seller, is with me."

There was a rustling sound ahead, and in the dim light Savn was able to make out Vlad turning his head. "Good," he said in a hoarse whisper.

"How are you feeling?"

"Weak. But a little better, I think."

"Great."

"Sorry I missed our appointment, Fird. Glad you got the note."

Fird was watching Vlad carefully. He said, "Note is arrived, but the wondering is from its means of travel."

"Does it matter?"

"Magic is that of the Easterner, is to wonder what else you is to have done or will do?"

"For one thing," said Vlad. "Give you a certain amount of gold, in exchange for answering some questions. Have you been to—" He paused and looked at Savn.

"Would you like me to leave?"

"Please," said Vlad. "I'm sorry, but I'd rather this not be overheard."

Savn shrugged his shoulders as if he didn't care, and, taking one of the burning torches, wandered back out of the cave. To his surprise, the larger of the jhereg accompanied him. He was even more surprised to realize that this no longer bothered him. Finding a comfortable-looking spot beneath a tree just outside the cave, he put out the torch and settled down with his back against the trunk. The jhereg perched on a low branch of the same tree.

Savn looked up at it, and it looked back, as if waiting for Savn to start the conversation. "I would like to know," said Savn obligingly, "what they're talking about in there."

The jhereg stared at him with unblinking, reptilian eyes.

"And while we're on the subject," he continued, "I'd like to know how close the searchers are getting to this cave. If I knew how long we had, I— well, I don't know what I'd do. But I'd like to know.

"And, since I'm asking questions, just what *did* Vlad do to Mae and Pae? I know, I know. He put a spell on them."

He frowned and studied the ground between his feet. He'd known since last night that Vlad had enchanted them, but it seemed to take a long time for the fact to make its way into his bones. There was something so *evil* about doing such a thing—about magically clouding someone's eyes, muffling his thoughts—that he couldn't really think of it as something done by the Easterner lying helpless a hundred yards into the hill.

And the thought that, even now, Mae and Pae were under the influence of whatever spell Vlad had cast was utterly foreign to his emotions; he didn't know how to look at it. The anger that ought to be his natural response simply wouldn't appear.

He tried to imagine himself confronting the half-dead Vlad and telling him off for it, but his imagination failed. He thought about doing nothing until Vlad felt better, but that didn't seem right either.

"What would you do?" he asked the jhereg.

It ducked its head under its wing and cleaned itself, then seemed to settle more fully onto the branch and looked around with, Savn imagined, an expression of mild curiosity.

"So, what am I waiting for? I'm not going to ask him about Mae and Pae. Why am I here? In case he has a relapse? But am I going to heal him after what he did? Of course I am; I can't let him *die*."

He stared at the jhereg, who seemed completely uninterested in his problems. He scowled at it. "What I *should* do is abandon Vlad and see what I can do for Mae and Pae. Sure. Good idea. But what can I do for them? They've been enchanted; I don't know anything about enchantments."

He stopped, feeling his eyes grow wide. "But Bless does. Bless knows all about curses of the gods, and whatever this Easterner did, it can't be *that* bad. That's it. Vlad can take care of himself; I have to find Bless."

And, with no more reflection or questions, he stood and dashed off toward town.

Twilight made the outlines of the livery stable indistinct as Savn came up over the top of the hill. He stopped and surveyed the city. There were a few people on the outskirts, talking, as there always were; Savn could make out Tif from her posture and Boarder from his hair, and there were others he didn't yet recognize. At the far end a few people moved about, but they were too far away to identify. However, he was certain he saw a two-horse wagon not far from Speaker's, and Bless was one of the few (as was Savn's family) who drove two horses.

He started down the hill, and couldn't help but notice how the gossips outside of Feeder's stopped talking and watched him pass. It was creepy. But they didn't say anything to him, and he didn't see any of his friends.

Bless and Ori came out of Speaker's house and climbed into the wagon. Savn ran up to them, waving. Bless saw him, checked the horses, and waited. Ori looked at him with mild curiosity. Bless's face was round, his eyes were very widely set, and the look on his face seemed suspicious, as if he wasn't certain Savn was doing what he was supposed to do.

"The evening's rain to you, sir."

"And to you, young man. Where have you been this last day?"

"Where have I been, sir?"

"Yes, the whole town has gathered to look for this Easterner, and your absence was noticed."

"I didn't know. Why were you looking for him, sir?"

"That is none of your concern, young man. You should be glad that it is I and not Speaker who wants to know, or you can be sure the questions would be rougher in the asking and quicker in the answering."

"Yes, sir." Savn didn't look at Ori, but he was aware of him there, watching, and it made Savn angry and uncomfortable.

"So where *were* you?" asked Bless.

Savn heard himself answer, "I was looking for him, too."

"*You* were?"

"Yes, sir. I saw what happened, and he was hurt, and I thought he might need physicking, and—"

"*Physicking!*" thundered Bless. "Of all the nerve! This Easterner killed—actually *killed*—three of His Lordship's men-at-arms, and you want to physick him?"

"I'm sorry, sir."

"I should hope so! He has already done more evil here than you can imagine."

"I know, sir. That's what I wanted to ask you about."

That seemed to catch Bless up short. "Eh? Is there something I don't know about?"

"Yes, sir. It's Mae and Pae."

"Well? What about them?"

"I wonder if you could . . . that is, I think they've been enchanted."

Bless made a peculiar sound with his mouth and nose. "Enchanted?" he said. "And by whom?"

"By Vlad, the Easterner."

"Oh, he's a wizard, is he?"

"No, sir, a witch."

"Rubbish," said Bless. "A witch can't do anything to you unless you believe he can. Have you spoken to Master Wag about this? What does he say about witches?"

"The same as you, sir, only—"

"Well, there you have it."

"But—"

Bless sighed. "Very well. What makes you think this witch has done something to them?"

"They've been acting funny. I mean, *really* funny."

Bless sniffed. "Maybe they're concerned about you."

"That's just it. They're *not*."

"What do you mean?"

"Well, they don't seem to care what I do."

"Eh? That's the first time I've heard that complaint from a young man. What did you do that they didn't care about?"

Savn realized that he was in dangerous waters. He wanted to say enough to convince Bless to do something, but not so much that Bless would know what he'd been up to.

"Well, I stayed out playing, and they didn't do anything about it. They didn't seem to even notice."

"I see. And because of this you think they're enchanted?"

"Well, yes. If you'd seen the way they've been acting—"

"I saw them two days past, and they seemed quite fine to me."

"It hadn't happened yet."

"Young man, I believe that you are suffering from a disease called bad conscience. Instead of seeing mysterious enchantments everywhere, I'd rec-

ommend you start doing what you should be doing, and I suspect everything will be fine."

"But—"

"But at the moment, I've got bigger problems. While this Easterner may
not be casting spells on everyone's mother, he *is* out there somewhere,
and I must see to it that he is found before he does any more damage.
Now be on your way."

Without waiting for Savn's answer, Bless motioned for Ori to drive off.
Savn clenched his fists with frustration. Why did everyone only see what
he wanted to?

Savn looked around to make sure he hadn't attracted any attention,
and saw, to his dismay, Lan and Tuk walking by on the opposite side of
the street, staring at him. They looked away when he stared back, which
was almost worse than if they'd tried to beat him up again.

He turned and headed for home. Maybe Polyi would say something
that would cheer him up.

The walk home was long, and it was nearly dark by the time he got
there. Mae and Pae were still busy, and when they bid him a good day,
it seemed that they were even further away than they had been.

Savn wondered if perhaps he was exaggerating their condition to himself. He couldn't be sure, but he didn't think so.

Polyi was in the house, and her first words were, "Are they sick, Savn?"

He thought about giving her an honest answer, but couldn't make himself do it. He said, "I don't know what's wrong, Polyi. I just don't know."

"Should we ask someone?"

"Who?"

"Well, Master Wag, maybe?"

"I don't think they're sick."

"Well *something's* wrong with them."

Savn sighed. "Yes, I know. Let me think about it."

"What good will thinking about it do? We have to—"

"I know, we have to do something. But I don't know—What in the
world was that?" There had come some sort of rapping, scraping sound
from the roof.

Polyi rushed out the door, Savn right at her heels. They turned and
looked up at the roof. Polyi screamed. Savn, though he had become used
to such things, felt very much like doing the same.

*For an hour or so after the large soft one left, the Provider seemed fine,
and even after that, she couldn't really tell that something was wrong, but*

her lover began to grow agitated, then worried, and finally almost frantic. He began to fly around, nearly hurting himself against the cave walls.

She came to understand that the Provider was not well, and she wondered if the large soft one had done something to him, and if she should track him down and kill him. No, she was told, it had nothing to do with that one, it had to do with how he had gotten hurt before.

This puzzled her, because it seemed that one would either be injured or healthy: the Provider had been injured and was now getting healthy again, so how could the same injury account for two illnesses? But her lover was in no mood to explain such things, so she didn't ask.

As he grew more frantic, however, she began to catch his mood. Desperate to do something that would alleviate his misery, she at last suggested that, if he had been cured before by something one of the Provider's species had done, couldn't it happen again?

Her lover calmed down at this suggestion, only to become angry again, this time at himself, because he seemed to feel he ought to have thought of that before. But he seemed disinclined to waste too much time with such thoughts; almost at once he turned and flew out of the cave.

She had nothing better to do, so she followed.

14

I will not marry a sly intendant,
I will not marry a sly intendant,
I'd make money and he would spend it.
Hi-dee hi-dee ho-la!
Step on out . . .

POLYI CLUTCHED SAVN'S ARM and stared. The day's light was nearly gone but there was enough to see, without possibility of error, what was sitting on the roof. Even to Savn, there was something horribly invasive in the jhereg's perching on his own house; whatever they were, and however friendly they were, they didn't belong here.

It was only much later that it struck Savn as odd that neither he nor Polyi thought of calling Mae and Pae, which would have been their automatic reaction only three days before.

At last Polyi said in a whisper, "What are they doing?"

"Watching us."

"I can see that, chag-brain. I mean *why* are they watching us."

"I don't know."

Savn stared back at them, refusing to be intimidated. That there might actually be intelligence behind those quick, tiny eyes made it worse. *Well,* he wanted to say. *What do you want with me?*

Could Vlad have sent them?

Maybe. But, if so, why not give them a note, like he gave to Fird?

Perhaps because he couldn't.

But, if he couldn't, how could he have sent the jhereg?

Savn scowled. He just didn't know enough about Vlad's relationship with these things. It was a matter of witchcraft, and—

Witchcraft.

Just like the spell he'd put on Mae and Pae.

He broke free of Polyi, turned, and walked away from the house. Behind him, Polyi was asking something, but he didn't really hear her.

Vlad was in trouble, maybe dying; that was the only possible explanation.

Vlad had, for whatever reason, laid enchantments on Mae and Pae.

Vlad needed help.

Vlad didn't deserve help.

Savn slammed back into the house and got a small cooking pot, two wooden bowls, a little barley (Vlad could pay for that at least, and he'd better!), and some three-season herb, which was another thing Master Wag had recommended against fever.

Polyi came back in. "Where are you going?"

"Vlad's gotten sick again," he growled.

"How do you know?"

"I just do."

He rolled up his sleeping furs and tied them into a bundle.

"Aren't you coming back?" said Polyi.

"Yes, I'm coming back, I just don't know when."

Prairiesong grew next to the road; he could pick some on the way. What else did he need?

"What do you mean, you don't know when?"

"I'm going to stay with Vlad until he's well, or until he dies, or until they find us. And, when he's well, I'm going to make him—I'm going to talk to him about some things."

He carefully wrapped Pae's best kitchen knife in a towel and stowed it among his furs.

"But," said Polyi, "that could take—"

"I know."

"Mae and Pae—"

"Won't even notice."

Polyi shut up. Savn continued to pack as quickly as possible, ending up with one large roll that fit over his shoulder and a light sack that he could carry.

"I'm going with you," announced Polyi.

Savn looked at her in the light of the stove. Her hair, which always gave her trouble, looked completely disorganized; her thin brows were drawn together in a line, and her mouth was set in an expression that he'd often seen before and thought of as stubborn; now it looked determined. He wasn't certain what the difference was, but he knew it was there.

"Of course you are," he said. "Hurry up and get ready. We have to take the long way around, and I don't want to waste any time."

THE TWO JHEREG SHADOWED them as they walked. It was too dark to see them, but Savn and Polyi heard the occasional *thwp thwp* of their wings, which made Savn nervous, though he didn't mention it. Polyi didn't mention it, either. In fact, Polyi didn't say anything at all, though a couple of times Savn tried, halfheartedly, to engage in her conversation. The only thing she said was, "How are we going to see in the cave? It's bad enough out here."

"I left a torch just outside; maybe we can find it."

Their progress through the woods was very slow. There was no light at all save for the diffuse glow from the sky and the faraway beacons from His Lordship's manor house, which, faint as it was, got fainter as they went further from Manor Road and into the woods above Bigcliff. Savn was afraid they would miss the path altogether and step off the cliff itself. He made Polyi take hold of his arm, and he went very slowly, feeling for low branches with his free hand and exposed roots with his feet.

"I'm glad you came along," he said. "This would be even scarier alone."

Polyi didn't answer.

Soon the light from the manor house was gone entirely, and Savn was afraid he'd lose his sense of direction and wander the woods all night, but shortly thereafter they emerged, and he realized that the soft glow from the sky was enough to allow him to pick his way with care down the path to the caves.

Finding the torch proved difficult indeed, and he might not have managed it if he hadn't bumped into the tree he'd been leaning against earlier. He scraped his cheek slightly, but was otherwise unhurt, and by feeling around at the tree's base, discovered the torch he'd brought out of the cave.

It was only then, with the unlit torch in his hand, that he realized that it was chilly. "Are you cold?" he asked Polyi.

"Yes," she said, "but I'm all right. Hurry up and light the torch so we can go."

While Polyi waited by the cave mouth, Savn pushed together a pile of leaves that weren't too damp and succeeded in making a fire. The glow hurt his eyes so much, he had to look away while igniting the torch, and once he'd managed to do so, he had to look away from both while he stamped out the fire. When he'd done this, he hesitated, wanting to wait until his eyes adjusted to the light, but not wanting to remain outside the cave where the light could be observed.

As he stood, undecided, Polyi said, "Come *on*, Savn," so he squinted as best he could and headed into the cave. The jhereg, visible now in the torchlight, stayed with them, as if to be certain they completed their journey.

At last they reached the chamber where Vlad lay. Savn put the torch in the wall, lit another from the stack on the floor, brought it over to the Easterner, and gasped.

"Savn, what's wro—"

"Hand me the sack, Polyi. Thanks. Now, find the mortar and pestle. Quick."

"Where? Oh, here it is."

Savn dumped the contents of the sack on the floor, and found the prairiesong. "Crush this up with some water," he said.

"Where's the water?"

"I don't know, look around. Wait, in the wineskin, against the wall, below the torch. No, the brown wineskin; that one still has wine. Yes."

"How much water?"

"After you've crushed the prairiesong, fill the bowl. Wait, give me the water first."

Savn inspected Vlad, looking at each wound carefully, then got a cloth wet and put it around Vlad's head. Then he began fanning him.

"What happened?" said Polyi.

"The Imps of Fever have entered his body, but I don't know how. His wound isn't infected."

"What do we do?"

"Have you mixed the prairiesong yet?"

"Yes."

"Then we will help him drink it."

"Then what?"

"Then we'll get the fire started again. Is there any wood left?"

"Not much."

"After he's had the prairiesong, take a torch with you and get some wood. Don't stay out there any longer than you have to. Be careful not to be seen."

"All right. What will we do when we've got the fire going?"

"We will sit here with him, keeping him cool, chanting the charms against fever, and feeding him water with prairiesong until his fever breaks."

"What if it doesn't break?"

"It will," said Savn.

"But what if it doesn't?"

"It will. Here. I'll hold his head, you open his lips and pour. Slowly, we don't want to spill any."

They helped the Easterner drink. He was only semiconscious, but he was able to swallow normally. His skin was still very hot. Savn wiped Vlad's forehead again, while Polyi got the firewood. He reviewed the chants against fever, while he ground up more prairiesong and set it aside, then began fanning Vlad. *I'll have to send Polyi out for more water,* he thought, *but that can wait until the fire's going.*

He began the chant clumsily. It was difficult to perform the invocation with the proper rhythm while fanning Vlad, until he managed to adjust his fanning to the rhythm of the incantation. After that it was easier.

Polyi returned with the firewood, and built up the fire, got more water, then sat down next to Savn. "How is he?"

"He burns," said Savn, his voice already hoarse. "Come, listen to the chant so you can help me with it. I'll fan him, you make sure the cloth on his forehead stays damp, and we'll perform the healing together."

"All right," said Polyi.

Vlad moaned softly then, and mumbled something. Polyi made a soft exclamation. Savn glanced at her and said, "We do not pay attention to the ravings of those under our care." Then he resumed chanting. Presently his sister joined him.

Several hours later, when both of their voices were raw and sore, when Savn felt more exhausted than he ever had in his life, when he was afraid that his arm lacked the strength to lift up Vlad's head one more time, he felt his forehead and found it was cool to the touch.

"You can stop, Polyi," he said.

She kept chanting, stumbling a little, slowing down, then at last ran down like a spinning doll at the end of its string. She looked at him blankly, as if unable to comprehend the silence. Perhaps they said something to each other—Savn later had a memory that they exchanged a hug, but he was never certain. All he knew was that within a minute after the sudden silence boomed through the cave, he was sound asleep.

*   *   *

WHEN SAVN AWOKE, THE first thing he did was stifle a cry and look at Vlad. Then he realized that he'd only dreamed that he'd fallen asleep while Vlad's life was still at stake, and he relaxed. The Easterner slept, but his color looked good and his forehead felt cool, though perhaps slightly clammy.

The next thing he did was make sure Polyi was all right. She was still asleep (or, for all he knew, asleep again). He badly wished for tea. Then he noticed a dead norska lying by the fire. He looked at the two jhereg who stood over it, either guarding it or showing off, and said, "Now, I suppose, you're going to want me to skin it and cook it, aren't you? Haven't we been through this already? Fortunately for you, I have a stew-pot, because I wouldn't want to risk the smell of roasting it again."

The smaller of the jhereg hopped over to him, jumped coolly onto his arm, and licked his ear. Savn wondered why this didn't bother him, and, moreover, how the jhereg knew it wouldn't bother him.

He built up the fire, skinned the norska, and put it in the pot with water and more three-season herb than probably ought to go in. That was all right; it might make the stew a little sweet, but it should still be edible. The smell woke up Polyi, and, at almost the same time, Vlad.

Savn realized the Easterner was awake when the two jhereg suddenly stopped nibbling at the norska skin and flew over to land next to his face. Savn followed them, knelt down, and said, "How are you?"

Vlad blinked, cleared his throat, and said, "What did I say this time?"

"I have no idea," said Savn. "You sound stronger than you did yesterday."

"Do I? I think I feel a little better, too. How odd."

"Did Fird do something to you?"

"No, I don't think so. I don't think he could have done anything I wouldn't have noticed, and he doesn't seem to be the type that would try anything, anyway. No, I think it just happened."

"You *do* sound better."

"Thanks. I really didn't say anything?"

"I wasn't paying attention. What was Fird doing here, anyway?"

"Giving me some information I'd paid him to find out."

"Oh. I hope it was worth it."

Vlad laughed, weakly. "Oh, yes. It was worth it."

Savn grunted and stirred the stew, spilling some, which made the fire hiss, and thick smoke curled up into his eyes. He waved it away and stepped back. He added a little wine, figuring it couldn't hurt anything and remembering Vlad's comments last time.

He glanced back at Vlad, who had struggled to a sitting position on his own, and was leaning against the wall, breathing heavily, his eyes closed.

"You're going to make it," said Savn quietly.

"Eh?" said Vlad.

"Nothing. Rest now and I'll wake you when the food's ready."

"Thanks, but I want to be awake. I need to think."

"Are you afraid they'll find you?" He didn't think the stew smelled as strongly as the roasted norska had, and hoped that the smell wouldn't manage to sneak its way out of the cave.

"Are they still looking?" asked Vlad.

"Yes."

"Hmmm. Well, that's part of it. If they found me now I wouldn't be able to give them much sport. But even if they don't find me, I have to figure out what to do."

"About what?"

"About Loraan, of course. Excuse me, I mean Baron Smallcliff."

"Oh."

Eventually the food was ready. Polyi splashed water on her face, visited the cave they'd designated as a privy, and rejoined them, still looking groggy. They ate in silence, not even commenting on the quality of the stew, which Savn thought was fine (although, as he had feared, a bit sweet), even if it was not as exciting as the roasted norska had been the first time.

They had to share bowls, since Savn had only thought to bring two, but they finished every morsel. When they had given the bones and scraps to the jhereg, Vlad rested for a while. Savn thought he was looking better and better, but resolved not to leave him unattended until he was certain there would not be another relapse.

Polyi, who, as usual, had been the last to finish eating, watched Vlad as he rested. Savn wondered what she was thinking about, a question which was answered when she suddenly said, "What did you mean about not wanting to work again?"

Vlad opened his eyes. "Excuse me?"

"When you were feverish, you said you never wanted to work again, and you wouldn't, and swore by Verra. Or maybe at Verra, I couldn't tell."

Vlad looked reproachfully at Savn, who said, "When did he say that, Polyi?"

"While we were chanting."

Savn looked at Vlad. "I didn't notice," he said.

"I meant," said Vlad, "that, basically, I'm a pretty lazy fellow. What else did I say?" The Easterner was staring at Polyi, and Savn felt the intensity of that stare.

"Stop it," he said.

Vlad turned to him. "Excuse me?"

"I said, stop it."

"Stop what?"

"Whatever you were about to do to her."

The Easterner seemed genuinely confused. "I wasn't about to do anything to her; what are you talking about?"

"You were about to cast a spell on her."

"No, I wasn't. What makes you think I was?"

"I saw how you were looking at her, and I know what you did to Mae and Pae."

"Oh," said Vlad softly. His features were still and silent; only his eyes seemed troubled as he looked at Savn.

"*What?*" cried Polyi, rising to her feet.

Damn my big mouth, thought Savn. He stepped between her and Vlad and said, "Wait—"

"*What did he do to them?*"

"How did you know?" said Vlad quietly.

Savn ignored him, gripped his sister's shoulders and said, "Polyi, please—"

"How long have you known?" said Polyi.

"I guessed yesterday, when we went home, but I wasn't certain."

She tried to twist free, but Savn was stronger. He said, "Wait, Polyi. Let us at least listen to what he has to say—"

Vlad, abruptly, started laughing. Polyi stopped struggling and stared at him. Savn did the same. "What's so funny?" he asked.

"I'm almost tempted," said Vlad, still laughing, "to tell you to let her go. After everything I've done, the idea of falling at last to the wrath of a Teckla girl appeals to my sense of irony. And right now, she could do it. At least," he added, sobering suddenly, "it wouldn't be Morganti."

Savn felt his stomach turn at the word. At the same time, he noticed that the two jhereg were watching Polyi with, it seemed, great intensity, and he remembered that they were poisonous—it was certainly best that Polyi be kept from attacking Vlad, even if Vlad was, as he claimed, "almost tempted."

The Easterner continued. "In any case, I wasn't about to put a spell on your sister. I wasn't doing anything except, maybe, trying to intimidate her a little."

"Why should I believe you?" said Savn.

"Why indeed?" said Vlad. "At any rate, I haven't denied what I did to your Mae and Pae."

"No, but you've lied about everything else."

Vlad shook his head. "Very little, in fact," he said. "I've mostly refused to answer because I really don't like lying to you. Although I'm willing to do so, if it will preserve my life and my soul."

His voice hardened as he said this, but Savn refused to be put off by it. "How did putting a spell on Mae and Pae help preserve your life?"

Vlad sighed and looked away. "I'm not sure it did," he said eventually. "I was being careful. How could you tell there was a spell on them? And, for that matter, how did you know it was me?"

Savn snorted. "Who else could it have been? And it wasn't very difficult to see they'd been enchanted. They've been acting like they're living in a dream-world. They haven't seemed to care what Polyi and I do. They—"

"I see," said Vlad. "I overdid it, apparently."

"What were you trying to do?"

"It's a long story."

"I'm not going anywhere."

He looked at Polyi, who hesitated, then sat down and looked at the Easterner expectantly.

Vlad took a deep breath and nodded. "I thought I might need your help," he said. "And, in fact, I did, though not the way I had anticipated." He smiled a little, looking down at himself as if to inspect Savn's work.

"How had you anticipated you'd need my help?"

Vlad shrugged. "Once I knew what had happened to Reins, I thought I might need the eyes, ears, and memory of a local. And I did, but it didn't turn out to be you, because I found Sara and Fird."

Polyi said, "What does that have to do with putting a spell on Mae and Pae?"

Vlad sat up, resting his back against the stone wall. He spread his hands. "If I wanted you to look around for me, I couldn't have you disturbed by parents wanting to know where you were and what you were doing. It wasn't supposed to be that strong, however."

Savn nodded. "You did it when you brought me home that night, didn't you?"

"That was when I triggered it, you might say, but I'd already set it up."

"How? You weren't anywhere near them before that."

"Yes." Vlad sighed. "Remember that green stone I gave you?"

"What green stone?"

"Remember when we met?"

"Sure. On Manor Road, by the Curving Stone."

"Yes. I gave you something."

"I don't remember . . . Wait. Yes. You said it was the custom of your land—" He broke off suddenly. "Why had I forgotten that? What did you do to me?"

Vlad winced, then looked away. After a moment he shook his head, as if to himself. "Not very much, actually," he said. "You can blame my friends here"—he gestured at the jhereg on the ground, who were still watching Polyi and Savn—"for not keeping good watch. You saw me doing something I didn't want known, so I gave you that stone, and through it, I suggested that you not talk about me, and that you not remember the stone. And I used the stone to work the other spells, the ones you noticed. When I took you home that night, I'd already prepared—"

Savn stared. "You've been putting spells everywhere, haven't you?"

"It may seem like that—"

"What did you do to Polyi?" he said fiercely, ready to strangle the Easterner, jhereg or no.

"Nothing," said Vlad. "But, as I said, I did use the stone to cast a spell on your parents, through you, that would allow you to be more useful to me. So if you're looking for a grievance, you have one."

Savn spat, then glared at the Easterner. Vlad met his eyes calmly.

"Well, I've been useful, haven't I?" said Savn bitterly. "I've saved your life—"

"I know."

More implications began to sink in. He said, "I assume you made me physick you? That was why I found you so easily?"

"No," said Vlad.

"What do you mean, No?"

Vlad adjusted his position against the wall. "I was unconscious, and even if I wasn't, it wouldn't have occurred to me that you'd be able to heal me." He paused. "How *did* you find me?"

"I remembered what you said about spells to make teleports easier, and I remembered what you'd been doing in the road, and I thought about how quickly you'd teleported, and I just put it together."

Vlad gave one of his characteristic laughs—a small chuckle that never left his chest. "Virtue, I've been told, is its own reward."

"What does *that* mean?"

"I almost blocked out your memory of what I'd been doing, but I didn't want to do more to your memories than I had to."

"That's bleeding noble of you," said Savn.

"So to speak," said Vlad.

"How can you do things like that?" said Polyi, in a tone more curious than reproachful.

"I'll do what I have to, to save my life," said Vlad, giving her the briefest of glares. "Who wouldn't?"

"I wouldn't," said Polyi firmly. "Not if to save my life I had to go into people's heads and change them. That's *evil*. It's better to just kill them."

"Maybe it is," said Vlad. "But if they're alive, they can change again, and perhaps recover. If they're dead, it's all over."

"But—"

"But yes, I know, altering someone's mind is an ugly thing to do. Don't think I don't know it. But don't think that you can pretend these questions are easy, because they aren't, and anyone who says they are is lying."

"You'd know a lot about lying, wouldn't you?" said Savn.

"Yes," said Vlad. "I've done a great deal of it. Also killing. Also, tricking people into doing what I wanted them to do. I'm neither proud nor ashamed of any of this—I do what I must."

"It sounds," said Polyi, "like you'll do anything to anyone, as long as it's useful to you."

Vlad took a deep breath, as if he was about to shout at her, then let it out slowly. "You may be right," he said.

"Is that why you taught me witchcraft?" said Savn. "Because you thought it would be useful to you?"

Once again, the chuckle. "No." Vlad shook his head and closed his eyes. Savn waited. After a moment, the Easterner sighed. "I guess, what with one thing and another, I owe you the truth."

Savn nodded, but didn't say anything. He felt Polyi looking at him, but she, too, waited.

Vlad said, "The first time, here in this spot, I didn't teach you anything. I just put you to sleep for a while so I could explore."

"I don't understand. Why did you bother putting me to sleep?"

Vlad turned his palms up. "I didn't want your company while I explored."

"Then why have me along at all?"

"You knew where this place was," he said, gesturing at the cave around them.

"This place? I don't understand."

"I knew there had to be an underground waterway, and Dark Water can be useful against the undead, and I was looking for a way into Loraan's manor house. I thought you might know how to find it, so I—"

"So you asked me leading questions until I found it for you."

"Yes," said Vlad. "That's right." He closed his eyes briefly. When he opened them again, his face was, once more, without expression.

"And the second time you pretended to teach me witchcraft? What was that about? That time, you even had me convinced you'd taught me something."

"I did. That time there was no trickery, Savn. I taught you because you wanted to know, and because I'd started to like you. I hate to sound trite, but you remind me of myself. Take that for what it's worth."

"I will," said Savn, hearing the bitterness in his own voice. Then he said, "Do you remember when we were talking about Athyra?"

"Yes."

"Do you remember how you said those who explore the world see people as objects, and mystics act like people don't really exist at all?"

"Yes," said Vlad. And, "Oh."

He looked down, and chewed on his lower lip. No one said anything, because there seemed to be nothing more to say.

15

I will not marry an acrobat,
I will not marry an acrobat,
He'd always think that I'm too fat.
Hi-dee hi-dee ho-la!
Step on out . . .

At last Vlad broke the silence. "Maybe you're right," he said. "Maybe I'm no better than your Baron. But all I know is that he's killed someone who once helped me. And years ago he nearly destroyed a close friend of mine. And now he is cooperating with a Jhereg assassin who plans to kill me—"

It took a moment before Savn realized that when Vlad said Jhereg he meant the House, not the animals. Then Savn gasped. "What?"

"That's what Fird told me, though I'd already guessed it. There's an assassin staying with Baron Smallcliff at the manor house, and I don't think he's here because he likes linseed-flavored wine. The Baron is cooperating with the Jhereg to assassinate me."

"I don't believe you," said Savn.

Vlad shrugged.

"Why would he do that?" said Savn.

"They both hate me; it makes sense that they'd work together."

"The Jhereg hates you?"

"Oh, yes."

"Why?"

"I picked an unfortunate method of terminating my relationship with them."

"What do you . . . you mean, you're a Jhereg?"

"I used to be."

"What did you do?"

Vlad took a deep breath and met Savn's eyes. "I killed people. For money."

Savn stared at him, but couldn't think of anything to say.

"I reached a point where I couldn't do it anymore, and I left. In the process, I killed someone important, and I threatened the House representative to the Empire—sort of like your Speaker. So now they want to kill me. I can't really blame them, but I'm hardly going to cooperate, am I?"

"I don't believe you," said Savn.

"Then I doubt I can convince you. But don't you wonder why the Baron attacked me?"

"Because you killed Reins—or because he thought you did."

"Is that the way justice usually works around here? If someone is suspected of a crime, your Baron Smallcliff sends his soldiers to kill them? You'll notice they made no effort to arrest me."

"I don't know," said Savn. "I never said I understood everything. But I know His Lordship wouldn't hire an assassin."

"Not hire," said Vlad. "Merely help."

"He wouldn't do that."

"Why is it that, just at the time I happen to be coming by, Loraan decides to leave his home and take up residence in his manor house, which just happens to be near the place I'm passing by? You think this has nothing to do with me?"

"I don't know."

"And then Reins dies, which is enough to keep me here—"

"I don't believe you."

Vlad sighed and shook his head. "Why does everyone only see what he wants to?"

Savn twitched, started to speak, then realized he had no answer. He sat on the floor of the cave, looking down.

At length, Vlad broke the silence. "What are you going to do?" he said.

"About what?" said Savn.

"I'd like to know if you plan to tell your Baron where I am, or perhaps the townspeople."

"Oh. Well, you never told me your plans; why should I tell you mine?"

Vlad chuckled. "Well taken. Whatever you decide, you should probably get home soon."

"What difference does it make?"

. "I would think," said Vlad, "that your Maener and Paener would be getting worried by now."

Savn looked at him closely. "Is it that easy?"

"To undo? Yes. The spell, at any rate, is easy to undo. And there shouldn't be any direct aftereffects."

"What do you mean, 'direct'?"

"I mean that they'll probably figure out that they've been under a spell. I don't know what that will do to them. Maybe nothing."

Savn glanced at Polyi, who was staring at the ground and frowning.

"Do you want to go home?" Savn asked her.

She looked up. "Do you?"

"Not right now. I want to stay for a bit and—"

"See how it comes out?" said Vlad ironically.

Savn shrugged and asked Vlad, "What do *you* intend to do?"

"I'm not sure. It depends how much time I have. If I had to teleport right now, I might be able to. Then again, I might not. I'd rather not have to. If I can get a couple of days to recover, I'll have the choice of getting out of here to someplace safer. If, on the other hand, I'm found, I'll have to try to escape as best I can."

"So your intention is to get out?"

"Oh, no. That's only if I have no choice. You know very well what I want to do."

"You're crazy," said Polyi. "You can't kill His Lordship! No one can."

Vlad shook his head. "I'm going to kill him. The only questions are when and how. If I can't do it now, I'll have to wait for a better time. But now would be best. I'd like to have it over and done with."

"Heh," said Polyi. "You won't feel that way when it *is* over and done with."

Savn knelt down next to Vlad and felt his forehead. He was relieved to find that it was still cool, though his face seemed a trifle flushed. Vlad watched him intently.

"How do you feel?" said Savn.

"Tired. Weak. Not bad other than that."

"You should rest."

"I doubt I can," said Vlad. "There's too much on my mind."

Savn was suddenly and comically reminded of how he would explain to Maener that he was too excited about Pudding Morn to go to sleep, and how she would smile and tell him that he should just rest his eyes then, and how he would fall asleep. He said, "That's all right, just close your eyes and—"

Vlad laughed. "Very good, Paener. I get the idea. Wake me if they come to kill me."

He slid over to his blankets, threw one arm over his eyes, and, as far as Savn could tell, went instantly to sleep.

THEY WATCHED HIM SLEEP for an hour or two; then Savn decided they should talk. He whispered to Polyi, and she agreed, so he took a torch and guided her back through the cave until he was certain they were far enough away that Vlad couldn't hear them.

"What should we do?" he said.

"I think we should go home," said Polyi. "If Mae and Pae really are worried—"

"What will we tell them?"

"The truth," said Polyi.

"Oh?"

She frowned. "Well, it isn't our problem, is it? Savn, you heard him. Now we *know* he wants to kill His Lordship. I mean, we know he can't, but what if he does?"

"Well," said Savn. "What if he does?"

"We have to stop him, that's all."

"Do we?"

"You heard what he is. He's an assassin. He kills people for money. He—"

"He *used* to be an assassin. And what about His Lordship?"

"You don't believe all that stuff he said, do you?"

"I don't know. Why would he admit to being an assassin, then lie about everything else? It doesn't make sense."

"He's an Easterner; maybe it makes sense to him."

"That's no answer."

"Why not? Do you know how they think?"

Savn didn't answer; in his mind, he kept hearing Vlad's voice, echoing his own: *Why do people only see what they want to?* An unanswerable question, certainly. If Master Wag would even admit that it was true, he'd just say that it didn't matter. And maybe it didn't; maybe it was always going to be frustrating for someone who knew things that most people didn't want to know. Maybe it was the way of the world.

But if what Vlad said was true, then, within a day, he'd been on both sides of the problem. He didn't much like either one. How were you supposed to know what to believe, anyway?

"Come on, Polyi," he said, and started back to the cavern where Vlad slept.

"You want to stay here?"

"I don't know, but right now I want to talk to Vlad."

"You know," said Polyi, "I'm getting tired of this cave."

Savn was tempted to tell her that she was along by her own choice, but decided it wouldn't be nice. He wedged the torch once more into the rocks and sat down next to Vlad. The jhereg, at first watching him carefully, seemed to relax and go back to resting. Funny how they knew he didn't intend to hurt Vlad. Maybe they had some means of knowing the truth. Maybe they were the only beings in the world who knew what was really going on, and they were secretly laughing at everyone else.

He laughed at the thought, and Vlad's eyes opened.

"What's funny?" said Polyi.

"I've just had a revelation," said Savn. "Truth is in the eyes of the jhereg."

Vlad blinked and shook his head. "Water?" he croaked.

Savn got him some, and said, "How do you feel?"

"Better," he said. He drank more water, then looked at Savn patiently.

"Vlad, how do you know what the truth is?"

The Easterner didn't laugh. He considered for a moment, then said, "Help me sit up."

Savn did so, then helped him to the wall, which he rested against for a few minutes, recovering his breath. To Savn's eye, he seemed to have made some improvement.

"Very often," said Vlad, "I learn what is true by trying something and having it fail."

"Oh," said Savn. "I know about that. Master Wag talks about learning from errors."

"Yes. I don't recommend it."

"You don't?"

"No. It's far better not to make mistakes, at least when your life is on the line."

"Well, yes."

Vlad chewed his lower lip. "It's not that I've never thought about it," he said. "I have. That happens when you associate with philosophers. The trouble is, you get different answers depending on whether you really want to know, or if you just want to argue about it."

"I don't want to argue about it," said Savn.

"I suspected that. That makes it harder."

Polyi said, "Savn, what are you doing?"

Vlad answered for him. "He's trying to make a very difficult decision."

Polyi snorted. "Savn, you're going to ask *him* how to decide whether you should turn him in? Well, that really makes sense, doesn't it?"

"I think it does," said Savn. He turned back to Vlad. "What were you saying?"

Vlad was frowning at the floor. He didn't look up. "I wasn't saying anything. I was thinking."

"Well?"

Then he did look up, squinting at Savn. "Let's start with this," he said. "Suppose everyone you know says there's no cave here. Is that the truth?"

"No."

"Good. Not everyone would agree with you, but I do."

"I don't understand."

"It doesn't matter." Vlad thought for a moment longer, then suddenly shook his head. "There's no easy answer. You learn things bit by bit, and you check everything by trying it out, and then sometimes you get a big piece of it all at once, and then you check *that* out. I know what your problem is. Everyone thinks that your Baron can't be killed, and, furthermore, he's a great guy, and here I am with a different story, and you don't know who to believe. I understand the problem. Sorry, I can't give you any answers.

"But," he resumed suddenly, as if a thought had just occurred to him, "I can point out a few things. First of all, the only reason you think he's so wonderful is because you know people from Bigcliff, who have a real scum of a Dzurlord. So what makes your Baron so great is that you have someone horrible to compare him with. As I recall, you weren't very impressed when you learned that I could have done worse things to you than I did, and you were right. As far as I'm concerned, saying someone could be much worse is not much of a recommendation."

Savn shook his head. "But he's never done anything to us."

Vlad's eyebrows twitched. "Doesn't he come by and pick the best portion of your crop, and take it for himself?"

"Well of course, but that's just—"

"I don't want to argue it," said Vlad. "There's no point in talking about all of the things you take as the natural order of life that I don't think are. But that's part of the answer to your question, which is just to ask questions of everyone, and of yourself. Try to identify the assumptions you make, and see if they stand up. Master Wag, you said, scoffs at witchcraft, doesn't he?"

"Yes."

"Well, why do you chant to drive fevers away? The incantations you use resemble witchcraft more than a little."

"Maybe they do," said Savn. "But I know witchcraft works, so why shouldn't the chanting?"

"Sure," said Vlad. "But how does Master Wag explain it?"

"Well, it's because the Fever Imps—"

"How do you know there are Fever Imps at all?"

"Because the chanting works."

"Fair enough. Why, then, do you also use herbs, and why go to such effort to keep me cool?"

"You need all those things."

"Are you sure? Maybe the herbs would work by themselves. Maybe the chanting would work by itself. Maybe all I'd need is to be kept cool. How do you know?"

"Well, I assume, since it's been done that way for years—"

"Don't assume, find out."

"You mean, I can't know anything until I've proven it for myself?"

"Hmmmm. No, not really. If someone learns something, and passes it on, you don't have to go through everything he learned again."

"But, then—"

"But you don't have to accept it on faith, either."

"Then what do you do?"

"You make certain you understand it; you understand it all the way to the bottom. And you test it. When you both understand why it is the way it is, and you've tried it out, then you can say you know it. Until then—"

"But can you ever *really* understand something?"

"Yes, I think so."

Savn fell silent. Eventually, Vlad cleared his throat and said, "I'm afraid I haven't helped you much."

Savn looked up at his odd face, with the thick black hair down in front of his ears and above his thin lip, more dark hair falling in waves inelegantly to his shoulders, with wrinkles of age on his forehead where none should yet be. Savn wondered how many people he had killed, and how rich he had become doing it, and why he had stopped.

"No," he said. "You've helped me a great deal."

Vlad gave a terse nod.

Savn said, "Would you like to tell me what you're going to do now?"

"What, before I know whether you plan to help me or betray me?"

"Haven't you been asking me to trust you, in spite of all the reasons you've given me not to?"

"I suppose I have," said Vlad.

"Well, then, why shouldn't I ask you to trust me, in spite of those very same reasons?"

Vlad looked at him for what seemed to be a long time. Never before had Savn wished so much to know what someone's thoughts were; he was very much aware of the two jhereg, sitting patiently at Vlad's side, with their poison fangs barely concealed by their reptilian jaws. Then, abruptly, Vlad laughed. "Well taken. I can't argue, so I concede. But what about you?" he added, looking at Polyi.

She stared back at him, then turned to Savn. "Whatever you do, I'll go along with it."

"Are you sure?" said Savn.

"Yes."

Savn turned back to Vlad. "Well?"

The Easterner nodded. "If you follow the waterway, you'll find it seems to run into a wall. If you go under the wall, it splits into several streams, none of which has much water, and all of which end in identical walls that look natural. Some of these—four, as far as I can tell—actually lead into the basement of the manor house. They are probably sorcerously controlled."

"Can you get past them?"

"Yes, given enough time."

"How?"

"You mostly wear your way through with diligence, patience, and a chisel."

"Can't you knock it down with sorcery?"

"Not without alerting him; he's very good."

"Then why can't he find you?"

"Because I'm very well protected against being found."

"So is that what you're going to do? Break through the wall and . . . and murder him?"

"Not a chance. He may be expecting me to do that, he may not, but he'll certainly be guarding against it. I might, however, make him think that's what I'm doing. It's the obvious way in."

"Then what will you do?"

"I haven't decided yet. I've got a few things going for me, but I haven't figured out how to make them work."

"What things?"

"The assassin. He's not getting along with Loraan at all."

"How do you know that?"

"Because he's been there for more than a week, and Loraan made that attack on me."

"I don't understand."

"The Jhereg," said Vlad, looking straight at Savn, "want me to be killed with a Morganti weapon. Loraan's attacks were not bluffs—he tried to kill me and almost succeeded. He—"

"Wait a minute. Attacks?"

"Yes. There have been two so far."

"I only know of the one at Tem's house."

"The other happened the day before. I got careless and allowed myself to be seen too close to his manor house, and he made a sorcerous attack on me."

"And it failed?"

"I have," said Vlad, "a few tricks up my sleeve. I was really sloppy in staying at Tem's house long enough for them to find me. My only excuse is that it's been some years now since I've had to worry about that sort of thing. In any case, neither attack would have been Morganti; neither would have satisfied the Jhereg. So my conclusion is that Loraan is just barely cooperating with them, and they are just barely cooperating with him. They need each other, because this is Loraan's area and because the Jhereg have the expert assassins. But neither of them like it. That's what I hope to use. I'm not certain how to go about it, though."

"I see," said Savn.

"Have I answered your questions?"

"Yes."

"Then, do you care to tell me what you're going to do?"

"I won't turn you in," said Savn.

That seemed to satisfy Vlad, who closed his eyes and breathed deeply, leaning against the wall.

"You tire easily, don't you?"

"I think," he said, "that I'll be able to begin healing myself in a day or two. After that, it shouldn't be long."

"So the idea is to keep you safe for two days."

"More or less. Less, I hope."

"Do you think this place is secure?"

Vlad frowned, then looked at the jhereg, who rose and flew out of the cave. "Maybe," said Vlad. "But, in any case, we will now be warned of anyone approaching, so, as long as they don't put a teleport block up over the entire area, I'll have a chance to get out."

"A *what* over the area?"

"Never mind. Loraan would either have to know exactly where I was, or be willing to use a great deal of power to cover the entire area."

"I don't understand."

"Skip it. I'm saying that whatever happens, at least we'll be warned."

Savn stared at the place where the jhereg had disappeared into the narrow corridor that accompanied the subterranean stream. "Yes," he said. "At least we'll be warned."

S
AVN AND POLYI CLEANED up the cooking pot, which Savn put back into the bag. He carefully wrapped the good kitchen knife. They assisted Vlad once more to get to his blankets; he needed less help than he had before.

It didn't seem to matter that outside the cave, which was already beginning to feel like another world, it was early afternoon; Polyi claimed to be tired, and so lay down among her furs, and soon began to breathe evenly. Savn lit fresh torches and tidied up the area. Was it Endweek again? If he were at home, would he be cleaning? What would Mae and Pae say when they saw him again? Were they really worried?

Could he trust anything Vlad said?

While Vlad and Polyi slept, Savn thought over all that Vlad had told him. What if the herbs were unnecessary to combat fever, and they'd just been used from the custom of years uncounted? What if *any* custom could be wrong? What if His Lordship was undead?

He considered truth and knowledge and trust, and responsibility, until they whirled around in his head empty of meanings, only occasionally coming to light on some real example of deceit, ignorance, betrayal, or neglect, which would give him some hint of understanding before vanishing once more into the whirlpool of half-understood platitudes and questionable wisdom.

He kept returning to one phrase the Easterner had let fall: "Don't assume, find out."

He thought about this very carefully, feeling the truth in the phrase, and asking himself if he was trusting the Easterner, or logic.

Even after he'd decided, he hesitated for some time before taking the obvious next step.

Savn stood at the Curving Stone for a long time, staring down the road that led to the door of His Lordship's manor house, which was itself out of sight behind a curve in the road. A score of years before, he and his friends had played on the grounds, hidden from all the glass windows except the one in the highest dormer, enjoying the feeling of danger, though safe in the knowledge that the manor house was empty.

Now His Lordship was in residence, and now Savn, though he wasn't certain what he was doing, was not playing. He walked on the road as if he belonged there, step by step, as if he were himself a visiting noble, although he had heard that these people teleported instead of walking, even when they only needed to go ten or twenty miles.

The manor house came in sight—a wide, tall building, full of sharp angles. In the years since he had seen it up close, he'd forgotten how big it was, or else decided it was only the exaggeration of a child's memory. Now he stared, remembering, taken again with the feeling that the magnificence of the house must reflect the power of he who dwelled within.

The roof looked like the edge of a scythe, with dormers on either side like wisps of straw. The brick of the house itself was pale green, and high on the front wall were wide windows made of glass—Savn could even see light creeping around the edges of the curtains inside. He strained his eyes, looking for movement. He looked for and eventually found the gully he had daringly played in so many years ago, as close to the house as one could get without being seen. There were glass windows on that side, too, but he remembered quite clearly that if you kept your head down you were only visible from the one lonely window high on the side.

Oddly enough, it was only then, looking at all the windows, that he realized it was becoming dark, and was surprised once more by how fast time went by in the cave. At that moment, more light began to glow around the far side of the house. He stopped where he was, and soon a servant appeared from around that side. Savn watched as the servant walked around the house using a long match to light lamps that were stuck onto the house at various points. When he was finished, the entire house was lit up as if it were burning.

When the servant was gone, Savn watched the house a little longer, then resumed his walk along the road, directly toward the house, and up to the large front door. He felt very much as he imagined a soldier would feel marching into battle, but this was another thought he didn't care to examine closely.

He stood before the door and stared at it. It seemed like such a plain door to be part of His Lordship's manor house—just wood, and it opened and closed like any other door, although, to be sure, it had a brass handle that looked too complicated for Savn to operate. He took a deep breath, closed his eyes, opened them, and clapped.

Nothing happened.

He waited for what seemed like several hours, although in fact it was hardly more than a minute. Still, he felt his courage slipping away. He tapped his foot, then stopped, afraid someone would see.

Why didn't someone come to the door?

Because he couldn't be heard, of course; the door was too thick.

Well, then, how was someone supposed to get the attention of His Lordship's servants?

He looked around, and eventually saw a long rope hanging down in front of the door. Without giving himself time to think, he gave it one long, hard pull, and almost screeched when he heard, from inside, a rattling sound as if several sticks or logs were rolling against each other.

His heart, which had been beating fast for some time, began to pound in earnest. He was, in fact, on the point of turning and bolting, when the door opened and he found himself looking up at a slight, sharp-featured man in the livery of Baron Smallcliff. After a moment, Savn recognized him as someone called Turi, one of His Lordship's servants who occasionally came into town for supplies. Come to think of it, Turi had been doing so ever since Reins had quit—

He broke off the thought, and at the same time realized he was staring. He started to speak but had to clear his throat.

"Well?" said the servant, frowning sternly.

Savn managed to squeak out, "Your pardon, sir."

"Mmmmph."

Savn took a breath. "May I request an audience with His Lordship? My name is Savn, and I'm the son of Cwelli and Olani, and I—"

"What do you want to see His Lordship about, boy?" said Turi, now looking impassive and impenetrable.

"If it please His Lordship, about the Easterner."

Turi slowly tilted his head like a confused dog, and simultaneously raised his eyebrows. "Indeed?"

"Yes, sir."

"You have information for His Lordship?"

"I . . . that is—"

"Well, come in and I will see if His Lordship is available. Your name, you said, is Savn?"

"Yes, sir."

"And you are a peasant?"

"I'm apprenticed," he said.

"To whom?"

"To Master Wag, the physicker."

At this Turi's eyes grew very wide, and for a moment he seemed at a loss for words. Then he said, "Come in, come in, by all means."

The inside of the house was even more magnificent than the outside, especially when it became clear to Savn that the room he stood in—which contained nothing but some hooks on the wall and another door opposite the one he'd come in—existed for no other purpose than as a place for people to wait and to hang up their cloaks.

"Wait here," said the servant.

"Yes, sir," said Savn as Turi went through the inner door, closing it behind him.

He stared awestruck at the fine, dark, polished wood, realizing that this one, unfurnished room must have cost His Lordship more than Savn's entire house was worth. He was studying the elaborate carved brass handle on the inner door, trying to decide if there was a recognizable shape to it, when it turned and the door opened. He braced himself to face His Lordship, then relaxed when he saw it was Turi again.

"This way, boy," said the servant.

"Yes, sir," said Savn, and, though his knees felt weak, he followed Turi into a place of splendor greater than his mind could grasp. The walls seemed to shimmer, and were adorned with richly colored paintings. The furniture was huge and came in amazing variations, and Savn couldn't imagine sitting on any of it. Bright light filled every corner of the room, glittering against objects of incomprehensible purpose, made of crystal, shiny metal, and ceramics that had been glazed with some unfathomable technique that made the blues and reds as deep and rich as the soil.

"Watch your step," said Turi sharply.

Savn caught himself just before walking into a low table that seemed made entirely of glass. He continued more carefully, while still looking around, and it suddenly came to him that some of the crystal and metal objects were drinking vessels. He didn't think he'd be able to drink from such objects—his hand would be shaking too much.

The shape and color of his surroundings changed. He had somehow entered another room, which might as well have been another world for all the sense he could make of anything around him, until he realized that every one of the objects that filled the room were books—different books—more books than a man could read in his entire lifetime—more books than Savn had thought had ever been written. There were hundreds and hundreds of them. These were cases that had obviously been made just to hold them. There were tables on which they lay, carelessly flung open to—

His gaze suddenly fell on a figure standing before him, dressed in a gleaming white shirt, which set off a bright red jewel suspended from a chain around his neck. The pants were also perfectly white, and baggy, falling all the way to the floor so that the figure's feet were invisible. Savn looked at his face, then looked away, terrified. On the one hand, though he was big, it seemed odd to Savn how human he looked; the thought, *He's just a man, after all,* came unbidden to his mind. But even as Savn was thinking this, he discovered that he had fallen to his knees and was touching his head to the floor, as if in response to something so deeply buried within him that it went beyond awareness or decision. As Savn knelt there, confounded and humbled, with the image of the Athyra nobleman burned into his mind, it struck him that His Lordship had seemed very pale.

Unnaturally pale.

Savn tried not to think about what this might mean.

When His Lordship spoke, it was with an assurance that made Savn realize that Speaker, with all his shouting, raving, and fits of temper, had only pretended to have authority—that real authority was something stamped into someone from birth or not at all. He wondered what Vlad would say about that.

"What is it, lad?" said His Lordship. "My man tells me you have something to say about the Easterner. If you want to tell me where he is, don't bother. I know already. If you are here asking about your Master, I'm not finished with him yet. If you want to tell me what sort of condition the Easterner is in, and what his defenses are like, that is another matter; I will listen and reward you well."

Savn's head spun as he tried to make sense out of this strange collection of ideas.

Your Master.

Master Wag?

Not finished with him yet.

Savn managed to find his voice, and croaked out, "I don't understand, Your Lordship."

"Well, what are you here for? Speak up?"

"Your Lordship, I—" Savn searched for the words, hindered in part by no longer being certain what he wanted to find out, or if he dared ask any of it. He looked up, and his eye fell on someone who had apparently been there all along, though Savn hadn't noticed him. The man, who Savn was certain he'd never seen before, stood behind His Lordship, absolutely motionless, his face devoid of the least hint of expression or of feeling, dressed in grey from head to foot, save for a bit of black lace on the ruffles of his shirt, and his high black boots. In some indefinable yet definite way, he reminded Savn of Vlad.

Below the collar of his cloak was the insignia of the House of the Jhereg, as if Savn needed that, or even his colors, to know that this was the assassin Vlad had spoken of.

Savn couldn't take his eyes off him, and, for his part, the stranger stared back with the curiosity of one looking at an interesting weed that, though it didn't belong in one's garden, had some unusual features that made it worth a moment's study before being pulled and discarded.

"Speak up, boy," snapped His Lordship, but Savn could only stare. Speech was so far from him that he couldn't imagine ever being able to talk again—the command of His Lordship, compelling though it was, belonged to another world entirely; surely His Lordship couldn't imagine that he, Savn, would be able to form words, much less sentences.

"What do you have to tell me?" said His Lordship. "I won't ask again."

Savn heard this last with relief; at this moment, all he wanted from life was for His Lordship not to ask him to speak anymore. He thought about getting up and bowing his way out of the room, but he wasn't certain his legs would support him, and if it wasn't the proper thing to do, he might never get out of the house alive. The complete folly of coming here hit him fully, rendering action or speech even more impossible.

His Lordship made a sound of derision or impatience and said, "Get him out of here. Put him with the other one. We don't have time now, anyway."

Another voice spoke, very softly, with a bite to the consonants that made Savn sure it was from the Jhereg: "You're an idiot, Loraan. We could find out—"

"Shut up," said His Lordship. "I need your advice now less than—"

"Indeed," interrupted the other. "Less than when? Less than the last time you ignored me and—"

"I said, shut up," repeated His Lordship. "We don't have time for this; we've got an Easterner to kill, and the troops should be in position by now."

"And if they find him before morning I'll eat my fee."

"I'll bring you salt," said His Lordship. "We know where to begin looking, and we have enough manpower that it won't take more than two or three hours."

At that moment, rough hands grabbed Savn's shoulders. The Jhereg and the Athyra did not seem to notice.

"He'll be gone before you find him," the Jhereg said.

Savn was pulled to his feet, but his knees wouldn't support him and he fell back down.

"Unlikely, I've put a block up."

"Around three square miles of caves?"

"Yes."

Savn was grabbed once more, held under his armpits by very strong hands.

"Then he's already alerted," said the Jhereg.

Savn was dragged away. He got a last glimpse of His Lordship, hands balled up in fists, staring at the Jhereg, who wore a mocking smile that seemed the twin of the one Vlad had put on from time to time. His Lordship said, "Let him be alerted. I have confidence in your . . ." and His Lordship's voice was drowned out by a sound that Savn realized was his own boots scraping along the floor as he was taken off.

He was completely unaware of the places he passed through, and wasn't even aware of who was dragging him, despite the fact that he heard a man's voice and a woman's, as if from a distance, telling him to walk on his own if he didn't want to be beaten flat. The voices seemed disconnected from the hands pulling him along, which felt like forces of nature rather than the work of human beings.

They came to the top of a stairway, and the woman, laughing, suggested they throw him down. He thought, *I hope they don't,* but knew he couldn't do anything about it in any case.

However, they continued to drag him down the stairs, and then through a dimly lit corridor, until at last they arrived at a large wooden door, bound with iron strips, with a thick bar across it as well as a locking mechanism. They leaned Savn against a wall, where he promptly sagged to the floor. He heard sobbing and realized it was his own. He looked up for the first time, and saw who had been dragging him—two people in the livery of the Athyra, both armed with large swords. The woman had a heavy-looking iron key. She unlocked the door and removed the bar. They opened the door, picked up Savn, and pushed him inside, where he lay face down.

The door was closed behind him, and he could hear the lock turning and the bar falling. At first it seemed dark inside, since there were no lanterns such as there had been along the corridor, but then he realized there was some light, which came from a faintly glowing lightstone—a device Savn had heard about but never seen. It was high up in the middle of the ceiling, which was a good twelve feet overhead. In other circumstances Savn would have been delighted to have seen it, and studied it as best he could, but for now he was too stunned.

He saw now that what he'd at first taken to be a bundle of rags was actually a person, and he remembered His Lordship saying something like *Put him with the other*. He looked closer, and as his eyes adjusted to the dimness of the room, he recognized Master Wag. He approached, and realized there was something wrong with the way the Master's arm was lying above his head. He stared, hesitating to touch him, and was gradually able to see some of what had been done to him.

The room spun, the light faded in and out. Savn could never remember the next few minutes clearly; he spoke to the Master, and he shouted something at the closed door, and looked around the room for he knew not what, and, after a while, he sat down on the floor and shook.

She flew low, well below the overcast, starting out near to her lover, then gradually getting further away as their search took them apart.

The Provider had told them to be careful, to be certain to miss nothing, so they covered every inch of ground below them, starting in a small circle above the cave-mouth and only widening it a bit at a time.

She was in no hurry. Her lover had relaxed, now that the Provider seemed to be out of danger, and it was a fine, cool day. She never forgot what she was doing—she kept her eyes and her attention on the ground below—but this didn't prevent her from enjoying the pleasures of flight. Besides, her feet had started hurting.

She recognized the large rock, the nearby house, and the winding, twisting road as things she'd seen before, but they didn't mean a great deal to her. For one thing, there was no meat there, living or dead. At the same time she could feel, in her wings and her breath, the difference in the feel of the air when she flew over fields or over forests, over water or over bare ground where only a stubble of growth was now left. All of these added to the pleasure of flying.

She could always feel where her mate was, and they spoke, mind to mind, as they flew, until at last she looked down and saw one of the soft ones below her. This seemed strange, and after thinking about it for a moment, she realized it was because he could not have been there a moment before, and she ought to have seen him approach. She swept back around, and there was another, and no more explanation of how this one had appeared. She recalled that the Provider could do something like this, and decided that she ought to mention it. She came back around again, and by now an entire herd of the soft ones had appeared, and they were walking along the road that cut through a thin, grassy forest.

She called to her mate, who came at once. He studied them, knowing more about their habits than she; then he told the Provider what they had discovered. They watched a little longer, until the herd left the road and began to walk down the narrow, curving path that led toward the caves.

Then they returned to the Provider, to see what he wanted them to do.

16

I will not marry an aristocrat,
I will not marry an aristocrat,
He'd treat me like a dog or cat.
Hi-dee hi-dee ho-la!
Step on out . . .

COHERENT THOUGHT GRADUALLY RETURNED, bringing sensations with it like trailing roots behind a plow. Savn lay very still and let the mists of his confused dreams gradually fade away, to be replaced by the vapors of true memory. He looked to see if Master Wag was really there; when he saw him, he squeezed his eyes tightly shut, as if he could shut out the sympathetic pain. Then he looked around, staring at anything and everything that wasn't his Master and wasn't so terribly hurt.

The room was about ten feet on a side, and smelled slightly dank, but not horribly so. He listened for the sounds of scurrying rodents and was relieved not to hear any. There was a chamber pot in a far corner; judging from the lack of odor, it had not been used. Things could, Savn decided, be much worse.

The light hadn't changed; he could still see Master Wag huddled against a wall; the Master was breathing, and his eyes were open. Both of his arms seemed to be broken or dislocated, and probably his left leg, too. There were red marks on his face, as from slaps, but no bruises; he hadn't been in a fight, he had been tortured.

On seeing that Savn was looking at him, the Master spoke, his voice only the barest whisper, as Vlad's had been after the first fever had broken, but he spoke very clearly, as if he was taking great care with each word. "Have you any dreamgrass?"

Savn had to think for a moment before replying. "Yes, Master. It's in my pouch."

"Fetch some out. We have no food, but they've left us water and a mug, over in the corner. I haven't been able to move to get it."

Savn got the mug of water and brought it back to the Master. He gave him a drink of plain water first, then mixed the dreamgrass into it as best he could without a mortar and pestle. "That's good enough," whispered the Master. "I'll swallow it whole. You'll have to help me, though. My arms—"

"Yes, Master." Savn helped him to drink again and to swallow the dreamgrass.

The Master nodded, took a deep breath, and shuddered with his whole body. He said, "You're going to have to straighten out my legs and arms. Can you do it?"

"What's broken, Master?"

"Both legs, both arms. My left arm both above and below the elbow. Can you straighten them?"

"I remember the Nine Bracings, Master, but what can we splint them with?"

"Never mind that, just get them straightened. One thing at a time. I don't wish to go through life a cripple. Am I feverish?"

Savn felt his forehead. "No."

"Good. When the pain dulls a bit, you can begin."

"I . . . very well, Master. I can do it, I think."

"You think?"

"Have some more water, Master. How does the room look? Does your face feel heavy?"

The Master snorted and whispered, "I know how to tell when the dreamgrass takes effect. For one thing, there will be less pain. Oh, and have you any eddiberries?"

Savn looked in his pouch, but had none and said so.

"Very well, I'll get by without them. Now . . . hmmm. I'm starting to feel distant. Good. The pain is receding. Are you certain you know what to do?"

"Yes, Master," said Savn. "Who did this to you?"

His eyes flickered, and he spoke even more softly. "His Lordship had it done by a couple of his warriors, with help from . . . There is a Jhereg here—"

"I saw him."

"Yes. They tied me into a chair and . . . they wanted me to tell them where the Easterner was."

"Oh. Did you tell them?"

The Master's eyes squeezed tightly shut. "Eventually," he said.

"Oh," said Savn. The importance of this sank in gradually. He imagined Vlad, lying quietly in the cave with no way of knowing he'd been betrayed. "I wish there was some way to warn him."

"There isn't."

"I know." But the Easterner had means of receiving a warning. Maybe he'd escape after all. But he'd think that Savn, who had vanished, had been the betrayer. Savn shook his head. It was petty of him to worry about that when Vlad's life was in danger, and pointless to worry about Vlad's life when Master Wag was in pain that Savn could do something about. "Can we get more light in here?"

"No."

"All right." Savn took a deep breath. "I'm going to undress you now."

"Of course. Be careful."

"Then I will—"

"I know what you're going to do."

"Do you need more dreamgrass?"

"No." The Master's voice was almost inaudible now. He said, "Carry on, Savn."

"Yes. It is true and it is not true that once there was a village that grew up at a place where two rivers came together. Now, one river was wide, so that one—"

"Shallow and wide."

"Oh, yes. Sorry. Shallow and wide, so that one could walk across the entire length and still be dry from the knees up. The—"

Master Wag winced.

"—other was very fast, and full—I mean, fast and deep, and full of foamy rapids, whirlpools, rocks, and twisting currents, so that it wasn't safe even to boat on. After the rivers came togeth—"

The Master gasped.

"—er, the river, which they called Bigriver, became large, deep, fast, but tame, which allowed them to travel down it to their neighbors, then back up, by means of—"

The Master began moaning steadily.

"—clever poles devised for this purpose. And they could also travel up and down the wide, slow river. But no one could travel on the fast, dangerous river. So, as time went on—"

The moans abruptly turned to screams.

"—the people of the village began to wonder what lay along that length, and talk about—"

The screams grew louder.

"—how they might find a way to travel up the river in spite of the dangerous rapids and the swiftness of the current. Some spoke of using the wind, but . . ."

Soon Savn no longer heard either his own voice or the Master's cries, except as a distant drone. His attention was concentrated on straightening the bones, and remembering everything his Master had taught him about using firm, consistent pressure and an even grip with his hands, being certain that no finger pressed against the bone harder or softer than it should, which would cause the patient unnecessary pain. His fingers felt the bones grinding against one another, and he could hear the sounds they made, even through the drone of his own voice, and his eyes showed him the Master turn grey with the pain, in spite of the dreamgrass, but he neither stopped nor slowed in his work. He thought the Master—the *real* Master, not this wrecked and broken old man he was physicking—would be proud of him.

The story told itself, and he worked against its rhythm, so that the rise in his voice and the most exciting parts of the story came when his hands were busiest, and the patient most needed to be distracted. Master Wag turned out to be a good patient, which was fortunate, because there was no way to render him immobile.

But it seemed to take a very long time.

SAVN LOOKED AT HIS Master, who lay back moaning, his ankles cross-bound with strips of his own clothing and his face covered with sweat. Savn's own face felt as damp as the Master's looked. Savn started to take a drink of water, saw how much was left, and offered it to the Master along with more dreamgrass. Master Wag accepted wordlessly.

As Savn helped the Master eat and drink, he noticed that his own hands were shaking. Well, better now than while he'd been working. He hoped he'd done an adequate job. The Master opened his eyes and said, "They were about to start on my fingers. I couldn't let them—"

"I understand, Master. I think I would have told them right away."

"I doubt that very much," said the Master, and closed his eyes. Savn moved back against the wall to relax, and, when he tried to lean against it, found that there was something digging into his back. He felt around behind himself, and discovered a bundle jammed into the back of his pants. It took him a moment to recognize it as the good kitchen knife, all wrapped up in a towel.

He unwrapped it, took it into his hand, and stared at it. He had cleaned it carefully after cutting the norska to make the stew for Vlad, so it gleamed even in the feeble light of the cell. The blade was ten inches long, wide near the handle, narrowing down toward the point, with an edge that was fine enough to slice the tenderest bluefish, but a point that was no better than it had to be to pry kethna muscle from the bone. As he looked, he wondered, and his hands started shaking harder than ever.

He imagined himself holding the knife and fighting his way past all of His Lordship's guards, then rescuing Vlad at the last minute. He knew this was impossible, but the thought wouldn't go away. How would he feel, he wondered, if he allowed the Easterner to be killed, and maybe Master Wag as well, when he had a knife with him and he never tried to use it? What would he say to himself when he was an old man, who claimed to be a physicker, yet he had let two people in his care die without making any effort to stop it? Or, if he left home, he would spend his life thinking he was running away from his own cowardice. It wasn't fair that this decision, which had become so important, should be taken away by something that wasn't his fault.

He turned the knife this way and that in his hand, knowing how futile it would be to challenge a warrior with a sword when he had nothing but a cooking knife, and had, furthermore, never been in a knife fight in his life. He had seen Vlad fighting some of His Lordship's soldiers, and couldn't imagine himself doing that to someone, no matter how much he wanted to.

He shook his head and stared at the knife, as if it could give him answers.

He was still staring at it some half an hour later, when there came a rattling at the door, which he recognized as the opening of the lock and removal of the bar. He stood up and leaned against the wall, the knife down by his side. A guard came into the room and, without a glance at Savn or Master Wag, slopped some water into the mug.

He seemed very big, very strong, very graceful, and very dangerous.

Don't be an idiot, Savn told himself. *He is a warrior. He spends all of his life around weapons. The sword at his belt could slice you into pieces before you took two steps. It is insanity. It is the same as killing yourself.* He had been telling himself these things already, but, now that it came to it, with the guard before him, the mad ideas in his head would neither listen to reason nor bring themselves forward as a definite intention. He hesitated, and watched the guard, and then, while the man's back was turned, Savn inched his way closer to the door, the knife still held down by his side.

It's crazy, he told himself. *If your knife had a good point, you could strike for his kidneys, but it doesn't. And you aren't tall enough to slit his throat.*

The guard finished and straightened up.

The knife is heavy, and there is some *point on it. And I'm strong.*

Still not deigning to look at Savn or Master Wag, the guard walked to the door.

If I strike so that I can use all of my strength, and I find just the right place, then maybe . . .

Savn was never aware of making a conscious decision, but, for just a moment, he saw an image of His Lordship standing next to the Jhereg as they broke the Master's bones. He took a deep breath and held it.

As the soldier reached the door, Savn stepped up behind him, picked his spot, and struck as hard as he could for a point midway down the guard's back, next to his backbone, driving the knife in, turning it, and pulling toward the spinal cord, all with one motion. The jar of the knife against the warrior's back was hard—shock traveled all the way up Savn's arm, and he would have been unable to complete the stroke if he had attempted anything more complicated. But it was one motion, just as Master Wag had done once in removing a Bur-worm from Lakee's thigh. One motion, curving in and around and out. Removing a Bur-worm, or cutting the spine, what was the difference?

He knew where he was aiming, and exactly what it would do. The guard fell as if his legs were made of water, making only a quiet gasp as he slithered to the floor jerking the knife, which was stuck against the inside of his backbone, out of Savn's hand. The man fell onto his left side, pinning his sword beneath him, yet, with the reflexes of a trained warrior, he reached for it anyway.

Savn started to jump over him, but couldn't bring himself to do it. The guard seemed unable to use his legs, but he pushed himself over to the other side and again reached for his sword. Savn backed into the cell, as far away from the guard as he could get, and watched in horrified fascination as the warrior managed to draw his sword and began to pull himself toward Savn with his free hand. He had eyes only for Savn as he came, and his face was drawn into a grimace that could have been hate or pain or both. Savn tried to squeeze himself as far into the corner as he could.

The distance between them closed terribly slowly, and Savn suddenly had the thought that he would live and grow old in a tiny corner of the cell while the guard crept toward him—an entire lifetime of anticipation, waiting for the inevitable sword thrust—all compacted into seven feet, an inch at a time.

In fact, the warrior was a good four feet away when he gasped and lay still, breathing but unable to pull himself any further, but it seemed much closer. Savn, for his part, didn't move either, but stared at the man whose blood was soaking through his shirt and beginning to stain the floor around him, drip by fascinating drip.

After what was probably only a few minutes, however long it felt, he stopped breathing, but even then Savn was unable to move until his sense of cleanliness around a patient overcame his shock and led his feet across the cell to the chamber pot before his stomach emptied itself.

When there was nothing more for him to throw up, he continued to heave for some time, until at last he stopped, shaking and exhausted. He rinsed his mouth with water the guard had brought, making sure to leave enough for Master Wag when he awoke. He didn't know how the Master was going to drink it, but there was nothing he could do about that now. He moved it next to him, in any case, and checked the Master's breathing and felt his forehead.

Then he stood and gingerly made his way around the corpse. It was funny how a man's body could be so like and yet unlike that of a dead animal. He had butchered hogs and kethna, poultry and even a goat, but he'd never killed a man. He had no idea how many dead animals he had seen, but this was only the second time he'd looked closely at a dead man.

Yes, an animal that was dead often lay in much the same way it would as if resting, with none of its legs at odd angles, and even its head looking just like it should. And that was fine. But there ought to be something different about a dead man—there ought to be something about it that would announce to anyone looking that life, the soul, had departed from this shell. There should be, but there wasn't.

He tried not to look at it, but Paener's best kitchen knife—a knife Savn had handled a thousand times to cut fish and vegetables—caught his eye. He had a sudden image of Paener saying, "You left it in a man's body, Savn? And what am I going to trade for another knife? Do you know how much a knife like that costs in money? How could you be so careless?" Savn almost started giggling, but he knew that once he started he would never stop, so he took a deep breath and jumped past the corpse, then sagged against the wall.

Because it felt like the right thing to do, he shut the door, wondering what Master Wag would think upon waking up with a dead soldier instead of a living apprentice. He swallowed, and started down the corridor, but, before he knew it, he began to trot, and soon to run down the hallway he'd been dragged along only a few scant hours before. Was the man he'd killed the same one who'd helped to push him into the cell? He wasn't sure.

When he reached a place where a stairway went up while the hall sloped down, he stopped, licked his lips, and caught his breath. *Think, Savn. What now? Which way?*

Upwards meant escape, but upwards was also where His Lordship was, as well as the Jhereg. The hallway could lead to almost anywhere—anywhere except back out. There was no point in going on, and he couldn't go up. Neither could he return to his cell, because the corpse was still there, and he thought he'd go mad if he had to see it again.

I'm trying to reason it out, he thought. *What's the point? It isn't a reasonable situation, and I might as well admit that I don't have the courage to go back up and risk meeting His Lordship. And they're going to find the body. And they'll kill me, probably in some horrible way.* He thought about taking his own life, but the kitchen knife was still in the dead man's body.

Then he remembered the caves.

Yes. The caves that Vlad had said must lead into the manor. If so, where in the manor would they be? Down. They could only be down.

There was no way to go but down the sloping hall, then—perhaps, if he didn't find a way to the caves, he'd find a place to hide, at least for a while, at least until he could think.

SAVN REALIZED THAT HE had been standing in darkness for some few minutes. He tried to reconstruct his path, and vaguely remembered going down a long stairway to a door at the bottom, finding it open, walking through it, and, as the door closed behind him, finding there was no light.

He had never before been in darkness so complete, and he wondered why he wasn't panicking—it was more fascinating than frightening, and, oddly enough, peaceful. He wanted to sit right where he was and just rest.

But he couldn't. He had to be doing something, although he had no idea what. They would be searching for Vlad, and if they found him, he would have no choice but to risk teleporting, and he had said himself he might not—He remembered fragments of conversation.

Unlikely, I've put a block up.

Around three square miles of caves?

Yes.

And—

As long as they don't put a teleport block up over the entire area . . .

Understanding seeped into Savn's brain. The one chance Vlad had of escaping was gone, and he was in no condition to fight. Oh, certainly his jhereg would fight for him, but what could they do against all of His Lordship's men?

And, if Vlad had told the truth about the assassin, which now seemed likely, then that assassin was carrying a Morganti weapon.

If only he could reach Vlad. But even if he could, what could he tell him?

The way out, of course.

Suddenly, it was just as it had been when he'd been healing the Easterner. There *was* a solution; there *had* to be a way. If only—

Witchcraft? Speaking to Vlad mind to mind?

But, no, Vlad had that amulet he wore, which prevented such things. On the other hand, there was the chance that . . .

It was a very ugly thought, and Savn didn't know if he was more afraid of failure or success, but it was the only chance Vlad was going to have.

Savn sat down where he was, lost in the darkness, and took a deep breath. At first he did nothing else, just sat there thinking about breathing, and letting the tension flow out of his body. His mind didn't want to cooperate—it kept showing him what would happen if he failed, or if he was too late. But he looked at each scene of death or torment, viewed it carefully, and set it aside, and as he did so, he told himself to relax, just as Vlad had taught him, starting at the top of his head, and working down.

It took longer than it should have, but he knew when he was there—floating apart from the world, able to move at will, everywhere and nowhere.

He imagined the cave, imagined the Easterner lying there, his eyes closed, the two jhereg around him, unaware of what was happening. Or maybe Vlad was awake, but unable to do anything about it.

He got a picture of the larger of the two jhereg, and concentrated on it, trying to talk. Did it understand? How could he communicate to such a beast; how would he know if he was succeeding?

He tried to imagine what its mind might feel like, but couldn't conceive of it. He imagined it, and imagined himself, calling to it, and imagined it answering him, but as far as he could tell, nothing happened. In desperation, he shouted his message to it, but it was as if he shouted to the air.

After some time—he didn't know how much—he came to himself, feeling shaky and exhausted. He opened his eyes, but was still in darkness, and now the darkness began to terrify him. He forced himself to stand slowly, and reached out with his hands. But wait, which way had he come in? He had sat down without turning, so he should turn now. He did so, reached out again, and again felt nothing.

Don't panic. Don't panic. It can't be far.

He tried taking a step, didn't run into anything, and reached out once more. Still nothing. He risked one more step, and this time he felt the cool, damp stone of a wall. He wanted to kiss it.

He slid forward until he was practically hugging the wall, and reached out in both directions, and so found the door. Now the darkness was becoming even more threatening, so it was with great relief he found that the door opened easily on its leather hinges. Very little light came through it, and as he stuck his head out, he saw that what there was came from a single lantern placed at the top of the stairs. He wondered how often these lanterns were checked, and who filled them, and how long it would be before someone missed it, and, for that matter, how much more kerosene it contained.

But there was no time for that. He went back up the stairs, fetched the lantern down, and went through the door once more. The room turned out to be big, and, except for several wooden tables, empty. He looked at the floor, and was unsurprised to find the remains of faint markings on it—this had been one of the places His Lordship had been accustomed to practice his wizardous work. But, while he didn't know exactly what he was looking for, he knew that wasn't it.

One wall, the one furthest from the door, looked odd. He crossed over to it, being careful to walk around the markings on the floor, and held up the lamp. There were several—four, in fact—odd, door-like depressions in the wall, each one about ten feet high and perhaps five feet wide at the bottom, curving at the top. And carved into the floor in front of each was a small, straight gutter that ran the length of the room and ended, as he followed them, in what looked to be a dry, shallow well.

He returned to the far wall and looked at the doors again. They looked almost like—

Almost like tunnels.

Or waterways.

Yes, there they were, just where they ought to be. He stared at them until the lamp flickered, which broke his reverie and reminded him that if he was going to do something, now would be a good time. He looked around the room, hoping to see some tool with which to open the gates, but the room was empty. He remembered Vlad saying something about traps and alarms, but there was no point in worrying about setting those off if he couldn't figure out a way to get the waterways open in the first place.

He approached one, and struck it with the side of his fist, and it did, indeed, sound hollow. He studied the wall around it, the floor below it, the ceiling above it.

And there it was, a chain, hanging down from the ceiling, as if there were a sign on it saying, "Pull me." And, in case it wasn't obvious enough, there were three more, one in front of each door. Well, on reflection, why should His Lordship have made it difficult for himself in his own work area?

So, Savn asked himself, *what now?* If he pulled the chain, the waterway would open, and all sorts of alarms would go off, and, no doubt, His Lordship would appear as fast as he could teleport. Then what? Could Savn escape, maybe swimming underwater for all he knew, before His Lordship caught him?

Not a chance.

He thought about trying once more to reach one of the jhereg, but at that moment he was startled almost out of his wits by a soft *tap tap* that came from somewhere he couldn't place.

He looked around, wildly, and it came again.

Could he have reached the jhereg after all?

Tap tap . . . tap tap.

He followed the sound, and discovered that, without doubt, it came from behind one of the waterways.

He hesitated no more. He stood in front of it, straddling the small gutter, then reached up and took the chain. It felt grimy with old rust, but he was able to get a good grip. He pulled.

At first it didn't move, as if rusted from long disuse, but he put his whole weight on it, and all of a sudden it gave.

In the dim light of the lantern, it looked for a moment as if the wall was moving backward, but then the reality of it became clear. The door in front of him creaked open noisily and admitted a small stream of water; a pair of jhereg; Polyi, dripping wet and looking frightened; and one very wet, very pale, very shaken-looking Easterner who stumbled forward and collapsed onto the floor at Savn's feet.

At that moment, as if Vlad's weight were enough to shake the entire manor, the floor began to vibrate. Savn looked around, but, for a moment, nothing happened. And then there was the sudden pop of displaced air, and Savn was looking at His Lordship and the Jhereg assassin, standing not ten feet away from him. His Lordship seemed very tall, with his hands out in front of him as if to touch the air, while the Jhereg crouched on the balls of his feet, holding a long, gleaming knife before him.

And there was a feeling Savn had never had, but could not possibly mistake for anything else: the knife in the Jhereg's hand was certainly Morganti.

17

I'm gonna marry me a bandit,
I'm gonna marry me a bandit,
Rich and free is how I've planned it.
Hi-dee hi-dee ho-la!
Step on out . . .

SAVN GRABBED POLYI WITH his free hand and pulled her back against the wall. Vlad remained where he was, on his hands and knees, looking up at His Lordship and the Jhereg assassin, who stood about ten feet away, motionless. The pair of jhereg took positions on either side of Vlad, and everyone waited.

Then Vlad slowly rose to his feet. He seemed to have some trouble standing, but managed. The jhereg flew up to land on either shoulder. Savn noticed that Vlad held a flask in his right hand.

"Careful," said His Lordship. "He's probably not hurt as badly as—"

"Shut up," said the Jhereg.

"Tsk," said Vlad. "No squabbling, now. It's unseemly. I have something for you, Loraan." He started forward, and there was a flash. Polyi screamed, but the knife didn't strike Vlad; it struck the flask in his hand.

Vlad chuckled and dropped it. "Well, it was a good idea. Nice throw, Ishtvan."

"Thanks, Taltos," said the assassin. "I try to keep my hand in."

"I know," said Vlad. "That's why I hired you."

His Lordship said, "Keep your mouth shut, East—"

"You're right," said the Jhereg. "Pardon us." Then he turned to His Lordship and said, "Immobilize him, and let's get this over with."

There was a tinkling sound from around Vlad's knees, and Savn noticed that Vlad now held in his left hand something that looked like a length of gold chain. His Lordship evidently saw it too, because he cried, "That's mine!"

"Yes," said Vlad. "Come and take it." But his strength wasn't the equal of his words; even as he spoke, his knees seemed to buckle and he stumbled forward. His Lordship took a step toward him and lifted his hands.

Without thinking about it, Savn ripped the top off the lantern and splashed the burning kerosene against the wall behind him. The room became very bright for a moment, then was plunged into total darkness.

Polyi screeched. Savn pulled her away, thinking that no matter what happened, they ought to be somewhere other than where they'd been standing when he put out the light. He took a few steps, found that he was standing in running water, and decided that was just as well with kerosene splashed everywhere. "Are you all right?" he asked in a whisper that sounded much too loud.

"You burned me," she whispered back.

"Sorry."

Why didn't someone make a light? Whole seconds had passed since he'd plunged the room into darkness; you'd think someone would want to see what was going on. And no one was moving, either.

Well, that might not be true; Vlad might still be able to move silently, and the Jhereg almost certainly could. And His Lordship was a sorcerer; for all Savn knew, there was a spell that would allow him to move silently. So maybe they were all moving all over the place, with Savn and Polyi the only ones fooled.

He thought about screaming, but was afraid it would upset his sister.

He heard a very faint *whsk whsk* that had to be the sound of jhereg wings. Shortly thereafter there was a very, very bright flash, but it showed him nothing; it only hurt his eyes and left blue spots in them. Polyi clung to him tightly; she was trembling, or he was, or maybe they both were—he couldn't tell.

He heard the flapping again, this time closer—he flinched even though he knew what it was. There was more movement, and another flash. This one wasn't as bright and lasted longer; he caught a quick glimpse of the Jhereg, crouched over holding the dagger out in front of him, and Vlad, on his feet once more, leaning against a wall, his sword in one hand, the gold chain swinging steadily in the other.

The flapping came again, even closer, and it seemed the jhereg hovered for a moment next to Savn's ear. He held his breath, half expecting what would come next, and it did—there was a touch on his shoulder, and then a gentle weight settled there. Savn, who had been standing motionless, froze—a difference hard to define but impossible to miss. Water soaked through his boots, but he was afraid to move.

"Savn? What happened?"

"Hush, Polyi."

Why had it landed on his shoulder? There must be a reason. Did it want him to do something? What? What could he do? He could panic—in fact, it was hard not to. What else could he do? He could get himself and Polyi out of there, if he had a light. Was the jhereg trying to tell him something?

He felt its head against his neck; then suddenly it jumped down to his right hand, which still held the empty lantern. He almost dropped it, but held on, and the jhereg hopped back up to his shoulder.

How had Vlad known to escape the searchers by entering the manor house through the cave? Was it desperation and lack of any other way, or had he, Savn, actually managed to get through to Vlad? If he had, then . . .

He tried to recapture the feeling he'd had before, of emptiness, of reaching out. He discovered that standing frozen in place with unknown but murderous actions going on all around was not conducive to the frame of mind he associated with witchcraft.

He had just reached this conclusion when Vlad began speaking. "I have to thank you for the loan of your device, Loraan. It's proven useful over the years. Have you missed it?"

"Don't speak," said the Jhereg. "He's trying to distract you. Ignore him."

"He's right," said Vlad. "Ignore me. But, just for something to think about, consider that your partner has a Morganti weapon, one of the few things that can destroy you, and consider that he's an assassin, and that assassins are very uncomfortable leaving witnesses alive. Any witnesses. Think about it. How have you two been getting along, by the way? Just curious—you don't have to answer."

Savn heard a chuckle from the vicinity of the Jhereg. "Give it up, Taltos. We have a deal."

"I'm certain he knows what a deal with you is worth."

"What's your game, Taltos?"

"Use your imagination, assassin."

Polyi whispered, "Savn, when he said witnesses, could that mean us?"

Savn swallowed. He hadn't thought of that.

If he had light, he'd be able to sneak out through the manor house, or maybe even the caves. Putting out the light, it seemed, hadn't helped anyone.

The jhereg bumped Savn's neck with its head again, and, once more, landed on the hand that held the lantern. It stayed there for a moment, flapping its wings for balance, then returned to Savn's shoulder.

It was, without doubt, trying to tell him something—something about the lantern, maybe. That he should light it? If so, it was too late, the oil was gone, although perhaps that was too complex an idea for a jhereg.

He started to say, "Are you trying to tell me something?" but stopped himself, realizing that it could be very dangerous to speak aloud. The jhereg bumped his neck again, as if in answer to his unspoken question.

He formed the sentence, "Was that an answer?" but didn't speak it.

Bump. At the same time, he imagined he heard a very tiny voice, located somewhere inside the very base of his head, voicelessly saying, "*Yes, idiot.*"

"*Who are you?*" he thought back.

"*Vlad, idiot,*" it told him.

"*How can we be talking like this?*"

"*I've removed the amulet, and that's really what's important right now, isn't it?*"

"*Sorry. What should I do?*"

"*Take your sister and get out of here. Loiosh will guide you.*"

"*I—*"

"*Damn it!*"

"*What?*"

"*Loiosh says he won't guide you. I'll—*"

"*It doesn't matter, Vlad. I want to help you.*"

"*You've already helped me. From here on out—*"

There was another bright flash of light. This time, Savn got a glimpse of His Lordship, both hands stretched out in front of him, just a few feet from the Jhereg.

"*Almost got me, that time,*" said Vlad. "*Look, I can't hold them off much longer, and I'm finished anyway. Take your sister and—*"

"*What's going on?*"

"*About as much sorcery as I've seen in one place at one time. They've got some sort of spell that keeps the jhereg from getting to them, and Loraan keeps shooting things at me, and the assassin is trying to maneuver into a position to nail me—the idiot thinks I'm faking or he'd just move in and have done with it—and Loraan's personal cutthroats are going to be here any minute. So, would you please—*"

There was more scuffling, then Vlad said, *"That was close."*

Then he spoke aloud, "Careful, Loraan. You're getting too near our assassin friend. He's quick."

"Shut up," growled His Lordship.

"Oh, you're safe until he's gotten me, I'm sure. But you'd better think about what happens after that. Or have you? Maybe I've got it backwards. Maybe you're already planning to do him. I'm sorry I won't be around to watch it."

"It's not working, Easterner," said His Lordship. "Ishtvan, he's getting desperate. Maybe he really is hurt. Why don't you just finish him? I've got all the protections up; I don't think he can do anything about it."

"Yes," said Vlad. "Why don't you, Ishtvan? Finish me, then he'll finish you. Why don't you ask *him* to finish me? Afraid you will lose the wages, my lord? Of course not, because you've already been paid, and you know very well you're going to have to kill him any—"

There was still another flash, and Savn saw His Lordship, hands now raised high above his head. At the same time, Vlad gasped.

"Vlad, are you all right?"

"Barely."

"Isn't there something you can do?"

"I don't carry poison darts anymore, and I don't have the strength to throw a knife. You have any ideas?"

Another flash of light illuminated the scene. The assassin had moved around to Vlad's right, but was still keeping his distance. Vlad had moved a foot or so to his left, and was still swinging the gold chain. Loiosh gripped Savn's shoulder, and occasionally squeezed with his talons. Savn wished he knew what Loiosh was trying to tell him. It would almost be funny if some brilliant idea for escaping were locked up in that reptilian brain but the poor thing couldn't communicate it. But of course that couldn't be the case, or Loiosh would have told Vlad. Unless, perhaps, it was something Vlad wouldn't approve of. But what wouldn't Vlad approve of if it would get him out of this?

Well, Vlad apparently wouldn't approve of Savn doing anything risky, whereas Loiosh probably wouldn't care. But what could he, Savn, do, anyway? He could hardly attack an assassin, barehanded, in the dark. And to do anything to His Lordship was both impossible and unthinkable.

You're so convinced that your Baron Smallcliff is invincible and perfect that you'd stand there and let him kill you rather than raising a finger to defend yourself.

Vlad had been right about that, just as he'd been right about the assassin, and the Morganti weapon, and even about His Lordship being . . .

He could imagine the jhereg saying, "You've finally figured it out, fool." Because he *had* figured it out, only now he didn't know if he had the courage to do anything about it.

You're so convinced that your Baron Smallcliff is invincible and perfect that you'd stand there and let him kill you rather than raising a finger to defend yourself.

It had rankled because it was true, and now, when he thought he knew what he could do about it, it rankled even more.

"*Savn, don't,*" said Vlad. "*Just get out of here.*"

Savn ignored him. He knelt down into the slowly flowing water and filled up the lamp.

"*Savn!*"

His sister whispered, "What are you doing?"

"Wait," he whispered back. "Don't move."

He stood up, and as best he could, walked quickly and firmly toward where he had last seen His Lordship, holding before him the lamp filled with Dark Water, stagnant and contained. *When stagnant and contained, it can be used to weaken and repel the undead. . . .*

His Lordship's voice came from directly in front of him. "What are—Ishtvan! Kill this Teckla brat for me."

Savn felt his hand shaking, but he continued walking forward.

The Jhereg answered, "I can't see anymore."

"Then make a light. Hurry! I can't do anything while—"

"The Easterner—"

His Lordship made an obscene suggestion concerning the Easterner, which Savn noticed indifferently as he continued to walk forward. He hardly blinked when a soft light filled the room, and, oddly enough, it hardly mattered that he could now see His Lordship, about five feet away, walking slowly backward, and glaring.

Savn wondered, in a familiar, detached way, how he could survive an attack by a Jhereg assassin. But the attack didn't come, because at that instant, Loiosh left Savn's shoulder.

Savn couldn't help it—he turned and watched as Loiosh and his mate simultaneously attacked. Evidently, His Lordship's spells that had kept them away were now gone. Ishtvan snarled and cut at the jhereg with the Morganti dagger. He turned, and apparently realized, at the same time as Savn did, that he was offering his back to Vlad, and that he was within range of the Easterner's sword.

He tried to spin back, but it was already too late. It made Savn wince to see Vlad, in his condition, execute a maneuver so demanding, but the Easterner managed it—the point of his sword penetrated deeply into the assassin's back right over his heart. At the same time, Polyi was shrieking—"Savn!" and Vlad continued forward, falling limply onto his face as the assassin screamed and the Morganti dagger went flying into the air—

—and the lamp was struck from Savn's hand to land and shatter on the floor. He turned in time to see His Lordship recovering from delivering a kick that must have been very difficult for him, judging by the look of concentration and effort on his face, and Savn felt an impossible combination of pride and shame in having caused His Lordship such distress. He wondered what His Lordship would do now, but—

—he didn't know, because the assassin's light-spell faded, and the room was suddenly pitched into darkness. It seemed that proximity to the Dark Water had taken His Lordship's magical powers, but hadn't actually hurt him—he could still kick. Which meant he might also be able to simply grab Savn and throttle him. Savn started to back away, but he was struck a blow that knocked him onto his back and caused him to crack his head sharply on the floor.

He decided he was glad he hadn't hit his head harder, when he realized that he *had* hit his head harder, that he was sick and dizzy and was almost certainly about to die, and, worst of all, he wasn't certain that he didn't deserve to.

It came to him that he had once again achieved the state of witchcraft, this time by the accident of bumping his head. He didn't have anything to do, but it was much more pleasant here, flying over walls, and cavorting in the air like a disembodied jhereg. There were terrible things happening to his body, and he had done terrible things himself, but they didn't matter anymore. He could—

There, before him, was His Lordship, grinning a terrible grin, his hand looming large, ready to smash him down as Savn would swat an insect.

I am not an insect, cried Savn in a voice no one could hear as, in helpless rage, he flew right into His Lordship's face, defying him, and waiting for his consciousness to end, for the sleep from which there is no waking.

He felt something break, but it didn't seem to matter, even though it was himself. He hoped somehow Vlad would survive, but he didn't see—

—he didn't see anything, because the room was dark, and his thoughts, all that remained, were becoming scattered, misty, and going away.

What he asked was impossible.

Not physically impossible; the evil thing spun and twirled right in front of her, and plucking it out of the air would be no problem at all, even in the total darkness. She could feel exactly where it was all along its path through the air. But it was still impossible. To touch such a thing was—

But her mate was insistent. Her lover was saying that if she didn't, the Provider would die. She didn't understand how this could be, or why it would be too late if she didn't do it now, as the evil thing reached the top of its arc and began to fall to the ground.

She didn't understand what it was, but she hated the idea of coming near it more than she had ever hated anything in her life. Did he understand that—

And her mate told her that there was no more time, she must get it now, because the undead soft one was going to kill the Provider, and, even if he didn't, couldn't she hear the footsteps of more of the soft ones coming? She should trust him, he said—these were not friends.

And what was she supposed to do when she had it? she wondered, but she nevertheless did as she was asked—she took it from the air, wrapping her feet around the bone part, trying to keep as far from the metal part as she could and—

Is that what she was supposed to do? How?

The other soft one, the one the Provider had been spending so much time with, the one who had saved him, was somewhere near here, but she couldn't see him.

Her mate could feel him? Well enough to know where his hand was? To direct her to . . . Oh, very well, then.

And so he guided her, and she went where he said, and, at the right time, she let the evil thing fall into the hand of the soft one who had saved the Provider—although it seemed odd to her that someone who would do that would have a use for such a thing. What would he do with it?

Although she couldn't see, she was able to tell what use he had for it— he plunged it into the side of the other soft one, the undead, who was on top of him, strangling the life out of him.

The odd thing was that both of them screamed—first the one who had been stabbed, then the one who did the stabbing, and they both screamed where she could hear it more within her mind than in the room, and both screams went on for a long time.

In fact, the one who was still alive didn't stop screaming with his mind at all, even after he had stopped screaming with his voice. He kept scream-

ing and screaming, even after the Provider managed to make a small amount of light appear, and to gather them all together, and to take them all far, far away from the place where the evil thing lay with the two bodies in the dark cavern.

Epilogue

THE MINSTREL SENT THE Easterner a look containing equal portions of disgust and contempt. It didn't seem to bother him; he was used to such things. But he avoided looking at the girl who sat by the fire, holding her brother's hand. The two jhereg sat complacently on the Easterner's shoulders, not terribly bothered by anything now that—in their reptilian opinions—the crisis was past. They finished up the scraps of the roasted athyra.

"Well?" said Sara.

"I'm glad you made it here."

"Your jhereg are good guides," said Sara. "I had a pretty good idea what they wanted."

"I thought you might. Thanks for coming."

"You're welcome," she said. And repeated, "Well?"

"Well what? If you're asking after my health, breathing doesn't hurt as much as it did a couple of days ago."

"I'm not asking after your health, I'm asking after *his*."

Vlad apparently didn't need to follow her glance to know of whom she was speaking—Savn sat staring into the fire, oblivious of the conversation, and of everything else going on around him.

"His health is fine. But, as you can see—"

"Yes. As I can see."

"I suppose I'm being hunted as a kidnapper."

"Among other things, yes. The village Speaker has appealed to the Empire, and he's been ranting about gathering the entire region to hunt for you tree by tree and stone by stone. And their parents are in agony, wondering where they are, imagining you've killed them or used them for some Eastern ritual or something. I don't know why I don't summon—"

"Summon who? The Jhereg? That's been tried."

"Yes, I suppose it has. They found the body next to His Lordship's. And they found the village physicker there, too."

"Wag? Really? Was he dead?"

"No, barely alive. Did you do that to him?"

"Do what?"

She searched his eyes, trying to see if he was lying. Then she shrugged. "He'd been tortured."

"Oh. No, I imagine that Loraan and the assassin did that. It makes sense, at any rate; that's probably how they found me."

"Well, he's going to live. He says Savn physicked him. The child will be a good physicker, if he ever comes out of it."

"Yes. If."

Polyi glared at him. Sara guessed that there hadn't been much small talk between Vlad and the girl in the two days since the death of Baron Smallcliff.

Sara said, "So Loraan and the Jhereg found you. How did you beat them?"

"I didn't. He did."

Sara's eyes turned to the Teckla boy, and widened. "*He* did?"

"Yes. He nullified Loraan's magic, helped distract the assassin, and, in the end, killed Loraan."

"I don't believe you."

"I couldn't care less."

Sara chewed her lip. "Exactly what happened to him, anyway?"

"I don't know for certain. My guess is that the shock of even holding, much less using, a Morganti dagger was pretty severe, and I think he hit his head and was dazed before that happened, and then he killed his own lord. He woke up after I teleported us out of there, stared at his hand, bit it, screamed, and hasn't said a word since."

"Oh," said the minstrel.

"He'll do what he's told, and he'll eat, and he keeps himself clean."

"And that's all."

"Yes."

"What are you going to do?"

"I'm going to keep moving. It would be a shame to let the townsfolk kill me after escaping Loraan and the Jhereg."

"And you want me to see to it the boy and his sister are returned home?"

"No, only the sister."

"What do you mean?"

"Think about it. The boy was seen with me, his friends tried to beat him up, and everyone's going to figure out that he at least helped kill His Lordship, who was a pretty well-liked bastard, for an undead. What sort of life is the kid going to have around here?"

"What are you talking about?"

"I'm talking about the fact that he saved my life, several times, and his only reward was being given such a shock that he has gone mad."

"What can you do about it?"

"I can try to cure him, and keep him safe in the meantime."

"You're going to wander around, running from the Jhereg, and keep a child with you?"

"Yes. At least until he's cured. After that, I don't think he'll be a child anymore, and he can make up his own mind."

"What makes you think he won't hate you?"

"He probably will."

"What makes you think you can cure him?"

Vlad shrugged. "I have some ideas. I'll try them. And I know people, if I get desperate."

"So you're going to take him away from his family—"

"That's right. Until he's cured. Then it's up to him."

Sara stared at him for a long moment, then burst out, "You're crazy!"

"No, just in debt. And intending to discharge the debt."

"I—"

"You can take the girl back to her family, and explain what I'm doing."

"They'll never let you do this. They'll hunt you down and kill you."

"How? I've avoided the Jhereg for more than two years, I can certainly avoid a few peasants long enough to see the boy cured."

Sara turned and looked at Savn, who continued to stare into the fire, and Polyi, who looked at her brother with red eyes. Sara said, "Polyi, what do you think of all this?"

"I don't know," she said in a small voice. "But he did this to Savn, so he ought to cure him, and then bring him back."

"That's my opinion," said Vlad.

"Don't you realize," said Sara slowly, "that traveling with the boy is going to make you ten times—a *hundred* times as easy a target for the Jhereg?"

"Yes."

"Work fast," said Sara.

"I intend to," said Vlad.

"Do you even have supplies for the journey?"

"I have gold, and I can teleport, and I can steal."

Sara shook her head.

Vlad stood up and reached a hand out. "Savn, come on."

The boy obediently stood, and Sara glanced at his eyes; they seemed empty. "Can you really heal his mind?" she asked.

"One way or another," said Vlad. "I will."

Polyi stood and hugged her brother, who seemed not to notice. She stepped back, gave Vlad a look impossible to describe, went over to Sara, and nodded.

"I don't know what to tell you, Easterner," said Sara.

"You could wish me luck."

"Yes. Good luck."

"Thanks."

He took the boy's arm, and led him off into the woods, walking slowly as if his wounds still bothered him. Sara put her arm around the girl, who didn't resist, and they watched the Easterner, the human, and the two jhereg until they disappeared. "Good luck," Sara repeated softly to their backs.

Then she turned to the girl and took her hand. "Come on," she said. "Let's get you home. Your Harvest Festival is beginning, and the gods alone know what sort of animals live out here."

The girl said nothing, but held onto Sara's hand, tightly.

ORCA

In memory of my brother,
Leo Brust, 1954–1994

Acknowledgments

My thanks to the Scribblies: Emma Bull, Pamela Dean, and Will Shetterly for their help with this one, and also to Terri Windling, Susan Allison, and Fred A. Levy Haskell. Thanks as well to Teresa Nielsen Hayden, who recommended a book that turned out to be vital; to David Green, for sharing some theories; and, as always, to Adrian Charles Morgan.

And to the fan who actually suggested the whole thing in the first place: Thanks, Mom.

Prologue

My Dear Cawti:

I'm sorry it has taken me so long to answer your letter, but the gods of Coincidence make bad correspondents of us all; I am not unaware that the passing of a few weeks to you is a long time—as long as the passing of years is to me, and this is long indeed when one is uncertain—so I will plead the excuse that I found your note when I returned from traveling, and will answer your question at once: Yes, I have seen your husband, or the man who used to be your husband, or however you would describe him. Yes, I have seen Vlad—and that is why it has taken me so long to write back to you; I was just visiting him in response to his request for assistance in a small matter.

I can understand your concern for him, Cawti; indeed, I will not try to pretend that he isn't still in danger from the Organization with which we are both, one way or another, still associated. They want him, and I fear someday they will get him, but as of now he is alive and, I can even say, well.

I don't pretend that I think this knowledge will satisfy you.

You will want the details, or at least those details I can divulge. Very well, I consent, both for the sake of our friendship and because we share a concern for the mustached fellow with reptiles on his shoulders. We will arrange a time and a place; I will be there and tell you what I can—in person, because some things are better heard face-to-face than page-to-eye. And, no, I will not tell you everything, because, just as there are things that you wouldn't want me to tell him, there are things he wouldn't want me to tell you—and, come to that, there are things I don't want to tell you, either. It is a mark of my love for you both that I keep these secrets, and trust you with those I can, so don't be angry!

Come, dear Cawti, write back at once (you remember that I prefer not to communicate psychically), and we will arrange to be alone and I will tell you enough—I hope—for your peace of mind. I look forward to seeing you and yours again, and, until that time, I remain,

                                                    Faithfully,
                                                    Kiera

1

VLAD KNEW ALMOST AT once that I was in disguise, because I told him so. When he called out my name, I said, "Dammit, Vlad, I'm in disguise."

He looked me over in that way of his—eyes flicking here and there apparently at random—then said, "Me, too."

He was wearing brown leather, rather than the grey and black of the House of the Jhereg he'd been wearing when I last saw him; but he was still an Easterner, still had his mustache, and still had a pair of jhereg on his shoulders. He was, I assumed, letting me know that my disguise wasn't terribly effective. I didn't press the issue, but said, "Who's the boy?"

"My catamite," he said, deadpan. He faced him then and said, "Savn, meet Kiera the Thief."

The boy made no response at all—didn't even seem to hear—which was a bit creepy.

I said, "You're joking, right?"

He smiled sadly and said, "Yes, Kiera, I'm joking." Loiosh, the male jhereg, shifted its weight and was probably laughing at me. I held out my arm to it; it flew across the four feet that separated us and allowed me to scratch its snakelike chin. The female, Rocza, watched us closely but made no move; perhaps she didn't remember me.

"Why the disguise?" he said.

"Why do you think?"

"You don't want to be seen with me?"

I shrugged.

He said, "Well, in any case, our disguises match." He was referring to the fact that I was wearing a green blouse and white pants, rather than the same black and grey he'd once worn. My hair was also different—I'd brushed it forward to conceal my noble's point so I'd look more like a peasant. But perhaps he didn't notice that; for an assassin, he can be amazingly unobservant sometimes. Still, you wear a disguise, first, from the inside, and perhaps that can in part explain the fact that my disguise didn't fool Vlad; I've always trusted him, even before I had reason to.

"It's been a long time, Vlad," I said, because I knew that to him, who could only expect to live sixty or seventy years, it would have seemed like a long time.

"Yes, it has," he agreed. "How odd that we should just happen to run into each other."

"You haven't changed."

"There's less of me," he said, holding up his left hand and showing me that the last finger was missing.

"What happened?"

"A very heavy weight."

I winced in sympathy. "Is there someplace we can talk?" I said.

He looked around. We were in Northport, quite a distance from Adrilankha, but it was the same ocean, and the docks, if older, were pretty much the same. There was a small, two-masted cargo ship unloading about fifty yards away, and there was a fishermen's market nearby; between them, on the very edge of the ocean, we were in plain view of hundreds of people, but no one was near us. "What's wrong with here?"

"You don't trust me," I said, feeling a bit hurt.

I could see a snappy answer get as far as his teeth and stop there. Vlad and I had a great deal of history; none of it should have given him any reason to be suspicious of me. "Last I heard," he said, "the Organization wanted very badly to kill me; you still work for the Organization. Excuse me if I'm a bit jumpy."

"Oh, yes," I agreed. "They want you very badly indeed."

The water lapped and gurgled against the dock that had stood since the end of the Interregnum; I could feel the spells that kept the wood from rotting. The air was thick with the smell of ocean: salt water and dead fish; I've never really liked either.

"Who *is* the boy?" I asked him, as much to give him time to think as because I wanted to know. Savn, as Vlad had called him, seemed to be a handsome Teckla youth, probably not more than ninety years old. He still had that look of strength and energy that begins to diminish during one's second century, and his hair was the same dusky brown as his eyes. It annoyed me that I could conceive of him as a catamite. He still hadn't responded to me or to anything else.

"A debt of honor," said Vlad, in the tone he uses when he is trying to be ironic. I realized that I'd missed him. I waited for him to continue. He said, "Savn was damaged, I guess you'd say, saving my life."

"Damaged?"

"Oh, the usual—he used a Morganti weapon to kill an undead wizard."

"When was this?"

"Last year. Does it matter?"

"I suppose not."

"I'm glad you got my message, and I'm glad you came."

"You're still psychically invisible, you know."

"I know. Phoenix Stone."

"Yes."

"How is Aibynn?"

Aibynn was one of the last people Vlad wanted to ask about; he knew it and I knew it. "Fine as far as I know. I don't see him much."

He nodded. We watched the bay for a while, but it didn't do much. I turned back to Vlad and said, "Well? I'm here. What is it?"

He smiled. "Maybe I've come up with a way to get the Organization to forgive and forget."

I laughed. "My dear Vlad, if you managed to loot the Dragon Treasury to the last orb and deposited it all at the feet of the Council they wouldn't forgive you."

His smile disappeared. "There's that."

"Well then?"

He shrugged. He wasn't ready to talk about it yet. That was all right, I can be a very patient woman. "You know," I said, "there aren't all that many Easterners who walk around with a pair of jhereg on their shoulders; are you quite certain you aren't too conspicuous?"

"Yeah. No professional would try anything in a place like this, and any amateur who wants to is welcome to take a shot. And by the time word gets around so someone who knows his business can set up something, I'll be gone."

"But they'll know where you are."

"I don't plan on being here for more than a few days."

I nodded.

He said hesitantly, "Any news from home?"

"None I can tell you."

"Excuse me?"

"You're asking about Cawti."

"Well—"

"I've promised not to say anything except that she's fine."

"Oh." I watched his mind work, but he didn't say anything else. I very badly wanted to tell him what was going on, but a promise is a promise, even to a thief. Especially to a thief.

I said, "How have you been getting by?"

"It's been harder since I acquired the boy, but I've managed."

"How?"

"I mostly stay away from towns, and you know the forests are filled with bandits of one sort or another."

"You've become one?"

"No, I rob them."

I laughed. "That sounds like you."

"It's a living."

"That sounds like you, too."

He shifted his weight as if his feet were causing him pain; it made me think about the amount of walking he must have been doing in these past three years and more. I said, "Do you want to sit down?"

"You don't miss much," he said. "No, I'm fine. Ever heard of a man named Fyres?"

"Yes. He died a couple of weeks ago."

"Other than that, what do you know about him?"

"He had a great deal of money."

"Yes. What else?"

"He was, what, a baron? House of the, uh, Chreotha?"

"Orca."

"All right. Then that tells you what I know about him."

Vlad didn't answer, which meant that I was supposed to ask him a question. I thought over a number of things I'd have liked to know, then settled on, "How did he die?"

"They've found no evidence of murder."

"That's not—Wait. You?"

He shook his head. "I don't do that sort of thing anymore."

"All right," I said. Vlad has always had the ability to make me believe him, even though I know what a liar he is. "Then what do you think happened?"

His eyes were in constant motion, and the jhereg, too, never stopped looking around. "I don't know," he said, "and I have to find out."

"Why?"

For just an instant he looked embarrassed, and "Oh ho!" passed through my head, but I sent it on its way—Vlad could be embarrassed by the oddest things. "It doesn't matter," he said. "Let me tell you what I'd like you to do."

"I'm listening."

One thing I like about Vlad is that he understands details. He not only gave me every detail of every alarm I was likely to encounter but also told me how he found out, so I could do my own checking. He told me where the stuff was likely to be and why he thought so, and the other places it might be located if he was wrong. He gave me the schedules of the patrols in the area and explained exactly what he hadn't been able to discover. It took about an hour, at the end of which time I knew the job would be well within my capabilities—not that there are many jobs that aren't, if they involve stealing.

I said, "There will be a price."

"Of course," he said, trying to hide that I'd hurt his feelings.

"You have to tell me why you want it."

He bit his lip and looked at me carefully; I kept my face expressionless, because I didn't want him learning too much. He nodded abruptly, and the deal was made.

IT TOOK ME TWO days to check everything Vlad had told me—two days that I spent working out of a reasonably comfortable room in a hotel in the middle of Northport; on the third I went to work. The place I was to burgle was situated a couple of miles east of Northport, and the walk there was the most chancy part of the operation—if anyone saw me and saw through my disguise as easily as Vlad had, it would arouse curiosity, and that would lead to investigations and that would lead to this and that. I solved the problem by staying off the roads and sticking as much as I could to the thin-wooded areas to the side. I didn't get lost, but it was several hours before I reached the bottom of a small hill, with Fyres's mansion looming above me.

I spent a couple of hours walking a wide circuit around it, taking a long, slow look at the place. One of the things Vlad hadn't given me was a set of blueprints, but with this newer work you can almost create the inside by seeing the outside; for some reason post-Interregnum architects object to having rooms without windows, which means the dimensions indicate the layout. You can also identify windowed corridors because (again, I don't know why) the windows are invariably smaller than those in rooms. By the time I'd finished my walk, I pretty much knew what it looked like, and I'd found the most obvious places for an office.

I spent the last hours of daylight watching for any signs of activity. There were none, which was as it should be—Fyres's family (a wife and three children) didn't live there, his mistress had abandoned the place, the staff were, no doubt, ensconced within, and all of the remaining protection was sorcerous and automatic. I took out a few of the devices I use to identify such things and set to work.

Darkness came as it always does, with shadows becoming dusk—shadows that were a bit sharper here than in Adrilankha, I suppose because the westerly winds thin out the overcast, so the Furnace is more apparent. Everything is brighter in the west of the Empire, as it is in the far east; all of which makes the darkness seem even darker.

The protections weren't bad, but not as thorough as I would have expected. The first was very general and nearly useless—all you had to do was pretend you belonged there and it would let you burn down the place without raising a fuss. The recognition spell was only marginally trickier, requiring me to cause it to bend around and past me; but there was no spell monitoring whether the recognition spell was being bent, so, really, they might as well not have bothered with it. There were the usual integrity detectors on the doors and windows, but these are easily defeated by transferring the one you want to pass to another door or window. These, in fact, did have monitor spells to watch for just this, but they'd been cast almost as an afterthought and without anything to let the security people know the monitor had been removed—I could take it down just by identifying the energy committed to that spell and absorbing it into a working of my own.

I considered the significance of how poorly the mansion was protected. It might mean that since the place was abandoned and its owner was dead, no one felt the need to use high-level protections. It might also mean that the Orca weren't as sophisticated as the Jhereg. Or it might mean that there were some traps concealed that I hadn't found yet. That possibility was worth an extra hour of checking, and I took it.

I went through enough gear to stock a small sorcery shop and found fertility spells that had probably been placed on the ground before the mansion was built, spells that kept the latrines from smelling, spells that kept the mansion from sinking into the ground, spells that kept the stonework from crumbling, and spells to make the row of rednut trees that flanked the road grow just so—but nothing else that had anything to do with security. I even used a blue stone I'd picked from the pocket of Vlad's friend Aliera, but the only signs of elder sorcery were distant echoes from the explosion that had dissolved Dragaera City at the start of the Interregnum.

I was satisfied. I climbed the hill slowly, keeping my eyes open for more mundane traps, although I didn't expect to find any, and I didn't. I eventually reached the edge of the mansion, which, I suppose I should have mentioned, demonstrated the sort of post-Interregnum aesthetic that thinks monoliths attractive for their own sake, producing big blocks of stone with the occasional bit of decoration, usually a wrought-iron animal, sticking out as an afterthought. Buildings like this are exceedingly easy to burglarize, because you know exactly where everything is relative to everything else, and because the regularity of the construction makes those who live there believe that it is difficult to conceal oneself while climbing up a wall, which is silly—I once challenged three friends to try to spot me while I scaled three stories of a blank wall, after telling them which wall I was going up and when I was going to do it. They couldn't find me. So much for the difficulty of concealment.

It took me about ten seconds to levitate up to the level of the window; I rested on the ledge and considered that idiotic spell I already mentioned that was supposed to make certain the integrity of the window wasn't broken. There was, indeed, nothing fancy about it, but I was careful and spent some time circumventing the alarm. The window, by the way, was filled in, as were all of them, with a solid sheet of glass cunningly worked into slots in a wood and leather contrivance that, in turn, fitted snugly into the window; a silly luxury that would need to be replaced in a hundred years or so, even if the fragile thing weren't broken in the meantime.

I broke it carefully, first covering it with a large sheet of paper smeared with an extremely tacky gel and then pushing slowly until the glass gave and the shards stuck to the paper rather than falling and making noise. There were jagged bits of the stuff all around the wooden frame so I had to be careful entering the room, but I was able to enter without cutting myself; then I hung the paper in the window where the glass had been so I could illuminate the room without the light appearing to anyone outside (if there was, by chance, someone outside).

I used another several seconds sensing for spells in the room, then lit a candle, squinted against the glare, and glanced around quickly. No matter how many times you've been through this, you always half expect to see someone sitting in the room waiting for you with all sorts of arguments to hand. It has never happened, and it didn't this time, but it's one of those things that pass through your mind.

I closed my eyes and stood very still for a while, listening for anyone moving around and for whatever creaks and groans might be usual for this building. After a minute, I opened my eyes and took a good look.

Office or study, said that part of my brain that wants to rush in and categorize before all of the details are individually assimilated. I let it have its way, ignored its opinion, and made some mental notes.

The room was dominated by two large cabinets against the far wall, both of some dark wood, probably cherry, and showing signs of careful but uninspired construction. In front of them was a small desk, facing the room's other window, with a chair behind it. From the chair, the occupant, presumably Fyres, could reach back to either cabinet. On top of the desk were a set of books that would probably reward some study, several sheets of paper, blotter, inkwell, and quill; several other quills were all set in a row to one side, as if awaiting their call. The desk and the room were neither unusually tidy nor remarkably messy, except for between one and four weeks' worth of dust over everything, which would be about right if no one had been in here since his death. Why would no one have been in his office since his death? No, questions later.

I checked all the desk drawers and cabinets and found both sorcerous alarms on each. None of them were terribly complicated and I wasn't in a big hurry, so I took my time disabling them (unnecessarily in all probability—they were almost certainly keyed directly to Fyres, who wouldn't be receiving any messages—but it is always best to be certain). I also looked for more mundane sorts of alarms—easily identified by thin wires hidden against desk legs or along walls—but there weren't any. It occurs to me now, as I relate this, that it may seem as if Fyres took insufficient precautions against theft, and I ought to correct this impression; most of his precautions probably involved guards, and, chances are, the guard schedule had been obliterated with Fyres's life. And the magical alarms were really quite good; it's just that I'm better.

It took maybe two minutes to assure myself that there were no secret drawers in the desk, another ten to be certain about the cabinets. The rest of the room took an hour, which is a long time to be on the scene, but I didn't think the risk was too great.

Once I was certain I hadn't missed anything, I began going through his papers, looking for anything that seemed like what Vlad was after. The longer I sat there, the harder it was to make myself go slowly and be careful not to miss anything, but, after four hours or so, I was pretty sure I had the information. It made a neat little bundle, which I tied up and slung over my back. I still had an hour or so before dawn.

I restored order to the papers and books I'd messed up, then slipped across the hall to the master bedroom. Everything was very still, and I could hear—or maybe I just imagined it—servants breathing from their quarters above me. The bed was made, the clothes were neatly arranged in the wardrobe, and, unlike the office, everything was freshly dusted—obviously the staff had been given orders to stay out of the other room, and they were still scrupulously following them. I opened drawers and scattered things about as if a thief had been looking for valuables. I did, in fact, find a safe, so I spent a few minutes marking it up as if I'd attempted to open it, then I went back to the study, out the window, and down.

I was back in town before the first light. I found my hotel and climbed into my second-story window so I wouldn't have to go past the desk clerk. I put the booty under my pillow and slept for nine hours.

Mʏ ʀᴇɴᴅᴇᴢᴠᴏᴜs ᴡɪᴛʜ Vʟᴀᴅ took place in one of those dockside inns that feature thick beer and harshly spiced fish stew. Vlad availed himself of the latter; I abstained. It was too early in the day for there to be much business; only a table or two was filled. Neither of us attracted much attention. I've always wondered how Vlad (even with a jhereg on his shoulder—only one today) managed to avoid making himself conspicuous wherever he went.

"Where's the boy?"

"With friends."

"You have friends?" I said, not entirely being sarcastic.

He gave me a brief smile and said, "Rocza is watching him."

He accepted the bundle of ledgers and papers, trying not to look eager. I made faces at Loiosh while he perused them; at last he looked up and nodded. "This is what I'm after," he said. "Thanks."

"What do they mean?"

"I haven't any idea."

"Then how do you know—?"

"From the notations at the top of the columns."

"I see," I lied. "Well, then—"

"What am I after?"

"Yes."

He looked at me. I'd seen Vlad happy, sad, frightened, angry, and hurt; but I'd never before seen him look uncomfortable. At last he said, "All right," and began speaking.

2

On the wall of a small hostelry just outside of Northport someone had written in black, sloppy letters: "When the water is clean, you see the bottom; when the water is dirty, you see yourself."

"Deep philosophy," I remarked to Loiosh. *"Probably a brothel."*

He didn't laugh. Call me superstitious, but I decided to find another place. I nodded to the boy to follow. I'm not sure when he started responding to nonverbal cues; I hadn't been paying that much attention. But it was a good sign. On the other hand, that had been the only improvement in the year he'd been with me and that was a bad sign.

Wait for it, Kiera; wait for it. I've done this before. I know how to tell a Verra-be-damned story, okay?

So I kept walking, getting closer to Northport. I'd come to Northport because Northport is the biggest city in the world—okay, in the Empire—that doesn't have any sort of university. No, I have nothing against universities, but you must know how they work—they act like magnets to pull in the best brains in an area, as well as the richest and most pretentious. They are seats of great learning and all that. Now I had a problem that required someone of great, or maybe not-so-great learning, but walking into a university, well, I didn't like the idea. I don't know how to go about it, and that means I don't know how to go about it without getting caught. For example, what happens if I go to, say, Candletown, and inquire at Lady Brindlegate's University, and someone is rude to me, and I have to drop him? Then what? It makes a big stink, and the wrong people hear about it, and there I am running again.

But I figured, what if I find a place with a lot of people but no institution to suck up the talented ones? It means it's going to be a place with a lot of hedge-wizards, and wise old men, and greatwives. And that's just what I was looking for—what I had been looking for for most of a year, and not finding, until I hit on this idea.

I'll get to it, I'll get to it. Trust me.

I got a little closer to town, stopped at an inn, and—look, you don't need to hear all this. I stayed out of a fight, listened to gossip, pumped a few people, went to another inn, did the same, repeat, repeat, and finally found myself at a little blue cottage in the woods. Yes, blue—a blue lump of house standing out from all the greens of the woods surrounding Northport. It was one of the ugliest objects I've ever seen.

The first thing that happened was a dog came running out toward us. I was stepping in front of Savn and reaching for a knife before Loiosh said, *"His tail is wagging, boss."*

"Right. I knew that."

It was some indeterminate breed with a bit of hound in it—the sleek build of a lyorn with the sort of long, curly, reddish hair that needed cleaning and combing, a long nose, and floppy ears. It didn't come up to my waist, and it generally seemed pretty nonthreatening. It stopped in front of me and started sniffing. I held out my left hand, which it approved, then it gave a half-jump up toward Loiosh, then one toward Rocza, went down on its front legs, barked twice, and stood in front of me waiting and wagging. Rocza hissed; Loiosh refused to dignify it by responding.

The door opened, and a woman called, "Buddy!" The dog looked back at her, turned in a circle, and ran up to her, then rose on its hind legs and stayed there for a moment. The woman was old and a foot and a half taller than me. She had grey hair and an expression that would sour your favorite dairy product. She said, "You're an Easterner," in a surprisingly flutelike voice.

"Yes," I said. "And your house is painted blue."

She let that go. "Who's the boy?"

"The reason I'm here."

"He's human."

"And to think I hadn't noticed."

Loiosh chuckled in my head; the woman didn't. "Don't be saucy," she said. "No doubt you've come for help with something; you ought to be polite." The dog sat down next to her and watched us, his tongue out.

I tried to figure out what House she was and decided it was most likely Tsalmoth, to judge by her complexion and the shape of her nose—her green shawl, dirty white blouse, and green skirt were too generic to tell me anything.

"Why do you care?" said Loiosh.

"Good question."

"Okay," I said. "I'll be polite. You're a—do you find the term 'hedge-wizard' objectionable?"

"Yes," she said, biting out the word.

"What do you prefer?"

"Sorcerer."

She was a sorcerer the way I was a flip-dancer. "All right. I've heard you are a sorcerer, and that you are skilled in problems of the mind."

"I can sometimes help, yes."

"The boy has brain fever."

She made a harrumphing sound. "There is no such thing."

I shrugged.

She looked at him, but still didn't step out of her door, nor ask us to approach. I expected her to ask more questions about his condition, but instead she said, "What do you have to offer me?"

"Gold."

"Not interested."

That caught me by surprise. "You're not interested in gold?"

"I have enough to get by."

"Then what do you want?"

"Offer her her life, boss."

"Grow up, Loiosh."

She said, "There isn't anything I want that you could give me."

"You'd be surprised," I said.

She studied me as if measuring me for a bier and said, "I haven't known many Easterners." The dog scratched its ear, stood, walked around in a circle, sat down in the same place it had been, and scratched itself again.

"If you're asking if you can trust me," I said, "there's no good answer I can give you."

"That isn't the question."

"Then—"

"Come in."

I did, Savn following along dutifully, the dog last. The inside was worse than the outside. I don't mean it was dirty—on the contrary, everything was neat, clean, and polished, and there wasn't a speck of dust; no mean trick in a wood cottage. But it was filled with all sorts of magnificently polished wood carvings—magnificent and tasteless. Oil lamps, chairs, cupboards, and buffets were all of dark hardwood, all gleaming with polish, and all of them horribly overdone, like someone wanted to put extra decorations on them just to show that it could be done. It almost made it worse that the wood nearly matched the color of the dog, who turned around in place three times before curling up in front of the door.

I studied the overdone mantelpiece, the tasteless candelabra, and the rest. I said, "Your own work?"

"No. My husband was a wood-carver."

"A quite skillful one," I said truthfully.

She nodded. "This place means a lot to me," she said. "I don't want to leave."

I waited.

"I'm being asked to leave—I've been given six months."

Rocza shifted uneasily on my right shoulder. Loiosh, on my left, said, *"I don't believe this, boss. The widow being kicked out of her house? Come on."*

"By whom?"

"The owner of the land."

"Who owns the land?"

"I don't know."

"Why does he want you to leave?"

"I don't know."

"Have you been offered compensation?"

"Eh?"

"Did he say he'd pay you?"

"Oh. Yes." She sniffed. "A pittance."

"I see. How is it you don't know who owns the land?"

"It belongs to some, I don't know, organization, or something."

I instantly thought, *the Jhereg,* and felt a little queasy. "What organization?"

"A business of some kind. A big one."

"What House?"

"Orca."

I relaxed. "Who told you you have to move?"

"A young woman I'd never seen before, who worked for it. She was an Orca, too, I think."

"What was her name?"

"I don't know."

"And you don't know the name of the organization she works for?"

"No."

"How do you know she really worked for them?"

The old woman sniffed. "She was very convincing."

"Do you have an advocate?"

She sniffed again, which seemed to pass for a "no."

"Then finding a good one is probably where we should start."

"I don't trust advocates."

"Mmmm. Well, in any case, we're going to have to find out who holds the lease to your land. How do you pay it, anyway?"

"My husband paid it through the next sixty years."

"But—"

"The woman said I'd be getting money back."

"Isn't there a land office or something?"

"I don't know. I have the deed somewhere in the attic with my papers; it should be there." Her eyes narrowed. "You think you can help me?"

"Yes."

"Sit down."

I did. I helped Savn to a chair, then found one myself. It was ugly but comfortable. The dog's tail thumped twice against the floor, then it put its head on its paws.

"Tell me about the boy," she said.

I nodded. "Have you ever encountered the undead?"

Her eyes widened and she nodded once.

"Have you ever fought an Athyra wizard? An undead Athyra wizard with a Morganti weapon?"

Now she looked skeptical. "You have?"

"The boy has. The boy killed one."

"I don't believe it."

"Look at him."

She did. He sat there, staring at the wall across from him.

"And he's been like this ever since?"

"Ever since he woke up. Actually, he's improved a little—he follows me now without being told, and if I put food in front of him, he eats it."

"Does he keep himself—?"

"Yes, as long as I remember to tell him to every once in a while."

She shook her head. "I don't know."

"He took a bash on the head at the same time. That may be part of the problem."

"When did it happen?"

"About a year ago."

"You've been wandering around with him for a year?"

"Yeah. I've been looking for someone who could cure him. I haven't found anyone." I didn't tell her how hard I'd been looking for someone willing and able to help; I spared her the details of disappointments, dead ends, aimless searches, and trying to balance my need to help him with my need to stay away from anywhere big enough for the Jhereg to be a danger—anywhere like Northport, say. I didn't tell her, in other words, that I was getting desperate.

"Why haven't you gone to a *real* sorcerer?" There was more than a hint of bitterness there.

"I'm on the run."

"From whom?"

"None of your business."

"What did you do?"

"I helped the boy kill an undead Athyra wizard."

"Why did he kill him?"

"To save my life."

"Why was the wizard trying to kill you?"

"You ask too many questions."

She frowned, then said, "We'll begin by looking at his head wound."

"All right. And tomorrow I'll start on your problem."

S~HE SPREAD OUT A~ few blankets on the floor for us, and that's where we slept. I woke up once toward morning and saw that the dog had curled up next to Savn. I hoped it didn't have fleas.

A few hours later I woke up for real and got to work. The old woman was already awake and holding a candle up to Savn's eyes, either to see if he'd respond to the light or to look into his mind, or for some other reason. Rocza was on the mantel, looking down anxiously; she'd developed a fondness for Savn and I think was feeling protective. The dog lay there watching the procedure and thumping its tail whenever the old woman moved.

I said, "Where are the papers?"

She turned to me and said, "If you'd like coffee first, help yourself."

"Do you have klava?"

"You can make it. The deed and the rest of my papers are in boxes up there." She gestured toward the ceiling above the kitchen, where I noticed a square door.

I made the klava and filled two cups. Then I found a ladder and a lamp, and took myself up to a large attic filled—I mean *filled*—with wooden crates, all of which were filled with junk, most of the junk being papers of one sort or another.

I grabbed a crate at random, brought it back down, and started going through it.

In the course of my career, Kiera, I've done a few odd things here and there. I mean, there was the time I spent half a day under a pile of refuse because it was the only place to hide. There was the time I took a job selling fish in the market. Once I ended up impersonating a corporal in the Imperial Guard and had to arrest someone for creating a disturbance in a public place. But I hope I never have to spend another week going through a thousand or more years' worth of an old lady's private papers and letters, just to find the name of her landlord, so I could sweet-talk, threaten, or intimidate him into letting her stay on the land, so she'd be willing to cure—Oh, skip it. It was a long week, and it was odd finding bits of nine-hundred-year-old love letters, or scraps of advice on curing hypothermia, or how to tell if an ingrown toenail is the result of a curse.

I spent about fourteen hours a day grabbing a crate, going through the papers in it, arranging them neatly, then bringing the crate back up to the attic and setting it in the stack of those I'd finished while getting another. I discovered to my surprise that it was curiously satisfying work, and that I was going to be disappointed when I found what I was looking for and would have to leave the rest of the papers unsorted.

Sometimes locals would show up, no doubt with some problem or an-other, and on those occasions I'd leave them alone and go walking around outside, which helped to clear my head from all the paperwork. If any of her customers had a problem with the boy or the jhereg, I never heard about it, and I enjoyed the walks. I got so I knew the area pretty well, but there isn't much there worth knowing. One day when I got back after a long walk the old woman was standing in front of the fireplace holding a crumpled-up piece of paper. I said, "Is that it?"

She threw the paper into the fire. "No," she said. She didn't face me.

I said, "Is there something wrong?"

"Let's get back to our respective work, shall we?"

I said, "If it turns out the lease isn't in any of these boxes—"

"You'll find it," she said.

"Heh."

But I did find it at last, late on the fifth day after going through about two-thirds of the crates: a neat little scroll tied up with green ribbon, and stating the terms of the lease, with the rent payable to something called Westman, Niece, and Nephew Land Holding Company.

"I found it," I announced.

The old woman, who turned out to have some strange Kanefthali name that sounded like someone sneezing, said, "Good."

"I'll go visit them tomorrow morning. Any progress?"

She glared at me, then said, "Don't rush me."

"I'm just asking."

She nodded and went back to what she was doing, which was testing Savn's reflexes by tapping a stick against his knee, while watching his eyes.

Buddy watched us both somberly and decided there was nothing that had to be done right away. He got up and padded over to his water bowl, drank with doglike enthusiasm, and nosed open the door.

"Are we going to kill someone tomorrow, boss?"

"I doubt it. Why? Bored?"

"Something like that."

"Exercise patience."

Loiosh and I went outside and tasted the air. He flew around while I sat on the ground. Buddy came up, nosed me, and scratched at the door. The old woman let him in. Loiosh landed on my shoulder.

"Worried about Savn, boss?"

"Some. But if this doesn't work, we'll try something else, that's all."

"Right."

I started to get cold. A small animal moved around in the woods near the house. I realized with something of a start not only that I'd come outside without my sword but that I didn't even have a dagger on me. The idea made me uncomfortable, so I went back inside and sat in front of the fire. A little later I went to bed.

I'D BEEN TO NORTHPORT a few years before, and I'd been hanging around the edges these last few days, but that next morning was really the first time I'd seen it. It's a funny town—sort of a miniature Adrilankha, the way it's built in the center of those three hills the way Adrilankha is built between the cliffs, and both of them jutting up against the sea. Northport has its own personality, though. One gets the impression, looking at the three-story inns and the five-story Lumber Exchange Building and the streets that start out wide and straight and end up narrow and twisting, that someone wanted it to be a big city but it never made it. The first section I came to was one of the new parts, with a lot of wood houses where tradesmen lived and had shops, but as I got closer to the docks the buildings got smaller and older, and were made of good, solid stonework. And the people of Northport seem to have this attitude—I'm sure you've noticed it, too—that wants to convince you what a great place they're living in. They spend so much time talking about how easygoing everyone is that it gets on your nerves pretty quickly. They talk so much about how it's only around Northport that you can find the redfin or the fatfish that you end up not wanting to taste them just to spite the populace, you know what I mean?

It was harder to find Westman than it should have been, because there was no address in the city hall for a Westman company. They did exist, they just didn't have an address registered. I thought that was odd, but the clerk didn't; I guess he'd run into that sort of thing before. The owner was listed, though, and his name wasn't Westman. It was something called Brugan Exchange. Did Brugan Exchange have an address? No. Was there an owner listed? Yeah. Northport Securities. What does Northport Securities do? I have no idea. You understand that the clerk didn't kill himself being helpful—he just pointed to where I should look and left it up to me, and it took three imperials before he was willing to do that. So I dug through musty old papers; I'd been doing that a lot lately.

Northport Securities didn't have an owner listed. Nothing. Just a blank space where the Articles of Embodiment asked for the owner's name, and an illegible scrawl for a signature. But, wonder of wonders, it did have an address—it was listed as number 31 in the Fyres Building.

Ah. I see your eyes light up. We have found our connection with Fyres, you think. Sort of.

I found the Fyres Building without any trouble—the clerk told me where it was, after giving me a look that indicated I must be an idiot for needing to ask. It was at the edge of Shroud Hill, which means it was almost out of town, and it was high enough so that it had a nice view. A very nice view, from the top—it was six stories high, Kiera, and reeked of money from the polished marble of the base to the glass windows on the top floor. The thought of walking into the place made me nervous, if you can believe it—it was like the first time I went to Castle Black; not as strong, maybe, but the same feeling of being in someone's seat of power.

Loiosh said, *"What's the problem, boss?"* I couldn't answer him, but the question was reassuring, in a way. There was a single wooden door in front, with no seal on it, but above the doorway "FYRES" was carved into the stonework, along with the symbol of the House of the Orca.

Once inside, there was nothing and no one to tell me where to go. There were individual rooms, all of them marked with real doors and all of which had informative signs like "Cutter and Cutter." I walked around the entire floor, which was laid out in a square with an open stairway at the far end. I said, *"Loiosh."*

"On my way, boss."

I waited by the stairs. A few well-dressed citizens, Orca, Chreotha, and a Lyorn, came down or up the stairs and glanced at me briefly, decided that they didn't know what to make of the shabbily dressed Easterner, and went on without saying anything. One woman, an Orca, asked if I needed anything. When I said I didn't, she went on her way. Presently Loiosh returned.

"Well?"

"The offices are smaller on the next floor, and they keep getting smaller as you go up, all the way until the sixth, which I couldn't get into."

"Door?"

"Yeah. Locked."

"Ah ha."

"Number thirty-one is on the fifth floor."

"Okay. Let's go."

We went up five flights, and Loiosh led the way to a tacked-up number 31, which hung above a curtained doorway. Also above the doorway was a plain black-lettered sign that read, "Brownberry Insurance." I entered without clapping.

There was a man at the desk, a very pale Lyorn, who was going over a ledger of some sort while checking it against the contents of a small box filled with cards. He looked up, and his eyes widened just a little. He said, "May I be of service to you?"

"Maybe," I said. "Is your name Brownberry?"

"No, but I do business as Brownberry Insurance. May I help you?"

He volunteered no more information, but kept a polite smile of inquiry fixed in my direction. He kept glancing at Loiosh, then returning his gaze to me.

I said, "I was actually looking for Northport Securities."

"Ah," he said. "Well, I can help you there, as well."

"Excellent."

The office was small, but there was another curtained doorway behind it—no doubt there was another room with another desk, perhaps with another Lyorn looking over another ledger.

"I understand," I said carefully, "that Northport Securities owns Brugan Exchange."

He frowned. "Brugan Exchange? I'm afraid I've never heard of it. What do they do?"

"They own Westman, Niece, and Nephew Land Holding Company."

He shook his head. "I'm afraid I don't know anything about that."

The curtain moved and a woman poked her head out, then walked around to stand next to the desk. Definitely an Orca; and I'd put her at about seven hundred years. Not bad if you like Dragaerans. She wore blue pants and a simple white blouse with blue trim, and had short hair pulled back severely. "Westman Holding?" she said.

"Yes."

The man said, "It's one of yours, Leen?"

"Yes." And to me, "How may I help you?"

"You hold the lease for a lady named, uh, Hujaanra, or something like that?"

"Yes. I was just out to see her about it. Are you her advocate?"

"Something like that."

"Please come back here and sit down. I'm called Leen. And you?"

"Padraic," I said. I followed her into a tiny office with just barely room for me, her, her desk, and a filing cabinet. Her desk was clean except for some writing gear and a couple large black books, probably ledgers. I sat on a wooden stool.

"What may I do for you?" she said. She was certainly the most polite Orca I'd ever encountered.

"I'd like to understand why my client has to leave her land."

She nodded as if she'd been expecting the question. "Instructions from the parent company," she said. "I'm afraid I can't tell you exactly why. We think the offer we made is quite reasonable—"

"That isn't the issue," I said.

She seemed a bit surprised. Perhaps she wasn't used to being interrupted by an Easterner, perhaps she wasn't used to being interrupted by an advocate, perhaps she wasn't used to people who weren't interested in money. "What exactly is the issue?" she said in the tone of someone trying to remain polite in the face of provocation.

"She doesn't want to leave her land."

"I'm afraid she must. The parent company—"

"Then can I speak to someone in the parent company?"

She studied me for a moment, then said, "I don't see why not." She scratched out a name and address on a small piece of paper, blew on it until the ink dried, and gave it to me.

"Thank you," I said.

"You are most welcome, Sir Padraic."

I nodded to the man in the office, who was too absorbed in his ledger to notice, then stopped past the door, looked at the card, and laughed. It said, "Lady Cepra, Cepra Holding Company, room 20." No building, which, of course, meant it was this very building. I shook my head and went down the stairs, sending Loiosh ahead of me.

He was back in about a minute. *"Third floor,"* he said.

"Good."

So I headed down to the third floor.

Do you get the idea, Kiera? Good. Then there's no need to go into the rest of the day, it was more of the same. I never met any resistance, and everyone was very polite, and eventually I got my answer—sort of.

It was well after dark when I returned to the cottage. Buddy greeted me with a tail wag that got his whole back half moving. It was nice to be missed.

"As long as you aren't fussy about the source."

"Shut up, Loiosh."

I walked in the door and saw Savn was asleep on his pile of blankets. The old woman was sitting in front of the fire, drinking tea. She didn't turn around when I came in. Loiosh flew over and greeted Rocza, who was curled up next to Savn.

I said, "What did you learn about the boy?"

"I don't know enough yet. I can tell you that there's more wrong with him than a bump on the head, but the bump on the head triggered it. I'll know more soon, I hope."

"What about curing him?"

"I have to find out what's wrong first."

"All right."

"What about you?"

"I'm fine, thanks."

She turned and glared at me. "What did you find out?"

I sat down at what passed for a kitchen table. "You," I said, "are a tiny, tiny cog in the great big machine."

"What does that mean?"

"A man named Fyres died."

"So I heard. What of it?"

"He owned a whole lot of companies. When he died, it turned out that most of them had no assets to speak of, except for office furnishings and that sort of thing."

"I heard something of that, too."

"Your land is owned by a company that's in surrender of debts, and has to sell it before the court orders it sold. What we have to do is buy the place ourselves. You said you have money—"

"Well, I don't," she snapped.

"Excuse me?"

"I thought I did, but I was wrong."

"I don't understand."

She turned back to the fire and didn't speak for several minutes. Then she said, "All of my money was in a bank. Two days ago, while you were out, a messenger showed up with information that—"

"Oh," I said. "The bank was another one? Fyres owned it?"

"Yes."

"So it's all gone."

"I might be lucky enough to get two orbs for each imperial."

"Oh," I said again.

I sat thinking for a long time. At last I said, "All right, that makes it harder, but not much. I have money."

She looked at me once more, her lined face all but expressionless. I said, "Somewhere there's someone who owns this land, and somewhere there's someone who is responsible for that bank—"

"Fyres," she said. "And he's dead."

"No. Someone is taking charge of these things. Someone is handling the estate. And, more important, there's some very wealthy son of a bitch who just needs the right sort of pressure put on him in order to make the right piece of paper say the right thing. It shouldn't disrupt anything— there are advantages to being a small cog in a big machine."

"How are you going to find this mythical rich man?"

"I don't know exactly. But the first step is to start tracing the lines of power from the top."

"I don't think that information is public," she said.

"Neither do I." I closed my eyes, thinking of several days' worth of my least favorite sort of work: digging into plans, tracing guard routes, finagling trivial information out of people without letting them know I was doing it, and all that just so we could perhaps get a start on how to address the problem. I shook my head in self-pity.

"Well?" said the old woman when she'd waited long enough and decided I wasn't going to say any more. "What are you going to do? Steal Fyres's private papers?"

"Do I look like a thief?"

"Yes."

"Thank you," I said.

She sniffed.

"Unfortunately," I added, "I'm not."

"Well, then?"

"I do, however, know one."

Interlude

"I SUPPOSE, IF ONE must lose a finger—"

"Yes. And it had healed cleanly."

"It hurts to think about it. I wonder what fell on it?"

"I don't know."

"You didn't ask?"

"He didn't seem inclined to talk about it. You know how he gets when there's something he doesn't want to talk about."

"Yes. A lot like you."

"Meaning?"

"There's a lot you aren't telling me, isn't there?"

"I suppose. Not deliberately—at least not yet. Later, there may be things I'd sooner not discuss. But if I told you everything I remember as I remember it, we'd still be here—"

"I understand. Hmmm."

"What is it?"

"I was just thinking how pleased he'd be if he knew we were spending a whole afternoon just talking about him."

"I shan't tell him."

"It doesn't matter."

"Should I go on?"

"Let's order some more tea first."

"Very well."

3

I LOOKED AT HIM after he'd finished speaking, struck by several things but not sure what to say or to ask. For one thing, I'd forgotten that when Vlad starts telling a story, you had best get yourself a tall glass of something and settle in for the duration. I thought this over, and all that he'd told me, and finally said, "Who did the boy kill?"

"A fellow named Loraan."

I controlled my reaction, stared at Vlad, and waited. He said, "I take it you know who he was?"

"Yes. I follow your career, you know. I'd thought he was pretty permanently dead."

Vlad shrugged. "Take it up with Morrolan. Or rather with Black-wand."

I nodded. "The boy saved your life?"

"The simple answer is yes. The more complicated answer would take a week."

"But you owe him."

"Yes."

"I see. What happened while you were waiting for me?"

"I learned everything about Fyres that was public knowledge, and a little that wasn't."

"What did you learn?"

"Not much. He liked being talked about, he liked owning things, he didn't like anyone knowing what he was up to. The accountants are going to be hard at work to figure out exactly what he owed and what he was worth—I imagine his heirs are pretty nervous."

"It'll be harder without those papers."

"Yeah. But I'll probably return them when I'm done. I'm in more of a hurry than they are."

"What else has happened?"

"Who do you mean?"

"With the boy."

"Oh. Nothing. She's still trying to figure it out. I guess it isn't easy to know what's going on in someone's head."

That, of course, was the understatement of Vlad's life.

"What's she done?"

"Stared into his eyes a lot."

"Notice any sorcery?"

"No."

I thought for a minute, then, "Take me to the cottage," I said. "I want to see it, and I want to meet this woman, and we can go over the information there as well as anywhere else."

"We?"

"Yes."

"All right."

We struck out for the cottage, walking. I like walking; I don't do enough of it. It was about four miles, deep in the woods, and the cottage really was painted bright blue so that it showed against the greens of the woods to a truly horrifying effect.

As we approached, a reddish dog ran out the door and stood in front of us, wagging its tail and letting its tongue hang out. It sniffed me, backed away with its head cocked, barked twice, and sniffed me again. After consulting with its canine sensibilities, it decided I was provisionally all right and asked us if we wanted to play. When we took too long to decide, it ran back toward the house. The door opened again, and a matron came out.

Vlad said, "This is my friend, Kiera. I'm not going to try to pronounce your name."

She looked at me, then nodded. "Hwdf'rjaanci," she said.

"Hwdf'rjaanci," I repeated.

"Kiera," she said. "You look like a Jhereg."

I could feel Vlad not looking at me and not grinning. I shrugged.

She said, "Call me Mother; everyone around here does."

"All right, Mother."

She asked Vlad, "Did you learn anything?"

"Not yet." He held up the parcel I'd given him. "We're just going to look things over now."

"Come in, then."

We did, the dog following behind. The inside was even worse than Vlad had described it. I didn't comment. Savn was sitting on a stool with his back to the fire, staring straight ahead. It was creepy. It was sad. "Battle shock," I murmured under my breath.

"What?" said the old woman.

I shook my head. Savn wasn't a bad-looking young man, for a Teckla—thin, maybe a bit wan, but good bones. Hwdf'rjaanci was sitting next to him, stroking the back of his neck while watching his face.

Hwdf'rjaanci said, "Will you be staying here?"

"I have a place in town."

"All right."

Vlad went over to the table, took out the papers, and began studying them. I knelt down in front of the boy and looked into his eyes; saw my own reflection and nothing else. His pupils were a bit large, but the room was dark, and they were the same size. A bit of spell-casting tempted me, but I stayed away from it. Thinking along those lines, I realized that there wasn't much of an air of sorcery in the room; a few simple spells to keep the dust and insects away, and the dog had a ward against vermin, but that was about it.

I felt the woman watching. I kept looking into the boy's eyes, though I couldn't say what I was looking for. The woman said, "So you're a thief, are you?"

"That's what they say."

"I was robbed twice. The first time was years ago. During the Interregnum. You look too young to remember the Interregnum."

"Thank you."

She gave a little laugh. "The second time was more recent. I didn't enjoy being robbed," she added.

"I should think not."

"They beat my husband—almost killed him."

"I don't beat people, Mother."

"You just break into their homes?"

I said, "When you're working with the mentally sick, do you ever worry about being caught in the disease?"

"Always," she said. "That's why I have to be careful. I can't do anyone any good if I tangle my own mind instead of untangling my patient's."

"That makes sense. I take it you've done a great deal of this?"

"Some."

"How much?"

"Some."

"You have to go into his mind, don't you?"

"Yes."

I looked at her. "You're frightened, aren't you?"

She looked away.

"I would be, too," I told her. "Breaking into homes is much less frightening than breaking into minds."

"More profitable, too," I added after a moment.

I felt Vlad looking at me, and looked back. He'd overheard the conversation and seemed to be trying to decide if he wanted to get angry. After a moment, he returned to looking at the papers.

I stood up, went over to the dog, and got acquainted. It still seemed a bit suspicious of me, but was willing to give me the benefit of the doubt. Presently Hwdf'rjaanci said, "All right. I'll start tomorrow."

BY THE TIME I got there the next morning, Vlad had covered the table with a large piece of paper—I'm not sure where he got it—which was covered with scrawls and arrows. I stood over him for a moment, then said, "Where's the boy?"

"He and the woman went out for a walk. They took Rocza and the dog with them."

"Loiosh?"

"Flying around outside trying to remember if he knows how to hunt."

He got that look on his face that told me he'd communicated that remark to Loiosh, too, and was pleased with himself.

I said, "Any progress?"

He shrugged. "Fyres didn't like to tell his people much."

"So you said."

"Even less than I'd thought."

"Catch me up."

"Fyres and Company is a shipping company that employs about two hundred people. That's all, as far as I can tell. Most of the rest of what he owned isn't related to the shipping company at all, but he owned it through relatives—his wife, his son, his daughters, his sister, and a few friends. And most of those are in surrender of debts and have never really been solvent—it's all been a big fraud from the beginning, when he conned banks into letting him take out loans, and used the loans to make his companies look big so that he could take out more loans. That's how he operated."

"You know this?"

"Yeah."

"You aren't even an accountant."

"Yeah, but I don't have to prove it—I've learned it because I've found out what companies he was keeping track of and looked at the ownership and read his notes. There's nothing incriminating about it, but it gives the picture pretty clearly if you're looking for it."

"How big?"

"I can't tell. Big enough, I suppose."

"What's the legal status?"

"I have no idea. I'm sure the Empire will try to sort it all out, but that'll take years."

"And in the meantime?"

"I don't know. I'm going to have to do something, but I don't know what."

Savn and Hwdf'rjaanci returned then and sat down on the floor near the fire. The woman's look discouraged questions as she took Savn's hands in hers and began rubbing them. Vlad watched; I could feel his tension.

I said, "You have to do something soon, don't you?"

He gave me a half-smile. "It would be nice. But this isn't the sort of thing I can stumble into. I should know what I'm doing first. That makes it trickier." Then he said, "Why are you helping me, anyway?"

I said, "I assume you've been making a list of all the companies you know about and who their owners are."

"Yeah. They've gotten to know my face real well at City Hall."

"That may be a problem later on."

"Maybe. I hope not to be around here long enough for it to matter."

"Good idea."

"Yes."

"No help for it, I suppose. Do you think it might be wise to pick one of these players and pay a visit?"

"Sure, if I knew what to ask. I need to figure out who really owns this land and—"

Loiosh and I reacted at once to the presence of sorcery in the room,

Vlad just an instant later. Our heads turned toward Hwdf'rjaanci, who was holding Savn's shoulders and speaking under her breath. We watched for maybe a minute, but there was no point in talking about it. I cleared my throat. "What were you saying?"

Vlad turned back to me, looking blank. Then he said, "I don't remember."

"Something about needing to find out who really owns this land."

"Oh, right." I could see him mentally shaking himself. "Yeah. What I really want is to get the picture of this thing as it's going to emerge when the Empire finishes its investigations, say two hundred years from now. But I can't wait that long."

"I might be able to learn something."

"How?"

"The Jhereg."

Vlad frowned. "How would the Jhereg be involved?"

"I don't know that we are. But if what Fyres was doing was illegal, and it was making a lot of money, there's a good chance for a Jhereg connection somewhere along the line."

"Good point," said Vlad.

Loiosh was still staring at the woman and the boy. Vlad was silent for a moment; I wondered what Vlad and Loiosh were saying to each other. I wondered if they spoke in words, or if it was some sort of communication that didn't translate. I've never had a familiar, but then, I'm not a witch. Vlad said, "You have local connections?"

"Yes."

"All right," he said. "Do it. I'll keep trying to put this thing together."

The woman said, "Cold. So cold. Cold."

Vlad and I looked at her. She wasn't shivering or anything, and the cottage was quite warm. Her hands were still on Savn's shoulders and she was staring at him.

"Can't keep it away," she said. "Can't keep it away. Find the cold spot. Can't keep it away." After that she fell silent.

I looked at Vlad and turned my palms up. "I might as well go now," I said.

He nodded, and went back to his paperwork. I headed out the door. The dog gave its tail a half-wag and put its head down between its paws again.

It was over two or three miles to Northport, but I had been there often enough to learn a couple of teleport points, so I went ahead and put myself into an alley that ran past the back of a pawnbroker's shop, startling a couple of local urchins when I appeared. They stared at me for a second, then went back to urchining, or whatever it is they do. I walked around the corner and into the dark little shop. The middle-aged man behind the counter looked up at me, but before he could say a word I said, "Sorry to disappoint you, Dor."

"What, you don't have anything for me?"

"Nope. I just want to see the upstairs man."

"For a minute there—"

"Next time."

He shrugged. "You know the way."

Poor Dor. Usually when I come into his place it's because I have something that's too hot to unload in Adrilankha, which means he's going to get something good for a great price. But not today. I walked past him into the rear of the shop, up the stairs, and into a nice, plain room where a couple of toughs waited. One, a very dark fellow with a pointy head, like someone had tried to fit him through a funnel, was sitting in front of the room's other door; the other one had arms that hung out like a mockman and he looked about as intelligent, although looks can be deceiving; he was leaning against a wall. They didn't seem to recognize me.

I said, "Is Stony in?"

"Who wants to know?" said Funnel-head.

I smiled brightly. "Why, I do."

He scowled.

I said, "Tell him it's Kiera."

Their eyes grew just a little bit wider. That always happens. It is very satisfying. The one stood up, moved his chair, opened the door, and stuck his head into the other room. I heard him speaking softly, then I heard Stony say, "Really? Well, send her in." There was a little more conversation, followed by, "I said send her in."

The tough turned back to me and stood aside. I dipped him a curtsy as I stepped in past him—a curtsy looks silly when you're wearing trousers, but I couldn't resist. He stayed well back from me, as if he were afraid I'd steal his purse as I walked by. Why are people who will walk into potentially lethal situations without breaking a sweat so often frightened around someone who just steals things? Is it the humiliation? Is it just that they don't know how I do it? I've never figured that out. Many people have that reaction. It makes me want to steal their purses.

Stony's office was deceptively small. I say deceptive because he was a lot bigger in the Organization than most people thought—even his own employees didn't know; he felt safer that way. I'd only found out by accident and guesswork, starting when someone had hired me to lighten one of Stony's button men and I'd come across pieces of his security system. Stony himself was pretty deceptive, too. He looked, and acted, like the sort of big, mean, stupid, and brutal thug that the Left Hand thinks we all are. In fact, I'd never known him to do anything that wasn't calculated—even his famous rages always seemed to result in just the right people disappearing, and no more. Over the years, I'd tried to puzzle him out, and my opinion at the moment was that he wasn't in this for the power, or for the pleasure of putting things over on the Guard, or anything else—he wanted to acquire a great deal of money, and a great deal of security, and then he planned to retire. I couldn't prove it, I reflected, but I wouldn't be at all surprised if someday he just packed up and vanished, and spent the rest of his life collecting seashells or something on some tiny island he owned.

Over the years, I had gradually let him know that I knew where he stood in the Organization, and he had gradually stopped pretending otherwise when we were alone. It was possible that he liked having someone with whom he could drop the game a little, but I doubt it.

All of this flashed through my mind as I sat in the only other chair in the room—the room just big enough to contain my chair, his chair, and the desk. He said, "Must be something big, for you to come here." His voice was rough and harsh, and fitted the personality he pretended to; I assumed it was contrived, but I've never heard him break out of it.

"Yes and no," I said.

"There a problem?"

"In a way."

"You need help?"

"Something like that."

He shook his head. "That's what I like about you, Kiera. Your way of explaining everything so clearly."

"My part isn't big, and what I need isn't big, but it's part of something big. I didn't want to ask you to meet me somewhere because I'm asking for a favor, and you don't get anything from it, so I didn't want to put you out. But it isn't a favor for me, it's for someone else."

He nodded. "That makes everything completely clear, then."

"What do you know of Fyres?"

That startled him a little. "The Orca?"

"Yes."

"He's dead."

"Uh-huh."

"He owned a whole lot of stuff."

"Yeah."

"Most of it will end up in surrender of debts."

"That's what I like about you, Stony. The way you have of reeling out information no one else knows."

He made a loose fist with his right hand and drummed his fingernails on the desk while looking at me. "What exactly do you want to know?"

"The Organization's interest in him and his businesses."

"What's your interest?"

"I told you, a favor for a friend."

"Yeah."

"Is it some big secret, Stony?"

"Yes," he said. "It is."

"It goes up pretty high?"

"Yeah, and there's a lot of money involved."

"And you're trying to decide how much to tell me just as a favor."

"Right."

I waited. Nothing I could say would help make up his mind for him.

"Okay," he said finally. "I'll tell you this much. A lot of people had paper on the guy. Shards. *Everybody* had paper on the guy. There are going to be some big banks going down, and there are going to be some Organization people taking sudden vacations. It isn't just me, but we're in it."

"How about you?"

"I'm not directly involved, so I may be all right."

"If you need anything—"

"Yeah. Thanks."

"How did he die?"

Stony spread his hands. "He was out on his Verra-be-damned boat and he slipped and hit his head on a railing."

I raised an eyebrow at him.

He shook his head. "No one wanted him dead, Kiera. I mean, the only chance most of us had to ever see our investment back was if his stuff earned out, and with him dead there's no way of it ever earning out."

"You sure?"

"Who can be sure of anything? I didn't want him dead. I don't know anyone who wanted him dead. The Empire sent their best investigators, and they think it was an accident."

"All right," I said. "What was he like?"

"You think I knew him?"

"You lent him money, or at least thought about it; you knew him."

He smiled, then the smile went away and he looked thoughtful—an expression I doubt most people would ever have seen. "He was all surface, you know?"

"No."

"It was like he made himself act the way he thought he should—you could never get past it."

"That sounds familiar."

He ignored that. "He tried to be polished, professional, calculating— he wanted you to believe he was the perfect bourgeois. And he wanted to impress you—he always wanted to impress you."

"With how rich he was?"

Stony nodded. "Yeah, that. And with all the people he knew, and with how good he was at what he did. I think that part of it—being impressive—was more important to him than the money."

I nodded encouragingly. He smiled. "You want more?"

"Yeah."

"Then I'd better know why."

"It's a little embarrassing," I said.

"Embarrassing?" He looked at me the way I must have been looking at Vlad when I realized that *he* was embarrassed.

"I have this friend—"

"Right."

I laughed. "Okay, skip it. I owe someone a favor," I amended untruthfully. "She's an old woman who is about to be kicked off her land because everybody is selling off everything to stave off surrender of debts because of this mess with Fyres."

"An old woman being foreclosed on? Are you kidding?"

"No."

"I don't believe it."

"Would I make up something like that?"

He shook his head, chuckling to himself. "No, I suppose not. So what do you plan to do about it?"

"I don't know yet. Just find out what I can and then think about it." Or, at any rate, if Vlad had had any other plan, he hadn't mentioned it to me. "What else can you tell me?"

"Well, he was about fourteen hundred years old. No one heard of him before the Interregnum, but he rose pretty quickly after it ended."

"How quickly?"

"He was a very wealthy man by the end of the first century."

"That is quick."

"Yeah. And then he lost it all forty or fifty years later."

"Lost it all?"

"Yep."

"And came back?"

"Twice more. Each time bigger, each time the collapse was worse."

"Same problem? Same sort of paper castles?"

"Yep."

"Shipping?"

"Yep. And shipbuilding. Those have been his foundations all along."

"You'd think people would learn."

"Is there an implied criticism there, Kiera?" His look got just the least bit hard.

"No. Curiosity. I know you aren't stupid. Most of the people he'd be borrowing from aren't, either. How did he do it?"

Stony relaxed. "You'd have to have seen him work."

"What do you mean? Good salesman?"

"That, and more. Even when he was down, you'd never know it. Of course, when someone that rich goes down, it doesn't have much effect on how he lives—he'll still have his mansion, and he'll still be at all the clubs, and he'll still have his private boat and his big carriages."

"Sure."

"So he'd trade on those things. You get to talking with him for five minutes, and you forget that he'd just taken a fall. And then his secretaries would keep running in with papers for him to sign, or with questions about some big deal or another, and it looked like he was on top of the world." Stony shrugged. "I don't know. I've wondered if he didn't have those secretaries pull that sort of thing just to look good; but it worked. You'd always end up convinced that he was in some sort of great position and you might as well jump on the horse and ride it yourself before someone else did."

"And there were a lot of us on the horse."

"A lot of Jhereg? Yeah."

"And in deep."

"Yeah."

"That isn't good for my investigation."

"You worried you might bump into the Organization? Is that it?"

"That's part of it."

"It might happen," he said.

"All right."

"What if it does?"

"I don't know."

He shook his head. "I don't want to see you get hurt, Kiera."

"Neither do I," I said. "How far beyond Northport does this thing go?"

"Hard to say. It's all centered here, but he'd begun spreading out. He has offices other places, of course—you have to if you're in shipping. But I can't say how much else."

"What was going on before he died?"

"What do you mean?"

"I have the impression things were getting shaky for him."

"Very. He was scrabbling. You wouldn't know it to look at him, but there were rumors that he'd stepped too far out and it was all going to crumble."

"Hmmm."

"Still wondering if someone put a shine on him?"

"Seems like quite a coincidence."

"I know. But I don't think so. As I said, I never heard any whispers, and the Empire investigated; they're awfully good at this sort of thing."

I nodded. That much was certainly true. "Okay," I said. "Thanks for your help."

"No problem. If there's anything else, let me know."

"I will." I stood up.

"Oh, by the way."

"Yes?"

He leaned back in his chair and looked at the ceiling. "Seen anything of that Easterner you used to hang around with?"

"You mean Vlad Taltos? The guy who screwed up the Organization representative to the Empire? The guy everyone wants to put over the Falls? The guy with so much gold on his head that his hair is sparkling? The guy the Organization wants so bad that anyone seen with him is likely to disappear for a long session of question and answer with the best information-extraction specialists the Organization can find? Him?"

"Yep."

"Nope."

"I hadn't thought so. See you around, Kiera."

"See you around, Stony."

4

My FIRST STEP WAS to fill Vlad in on what I'd learned; but I took a long, circuitous route back just in case I was being followed, so it took me almost until evening to get back to the cottage. When I turned the last corner of the path, Vlad was waiting for me, on the path, about fifty meters from the cottage. That startled me just a bit, as I'm not used to being seen so quickly even when I'm not trying to sneak, until I realized that Loiosh must have spotted me. I must remember to be careful if I ever have to sneak up on that Easterner.

He stood clothed only in pants and boots, his upper body naked and full of curly hairs, and he was sweating heavily, although he didn't seem to be breathing hard.

"Nice evening," I told him.

He nodded.

I said, "What have you been doing?"

"Practicing," he said, pointing at a tree some distance away. I noticed several knives sticking out of it. Then he touched his rapier, sheathed at his side, and said, "I've also punctured my shadow several times."

"Did it hurt?"

"Only when I missed."

"Did it get any cuts in?"

"No. But almost."

"Good to see you're keeping your hand in."

"Actually, I haven't been lately, but I thought it might be time to again."

"Hmmm."

"Besides, I needed to get out."

"Oh?"

"It's ugly in there," he said, gesturing toward the cottage.

"Oh?" I said again.

"The old woman is doing what she promised."

"And?"

He shook his head.

"Tell me," I said.

"He's all screwed up."

"That's news?"

Vlad looked at me.

"Sorry," I said.

"He keeps thinking he killed his sister, or he has to save her, or something."

"Sister?"

"Yeah, she was involved, too. He feels guilty about her."

"What else?"

"Well, he's a Teckla, and Loraan was his lord, and if you're a peasant, you don't do what he did. Deathgate, Kiera. Even touching a Morganti weapon—"

"Right."

"So if he didn't kill Loraan, he must have killed his sister."

I said, "I don't follow that."

"I'm not sure I do, either," said Vlad. "But that's what we're seeing. Or what we think we're seeing. It isn't too clear, and we've been doing a lot of guesswork, but that's how it looks at the moment. And then there's the bash on the head."

"What did that do?"

"She thinks there may be a partial memory loss that's contributing to the whole thing."

"Better and better."

"Yeah."

"What now?"

"I don't know. The old woman thinks we have to find some way of communicating with him, but she doesn't know how."

"Does he hear us when we talk? See us?"

"Oh, sure. But we're like dream images, so what we say isn't important."

"What *is* important? I mean, she probed him, right? What's he doing in there?"

He shrugged. "Trying to keep his sister away from me, or away from Loraan, or something like that."

"A constant nightmare."

"Right."

"Ugly."

"Yes."

"And there's nothing you can do."

"Nothing I can do about that, anyway."

"If you could go in there yourself, I mean, into his mind—"

"Sure, I'd do it. In a minute."

I nodded. "Then I might as well tell you what I learned today."

"Do."

"Do you want to go inside?"

"No."

"All right." He put his shirt on and nodded to me and I told him. He was a good listener; he stood completely still, leaning against a tree; his only motion was to nod slightly every once in a while; and he was spare with his questions, just asking me to amplify a point every now and then. Loiosh settled on his left shoulder, and even the jhereg appeared to be listening. It's always nice to have an audience.

When I was finished, Vlad said, "Well. That's interesting. Surprising, too."

"That the Organization is involved?"

"No, no. Not that."

"What?"

He shook his head and appeared to be lost in thought—like I'd told him more than I thought I had, which was certainly possible. So I gave him a decent interval, then said, "What is it?"

He shook his head again. I felt a little irritated but I didn't say anything. He said, "It doesn't make sense, that's all."

"What doesn't?"

"How well do you know Stony?"

"Quite."

"Would he lie to you?"

"Certainly."

"Maybe that's it, then. In any case, *someone* lied, somewhere along the line."

"What do you mean?"

"Let me think about this, all right? And do some checking on my own. I want to follow something up; I'll tell you about it tomorrow."

I shrugged. There's no reasoning with Vlad when he gets a mood on him. "Okay," I said. "I'll be back in the morning."

He nodded. Then he said, "Kiera?"

"Yes?"

"Thanks."

"You're welcome."

I SLEPT LATE THE next day, because there was no reason not to. It was around noon when I got to the cottage, and no one was there except the dog. It shuffled away from me. I devoted some effort to making friends with it, and of course I succeeded. I talked to it for a while. Most cat owners talk to their cats, but all dog owners talk to their dogs; I don't know why that is.

I'd been there an hour or so when the dog jumped up suddenly and bolted out the door, and a minute or so later Hwdf'rjaanci returned with Savn. I said, "Good day, Mother. I hope you don't mind that I let myself in. I've made some klava."

She nodded and had the boy sit down, then she closed the shutters. I realized that each time I'd been there during the day the windows had been shut. I got her some klava, which she drank bitter.

I said, "What have you learned, Mother?"

"Not as much as I wish," she said. I waited. She said, "I think the two biggest problems are the bump on the head and the sister."

"Can't the bump be healed?"

"It has healed, on the outside. But there was some damage to his brain."

"No, I mean, can't the damage be healed? I know there are sorcerers—"

"Not yet. Not until I'm sure that, if I heal him, I won't be sealing in the problem."

"I think I understand. What about the sister?"

"He feels guilty about her—about her being exposed to whatever it was that happened."

She nodded. "That's the real problem. I think he's somehow using guilt about his sister to keep from facing that. He creates fantasies of rescuing her, but always shies away from what he's rescuing her from. And then he loses control of the fantasies and they turn into nightmares. It's worse, I think, because he used to be apprenticed to a physicker, so he's even more tormented about what he did than most peasant boys would be."

I nodded. Speaking like this, she'd changed somehow—she wasn't an old woman in a cottage full of ugly polished wood carvings, she was a sorcerer and a skilled physicker of the mind. It now seemed entirely reasonable that, as Vlad had told me, the locals would come by from time to time to consult with her on whatever their problems might be.

"Do you have a plan?"

"No. There's too much I don't understand. If I just go blundering in, I might destroy him—and myself."

"I understand." I opened my mouth and closed it again. I said, "What are the walks for?"

"I think he's used to walking. He gets restless when he's sitting for too long."

"And the closed shutters? Are they for him, or do you just like it that way?"

"For him. He's had too much experience, there have been too many things for him to see and hear and feel all at once—I want to limit them."

"Limit them? But if he's trapped in his head, won't it help to give him things outside his head to respond to?"

"You'd think so, and you may even turn out to be right. But more often than not, it works best the other way. It's as if he's trying to escape from pressure, and everything he perceives adds to the pressure. If I was more certain, I'd create a field around him that shut him off from the world entirely. It may yet come to that."

"You've had cases like this before?"

"You mean people who were so pulled into themselves that they were out of touch with the world? Yes, a few. Some of them worse than Savn."

"Were you able to help them?"

"There were two I was able to help. Three I couldn't." Her voice was carefully neutral.

One way of looking at it was that the odds were against success. Another way was that she was due to win one. Neither was terribly productive, so I said, "How did you proceed?"

"I tried to learn as much as I could about how they got that way, I healed any physical damage when there was some, and then, when I thought they were ready, I took them on a dreamwalk."

"Ah."

"You know about dreamwalking?"

"Yes. What sort of dreams did you give them?"

"I tried to guide them through whatever choice they made that put them in a place they couldn't get out of, and give them another choice instead."

"And in three cases it didn't work."

"Yes. In at least one of those, it was because I didn't know enough when I went in."

"That sounds dangerous."

"It was. I almost lost my mind, and the patient became worse. He lost the ability to eat or drink, even with assistance, and he soon died."

I kept my face expressionless, which took some effort. What a horrible way to die, and what a horrible knowledge to carry around with you, if you were the one who had tried to cure him. "What had happened to him?"

"He'd been badly beaten by robbers."

"I see." I almost asked the next obvious question, but then I decided not to. "That must not be an easy thing to live with."

"Better for me than for him."

"Not necessarily," I said, thinking of Deathgate Falls.

"Maybe you're right."

"In any case, I understand why you want to be careful."

"Yes."

She went over and sat down in front of Savn once again, staring at him and holding his shoulders. In a little while she said, "He seems to be a nice young man, somewhere inside. I think you'd like him."

"I probably would," I said. "I like most people."

"Even the ones you steal from?"

"Especially the ones I steal from."

She didn't laugh. Instead she said, "How do you know I won't turn you over to the Empire?"

That startled me, although I don't know why it should have. "Will you?" I said.

"Maybe."

"Maybe you shouldn't be telling me that."

She shook her head. "You aren't a killer," she said.

"You know that?"

"Yes." She added, "The other one, the Easterner, he's a killer."

I shrugged. "What could you tell the Empire, anyway? That I'm a thief?

They know that; they've heard of me. That I stole something? They'll ask what I stole. You'll tell them, by which time Vlad will have hidden it, or maybe even returned it. Then what? Do you expect them to be grateful?"

She glared at me. "I wasn't actually going to tell them, anyway."

I nodded.

A few minutes later she said, "You can't have known the Easterner long—they don't live long enough. Yet you treat him as a friend."

"He is a friend."

"Why?"

"He doesn't know, either," I said.

"But—"

"What you're asking," I said, "is whether he can really do what he says he can do."

"And whether he will," she agreed.

"Right. I think he can; he's good at putting things together. In any case, I know that he'll try. In fact, knowing Vlad . . ."

"Yes?"

"He might very well try so hard he gets himself killed."

She didn't have anything to say to that, so she turned her attention back to Savn. Thinking about Savn didn't help me any, and thinking about Vlad getting killed was worse, so I went out and took a walk. Buddy came along, either because he liked my company or because he didn't trust me and wanted to keep an eye on me.

Good dog, either way.

BY THE TIME WE returned, it was getting dark, and Vlad was sitting at the kitchen table, with a bandage wrapped around his left forearm and no hair growing above his lip. I'm not sure which surprised me more. I think it was the lack of hair.

There was some blood leaking through the bandage, but Vlad didn't seem to be weak or even greatly disturbed. Buddy bounded up to him, asked him to play, sniffed at his wound, and looked hurt when Vlad pulled his arm out of reach. Loiosh watched the display with what I would have guessed to be disdain if I ever knew what jhereg were thinking.

He saw me looking at him and said, "Don't worry. It'll grow back."

"Well," I said. "You seem to have been busy."

"Yes."

"How long since you've returned?"

"Not long. Half an hour or so."

"Learn anything?"

"Yes."

I sat down opposite him. Savn was on the floor, resting. The old woman sat beside him, watching us.

"Shall we start at the beginning?"

"I'd like a glass of water first."

The old woman started to get up, but I motioned her to sit, went outside to the well, filled a pitcher, brought it in, filled a cup, and gave it to Vlad. He drank it all, slowly and carefully.

"More?" I said.

"Please."

I brought him more; he drank some of it, wiped his mouth on the back of his hand, and nodded to me.

I said, "Well?"

He shrugged. "The beginning was your own story."

"Go on."

He said, "It didn't make sense."

"So I gathered at the time. What part of it didn't make sense?"

He frowned and said, "Kiera, have you ever been involved in investigating someone's death—in trying to determine cause of death?"

"No, I can't say I have. Have you?"

"No, but I've been concerned with several, if you know what I mean."

"I know what you mean. And I have an idea of what's involved in an investigation like that." I shrugged. "What about it?"

"How long does it take to decide that someone wasn't murdered?"

"*Wasn't* murdered?"

"Yes."

"I don't know. Looking at the body—"

"Takes a day, maybe two, if he *was* murdered."

"Well, yes, but to prove a negative—"

"Exactly."

"They'd have to go over him pretty carefully, I suppose."

"Yes. Very carefully. And they look at everything else, too—such as if he was the sort of person likely to be murdered, or if there is anything suspicious in the timing of his death, or—"

"Exactly the sort of circumstances that surrounded Fyres's death."

"Yes. Fyres's death would set off every alarm they have. If you were the chief investigator, wouldn't you want to be extra careful before putting your chop on a report that stated he died of mischance attributable to no human agency, or however they put it?"

"What are you getting at?"

"Your friend the Jhereg told you that the Imperial investigators had determined the cause of death to be accidental."

"And?"

"And when did Fyres die?"

"A few weeks ago."

He nodded. "Exactly. A few weeks ago. Kiera, they *can't* have decided that this quickly. The only thing they could know this quickly is if it *was* a murder."

"I see your point. What's your conclusion?"

"That either your friend Stony lied to you or—"

"Or someone lied to Stony."

"Yes. And who would lie to Stony about something like this? Of those, who would he believe?"

"No one."

"Tsk."

"He's a naturally suspicious fellow."

"Well, but who would he believe?"

I shrugged. "The Empire, I suppose."

"Exactly."

"But the Empire wouldn't lie."

Vlad raised his eyebrows eloquently.

I shook my head. "You can't be implying that the Imperial investigators—"

"Yep."

"No."

"You don't believe it?"

"Why would they? How could they hope to get away with it? How many of them would have to be bought off, and how much would it cost? And consider how closely their report is going to be looked at, and think about the risks they run. They'd have to know they'd get caught eventually."

Vlad nodded. "Certainly valid points, Kiera. That's exactly what was bothering me yesterday when you told me about your conversation with Stony."

"Well, then—"

"Kiera, how about if I just tell you what I've been up to, and you form your own conclusions?"

I nodded. "Okay, I'm listening. No, wait a minute." I helped myself to a glass of water, set the pitcher next to me, sat down, and stretched out. "Okay," I said. "Go ahead."

Vlad took another drink of water, closed his eyes for a moment, then opened them and began speaking.

5

FIRST, OF COURSE, I had to find out who had carried out the investigation. I was afraid that the Empire had brought people in from Adrilankha and that these people had already returned, which meant a teleport to our beloved capital, about which idea I was less than thrilled, as you can imagine.

But one step at a time. I could have found a minstrel—I have an arrangement with their Guild—but news travels in both directions by that source, so I tried something different.

I made the tentative assumption that some things are universal, so I walked around until I found the seediest-looking barbershop in the area. Barbershops are more common in the East and in the Easterners' section of Adrilankha—barbers cut whiskers as well as head hair—but they exist everywhere. I'll bet you'd never thought of that, Kiera; whiskers aren't just a distinguishing feature; they have to be tended to. Fortunately, I have sharp enough blades that I don't have to go to barbershops for my own whiskers, but most Easterners don't have knives that sharp. But even in the East, Noish-pa tells me, barbershops are pretty much the same as they are here.

The barber, who seemed to be a Vallista, and a particularly ugly one at that, looked at me, looked at Loiosh, looked at my rapier, and opened his mouth—probably to explain that he didn't serve Easterners—but

Loiosh hissed at him before he had a chance to say anything. While he was trying to come up with an answer for Loiosh, I walked over to the chairs where customers waited. There was a little table next to them, and I found what I was looking for in about two seconds.

It had a title, *Rutter's Rag,* in big, hand-scrawled letters along the top, and it was mostly full of nasty remarks about city officials I'd never heard of, and it asked the Empire questions about its tax policy, implying that certain pirates were taking lessons from the Empire. It had a list of the banks that had closed suddenly—I assume it included the one our hostess used—and suggested that they were having a race to see which of them could clear out and vanish quickest, while wondering if the Empire, which allowed them to shut their doors on people who had their life savings in them, was really incompetent enough not to have known they were going under, or if this was now to be considered official Imperial policy.

It also, interestingly enough, made some ironic comments about Fyres's death—suggesting that those who had invested in his companies had gotten what they deserved. But that wasn't what I was after. Of course, it didn't give the real name of whoever produced it, but that didn't matter.

"What do you want?" said the barber.

"I want to know who delivers this to you."

That confused him, because I didn't look like a Guardsman, and, besides, they don't really care about sheets like this. But printing it was technically illegal, and those involved in it certainly wouldn't want to be known, so I knew I was going to have to persuade him. I tossed an imperial his way just as he was starting to shake his head. He caught it, opened his mouth, closed it, and started to toss it back. I put a couple of knives into the wall on either side of his head. Good thing I'd been practicing or I might have cut his hair. In any case, I do believe I frightened the man, judging by the squeaks he made.

He said, "A kid named Tip."

"Where can I find him?"

"I don't know."

I pulled another throwing knife (my last one, actually—I'd just recently bought them) and waited.

"He lives around here somewhere," squeaked the barber. "Ask around. You'll find him."

"If I don't," I said, "when do you expect him to deliver another one of these?"

"A couple of weeks," he said. "But I don't know exactly when. I never know when they'll show up."

"Good enough," I said. I took a step toward him and he moved away, but I was only going to get my knives. I put them away and walked back out, turned right at random, and stepped into the first alley I got to. And there they were—another eight urchins, mixed sexes, mixed Houses. Street kids don't seem to care much what your House is. There may be a moral there, but probably not.

I walked up to them and waited a moment to give them a good look. They studied me with a lot of suspicion, a little curiosity, but not much fear. I mean, I was only an Easterner, and maybe I had a sword, but there were still eight of them. Then I said, "Do any of you know Tip?"

A girl, who seemed to be about seventy and might have been the leader and might have been a Tiassa, said, "Maybe."

A boy said, "What you want him for? He in trouble?"

Someone else said, "You a bird?"

Someone else asked to see my sword.

"Yeah," I said. "I'm a bird. I'm going to arrest him as a threat to Imperial security, and then I'm going to haul him away and torture him. Any other questions?"

There were a few chuckles.

"Who are you?" said the girl.

I shrugged and took out an imperial. "A rich man who wants to spread his wealth around. Who are you?"

They all turned to look at the girl. Yes, she was definitely in charge. "Laache," she said. "Is that thing your pet?" she asked.

"Go ahead, explain it, boss."

"Shut up, Loiosh."

"His name is Loiosh," I said. "He's my friend. He flies around and looks at things for me."

"What does he look at?"

"For example, if I were to give this imperial to someone to bring Tip back, he'd fly around and make sure whoever I gave it to didn't scoot off with it. If someone took this imperial and told me where Tip could be found, Loiosh would wait with that person until I was certain I hadn't been fooled."

One of the boys said, "He can't really tell you where someone went, can he?"

Laache grinned at me. "You think we'd do something like that?"

"Nope."

"What reason do I give Tip for showing up?"

I brought forth another imperial. "For him," I said.

"You sure he isn't in trouble?"

"No. I've never seen him before. For all I know, he might have robbed the Imperial Treasury."

She gave me a very adultlike smile and held out her hand; I gave her one of the coins.

"Wait here," she said.

"I'm not going anywhere."

When she left, Loiosh flew off and followed her, which elicited a gasp from the assembled urchinhood.

With her gone, the mood changed—the rest of them seemed suddenly uncomfortable, like they didn't know quite what to do with me. That worked out all right, because I didn't know what to do with them, either. I leaned against a wall and tried to look self-assured; they clumped together and held quiet conversations and pretended they were ignoring me.

After about fifteen minutes, Loiosh said, *"She's found someone, boss. She's talking to him."*

"And . . . ?"

"Okay, they're coming."

"Hooray. Where are they now?"

"Just around the corner."

I said, "Laache and Tip will be here soon."

They looked at me, and one of them said, "How d'you—" and cut himself off. I smiled enigmatically, noticing the looks of respect and fear. Sort of the way my employees used to look at me, way back when. I wondered if I'd come down in the world. If I handled things just right, I could maybe take the gang over from Laache. Vlad Taltos—toughest little kid on the block. I was the youngest, too.

They appeared then—Laache with a young man who seemed to be about the same age as her, and who I'd have guessed to be an Orca—a bit squat for a Dragaeran, with a pale complexion, light brown hair, and blue eyes. Old memories of being harassed by Orca just about his age came up to annoy me, but I ignored them—what was I going to do, beat him up?

He was looking a bit leery and keeping his distance. Before he could say anything, I flipped him an imperial. He made it vanish.

"What do you want?" he said.

"You're Tip?"

"What if I am?"

"Let us walk together and talk together, one with the other, out of range of the eager ears of those who would thwart our intentions."

"Huh?"

"Come here a minute, I want to ask you something."

"Ask me what?"

"I'd rather not say out here where everyone can hear me."

Someone whispered something, and someone else giggled. Tip scowled and said, "All right."

I walked up to him and we walked down the alley about twenty yards, and I said, "I'll give you another imperial if you'll take me to the man who prints *Rutter's Rag*," and he was off down the alley as fast as his feet could carry him. He turned the corner and was gone.

"You know what to do, Loiosh."

"Yeah, yeah. On my way, boss."

I turned back and the kids were all looking at me—and looking at Loiosh flying off into the city.

"Thanks for your help," I called to them. "See you again, maybe."

I strolled on down the alley. It was, of course, possible that Laache had told Tip about Loiosh, but, as we followed him, he didn't seem to be watching above him.

He stayed with the alleys and finally, after looking around him carefully, stepped into a little door. Loiosh returned to me and guided me along the same path he'd taken, and to the door. It wasn't locked.

It seemed to be a storeroom of some sort; a quick check revealed that what was stored included a great deal of paper and drums of what had to be ink, judging by the smell coming off them and filling up the room.

"Ah ha," I told Loiosh.

"Lucky," he said.

"Clever," I suggested.

"Lucky."

"Shut up."

I heard voices coming from my right, where there was a narrow, dark stairway. I took the stairs either silently or carefully—they tend to be the same thing. But you know that, Kiera. When I reached the bottom, I saw them, illuminated by a small lamp. One was Tip, the other was an old man who seemed to be a Tsalmoth, to judge from the ruddiness of his complexion and his build. I couldn't see what colors he wore. He didn't see me at all. The man was seated in front of a desk that was filled with desk things. Tip was standing next to him, saying, "I'm sure he was an Easterner. I know an Easterner when I see one," which was too good an entrance line for me to ignore.

I said, "Judge for yourself," and had the satisfaction of seeing them both jump.

I gave them my warmest smile, and the Tsalmoth scrabbled around in a drawer in his desk and came out with a narrow rod that, no doubt, had been prepared with some terrible, nasty killing thing. I said, "Don't be stupid," and took my own advice by allowing Spellbreaker to fall into my hand.

He pointed the rod at me and said, "What do you want?"

"Don't blame the boy," I said. "I'm very hard to lose when I want to follow someone."

"What do you want?" he said again. His dialogue seemed pretty limited.

"Actually," I said, "not very much. It won't even be inconvenient, and I'll pay you for it. But if you don't put that thing down, I'm likely to become frightened, and then I'm likely to hurt you."

He looked at me, then looked at Spellbreaker, which to all appearances is just a length of gold-colored chain, and said, "I think I'll keep it in hand, if you don't mind."

"I mind," I said.

He looked at me some more. I waited. He put the rod down. I wrapped Spellbreaker back around my left wrist.

"What is it, then?"

"Perhaps the boy should take a walk."

He nodded to Tip, who seemed a little nervous about walking past me, so I stepped to the side. He almost ran to the stairs, stopping just long enough to take the imperial I threw to him. "Don't squander it," I said as he raced past me.

There was another chair near the desk, so I sat down in it, crossed my legs, and said, "My name is Padraic." Quit laughing, Kiera; it's a perfectly reasonable Eastern name, and no Dragaeran in the world is going to look at me and decide I don't look right. Where was I? Oh, yeah. I said, "My name is Padraic."

He grunted and said, "My name is Tollar, but you might as well call me Rutter; there's no point in my denying it, I suppose."

He was a frightened man trying to be brave; I've always had a certain amount of sympathy for that type. From this close, he didn't seem as old as I'd first thought him, but he didn't seem especially healthy, either, and his hair was thin and sort of wispy—you could see his scalp in places, like an Easterner who is just beginning to go bald.

He said, "You have me at a disadvantage."

"Sure," I said. "But there's no need to worry about it. I just need to find out a couple of things, and I took the easiest method I could think of."

"What do you mean?"

"I mean I ask you a couple of questions that you have no reason not to answer, and then I'm going to give you a couple of imperials for your trouble, and then I'm going to go away. And that's it."

"Yeah?" He seemed skeptical. "What sort of questions, and why are you asking me?"

"Because you have that rag of yours. That means you hear things. You pick up gossip. You have ways of finding out things."

He started to relax a little. "Well, yeah. Some things. Where should I start?"

I shrugged. "Oh, I don't know. What's the good gossip since the last rag came out?"

"Local?"

"Or Imperial."

"The Empress is missing."

"Again?"

"Yeah. Rumor is she's off with her lover."

"That's four times in three years, isn't it?"

"Yeah."

"But she always comes back."

"First time it was for three days, second time for nine days, the third time for six days."

"What else?"

"Imperial?"

"Yeah."

"Someone high up in the Empire dipped his hand into the war chest during the Elde Island war. No one knows who, and probably not for very much, but the Empress is a bit steamed about it."

"I can imagine."

"More?"

"Please."

"I'm better on local things."

"Know anything that's both local and Imperial?"

"Well, the whole Fyres thing."

"What do you know about that?"

"Not much, really. There's confirmation that his death was accidental."

"Oh, yeah?"

"That's what I hear."

"I hear the Empire is investigating his death."

He snorted. "Who doesn't know that?"

"Right. Who's doing the investigating?"

He looked at me, and I could see him going, "Ah ha!" just like me. He said, "You mean, their names?"

"Yeah."

"I have no idea."

I looked at him. He didn't seem to be lying. I said, "Where are they working out of?"

"You mean, where do they meet?"

"Right."

"City Hall."

"Where in City Hall?"

"Third floor."

"The whole floor?"

"No, no. The third floor is where the officers of the Phoenix Guard are stationed. There are a couple of rooms set aside for any senior officials who might show up. They're using those."

"Which rooms?"

"Two rooms at the east end of the building, one on each side of the hall."

"And they haven't gone back to Adrilankha yet?"

"No, no. They're still hard at it."

"How could they still be hard at it if they already know what the answer is?"

"I don't know," he said. "I imagine they're just tying up loose ends and doing their final checking. But that's just a guess."

"Which wouldn't stop you from printing it as a fact."

He shrugged.

I said, "Heard anything about their schedule?"

"What do you mean?"

"I mean when they expect to be finished."

"Oh. No, I haven't."

"Okay." I dug out three imperials and handed them to him. "See?" I said. "That wasn't so bad, was it?"

He wasn't worried anymore. He said, "Why is it you want to know all of this?"

I shook my head. "That's a dangerous question."

"Oh?"

"If you ask it, I might answer it. And if I answered it, the answer might appear as gossip in your lovely little sheet. And if that happened, I would have to kill you."

He looked at me and seemed like a frightened old man again. I stood up and walked out without a backward glance.

I TOLD YOU THEY were getting tired of seeing me at City Hall, which was another problem, so I tried out a disguise. The first problem was my mustache, so it went. It took a lot of time, too, because even after you shave it off, you have to scrape quite a bit at the whiskers to make sure they don't show at all. The next problem was my height. I found a cobbler who sold me some boots which he then put about eight extra inches on, leaving me about Aliera's height, which I hoped would be good enough. Then I had to practice walking in them and taking long strides. Have you ever tried walking in boots with eight extra inches of sole? Don't. Then I broke into a theater to steal a wig with a noble's point and get some powder to hide the traces of whiskers, then I bought some new clothes, including trousers long enough to hide the shoes but not long enough to trip on. I practiced swaggering just a bit. Kiera, this was not easy—I had to keep my balance, take strides long enough so it wouldn't look funny with my height, and *swagger,* for the love of Verra. I felt like a complete idiot. On the other hand, I didn't draw any funny looks while I was walking around, so I figured I had a chance of pulling it off.

I hid my clothes and my blade behind a handy public house half a mile or so from City Hall. So I did all that, dressing myself up like a Chreotha so people would feel free to push me around. You can learn a lot letting people push you around, and it's always nice knowing that you can push back whenever you want.

I told Loiosh to wait for me outside, which he didn't like but was unavoidable. Then I walked into the place like I knew my business, went up a flight of stairs to take me past the nice Lyorn who'd been helping me so far, found another flight of stairs, turned right, and looked down to the end of the hall. There were three or four people sitting on plain wooden chairs in the hall. Three men, one woman, all of them Orca except for one poor fellow who seemed to be a Teckla.

I leaned against a wall and watched for a while, until the right-hand door opened and a middle-aged Orca walked out. A moment later, as she was walking past me, one of those waiting went in. I walked past and entered the door to the left.

There was a sharp-looking young Dragonlord sitting at a desk. He said, "Good day, my lord."

How long was I a Jhereg, Kiera? Hard to say, I suppose; it depends when you start counting and when you stop. But a long time, anyway, and that's a long time spent getting so you can smell authority—so you know you're looking at an officer of the Guard before you really know how you know. Well, I walked through that door, and I knew.

He was, as I said, a Dragonlord, and one who worked for the Phoenix Guards, or for the Empire; yet he was dressed in plain black pants and shirt with only the least bit of silver; his hair was very short, his complexion just a bit dark, his nose just a bit aquiline; he rather looked like Morrolan, now that I think of it. But I've never seen Morrolan's eyes look quite that cold and that calculating; I've never seen anyone look like that except for an assassin named Ishtvan, who I used a couple of times and killed not long ago. It took me about a quarter of a second to decide that I didn't want to go up against this guy if I could avoid it.

I said, "My lord, you are looking into the death of Lord Fyres?"

"That's right. Who called you in?"

"No one, my lord," I said, trying to sound humble.

"No one?"

"I came on my own, when I heard about it."

"Heard about what?"

"The investigation."

"How did you hear?"

I had no idea how to answer that one, so I shrugged helplessly.

He was starting to look very hard at me. "What's your name?" he said. I was no longer his lord.

"Kaldor," I said.

"Where do you live, Kaldor?"

"Number six Coattail Bend, my lord."

"That's here in Northport?"

"Yes, my lord, in the city."

He wrote something down on a piece of paper and said, "My name is Loftis. Wait in the hall; we'll call you."

"Yes, my lord."

I gave him a very humble bow and stepped back into the hall, feeling nervous. I'm a good actor, and I'm okay with disguises, but that guy scared me. I guess I'd been working on the assumption that the Imperial investigators were on the take, and I'd gone from there to the assumption that they must be pretty lousy investigators. Actually, that was stupid; I know from my own dealings with the Guard that just because one of them is on the take doesn't mean he can't do his job, but I hadn't thought it through, and now I was worried; Loftis didn't seem to be someone I could put much over on, at least not without a lot more work than I'd put in.

So, of course, I listened. I assumed that they'd be able to detect sorcery, but I doubted they'd be looking for witchcraft, so I took the black Phoenix Stone off and slipped it into my pouch—hoping, of course, that the Jhereg wouldn't pick that moment to attempt a psychic location spell. I leaned my head back against the wall, closed my eyes, and concentrated on sending my hearing through the wall. It took some work, and it took some time, but soon I could hear voices, and after a bit I could distinguish words.

"Who do you think sent him?" I wasn't sure if that was Loftis.

"Don't be stupid." *That* was Loftis.

"What, you're saying it was the Candlestick?"

"In the first place, Domm, when you're around me, you'll be respectful when speaking of Her Majesty."

"Oh, well pardon my feet for touching the ground."

"And in the second place, no. I mean we have no way of knowing who sent him, and if we're going to do this—"

"We're going to do this."

"—we should at least be careful about it. And being careful means finding out."

"He could have given us his right address."

"Sure. And he could be the King of Elde Island, too. You follow him, Domm. And don't let him pick up on you."

"You want to put those orders in writing, *Lieutenant*?"

"Would you like to eat nine inches of steel, *Lieutenant*?"

"Don't push me, Loftis."

"Or we could just dump the whole thing on Papa-cat's lap and let him decide our next step. Want to do that? How do you think he'd feel about it?"

"I could tell him it was your idea."

"Sure. Do it. I'm sure he'll believe you, too. You know as sure as Verra's tits I'll roll on this as soon as I have a good excuse. Go ahead.

My protests are down in writing, Domm. How about you? Did you just shrug and say, 'Hey, sure, sounds like fun'? Probably. So go ahead."

"Lieutenant, sir, with all respect, my lord, you tire me."

"Tough. You've got your orders, my lord lieutenant. Carry them out."

"All right, all right. You know how much I love legwork, and I know how much you care about what I love. I'll wait until his interview is over, then pick him up. Should I bring some backup?"

"Yeah. Take Timmer; she's good at tailing, and she hasn't stirred her butt since she's been here."

"Okay. What should I tell Birdie about the interview?"

"Play it straight, see what he has to say, and try to keep the bell ringing."

"Huh?"

"Battle of Waterford Landing, Domm. Tenth Cycle, early Dragon Reign. A border skirmish between a couple of Lyorn over rights to—"

"Oh, now that's extremely useful, Loftis. Thanks. Why don't you skip the history, and the obscure references, and just tell me what you want Birdie to do."

"I mean Birdie should try to get him talking, and then just keep drawing him out until there isn't anything left to draw."

"And if he won't *be* drawn?"

"Then that'll tell us something, too."

"Okay."

"You got to admit this is better than just sitting here day after day pretending. At least it's doing something."

"I suppose. Mind if I put him in front of the queue so I don't have to wait all night?"

"Yeah, I mind. Nothing to make him suspicious. You can put him in front of the Teckla if you want."

"Okay. Hey, Loftis."

"Yeah?"

"You ever wonder why?"

"Why what? Why we got the word?"

"Yeah."

"That's a laugh. I haven't been doing anything *but* wondering why for the last two weeks."

"Yeah."

They stopped talking. I moved my head forward, replaced the Phoenix Stone around my neck, and didn't look as someone I didn't recognize walked out of the door and across the hall. An instant later he came back. I watched him, as did all of the others who were waiting, but he didn't look at me at all. Assuming that was Domm, my opinion of him went up a bit—it isn't easy to avoid taking even a quick glance at someone you're going to be following in a few minutes. I got the uncomfortable feeling that I was dealing with professionals here.

I sat there trying to decide if I should skip out now, which would mean I wouldn't have to worry about losing the tail and would give them something to wonder about, or if I should go ahead and let them interview me, and hope to pick up more information that way. I decided to gamble, because, now that I had a better idea of what was going on, as well as how they were going to handle me, I felt like I could maybe learn a bit. I was glad Domm had demanded the explanation for "keep ringing the bell," because it would have been a mistake to have asked Loftis myself.

Someone else showed up, went into the room I'd just come out of, then emerged and took a seat next to me. We didn't speak. None of us had so much as made eye contact with any of the others. But as I sat there waiting for about an hour and a half planning what kind of story I was going to tell them, I didn't get any less nervous.

When they finally called out "Kaldor," it took me a moment to realize that was the name I'd given them. I tell you, Kiera, I'm not made for a life of deception. But I shuffled into the office, still taking long strides and swaggering, but shuffling, too, if you can imagine it, where sat a fairly young, competent-looking Lyorn behind yet another desk. I've been seeing a great number of desks lately—it makes me miss my own. I don't know what it is about a desk that gives one a feeling of power—perhaps it is that, when you are facing someone behind a desk, you don't know what is concealed within it; the contents of a desk can be worse than a nest of yendi.

The chair he pointed me to was another of the inevitable plain, wooden chairs—there's something about those, too, now that I think of it.

He said, "I am the Baron of Daythiefnest. You are Kaldor?"

Daythiefnest? Birdie. I didn't laugh. "Yes, my lord."

"Number three Coattail Bend?"

"Number six, my lord." Heh. Caught that one, at least.

"Right, sorry. And you have come in on your own?"

"Yes, my lord."

"Why?"

"My lord?"

"What brought you here?"

"The investigation, my lord. I have information."

"Ah. You have information about Fyres's death?"

"Yes, my lord."

He studied me carefully, but, as far as intimidation went, he was nothing compared to Loftis. Of course, it wouldn't do to tell him so; it might hurt his feelings.

"And what is this information?"

"Well, my lord, after work—"

"What sort of work do you do, Kaldor?"

"I mend things, my lord. That is, I mend clothes, and sometimes I mend pots and pans, except my tools got took, which I reported to the Guard, my lord, and I mend sails for sailors sometimes, and—"

"Yes, I understand. Go on."

"I know that you aren't the gentlemen who are going to get my tools back, that's a different outfit."

"Yes. Go on."

"Go on?"

"After work . . ."

"Oh, right. Well, after work, on the days I have work, I like to go into the Riversend. Do you know where that is?"

"I can find it."

"Oh, it's right nearby. You just take Kelp down to where it curves—"

"Yes, yes. Go on."

"Right, my lord. Well, I was in there having a nice glass of ale—"

"When was this?"

"Last Marketday, my lord."

"Very well."

"Well, I'd been drinking a fair bit, and I'd gotten a kind of early start, so before I knew it I was seeing the room go spinning around me, the way it does when you know you've had more than maybe you should?"

"Yes. You were drunk."

"That's it, my lord. I was drunk. And then the room spun, and then I must have fallen asleep."

"Passed out."

"Yes, my lord."

"Well?"

"Yes, my lord?"

"Get on with it."

"Oh. Yes, my lord. I must have been sleeping five, six hours, because when I woke up, needing to relieve myself, you understand, I wasn't nearly so drunk, and I was lying on one of the benches they have in back, and the place was almost empty—there was Trim, the host, who was in the far corner cleaning up, and there was me, and there were these two gentlemen sitting at a table right next to me, and they were talking kind of quiet, but I could hear them, you know, my lord? And it was pretty dark, and I wasn't moving, so I don't think they knew I was there."

"Well, go on."

"One of them said, 'If you ask me, they didn't get anything.' And the other one said, 'Oh, no? Well, I'll tell you something, they got a lot, and it's going on the market next week,' and the first one said, 'What's it going for?' and the other one said, 'A lot. It has to be a lot. If someone is going to lighten Fyres, especially after he's dead, and not take anything but a bunch of papers, they must be important.' And the first one said, 'Maybe that's what he was killed for?' And the other one said, 'Killed? Naw, he just fell and hit his head.' And then, my lord, I sort of figured out what they were saying, even though I was still maybe a bit woozy, and I knew I didn't want to hear any more, so I moaned like I was just waking up, and they saw me, and they stopped talking right then. And I tumbled out of there, singing to myself like I was even drunker than I was, and I went out the back way and I beat it for home as quick as I could, and I didn't even settle up with Trim until the next day. But, as I was walking out, just at the last minute, I took a quick look at the two gentlemen. I couldn't see their faces too well, but I could see their colors, and they were both Jhereg. I'll swear it. And that's what I have, my lord."

"That's what you have?"

"Yes, my lord."

He stared at me like I was a rotten pear and he'd just bit into me, and he thought for a while. "Why did you come and see us now, and not two weeks ago?"

"Well, because I heard of the reward, and I was thinking about my tools that got stole, and—"

"What reward?"

"The reward for anyone who gives evidence about how Fyres died."

"There's no reward."

"There's no reward?"

"Not at all. Where did you hear such a thing?"

"Why, just yesterday, down at the Riversend, a lady told me that she'd heard—"

"She was deceived, my friend. And so were you."

"My lord?"

"There isn't any reward for anything. We're just trying to find out what happened."

"Oh." I tried to look disappointed.

He said, "How did you learn to come here, by the way?"

"How, my lord?"

"Yes."

"Why, the lady, she was a Tsalmoth, and she told me."

"I see. Who was this lady?"

"Well, I don't know, my lord. I'd never seen her before, but she was—" I squinted as if I was trying to remember. "Oh, she was about eight hundred, and sort of tall, and her hair curled, and she was, you know, a Tsalmoth."

"Yes," he said, nodding. "Well, I'm sorry to disappoint you, but there isn't any reward."

I looked disappointed but said, "Well, that's all right, my lord; I'm just glad to have done the right thing."

"Yes, indeed. Well, we know where to reach you if we have any more questions."

I stood up and bowed. "Yes, my lord. Thank you."

"Thank you," he said, and that was it for the interview.

I walked out the door without seeing anyone except those who were waiting for their turn, and I took my time going down the stairs. As I went, I said, "*Loiosh?*"

"*Right here, boss.*"

"*I'm going to be followed, so stay back for a while.*"

"*Okay. Who's going to follow you, boss?*"

"*I don't know, but I think the enemy.*"

"*Oh, we have an enemy now?*"

"*I think so. Maybe.*"

"*It's nice to have an enemy, boss. Where are you taking them?*"

"*Good question,*" I said. "*I'll let you know when we get there.*"

6

I STOOD ON THE street, just outside City Hall, not looking behind me and trying to stay in character while figuring out where to go and what to do. You don't get tailed all that often, at least when you know it's happening, and an opportunity like that ought not to be wasted.

"I've spotted 'em, boss. Two of 'em. Pros."

"What are they doing?"

"Waiting for you to do something."

"Good. Let them wait."

I'd done what I actually set out to do, of course—it was easy to fill in the missing pieces of Loftis's conversation with Domm, and the missing pieces said that they were faking their way through the investigation and putting out the results they were told to, and that was confirmed by the way the other one, Daythiefnest, had been more concerned with how I knew enough to find them and why I wanted to than with the information itself. But what now? Knowing the investigation was faked brought up the possibility (although not the certainty by any means) that Fyres was, in fact, murdered, but it got me no closer to learning who was pulling the financial strings, or who in the next few months and years would be.

But more than that, Kiera, I was bothered, just as you were when I first suggested it. Why would the Empire do something like that? I'd never heard of it being done, and it would take, well, someone very highly placed in the Empire, and a very strong need, to attempt it. The question was who—who in the Empire and who in Fyres's world? And I didn't know anyone who inhabited either realm.

I mentally ran through the notes I'd made when reading the files you lightened Fyres of. Based on what I picked up from the files, and based on what your friend Stony told you, I'd guess that Fyres's children were somewhere near the center of things—that is, he was certainly going to leave his kids in charge of as much as possible, divided up according to his best guess about who could handle what and how much. He had a wife, one son, and two daughters, as well as a few other scattered relatives.

The wife, I heard somewhere, used to be third mate in a man-o'-war, which might indicate leadership qualities, but according to the files, he never seemed to trust her; and she never had anything to do with his business. There was just enough gossip floating around about his son for me to get the idea that everything he touched turned to mud; over the years, Fyres trusted him with less and less. If I had to guess about the will, I'd say Fyres left him with a house or two, a bunch of cash, and nothing else.

That left the daughters: the younger, Baroness of Reega, and the older, the Countess of Endra. It seemed from Fyres's notes that, as time went on, he was giving them more and more responsibility and working them into his businesses. Right then, Kiera, I really wished I had my old organization, because I could have made one remark to Kragar—how's he doing, by the way?—and in two days I would know everything possible about them. I hate doing the legwork myself, and, more important, I just didn't have time to do it.

Well, if all I could do was blunder about, I might as well get to it, I decided, and I turned around and back into City Hall I went. I didn't see those tailing me scramble out of my way; in fact, I didn't see them at all.

The nice Lyorn didn't recognize me and were far more helpful to Kaldor the Chreotha than they'd been to Padraic the Easterner—what they would have thought of Vlad the Jhereg I don't even want to think about. Oh, and they weren't all Lyorn, either, just for the record—but the ones who weren't looked like they wanted to be. Enough said.

In two minutes I was in front of the collection of city maps, and it took me about half an hour to determine that neither a barony of Reega nor a county of Endra could be found in the area. So I puttered around some more and found out that neither one actually existed—they were titles without places to go with them, which I suppose I should have expected of Orca. I then dug into the citizen rolls, which took a fair bit of time. I could have done it faster by asking for help, but then, no doubt, my shadows would have been able to find out what I was up to and I wasn't sure that was a good idea.

Endra—that is, the person—lived high on Vantage Hill, overlooking a little town called Harper on the outskirts of Northport. It was, I calculated, only an hour's walk, and I liked the idea of Domm and Timmer getting blisters on their feet; besides, you know how I feel about horses. So I set out. The day was nice, with a mild breeze blowing in from the sea. As I walked, I made a few minor but important adjustments to my costume—you know, I turned up the collar, I fixed my hair, I straightened my buttons, and, generally, I made myself appear more prosperous, because I figured I had to reach a certain social level before I'd have a chance that Endra—or, more likely, whoever answered the door for her—would even consider letting me see her.

One thing I'd forgotten when I set out was that, since I was still in my disguise, I was wearing the platform boots that didn't fit me very well; about halfway there I started calling myself names, and Loiosh, trailing behind to keep an eye on my shadows, starting laughing at me. And I was a bit worried about not having my sword with me. And it made me nervous to know there were two people following me. In other words, I was not in a good mood by the time I reached Vantage Hill.

Endra's place was pretty simple, actually. It was a plain house, standing by itself on a little hillock, but it was certainly well built, and it struck me as comfortable. The grounds were well manicured with some nicely behaved trees in a neat row and trimmed grass and patches of garden, but not molded and tended like the Imperial Palace, or like The Demon's place, if you've ever been to—Oh, of course you've been there. Sorry.

I don't know. As I approached it, I was thinking that maybe I'd been spoiled by Castle Black and Dzur Mountain, but I had expected something more—I guess ostentatious is the word. But then I remembered your description of Fyres's place—the one he actually lived in as opposed to one of the places he used to impress people—and it wasn't as big and impressive as it could have been either, was it? I figured maybe it's a family trait. It was also interesting that there seemed to be no guards patrolling the area. Fyres's place had had plenty, but did one generation cause that big a drop-off in the need for security? I hate dealing with things I don't understand.

I pulled the door clapper and waited. Presently someone opened the door and frowned at me. I bowed and gave him Kaldor as a name, and asked if it would be possible for his mistress to spare me a few minutes of conversation.

He stared at me for a moment, as if he wasn't sure he'd heard me correctly. Then he said, "May I ask what your business is with the Countess?"

"I'm afraid it's private," I said.

He looked doubtful. I tried to look like I knew my business, which wasn't as easy as a Chreotha as it would have been in my usual guise, nor was he responding as well as I'd have expected when I looked like myself; I'm not certain why that is. Maybe there's more shock value in seeing an Easterner at one's door. Maybe I'd have been better off pretending to be a Dragonlord, but then I probably wouldn't have learned as much from the Imperial investigators.

Eventually, however, he let me in, and bid me wait while he found out if the Countess was available. I did what everyone has always done in that situation—I looked around. It was big, and it was impressive, and the stairway was white marble that swept up in a gracious curve and complemented the white, white walls broken by—ah, Kiera, my dear, if you'd been there, you'd still be drooling. I don't have the disposition of a thief, but I was tempted. There were gold plates on the wall, marble busts, crystal sculpture, a tapestry made of bloody damn pearls that would have made you cry. Stained glass embedded with gems. The place didn't speak of wealth, it screamed it. All of the ostentation I'd looked for on the outside was reserved for the inside, where it destroyed all my little notions about what a plain, simple, unassuming lifestyle this family chose. It was very strange, Kiera, and I couldn't help wondering at the sort of mind that had produced it.

And then it occurred to me that there was a similarity between the outside and the inside—and that was how little they said. I mean, sure, they screamed money, but what else? You can tell a lot about someone by seeing his home, right? Well, not these people. The place said nothing, really, except that she was rich. Was that because she was shallow, or because she didn't want anyone to know anything about her?

The servant appeared as I was considering this and said, "The Countess can spare you a few moments. She's in the library. Please follow me."

I did so.

The library. Yeah.

Remember those traps Morrolan has in his library? Oh, I imagine you do. Did you ever fall for them? No, I withdraw the question; sorry. But, yeah, everything in the library looked like Morrolan's traps—great huge tomes with jewel-encrusted covers chained to pedestals. Well, okay, so I'm overstating it a bit. But that was how the library felt—everything *looked* good, but it didn't give you the feeling you wanted to sit down and *read* anything. The library wasn't for reading, it was for meeting people in an atmosphere that tried to be intellectual. Or that's how it struck me, at any rate. I don't know. Maybe I've just never known enough rich people to have an opinion—maybe they have their own rules, or maybe they're trying to make up with money what they've been denied by birth; I don't know. I'm just giving it to you as it hit me at the time.

She was sitting at a table—not a desk, for a change—and reading a book, or pretending to. She looked up as I came in and gave me a quizzical half-smile, then rose to greet me; she was quite thin and had very short, light-colored straight hair—a "warrior's cut," in fact, which went oddly with her dress, which was a flowing blue gown. She had the Orca eyebrows—almost invisible—a largish mouth and thin lips, narrow, wide-set eyes, and a strong chin.

Her voice had a bit of the twang of the region, but not as much as our hostess has, or most of the people we've been running into around here, and it was quite musical sounding. She said, "Your name again was—?"

"Kaldor, my lady."

"You wished to speak to me?"

"Yes, my lady, if I may have a few moments."

"You may. Please sit. Here. What is your business?"

And here, Kiera, is where I paid the price of deceit. Maybe. Because it occurred to me that I might just be able to come out and ask her if she'd be willing to let us buy this land, or at least plead the case. But if she said no, and she was then questioned by Domm, they'd have no trouble tracing me back, and that could be unhealthy.

I said, "My condolences, my lady, on the death of your father."

She raised an eyebrow—it looked like a practiced maneuver—and said, "Yes, certainly."

I said, "It is the death of your father that brings me here."

She nodded again.

I said, "I have reason to believe the Empire is not looking into his death as seriously as they should."

"That's absurd."

"I don't think so, my lady."

"Why?"

"I can't tell you exactly."

"You can't tell me?"

I shook my head. I said, "If you would like, though, a friend of mine who knows something about it will come by, and he can tell you more—he just wanted me to find out if you cared."

"I care," she said. "But I don't believe it."

"But will you talk to my friend?"

She stared at me very hard, then said, "All right. When can I expect him?"

"I'm not sure."

"What's his name?"

"I'm not to say, my lady. He'll identify himself as my friend, though."

She looked at me for quite a while, then nodded and said, "All right."

I stood up and bowed. "I've taken enough of your time, I think."

She stood, which was a courtesy I hadn't expected, and as I left, the servant came and escorted me to the door. I left the way I'd come and began walking back to town.

What had I accomplished? I'm not certain, but I had left a way open for me to return in some other guise, even as myself, if it seemed appropriate.

I considered the matter as I walked. The day was still young, and I had a long way to go to reach the Baroness of Reega, and my feet were killing me.

Reega lived on a hill—I guess the rich always live on hills, maybe because the aristocrats do—called Winteroak, which was on the northern edge of Northport, overlooking the Kanefthali River Valley. It was quite a hike, so as soon as I was out of sight of Endra's place I sat down long enough to remove the black Phoenix Stone and perform a quick spell to make my feet feel better. I couldn't do a whole lot without letting the watchers know what I was up to, but it helped. I put the Phoenix Stone back on and continued. If they were like me when I was following someone, they would have noticed at once that they couldn't locate me either psychically or sorcerously, and they'd wonder about that, but my luck would have to be awfully bad for them to pick that moment to try again. Sometimes it's worth a certain amount of risk to alleviate discomfort.

This is a funny part of the world, Kiera. Have you noticed it? The landscape, I mean. Maybe it's because we're so far north of the equator, or because the Kanefthali Mountains start only a few hundred miles away—though I don't see how that can have anything to do with it. But it seems odd to me that you can walk from the east side of Northport to the west, or from hills overlooking the docks straight north, and you'll have four completely different landscapes. I mean, along the coast, it might as well be Adrilankha—you've got the same kind of ugly red cliffs and the sort of dirt that makes you think nothing could ever grow there no matter what you did. But just a little ways to the east you have these prairies that look like the area around Castle Black and west of Dzur Mountain, and there's lots of water and it looks like it might be good farmland. And the country around Endra's is all rocky and hard and pretty in the same way the southern tip of Suntra is pretty—unforgiving, but attractive, anyway. So you head north, along the river to where Reega lives, and it's like the big forests to the east of Dzur Mountain, almost jungle, only they've been cut back because there are a lot of people there, but it isn't hard to imagine running into a dzur or a tiassa prowling around. Isn't that strange? I wonder if there's some magic about it, or if it just happened that way.

But sorry, I've wandered away from the point. Reega's place was nestled in among a lot of trees and stuff, and looked completely untended—there were a good number of other houses in the area, so I had to ask directions a few times to figure out which it was. It was nice, Kiera. I mean it was smaller than Fyres's or Endra's, though still quite a bit bigger than this place, but it seemed to want to be a house, instead of a mansion that wanted to be a castle. Looking at it, I figured that when I clapped she'd answer the door herself, and, as a matter of fact, that's just what happened.

She was a bit shorter and a bit heavier than her sister, and her hair was longer and curled quite a bit, but they had pretty much the same face. She looked at me the way someone who lived in a house like that ought to look at you, as if she was a bit curious about why someone would want to talk to her—by which I mean, not like the daughter of someone as rich as Fyres ought to look at you. I wondered if I was at the wrong place. I said, "Baroness Reega?"

"That's right," she said. "And you are—?"

"Kaldor. May I speak to you for a moment?"

"Concerning what?" she asked. She still seemed polite and friendly, but she hadn't invited me in.

"Your father."

"My father?"

"You are the daughter of Lord Fyres, aren't you?"

"Why, yes I am."

"Well, then, what I have to say concerns you."

She gave me a contemplative look and said, "What is it, then?"

It seemed odd to be discussing this standing outside of her house, but it was her choice. I said, "I have reason to believe that the Empire is not looking into his death as thoroughly as they ought to be."

Her eyes narrowed to slits, and she studied me, and I was suddenly not at all sure of my disguise. She said, "Oh you do, do you?"

"Yes, my lady."

"And what business is that of yours?"

Ah ha. If you've been counting, Kiera, that was the third "ah ha" of the day.

"My lady?"

"Why do you care?"

"Well, I was hoping, you know, that . . . uh . . ."

"That there would be a reward in it for you?"

"Well—"

She gestured with her hand toward the road behind me. "You may leave now."

I couldn't think of anything else to do, so I bowed and left. It had been a long walk for a short conversation, but no walk is wasted if there's an "Ah ha" at the end of it. I shared this thought with Loiosh, who suggested that he could supply me with as many "ah ha's" as I wanted. I didn't have an answer handy, so I just headed back to town.

MY NEXT STOP WAS the Riversend, because I figured that would give my story some verisimilitude with my shadows, and because it had a back door in case I wanted to use it, and because I had my clothes and my weapons stashed there. If I needed to visit the son and the widow, I figured it would wait, because evening was coming on and my feet were hurting like blazes, and I wanted a good meal and a drink, which was another reason to stop at the Riversend.

But first things first. I asked Loiosh what my shadows were up to. He said, "*One's going around to the back, boss.*"

"*Is the other one coming in?*"

"*No.*"

"*Okay.*"

I walked through the tavern, opened up the back door, moved a few empty crates, recovered the bundle that I'd made of my possessions, recovered my sword from behind the garbage pile, and slipped back inside before Timmer or Domm or whoever it was got there. The inn wasn't very crowded, but no one particularly noticed me, anyway.

I sat down at a table and caused the host (whose name really is Trim, by the way) to bring me some wine, a bowl of fish soup, and whatever fowl they had roasting away over the spit and producing those amazing smells. They were apparently basting it with some sort of honey and lemon mixture that made the fire dance very prettily and made my stomach growl like a dzur.

Trim's service was very fast, and his food was very good; I hoped that they wouldn't question the poor bastard, or if they did, that they were nice about it.

I ate, drank, rested, and tried to figure out my next step. The last was the hard part, the others come pretty easy if you practice long enough. Loiosh was getting hungry, too, which I felt bad about, but I needed him to keep watching, so my meal was accompanied by his running complaints. I didn't allow this to detract from the food, however.

Then Loiosh said, *"Boss, the guy's coming inside."*

"Okay," I said, and I placed the sword against the wall behind me, resting it against a support beam where it would be, if not hidden, at least not horribly obvious. I made sure I had a dagger near to hand, then I finished sopping up the meal with the remains of the bread—a good black bread made with seeds of some kind.

In fact, they both came in—the man and the woman—and planted themselves in front of me; no doubt they'd received instructions from headquarters. I looked up at them with an expression of profound innocence, to which I tried to mix in a certain amount of alarm.

"Lord Kaldor?" said the man.

I nodded.

"May we speak with you for a moment?"

I nodded again.

"I'm Lieutenant Domm, this is Ensign Timmer, of Her Imperial Majesty's Guard."

I nodded for the third time. I was getting good at it.

They sat down, even though I hadn't invited them to; I think they felt that standing while I sat would make it harder for them to intimidate me. Meanwhile, I tried to act like I was intimidated but trying to act like I wasn't. I don't think I did very well—it's a lot easier to pretend to be tough when you're scared than to pretend to be scared when you're tough. Or, at least, it is for me.

"Need any help, boss?"

"Not yet, Loiosh."

"We'd just like to ask you some questions. We understand that you've been telling people that we're not conducting a thorough investigation into a certain matter. We'd like to know why you think so."

I was betting on Reega over Endra, so I said, "My lord, I went over to the city hall today, where they're—you're—talking to everyone, and I told them what I knew, and they didn't care, so I figured that must mean—"

"Bullshit," said Timmer, opening her mouth for the first time. "What's the real reason?"

"That's the only—"

She turned to Domm and said, "Let's take him back and work on him for a while. We don't have time for this."

"Be patient," said Domm. "I think he'll talk to us."

"Why bother? We can peel him like an onion."

Domm shook his head. "Not unless we have to. The big guy doesn't like us destroying people's brains unless there's no other choice."

"So who's going to tell him?"

"Let's try it my way first."

"Okay. You're the boss."

He nodded and turned back to me. It was becoming harder and harder to try to look frightened. People all around us in the inn had now moved away and Trim was giving us uneasy glances. A reassuring wave, I thought, would probably not be a good idea. Domm leaned over the table to bring his face right up to mine.

"Who are you, what do you know, how do you know it, and what are you after?"

I sank back into the chair and made my eyes get wide, which is as good as I can do at pretending to be afraid. I tried to figure out if there was any way to talk my way out of this without giving them anything. Nothing came instantly to mind. Domm said, "Am I going to have to let Timmer here work on you? It isn't how I like to do things, but if you don't give me any choice, I'm going to have to give you to her."

It suddenly occurred to me that, if they believed I was a professional, they wouldn't be trying to pull stuff like that on me—I was in a better position than I'd thought I was.

"Okay," I said. "I'll tell you what I know."

Domm sat down again and waited, but kept his eyes fixed on me. I'll bet he's pretty good at telling when people are lying. But then, I'm pretty good at lying.

I said, "There was this man. He asked me if I wanted to make some money—fifty imperials, he said, to go to a room in the city hall, say all these things, then walk around to a couple of places and say some more things. He told me what to say."

"Who is he?" snapped Timmer.

"I don't know. I'd never seen him before."

"Where did you meet him?"

"Here—right here."

Domm said, "How did he know to talk to you?" He was good, this guy.

"I don't know," I said.

"Oh, come on. You can do better than that. Do you expect us to believe he just walked in here and picked the first guy he saw to make this offer to?"

I shook my head. "I don't know."

Domm said, "What House was he?"

"Orca," I said. They looked at each other, which gave me the impression I'd scored a hit, although it was a pretty obvious thing to say.

Timmer said, "What did he look like?"

I started to make something up, then decided that Kaldor wasn't all that observant, and they could work for what they got. "I don't know, he was just, you know, just someone."

"How old do you think he is?"

"I don't know. Not too old. Twelve hundred or so."

"Tall? Short?"

"I don't know."

"Taller than you?"

"Oh, yes. Everyone's taller than me."

Domm stood up. "Taller than me?"

"Uh, I think so."

He sat down again. "Heavy-set?"

"No, no. Skinny."

"Long hair? Short hair? Straight? Curly?"

And so on. Eventually they got a pretty good description of the non-existent Orca, and I told them I hadn't realized I was so observant.

"All right," said Domm, nodding slowly after I'd finished. Then he paused, as if thinking things over, then he said, "Now let's have the rest of it."

"Huh?" I said, pretending to be startled.

"Who are you, and why did he come to you?"

Okay, this was the tricky part. As far as they were concerned, they'd gotten me beat, and it was just a matter of squeezing a little to get everything out of me. So I had to keep letting them think that, while still trying to pull my own game. This was, of course, made more difficult by the fact that I didn't know what my own game *was*—I was still trying to find out as much as I could about what was going on.

I gave a sigh, let my lips droop, and covered my face with my hands. "None of that," snapped Domm. "You know who we are, and you know what we can do to you. You have one chance to make this easy on yourself, and that's by telling us everything, right now."

I nodded into my hands. "Okay," I said to the table.

"Start with your name."

I looked up and, trying to make my voice small, I said, "What's going to happen to me?"

"If you tell us the truth, nothing. We may take you in for more questioning, and we'll need to know where we can reach you, but that'll be all—*if* you tell us the truth and the whole truth."

I gave Timmer a suspicious look.

"She won't do anything," said Domm.

"I want to hear her say it."

She smiled just a bit and said, "I stand by what the lieutenant said. *If* you tell us the truth."

Lying bastards, both of them. I gave them a suspicious look. "What about your commander? Will he go for it?"

Domm started to look impatient, but Timmer said, "If we give him the answers, he won't care how we got them."

"Is that the one I first talked to? What was his name, Loftis?"

"Yeah. He'll go for it."

I nodded, as if I was satisfied. I could feel them relax. "I should never have done this," I said in the tones of a man about to spill his guts. "I'm just a thief, you know? I mean, I've never hurt anyone. I know a couple of Jhereg who buy what I steal, but—wait a minute. You don't have to know the names of the Jhereg, do you?"

"I doubt it," said Domm.

"They'll kill me."

"It shouldn't be necessary," said Timmer comfortingly. "And we can protect you, anyway," she lied.

"All right," I said. "Anyway, it was stupid. I should have known better. But *fifty* imperials!"

"Tempting," said Domm.

"That's the truth," I said. "Anyway, my real name is Vaan. I was named after my uncle, who built—But you don't want to hear about that. Right?" I stopped and shook my head sadly. "I'm really in trouble, aren't I?"

"Yes," said Timmer.

"But you can get out of it," said Domm.

"Do you do this a lot? I mean, track people down and question them?" They shrugged.

"That must be fun."

Domm permitted himself a half-smile. "You were saying?"

"Uh, right." I remembered I had a glass with some wine still in it, so I drank some and wiped my face with the back of my hand. "You got onto me from the locals, didn't you? I mean, you're from Adrilankha—anyone can hear it from your voice—but you checked on me with the locals and they told you about me."

They grunted, which could mean anything, except that Timmer let slip a look that said they'd rather die than have anything to do with the locals. That was important, although it wasn't the big thing I wanted to find out. But I had them going now. They'd broken me, and they knew that I would tell them everything I knew about everything if they handled me right, and handling me right meant letting me talk, only nudging me if I got too far off course. So now I had to stay almost on course, and let them drift with me just for a bit.

I said, "The local Guards had me in once or twice, you know. They let me go because they could never be sure, but they know about me. They beat me once, too—they thought I knew something about some big job or another, but I didn't know anything about it. I never know anything about big jobs. Big jobs scare me. This one scared me, and I guess I was right to be scared." I drank some more wine and risked a look at them. They were relaxed now, and not paying all that strict attention—in other words, set up.

I shook my head. "I should have listened to my instincts, you know? I was telling some friends of mine just the other day that I had a bad feeling—"

All of a sudden Domm was no longer relaxed. "What friends?" he snapped. "What did you tell them?" Then he caught himself and looked at Timmer, who was looking at him and frowning. And that made the fourth "Ah ha" of the day, which I decided would have to be enough, especially because one of the things I learned from this one was that they—or at least Domm—had no intention of leaving me alive.

I reached back, grabbed my sword, and nailed Domm in the side of the head with the flat, trying to knock him both out and into Timmer, but I couldn't get quite enough power for either to work with my thin little blade. Timmer was fast. *Really* fast. She was up, weapon out, and coming at me before I'd stood up, and I had to squeeze into the corner and parry with both hands or she'd have spitted me; as it was she did violence to my arm, which I resented. But before she could withdraw her steel I cut at her forearm, then sliced up at her head, and—because of one move or the other—her blade fell to the floor. She bent over to pick up her weapon while I reached down and got my parcel of clothes from next to my chair. Among other things, it had my boots in it.

Domm was shaking his head—I'd at least slowed him down. Timmer came at me again, but I knocked her sword aside with my parcel, then hit *her* with the parcel, and I came up over the table and on the way by I thumped Domm's head with the pommel of my rapier. As I came over the table it tipped and I was able to put it between me and Timmer for a second, which then I used to turn and dash out the back door. I couldn't go as fast as I'd have liked, because of those Verra-be-damned boots, but I made it before they caught up with me.

I'd had an escape route planned, but I hadn't intended to be bleeding when I took it. I headed out of the alley and into another one while sheathing my weapon. I heard footsteps and I knew that Timmer was behind me. I wasn't terribly keen on killing her—you know as well as I do what sort of heat it brings to kill a Guardsman—but I was even less keen on her killing me, and there was no way I could escape her by running—not in those boots. And if I teleported, of course, she'd just trace the teleport; no future in that.

I was just considering where I should make a stand when I got lucky. I turned a corner and someone vanished—some guy had just stepped out of some shop and teleported home with his purchases. If I hadn't been wearing the black Phoenix Stone, which prevents Devine contact, I would have given a prayer of thanks to Verra; as it was, I ran right through the spot where he'd teleported from, held my arm against the parcel of clothes in the hopes that I wouldn't drip any more blood, and ran another twenty feet and through the curtained entrance to the shop.

It turned out to be a clothier, and there were a couple of customers in it. The man behind the counter—a real Chreotha—said, "May I be of some service to you, my lord?"

"Yes," I said, trying to catch my breath. "Do you have something in red?"

"You're bleeding!" said one of the customers.

"Yes," I said. "It's the fashion, you know."

"My dear sir—" said the proprietor.

"A moment," I said, and I pulled the curtain aside just a hair, just enough to see the end of Timmer's teleport. "Never mind," I said. "I think I like the pattern it's making. Good day."

I went back into the alley, and then to another one, and did my best not to leave a trail of blood. With any luck at all I had a good couple of minutes before Timmer realized that she'd followed the wrong man, and, I hoped, Domm was too far out of it to be a problem.

"Well, Loiosh?"

"You're in the clear for the moment, boss."

"Okay. Hang on for another minute, then join me."

I found a little nook I'd noticed before, and spent a minute and a half becoming a bleeding Easterner instead of a bleeding Chreotha. I put the remains of the Chreotha disguise in the bag, took off the gold Phoenix Stone, and teleported the bag to a spot I knew well just off the coast of Adrilankha, where it went to join a couple of bodies who wouldn't mind the intrusion. Loiosh arrived on my shoulder with a few choice words about how clever I thought I was compared to what a fool I'd been acting like. I thanked him for sharing his opinion with me.

Since I'd taken the chain off, anyway, there was no reason not to teleport back here, so I arrived at a point I'd memorized a little ways away into the wood, and here I am, Kiera, happy to see you as always, and has anyone ever told you that you're lovely when you're disgusted?

Interlude

"I'VE NEVER HEARD OF that Stony you talked to. If he's just sort of midlevel in Northport, what made you think he'd know anything about Fyres?"

"That's one of the things I can't tell you."

"Oh. There are a lot of things like that, aren't there?"

"I told you there would be, Cawti."

"Yes, I know. I've never known Vlad to use disguises before."

"Neither had I. It was probably something he picked up while traveling."

"What about the old woman? How was she taking all of this?"

"I suspect it bothered her a great deal, but she never let on. In fact, the whole time she had an attitude like none of it had anything to do with her."

"I can't blame her, I guess. It would be strange."

"Yes."

"It's funny, you're summarizing for me Vlad's report to you about his conversations with others, which is three steps removed from the actual conversations, but I can still almost hear him talking."

"You miss him, don't you?"

"I—"

"He misses you, Cawti."

"Let's not start on that, all right?"

"If you wish."

"It's complicated, Kiera. It's difficult. I don't know any of the answers. Yes, I miss him. But we couldn't live together."

"He's changed, you know."

"Are you trying to get us back together, Kiera?"

"I don't know. I think at least he should know about—"

"Let's not talk about it."

"All right. Maybe I should summarize even more."

"No, you're doing fine."

"I have to say, though, that I don't have a very good memory for conversations, so a lot of this I'm reconstructing and making up. But you get the gist of it."

"I do indeed. You must have had a few words for him when he got back to the house. I know I would have."

"Oh, yes."

7

"WELL," I SAID SLOWLY. "Congratulations, Vlad."

He looked at me and waited for the punch line.

I said, "You've now not only got the Jhereg after you but also the Empire, and, as soon as they tie you to the documents we stole, the House of the Orca will want you, too—and me, by the way. That leaves only fourteen more Houses to go and you'll have the set. Then you can start on the Easterners and the Serioli. Good work."

"It's a talent," he said. "I can't take credit for it."

I studied him while considering his story. He was looking—I don't know, *smug* wasn't quite right, but maybe something like, *amused with a veneer of self-satisfaction.* Sometimes I forget just how devious he is, and how good he is at improvising, and his skill at calculating odds and pulling off improbable gambits. Sometimes he thinks he's better at these things than he actually is, and it is likely to get him killed one of these days—especially now, when, between the gold and the black Phoenix Sx he wears, he is entirely cut off from those who would be most willing and able to help him.

"All right," I said. "Either Fyres was murdered or the Empire is afraid Fyres was murdered, and, in either case, the Empire doesn't want it known."

"Someone in the Empire," Vlad amended.

"No," I said. "The Empire."

"You mean the Empress—"

"I wouldn't say the Empress knows, but it doesn't matter either way."

"I don't understand."

"If it isn't the Empress, it's someone almost as important, and it's with the cooperation of the highest level of government."

"What makes you so sure? An hour ago you didn't even believe—"

"Your story was very convincing," I said. "And you told me things you probably didn't know you were telling me." I frowned. "The way Loftis talked to Domm, and the way Domm and Timmer talked to each other, tell me—"

"That Timmer doesn't—or, perhaps, *didn't*—know about it."

"That's not the point, Vlad. They were acting under orders, and they have support that not only goes high, it goes broad—widespread. At the Imperial level, too many people are involved for there to be just one person pulling the strings from behind a closet."

"Hmmm. I see your point. But with that many involved, how can it stay secret?"

"There's secret, and then there's secret, Vlad. If, in a year or two, the Empress starts to hear whispers about so-and-so having pulled a scam in the Fyres's investigation, there won't be much she can do about it, depending on who so-and-so is."

"In other words, it can leak, as long as it doesn't break."

"Something like that." I shrugged. "I'm just speculating, based on what I know about the Court, but it's a pretty good guess. You know," I added, "you're in over your head, Vlad. I'd call for help."

Vlad laughed without humor. "Call for help? From whom? Sethra Lavode? She's taken on the whole Empire before. You think she'd do it now? Without knowing why, or what's involved? And just what exactly are Iceflame and the power of Dzur Mountain going to do against a snotty little intrigue? Or maybe you mean Morrolan. He could solve the whole thing by inviting our hostess to move into Castle Black, but I don't think she'll go for it, and he doesn't have any connections in the House of the Orca. Aliera would love to go charging into this, Kiera, but subtlety isn't her strong suit—she'd just kill everyone who was acting dirty, and we'd have the same mess with a bunch of bodies to complicate things. Norathar would be the one who could solve it—if this was the Dragon Reign. But, last I heard, Zerika is still on the throne—at least technically."

I didn't quite know how to answer that, so I didn't. He said, "And remember, I don't really care what the Empire is doing or to whom, as long I can do what I promised Hid—Hwid—the old woman I'd do and she can help Savn. Do you care?"

That was tough. I *did* care—but . . . "No," I said. "You're right. But it may be that we have to deal with the whole thing in order to solve our little problem. I don't know."

"Neither do I," said Vlad.

"What do we know, then?"

"We know the Empire is covering up something—very possibly murder. We know that not all of the investigators know about it, and we know that not all of the ones who do are happy about it, but that the orders include killing anyone who knows what's going on. We know that there is a big tangle about who owns what parts of Fyres's property, and that finding out who owns this blue cottage and its environs is not going to be easy. And we know that something, somewhere, is very wrong."

"Wrong how?" I said.

"The timing—it's funny and I'm not laughing."

"Go on," I said, though I was starting to realize that I knew—that I'd been subconsciously aware of something being strange about how things had been happening.

"What's the hurry? When someone as rich as Fyres dies, it's sort of expected to take fifty or a hundred or two hundred years to sort out who owns what. But they're not only putting a coat of paint over this investigation, they're doing it in an awful hurry. And not just the Empire—everyone associated with it."

"What do you mean by everyone?"

"I mean," he said carefully, "that Fyres had been dead for maybe a week when our hostess was told to vacate, and she was given six months in which to do it. Now, that doesn't make any sense at all, unless there are two things going on: one, the land is valuable somehow; and, two, someone, somewhere, is panicking."

I nodded. Yeah, that was it. I said, "Almost. I agree about the panic, but the land doesn't have to be particularly valuable."

"Oh? Then why—"

"Someone wants to take it, get as much cash as he can for it, and be gone before it comes out that it wasn't his land to sell in the first place."

"Ah," said Vlad. "Yes, that makes sense." He thought for a moment. "Unfortunately, it doesn't help—it doesn't point to anyone in particular, and it doesn't even eliminate anyone."

"True," I said.

"Which still leaves us with the problem of finding out, which, in turn, brings up the next question: What now?"

I was able to answer that one, anyway. "Now," I said, "we sleep on it. It's late, and my brain is tired. We'll talk again in the morning."

"Okay. Meet here?"

"Yes."

"I'll cook breakfast."

"I'll bring something to cook."

"It's a pleasure working with you, Kiera."

I SPENT THE NIGHT trying to make sense of everything I'd learned; I'd have bet Juinan's Pearl against a pound of tea that Vlad did the same. And I'd have won, judging by the look on his face when I got there the next morning.

"Not much sleep?" I suggested sweetly.

He scowled and went back to making klava. I put the groceries on the counter next to him and said, "Goose eggs, sneershrimp, endive, cynth, orange and black fungus, and various sweet and hot peppers. Also a pound of flatbread. Make breakfast."

"Onions?"

"She has them growing in back."

"Garlic?"

"Hanging in a basket about six centimeters from your right hand. Observant, aren't we?"

"You can talk to Loiosh," he said.

Loiosh, curled up with Rocza near the cold hearth, twitched and probably said something to Vlad. Hwdf'rjaanci emerged from the back, toweling her hair dry. "You've made the klava," she said.

"Yeah," said Vlad. "I hope it isn't too strong."

"Don't make jokes," she said.

Savn was still wrapped up in his furs, but he was awake and staring at the ceiling. I noticed that Vlad was looking at him, too. The old woman said, "I'm going to go in today."

I heard Vlad's sharp intake of breath—or maybe it was mine. "Dreamwalk?" I said.

"No, I'm just going to heal the physical damage. There isn't much of it, and I've looked carefully—it won't hurt him, and it might start the healing process."

Vlad nodded, turned back to the kitchen, and began to prepare breakfast. Hwdf'rjaanci sat on the floor near Savn's head. I chopped things and sampled them. He didn't make any comments about my doing so, which meant either he was unique in my experience with cooks, or he was distracted, or he was uncomfortable because no one had done that since he and Cawti had broken up. I felt a little bad for him, but not bad enough to stop sampling things. The peppers were exquisite.

He said, "There are few sounds more beautiful than that made by a mess of onions landing on a cast-iron skillet with a layer of hot oil. The trick is getting them to just the right degree of done before you start adding other things, and then to not let them go too much further before you add the eggs—the eggs have to be last because they don't take as long—"

"What's on your mind, Vlad?"

He shrugged. "The same thing that's on yours, of course—are we going to be able to solve our hostess's problem without taking on, in effect, the whole Empire? And, if we do have to take on the Empire, how can we win? It's bound to be tricky."

"Tricky," I said. I shook my head. "You're nothing if not confident."

He shrugged. "It shouldn't be any problem. I'll just work my way through these special Guardsmen, find out who their boss is, kill him, take his position, use that to get close to the Empress, kill her, take the Orb, and rule Dragaera myself, exploiting the Empire ruthlessly in order to enrich myself and punish those who have offended me throughout my life, in preparation for conquering the East and eventually making myself ruler of the entire world." He paused from whipping the eggs, looked at me, and nodded somberly. "*Then* I'd meet some girls, I'll bet." He covered the pan. "Want to set the table for four?"

"Three," said our hostess, who was still seated next to the boy but was now staring down at him while holding both of his shoulders. "Savn will be needing his rest."

I looked at her, then at Savn, then at Vlad, who was looking at me. I opened my mouth to speak and then felt the casting of a spell. Vlad apparently felt it, too, or more accurately Loiosh did; in any case we both turned to watch, then looked again at each other. Vlad's eyes were a bit wide, but he shrugged.

"Don't let the food burn," I said.

"I shan't," said Vlad, and turned his attention back to the skillet. I set the table. The feeling of sorcery went away about two minutes after it had started, and then the old woman joined us at the table and we ate.

302Steven Brust

She didn't seem quite comfortable with Loiosh and Rocza joining us and eating scraps from Vlad's plate, even though she should have been used to it by now. But she didn't say anything. Buddy sat next to the table and spoke most eloquently with his eyes but got nothing for his trouble, poor beast. The food was good and there was no conversation for quite some time, until I noticed that Vlad was watching me.

I said, "What is it?"

"Don't you care for it?"

"Are you fishing for compliments?"

"No."

I shrugged. "I like it quite a bit."

"All right," he said.

I don't know anyone like Vlad: it's like his mind never shuts off. Even Morrolan relaxes from time to time, but I've never seen Vlad when he wasn't thinking. I very much wanted to know what he was thinking about just then, but there was no polite way to ask.

Vlad broke down before I did. He said, "Well, Mother?"

She said, "Yes?"

He cleared his throat. "How did—that is, is Savn all right?"

"You mean his injury?"

"Yes."

"Yes, I healed it. It isn't difficult if you know what you're doing. I'm not really a physicker, but I am a sorceress"—she looked at me as she said it, as if expecting me to argue—"and this is the sort of problem I'm most familiar with."

"So it went well?" asked Vlad. Vlad needing reassurance was something outside of my experience.

"Quite well."

"Uh, good," he said.

"What now?" I asked her.

"Now? Well, repairing the physical damage ought to help him, so now we see if there's any change in his behavior—better or worse. If not, then I'll go back to trying to understand the inside of his head well enough to risk a dreamwalk. If there is a change, well, then we'll just have to see what the change is and do our best from there."

"Oh," said Vlad. He glanced at Savn, who was sleeping peacefully, and fell silent.

We finished eating, and Vlad and I cleaned up. I took my time, because I wasn't in a hurry to go back to talking about how we were going to approach the problem. Vlad also seemed to be moving a bit slowly, I suspect for the same reason. I drew the water, he set it to heating, then we took our time sorting things that went into the compost from things to be burned and things to feed to Buddy. When the water was hot, I started in on the dishes. Vlad cleaned the table and the stove.

As we were finishing up, I said, "How's the arm?"

"Fine."

"Let's take a look at it."

"When did you become a physicker?"

"One learns a bit of everything in my line of work—or in yours."

"Yeah."

He took his shirt off. His chest was still full of hairs; I tried not to react. I unwrapped the bandage. Some people look at their wounds, others look away. Vlad looked, but he seemed a bit queasy. The lower wrappings of the bandage were bloody, but not horribly so, and the wound itself showed no signs of infection.

I said, "If you want to take the Phoenix Stone off, I can have that healed up in—"

"No, thanks," said Vlad.

"You're probably right," I said.

I washed it and rewrapped it. Hwdf'rjaanci watched but made no effort to help—maybe blood made her queasy; maybe she considered herself too much of a specialist to be bothered with simple wounds.

I said, "Okay, if you've changed your mind about ruling the world, and you don't want to ask anyone for help, what's our next step?"

"I went through the notes again last night, after you left," said Vlad.

"And?"

"And nothing. If we had all the files as well as the Imperial record, and maybe some of the records of a few Jhereg, and we combined those with what we've got, and we had a hundred accountants working full-time, we could probably find the answer—and maybe even find it soon enough to do some good. But we don't, so we're going to have to start from the other end."

"And the other end is?"

"The investigation. We have a piece of something—all I can think of to do is follow it and see where it leads."

I nodded. "Yeah. I was afraid it was going to come to that."

"Meanwhile," he said, "I'm going to see just how much money it will take to buy the land."

I nodded. "Yes. The amount should tell us if you're right about there being something valuable about this piece of property. If it comes down to nothing more than finding a sum of money, there are ways to do that."

I noticed Hwdf'rjaanci looking at us. Vlad said, "That, of course, is my end of things. What do you want to do?"

"I want to find out just who Loftis is working for, what his orders are, what he knows, what he guesses, and what he plans to do about it," I said.

"Good thinking," said Vlad. "How do you plan to go about it?"

"I don't know. I thought maybe I'd ask him."

"I can't see why that wouldn't work."

"Yeah."

"Then let's do it," said Vlad.

I finished bandaging him, and he put his shirt on, then his cloak, then his sword belt. He petted Buddy, recommended the cottage to him, collected Loiosh, and left with a sweeping bow.

"They're disgusting," said Hwdf'rjaanci.

"Who?"

"Easterners," she said.

I said, "Ah. I'll tell him you said so, Mother."

"Oh don't," she said, looking suddenly distressed. "It would hurt his feelings."

I collected my things and stepped out of the door. Unlike Vlad, I had no reason not to teleport, so I did, arriving at a place I knew where I could change my garb a little, which I did. I arrived outside of City Hall at just about the tenth hour, which was when things ought to begin moving there. I took a position across the street, became inconspicuous, and waited.

I'd been there for more than an hour when Vlad showed up and went in, and then nothing happened for quite some time, and I was beginning to think I'd missed Loftis—that he'd gotten in early—when I saw him on the other side of the street, just approaching; from Vlad's description, it had to be Loftis. I crossed over and walked past him, and even that brief a glance was enough to confirm that Vlad was right—this wasn't someone to mess around with casually. He was frowning as he walked, like he had something on his mind; it wasn't hard to guess what it was.

I found an inn that let rooms by the hour and rented one—this is a good way to find a place where you won't be disturbed and won't be talked about, even if you don't use the room for the reasons they expect you to. They had put in a real door, to ensure the guests had privacy, and

I liked that, too. Instead of a tag, it was Loftis's papers and possessions that I spread out on the bed; then I commenced to study them. He had not, in fact, been polite enough to be carrying a note that spelled out what he'd been asked to do, the reasons behind it, and the name of his superior officer, but we make do with what we have, and the pouch of an Imperial investigator can hardly fail to be revealing.

His name was, indeed, Loftis, a Dragonlord of the e'Drien line, same as Morrolan; and he was the Viscount of Clovenrocks Wood, which was in a far northeastern province, if I could trust a memory that wasn't my own. He had three Signets. I knew he'd have at least one, I was counting on it—but three indicated he was, indeed, high up in the counsels of the great and powerful who ran the Empire. And the oldest of the Signets— which included authorization to make arrests—was two hundred years old, which meant he'd have to have been in the Imperial Service at least two hundred and fifty years, which is a long time to only be a lieutenant— unless, of course, he was in one of those branches of the service where traditional ranks were meaningless, which would explain the irony Vlad had detected when he and Domm had called each other by their ranks.

I knew about four such services, all of them more or less independent. Well, there was a fifth, but that hadn't existed in some years except for one person—and whoever Loftis was, he wasn't Sethra Lavode. I considered the four services I knew about, and speculated uncomfortably about the possibility of there being one I hadn't heard of.

One of them was the Imperial Surveillance Corps. They were responsible to the Prime Minister, when there was one, or to the Minister of the Houses when there wasn't. The Minister of the Houses was presently an Issola named Indus, and I'd play cards with her only as long as she never got near the deck. She was tricky, but she was loyal—she'd do something like this if she was ordered to, and it might well fall within her province, but the order would have to come from Zerika. If anyone but the Empress tried to use Indus . . . well, anyone who knew enough about her to ask would know better than to try. So either it wasn't Indus, or the order came from the Empress, and I was convinced the order hadn't come from the Empress.

The same argument applied to "Third Floor Relic," which was named for the room where they supposedly met with Her Majesty. There were only about twenty or thirty of them at any one time, and, while they were very good at what they did, it took the Empress's orders to get them to do it. Also, it seemed unlikely that they'd be involved in something this widespread—narrow and specific objectives were more their style.

The other two units I knew about were both part of the military. One of them, the one that was publicly acknowledged to exist, was Division Six of the Imperial Army General Staff Consultants. They did most of their work on foreign soil, but could certainly be used in the Empire if the situation warranted. They were big, unwieldy, often confused, sometimes brilliant, and responsible to the Warlord. The Warlord wouldn't allow them to be used this way if the Empress didn't approve, but they were big enough that it just might be possible for someone in the hierarchy to have been corrupted. If it *was* Division Six, though, they'd be unlikely to be able to keep it secret very long—at least, not secret from those who knew where to look.

And then there was the Special Tasks Group, which was small, very well trained, easily capable of covering up mistakes by the other groups (and was often used for exactly that), and, in fact, perfect for jobs like this. But *they* reported to Lord Khaavren—he would never allow them to be used this way without orders from the Empress, and if the Empress did give such an order, he'd have another one of his temper tantrums and resign again.

I chewed it over as I put the contents of Loftis's pouch back together. Then I sat on the bed (the only piece of furniture in the room) and continued thinking it over. There were good reasons why it couldn't be any of those groups, but it seemed very unlikely that there was another team involved that I hadn't heard of—I keep very well abreast of what's happening around the Palace, on both sides of the walls, as they say.

I tried to remember everything Vlad had told me about his dealings with the group, including every nuance of expression he'd picked up. Of course, it isn't easy when you're twice removed from the conversation. And I didn't have long to figure it out, either. I checked the time. No, I didn't have long at all.

I went over all the information again and shook my head. If I had to guess, I'd say Surveillance, just because it involved the Empire and the House of the Orca and, above all, because under normal circumstances they're the ones who would conduct such an investigation—being checked up on, no doubt, by the Third Floor group. But it still didn't make sense. Could it be Division Six? While they were the most likely in that they'd think they could get away with it, they just didn't have the reputation for switching so easily from pulling cover-up jobs to rough stuff—they were mostly a bunch of clerks with a big budget, some half-competent thieves, and a lot of people who knew how to spread money around. No, Surveillance was more likely, only I had trouble squaring that with what I knew about Lady Indus—if a request like that fell into her lap, she'd—

Now, what did that remind me of?

Or we could just dump the whole thing on Papa-cat's lap.

That had been a threat. A threat to tell the man in charge what they were doing—which meant, first, that, although they were acting under orders, they weren't acting under orders of their own chief. And, second, that the man in charge was, in fact, a man, which neatly eliminated Indus.

Papa-cat.

Cat.

Tiassa.

Lord Khaavren.

As Vlad would say, "Ah ha."

There was the sound of heavy boots outside the room, and the door went crashing down. I was looking at a man and a woman, both of whom had swords drawn and pointed at me. I tossed the purse to the man and said, "In the first place, Loftis, tell Timmer to go back to City Hall, it's you I want to talk to. And in the second place, you'll be paying for that door out of your own pocket; I don't think Papa-cat will authorize it when he hears what it's for—*if* he hears what it's for."

They stared at me.

I said, "Well? What are you waiting for? Lose your associate, come in here, and sit down. Oh, Ensign, on your way out, set up a sound field around this room—I assume you're equipped for that, aren't you? And take care of anyone who might be coming up to look into the noise of the door breaking. Tell the host it's all right and your friend will pay for the damages. Which he will," I added.

She looked at Loftis. He gave her a bit of a half-smile, as if to say, "Whatever this is, it's bound to be good," then nodded. She gave me one quick glance, and I could see her committing me to memory, then she was gone. Loftis came in and leaned against the far wall, still holding his sword.

I said, "Put that thing away."

He said, "Sure. As soon as you explain why I shouldn't arrest you."

I rolled my eyes. "You think I'm a thief?"

He shook his head. "I *know* you're a thief—and quite an accomplished one, since you got this off me just passing in the street. But I don't know what *else* you are."

I shrugged. "I'm a thief, Lieutenant. I'm a thief who happens to know

your name, your rank, your associate's name and rank, and that you work
for Lord Khaavren's Special Tasks Group; and I'm so stupid that I took
your purse but didn't bother with a spell to prevent you from tracing the
Signets, didn't *ditch* the Signets, but instead just sat here waiting for you
to arrive so I could hand the purse back to you. That's right, Lieutenant,
I'm a thief."

He shrugged. "When someone starts reeling off what he knows like
that, it always makes me wonder if I'm supposed to be so impressed that
I'll start reeling things off, too. What do you say?"

He wasn't stupid. "That you're not stupid. But you're still pointing a
sword at me, and I find that irritating."

"Learn to live with it. Who are you and what do you want? If you
really went through all of that just to get me here, you're either very
foolish or you have some explanation that—"

"Do you remember a certain affair three or four years ago, that started
out with Division Six looking into the activities of a wizard working for,
uh, a foreign kingdom, and ending up with a Jenoine at Dzur Mountain."

He stared at me, licked his lips, and said, "I've heard about it."

"Do you remember what you—your group—was assigned to do after
Division Six had bungled it?"

He watched me very closely. "Yes," he said.

"That's what I'm here to do, only this time it's you who are making a
mess of things."

He was silent for a moment. "Possible," he said.

"Then let's talk. I'm not armed—"

He laughed. "Sure you're not. And Temping had no reserves at the
Battle of Plowman's Bridge."

I raised my eyebrows at him. He said, "Eighth Cycle, two hundred and
fifth year of the Tiassa Reign, the Whetstone Rising. The Warlord was—"

"I am not, in fact, armed," I cut him off. "At least, not with a conventional weapon."

He raised his eyebrows back at me.

I said, "What I've got for armament is a letter, being held quite safely,
that is ready to go to Her Majesty if I fail to appear. The object, in fact,
doesn't have anything to do with you, it's to make sure certain influential
parties are disassociated from this affair, and appear clean when it blows
up. What it will do to your career is, in fact, just a side effect, but that
won't change how it hits you when Lord Khaavren learns what you've
been up to. You know him better than I do, my dear lieutenant—what

will he do? And it won't help to try to keep the letter from reaching the Imperial Palace the way you, or your people, did in the Berdoign business, because the letter is already in the Palace. I think that's better than a conventional weapon, under the circumstances, don't you?"

"You are very well informed," he said. I could see him wondering if I was lying, then deciding he couldn't take the chance. He smiled, bowed his head slightly, and sheathed his sword. "Let's talk, then," he said. "I'm listening."

"Good. We'll start with the basics. You've been given an assignment that you dislike—"

He snorted. " 'Dislike' would cover it," he said, "if stretched very thin."

"Nevertheless," I continued, "you're doing what you were instructed to do. Whatever else you are, you're a soldier."

He shrugged.

I said, "I represent, as I said, certain interests very close to, but not quite the same as, those who required you to carry out this mission. I would prefer that our efforts were combined, to a limited extent, because my job, to put it simply, is to clean up after your efforts to clean up. I have a certain hold on you, but not, I know, a strong one—"

"You got that right," he said, smiling.

"—in that you'd prefer Lord Khaavren didn't learn what you're up to."

"Don't think you can push that too far, lady," he said.

"I know how far I can push it."

"Maybe. And what do I call you, by the way?"

"Margaret," I said. "I fancy Eastern names."

"Heh. You and Her Majesty."

He'd thrown that out, I assumed, to see if I was up on current gossip; I gave him a slight smile to show that I was. He said, "Very well, then, Margaret. For whom do you work?"

"For whom do *you* work?"

"But you know that—or, at least, you laid out a theory which I haven't disputed."

"No, I've told you that I know the organization you work for, not where the orders came from to slide through the Fyres's investigation."

"So do you know who gave those orders?"

"Why don't you tell me, Loftis?"

He smiled. "So we've found a piece of information you lack."

"Maybe," I said, returning his smile. "And maybe I'm just trying to find out if you're planning to be straight with me."

"Trade?" he suggested.

"No," I said. "You'd lie. I'd lie. Besides, in point of fact, I know, anyway."

"Oh?"

"There's only one possibility."

He looked inscrutable. "If you say so."

I shrugged.

He said, "All right, then. What do you want?"

"As I told you before, cooperation."

"What sort of cooperation? Be specific. You don't want to share information, because we'd both lie, and because you don't seem to need any, and because there's really nothing I need to know. So what *do* you want, exactly?"

"Wrong on several counts," I said.

"Oh?"

"As I told you, I'm here to keep this business from getting out of hand. I'll blow the whistle on you if I have to, but I, and those who've given me this job, would prefer I didn't. Now, what we have—"

"What cleanup are you talking about, Margaret?"

"Oh, come on, Loftis. Your security's been broken all over town. Didn't you just have someone show up out of nowhere, interrogate your interrogators, lead your shadows all over the region, pump them some more, and then almost kill them in a public inn? Is that your idea of secrecy?"

He studied me carefully, and I wondered if I'd gone too far. He grunted and said, "My compliments on your sources, Margaret."

"Well?"

"Okay, you've made your point. What do you want?"

"Let's start with the basics," I said. "I have to know what I'm working with."

"Heh," he said. "There's something you don't know?"

I smiled. "How many on your team?"

"Six, with another three on standby."

"How many know what you're up to?"

"Domm and I."

"And Timmer," I added, "as of last night."

He frowned. "Are you sure?"

I shrugged. "She may not know precisely, but she knows something's up, and, if she thinks about it, she'll probably figure out most of it. She isn't stupid."

He nodded. "Okay. What else do you want to know?"

"What actually happened to Fyres."

Loftis shrugged. "He was murdered."

I shook my head. "I know that. But who killed him?"

"An assassin. A good one. Hundred to one it was a Jhereg, and another hundred to one that we wouldn't catch him even if we were trying to."

"Yeah," I said. "Okay. Who had it done?"

"I don't know," said Loftis. "That isn't what we were trying to find out."

"Sure, but you probably have an idea."

"An idea? Hell, yeah. His wife hated him, his son loathed him, one daughter wants to be rich and the other one wants to be left alone. Is that good enough for a start?"

"No," I said.

He looked at me, then turned away. "Yeah, it wasn't them. Or, at least, it wasn't just them."

"Well, then?"

"The House of the Orca, I think. And the Jhereg. And someone, somewhere, high up in the Empire—like, maybe, whoever it was who hired you?" He'd slipped his right hand down behind his leg, where he was, no doubt, concealing something, and I hadn't even seen him do it.

"No," I said. "But good guess."

He shrugged. "What else do you want to know?"

I wanted to know how Loftis had been conned, or pressured, into doing this in the first place, but this was the wrong time to ask. I said, "That'll do for now. I'll be in touch."

"Okay. Pleasure meeting you, Margaret."

"And you, Lieutenant."

I got up and walked out of the room, my back itching as I passed him, but he made no move. On the way out of the inn, I flipped the host a couple of imperials and apologized about the door. I walked around some corners to make sure I wasn't being followed, then I teleported back to the blue cottage and went in.

Vlad was waiting for me. He said, "Well?"

One disadvantage of teleports is that they sometimes get you there too quickly—I hadn't had time to sort out my thoughts yet. I said, "Is there anything to eat?"

"No. I could cook something."

I nodded. "That would be good. I'm a bit tired."

"Oh?" said Vlad.

"I'll get to it."

He shrugged. Savn was near the hearth, sitting up and looking at nothing. Hwdf'rjaanci sat hear him, with Buddy at her feet. Buddy watched me as he always did, but wasn't unfriendly. Loiosh sat on Vlad's shoulder. I felt like I'd been through a pitched battle, and it was somehow amazing that no one in the house shared my exhaustion.

Vlad said, "Do you want to hear my news first, or after yours?"

I said, "Let's look at your arm."

Vlad shrugged, started to speak, and then apparently realized that I wasn't ready to think about anything quite yet. He wordlessly took off his shirt. I undid the bandage and inspected the wound, which seemed about the same as it had four hours earlier.

Only four hours!

I washed it and walked over to the linen chest to find something clean to wrap it in.

"It's fine," I said.

"I suppose so," said Vlad.

"You've been stabbed," said Savn.

8

EVEN BUDDY—TAIL THUMPING and floppy ears vainly trying to prick forward—was staring at him. He, in turn, was staring at Vlad's arm—an intense stare, a creepy stare; he was standing up, his whole body rigid. Savn's voice had the uneven rasp of long disuse, or of young adulthood, take your pick. He said, "You were stabbed with a knife."

"That's right, Savn," said Vlad, and I could hear him working to keep his voice even. He didn't move a muscle. Hwdf'rjaanci wasn't moving, either; for that matter, neither was I.

"Was it really cold when it went in? Did it hurt? How deep did it go?"

Vlad made some odd sort of sound from his throat. Savn's questions came slowly, as if there was a great deal of consideration behind them; but the tone was of casual curiosity, which in turn was at odds with his posture—it was very unsettling for me, and I could see that it was even more so for Vlad.

"Not all knives have points, you know," said Savn. "Some of them you can't stab with, only *cut*." As he said that word, he made a quick cutting gesture with his right hand; and that was creepy, too, because while he did it the rest of his body didn't move, and his face didn't change expression; it was only the arm movement and the emphasis in his voice.

"Only cut," he said again.

Then he didn't say anything else. We waited, not moving, for several

minutes, but he'd said what he had to say. Vlad said, "Savn?" and got
no response. Savn sat down again, but that also showed something—he
hadn't been told to. Vlad came over and knelt down facing him. "Savn?
Are you . . . are you all right?"

The boy just sat the way he'd been sitting all along. Vlad turned and
said, "What happened, Mother?"

"I don't know," she said. "But I think it's a good sign. I know it's a
good sign. I don't know how good, but we're getting somewhere."

"You think that came from healing the injury?"

"Maybe. Or maybe it was time. Or the right stimulus. Or some combination. Have you been cut in the last year?"

"Not even threatened," said Vlad.

"Then that may be it."

"What do we do now? Should I cut myself some more?" I wasn't certain he was joking.

"I'm not sure," she said. "Talk about knives, maybe."

I was watching Savn the whole time, and at the word "knives" there
was a perceptible twitch around the left side of his mouth. Vlad saw it,
too. He said, "Savn, do you want to talk about knives?"

The boy's expression didn't change, but he said, "You have to take care
of the good ones. A good knife is expensive. The good ones stay sharp
longer, too. Sometimes you have to cut people to heal them, and you
should use a really good one, and a really sharp one for that. You can
hurt someone more with a dull knife than with a sharp knife."

"Are you afraid of knives?" said Vlad.

Savn didn't seem to hear him. He said, "You should always clean it
when you're done—wash it and dry it. You have to dry it, especially. It
won't rust—the good ones are made so they don't rust. But if you leave
something on it, it can corrode, and that ruins it, and good knives are
expensive. Good knives stay sharp. They get sharper and sharper the more
they're used, until they get so sharp they can cut you right in half just by
looking at you."

"Knives don't get sharper on their own," said Vlad.

"And they can stab you, too. If the point is sharp, it can stab all the
way through you, and all the way through everybody, and stab the sky
until it falls, and stab all the way through everything."

Then he fell silent once more. After a couple of minutes, Vlad turned
around and said, "He isn't responding to what I say, Mother."

"No," she said. "But you got him started. That means, on some level,
he is responding to you."

Vlad turned back and looked at him some more. I tried to read the expression on Vlad's face, then decided I didn't want to.

He got up and came over to where Hwdf'rjaanci and I stood watching. He whispered to her, "Should I try again, or let him rest?"

She frowned. "Let him rest, I think. If he starts up again on his own, we'll take it from there."

"Doing what?" I said.

"I don't know. I'm encouraged, but I don't know."

"All right," said Vlad. "I'm going to make some klava."

By the time it was done, Savn had gone to sleep—perhaps talking for the first time after a year's silence had tired him out. We drank our klava standing on the far side of the room, near the stove and the oven. Hwdf'rjaanci eventually went over and sat down next to the boy, watching him while he slept. Vlad took a deep breath and said, "All right, let's hear it."

"Huh? Hear what?"

He laughed. "What you came in with an hour ago, and were so excited about that you had to take some time before you could talk about it. Remember?"

"Oh." I felt myself smiling. "Oh, that."

"Yeah. Let's hear it."

I nodded and gave him the short version, which took about ten minutes. He said, "Let's have it all."

"Do you really need it?"

"I won't know until I hear it."

I was going to argue, but then I realized that if he'd given me the short version of his sortie, I wouldn't have made the connection to Lord Khaavren, and my talk with Loftis would have gone rather differently. So I filled in most of the details, helped now and then by Vlad's questions. He seemed especially interested in exactly when everything had happened and in precisely how I'd fooled Loftis—that, in particular, he wanted me to go over several times, until I felt like I was being questioned under the Orb. I pleaded poor memory for the parts of it I didn't want to talk about and eventually he relented, but when I was done, he looked at me oddly.

"What is it?" I said.

"Eh? Oh, nothing, Kiera. I'm just impressed—I didn't know you had that in you."

"The deception or remembering the details?"

"Both, actually."

I shrugged. "And how was your day?"

"Much shorter, much simpler, much easier to report, and probably more mystifying."

"Oh?"

"In a word: they're closed."

"Huh?"

"Gone. Finished. Doors locked, signs gone."

"Who is?"

"All of them: Northport Securities, Brugan Exchange, Westman—all of them."

"The whole building?"

"About three-quarters of the building, near as I can tell—but all of the companies that were part of Fyres's little empire are gone."

"Verra! What did you do?"

"I went to City Hall—remember, you saw me there?"

"Yes, but for what?"

"Well, the building was still open; I thought I'd find out who owned it."

"Good thinking. And who owns the building?"

"A company called Dion and Sons Management."

"And?"

He shrugged. "And they're located right in the same building, and they're out of business, too."

"Oh."

"Yeah. So much for bright ideas."

"Well, what now, Vlad?"

"I don't know. How can they sell the land if the company that claims ownership doesn't exist? If they can't, we could just forget the whole thing right now; all we're really trying to accomplish is to keep the old woman on her land. But I'm afraid that, if we do that, someone will show up—"

"Is that it?"

"What do you mean and why are you smiling?"

"I just have a feeling that you're hooked on this thing now—you have to find out what's going on for its own sake."

He smiled. "You think so? Well, you may be right, I *am* curious, but you show me some proof that our hostess here is going to be able to keep her lovely blue cottage and I'll be gone so fast you'll only feel the breeze."

"Heh."

He shrugged. "What about you?"

"Me?"

"Yeah. Aren't you curious?"

"Oh, heavens yes. That's a big part of why I signed onto this. But I'm willing to admit it, and you—"

"Yeah, well, ask me again tomorrow and I might give you a different answer. Meanwhile—"

"Yes. Meanwhile, what next?"

"Well, any interest in starting at the top and trying to find out who in the Empire is behind all this?"

"No."

"Me, neither." He thought for a minute. "Well, I'm not sure if I've gotten anywhere with the daughters, so we can't count on that for anything, but we've got one foot in the door with our dear friend from the Tasks Group—thanks to you. And we've got another foot in the door with the Jhereg—thanks to you. So how about if we try for a third foot—anatomically interesting, if nothing else—and triangulate?"

"What did you have in mind?"

"Finding this bank that closed down."

I thought it over. "Not bad. Just keep worrying away at different sides of the problem and see what gives?"

He spread his hands. "That's all I can think of."

"It makes sense. Do you want me to do it?"

He nodded. "I think you'll be more effective dealing with bankers than I will. I'm going to hang tight right here, and see if I can do Savn any good."

He said it conversationally, but I could tell there was a lot of tension behind the words. I spoke lightly, saying, "Yes, that makes sense. I'll see what I can find."

"After lunch," he suggested.

Lunch, on this occasion, involved a loaf of bread which was hollowed out and filled with some kind of reddish sauce that had large chunks of this and that in it, featuring pieces of chicken with the skin but without the bones. Savn sat at the table with us, eating mechanically and appearing, once more, oblivious to everything around him. This dampened the conversation a bit. It seemed odd that Savn happily used the knife in front of him to eat with and didn't seem at all put out or unduly fascinated by it, but the ways of the mind are strange, I guess.

I suggested to Vlad that if the Jhereg really wanted to find him, all they had to do was keep track of garlic consumption throughout the Empire. He suggested that I not spread the idea around, because he'd as soon let them find him as quit eating garlic.

Then we got onto business. I said, "Mother, you said the bank closed?"

She nodded.

"Which bank?"

She glanced at me, then at Vlad, opened her mouth, closed it, shrugged, and said, "Northport Private Services Bank. Are you going to rob it?"

"If it's closed," I said, "I doubt there's any money in it—or anything else for that matter."

"Probably," said Vlad. Then he frowned. "Unless . . ."

"Unless what?"

"I'm remembering something."

I waited.

He said, "That gossip sheet, *Rutter's Rag,* said something about the banks."

"Yes?"

"It made a point of how quickly everyone got out of there." He turned to Hwdf'rjaanci. "Do you know anything about that, Mother?"

She said, "I know it closed down fast. My friend Henbrook—it was her bank, too, and I don't know *what* she's going to do—anyway, she was in town that day, and she said they were open just like usual at thirteen o'clock, and at fourteen there were these wagons there—the big wagons, with armed guards and everything—and by noon it was shut up tight."

Vlad nodded. "Two hours. They took two hours to clear the place out."

Hwdf'rjaanci agreed. "They had a hundred men, and wagons lined up all down the street. And the other banks, too, went the same way, at the same time, near as I can tell."

"In which case," said Vlad, "they can't have done a very good job of it."

"What do you mean?"

"I mean clearing things out. They were in a hurry to be gone before their customers got to them, and—"

"Then why not seal things inside?"

He shrugged. "Too much sorcery floating around. Get people mad enough, and at least one of them will be able to tear down the building."

"Okay," I said. "I'll buy that. But do you really think it likely that there's anything still in there?"

"Oh, I doubt there's any money in it, but you never know what might be left behind."

"You mean, papers and things?"

He nodded.

"If they went under, wouldn't they be careful to clean up anything worth looking at?"

"How much time would it take to clean up every last scrap of paper, Kiera? Could they do it in two hours?"

"Probably not. But all the important ones—"

"Maybe. But maybe not. I don't know how banks operate, but they're bound to generate immense amounts of paperwork, and—"

"And you're willing to wade through immense amounts of paper, just to see if there might be something useful?"

"Right now, any edge we can get amounts to a lot. Yeah, I don't mind taking an evening to go through their wastebaskets—or, rather, papers that missed the wastebaskets—and see if there's something that points us anywhere interesting."

I thought it over for a minute. "You're right," I said. "I'll look around and get what I can; it should be easy enough." I turned to Hwdf'rjaanci. "Where is it?"

"In town," she said. "Stonework Road, near the Potter's Field Road." She gave me more precise directions.

"Okay," I said. "I'll look around it today. Since you're so used to going to City Hall, can you—"

"Find out who owns it? Sure."

"But just get the name and address."

"Right. I should have cooked some vegetables to go with this."

"I wouldn't have had room for them," I said.

"That's true. You don't eat much, do you?"

"I'm trying to keep my slender girlish figure."

"Ah. That's what it is."

We finished, and, since I was doing the dangerous work, I allowed him to volunteer to clean up. Not that there was that much to clean up after Loiosh, Rocza, and Buddy got through with the plates.

"All right," I said, " 'Once more upon the path, and may the wind cry our tale.' "

"Villsni?"

"Kliburr." I headed out the door.

Vlad said, "I don't know how you do it, Kiera."

"Eh? You're the one with all the quotations. I was just imitating you."

"No, not that—teleporting right after a meal. I just don't know how you manage."

*　　*　　*

I MANAGED FINE, BRINGING myself, first, home to Adrilankha to acquire some tools, and then to the same teleport spot I'd used before, it being one of very few I knew in Northport. Then I set out to find the bank, which was easy from the directions I'd been given. I was looking forward to this. I'd never broken into a bank before, and certainly never in the middle of the day; the fact that the bank was now out of business only took a little of the fun away.

And it was, indeed, out of business—there was a large sign on it that spelled out "Permanently Closed," along with the water and hand symbol for those who couldn't read, and there were large boards over all the windows, and bars across the doors. I walked around it once. It was an attractive building, two stories high with a set of six pillars in front, and all done in very fine stonework. It took up about a hundred and forty meters across the front and went back about a hundred and ninety meters, and there were no alleys behind it—just a big cleared area that had become an impromptu produce market since it closed. The cleared area was, no doubt, to make sure that the guards had a good view.

On the other hand, now that it was closed, there seemed to be no security worth mentioning—certainly no one on duty there, and only the most basic and easily defeated alarm spells, proving that there was no money left in it. *Anyone* could have broken into the bank at this stage, and anyone would have done so just the way I was going to—which showed that no one thought there was anything at all of interest there. I shrugged. I'd know soon enough.

One of the devices I'd gotten from home was in the form of a tube that fit snugly into my hand. I palmed it and leaned against the building. I placed the tube against the wall, and in a few seconds I was seeing the inside of the building, and in a few more seconds I was seeing it clearly enough to teleport; no one was looking at me, so I did.

There was a minor spell inside to detect sorcery, so I disabled it before doing a light spell, then I started looking around.

There really isn't any point in going into the details. It was big, and it was empty, and there was a lot of small offices, two vaults, and a basement, and I looked at them all, and it took me about four and a half hours, and at the end of it I had a bag full of scraps of paper. The good news, or the bad news, was that I'd found right away a very large bin full of papers that they'd never gotten around to throwing into the stove—good news because it meant there was a lot of material, bad news because if any of it was important it would have been taken or destroyed. But I wasn't the one who had to go through them all.

I kept them sorted just a bit, in case Vlad would want to know which ones were found where. I knew that most of them, probably all of them, would be worthless, but Vlad would be stuck with going over them, so I had no problem doing the collecting. When I was done, I teleported directly back to the cottage. Buddy, who was outside, started barking when I appeared, but settled down quickly.

"Hey," I told him. "Don't worry. I got the goods."

He wagged his tail.

Vlad came to the door, probably in response to Buddy, and held it open for me. He said, "Well?"

I held up the sack full of papers. "Enjoy."

"No problems?"

"None. How about the boy?"

"He started talking about knives again—this time without any prompting at all. I can't decide if that's good or bad. Maybe it's both. And he's sleeping an awful lot."

I sat down. The boy was asleep. Hwdf'rjaanci was sitting by him, quietly singing what sounded like a lullaby. Vlad accepted the papers. He seemed a bit startled by how heavy the bag was; he weighed it in his hands and whistled appreciatively.

"What did you find out?" I asked him.

"The banker was—or is—Lady Vonnith, House of the Orca, naturally. She owned the bank completely, according to the paperwork at City Hall, which may or may not be reliable. She's also the 'pointer'—whatever that means—for three other banks, one of which has gone under and the other two of which are still solvent, but both of which have issued a 'Hold of Purchase'; again, whatever that is. She lives not too far from Endra." He gave me the address.

"Okay."

"What's a pointer?"

"I don't know where the term came from," I said. "But it means she's in charge of the business, she runs it, even if she doesn't own it. At a guess, she gets a whomping big cut of the profits, or she's a part owner, or, most likely, she's the full owner under a different name."

"Why do that?"

I smiled. "Because if one of her banks files surrender of debts, which just happened, she can keep running the others without the debts of one being assessed against the income of the others, which the Empire is supposed to do."

"Oh. Is that legal?"

"If she isn't caught."

"I see. What is a Hold of Purchase?"

"It means the bank has the right to keep your money."

"Huh?"

"It was a law passed in the twelfth Teckla Reign. It prevents everyone from pulling his money out all at once and driving the bank under. There are all sorts of laws about when it can be invoked, and for how long, and what percentage of their cash they have to release, and to whom, and I don't really understand it myself. But it may mean they're in trouble, or, more likely, it means that with banks going under they're afraid of a general panic and they're taking steps to prevent one."

"They," he repeated. "The owners of the bank, or the Empire?"

"The owners request it, the Empire grants it—or doesn't."

"I see. That's interesting. Who in the Empire would they go to to get such an order?"

"The Minister of the Treasury's office."

"Who's the Minister of the Treasury?"

"His name is Shortisle."

"Shortisle," said Vlad. "Hmmm."

"What?"

"That name came up in Fyres's notes, somewhere. Something about it struck me as odd, but I didn't pay much attention, and now I can't remember what it was. I guess they met for dinner or something."

"Hardly surprising," I said. "The Minister of the Treasury and a major entrepreneur? Sure."

"Yes, but . . . never mind. I'll think about it. House?"

"Shortisle? Orca."

He nodded, and fell into a reverie of contemplation.

"Is there anything else?"

"Huh? Yeah. Go home. I'll go over your booty tonight, which should leave me with, oh, at least half an hour to sleep. Tomorrow you make contact with the banker and see what you can learn."

"All right," I said. "Should I check with you first, to see what you've found out?"

"Yeah. But don't hurry—I want a chance to at least close my eyes and snore once before you show up."

"Okay. Sleep well."

He looked at the bag full of dusty scrap paper in his hand and favored me with a thin smile. Loiosh stretched his wings and hissed, as if he were laughing at us both.

W̲HEN I RETURNED IN the morning, the table near the stove was filled with the papers I'd discovered, all neatly sorted into four stacks, and, if I remembered the quantity correctly, reduced by about three-quarters. Vlad had the bleary-eyed look of someone who had just woken up, and Savn was still asleep by the hearth, Loiosh, Rocza, and Buddy curled up with him. Buddy thumped his tail once, gave a dog yawn, gave a whiny sigh, and put his head down on his paws. There were pieces of charcoal on the floor, more testimony to Vlad's state; the water was boiling, and I could see the klava tin next to it, and Vlad was staring at them like he'd forgotten what they were for.

I said, "What did you learn?"

He said, "Huh?"

"Make the klava."

"Yeah. Right."

"The water goes into the inverted cone sitting on the—"

"I know how to make Verra-be-damned klava."

"Right."

He completed the operation, not spilling any water, which impressed me, then he scowled at the floor and went looking for a broom. I said, "I take it it will be a while before I get my answers."

"Huh? Yeah. Just let me drink a cup of this poison."

"Poison? I thought you liked klava."

"She's out of honey," he said, practically snarling.

"Back in a minute," I said.

By the time the klava was done, I was back with a crock of honey, and Vlad said, "You must be sure to permit me to be cut into pieces for you sometime."

"Been reading Paarfi again?"

"I don't know how to read. In an hour, maybe I'll know how to read."

He put honey into the mugs, pressed the klava, and poured a little bit more than two mugs' worth into two mugs. He cursed. I said, "I'll clean it up."

"I'll also be immolated for you whenever you wish."

"Noted," I said.

Half an hour later he was himself again, more or less. I said, "Okay, what did you learn?"

"I learned," he said slowly, "that either it takes a trained expert to learn things from pieces of scrap paper, or it takes an amateur a long, long time to look for a greenstalk in the grass."

"In other words, you learned nothing?"

"Oh, I wouldn't say *nothing*."

He was smiling. He'd gotten something. I nodded and waited. He said, "Most of it was numbers. There were a lot of numbers. I didn't pay much attention to them, until I realized they probably meant money; then they caused me a certain distress. But that still wasn't helpful. I haven't thrown them away, because you never know, but I did set them aside."

I kept waiting.

"A few of those scraps of paper had names, sometimes with cryptic notes. Those I paid more attention to. I sorted them into three groups. One pile has mostly numbers but maybe a name, or a word that might be a code word, or something like that. Another has messages—things like, 'Lunch, Firstday, Swallowtail, Lady Preft,' or 'Modify collateral policy on mortgage holdings—meeting three o'clock.' The third pile—"

He stood up, walked over to the table, and picked up a few pieces of paper. "The third pile contains the results of going through the other two—these are scraps I came up with after looking at and rejecting a lot more. There isn't much, but there may be something."

He brought them over and handed them to me. "Okay, Kiera," he said. "Let's see if you're as devious as I am. Take them one at a time, in order, and try to put it together."

"Okay," I said. "I like games."

There were four slips of paper—two of them obviously torn off from larger sheets, the other two on very plain paper. The one on top, one of the torn fragments, was written in a very elegant, precise hand, an easy one to read. It read, *5D for BT, 5&10, 8:00, Skyday, Cklshl.*

I said, "Well, 5D, if we were talking about money, is probably five dots: five thousand imperials. But that's a Jhereg term—I wouldn't have expected a banker to use it."

"Yep. That's exactly what caught my eye. Keep going."

I shrugged. "Skyday is easy, and so is 8:00. But I don't know what BT means, 5&10, or what cee kay ell ess aech ell spells."

He said, "Start with the last. There's a small inn, not far from the bank, that's marked by a sign of a seashell, and it's called the Cockleshell. Our hostess told me about it. She says it isn't the sort of place one might normally find a banker."

"Hmmm. This _is_ getting interesting. A payoff of some sort?"

Vlad nodded. "Look at the time again."

I did so. "Right," I said. "Whether it's eight in the morning or eight at night, it isn't at a time when banks are open."

"Exactly. Now, what do you make of the 5&10?"

"Five- and ten-imperial notes, or pieces?"

He nodded. "That's my guess. Coins, probably. Clumsy to carry, but safer to negotiate."

"Then it _is_ a payoff. And BT is the person being paid off—out of bank funds. Any idea who that is?"

"Try the next note."

It was just like the first—same hand, same amount, different day and time, only no place was mentioned, and the "5&10" was missing. It had been crumbled up, like someone had thrown it at a wastepaper basket and missed. I said, "Well? They did it at the bank?"

"Maybe. Or maybe we've found an early one and a late one, and there was no need to name the place or the denominations because by now she knew it. And another thing: look at the blotting on both of them."

"It's sloppy."

"Right. They were just notes by—I presume—Lady Vonnith to herself. If they were ever turned into official copies, those were filed, processed, and taken—or, more likely, destroyed. But she scribbled these while doing calculations or talking to someone, and then apparently tossed them at the wastepaper basket and missed."

"Yes," I said. "And this one is fairly recent—like, perhaps, the day they closed down."

"Right."

I nodded. "I recognize the hand, by the way."

"You recognize it?"

"Only in the sense that I remember where these came from, and there was a lot of paper there, most of it, like this, crumbled up into balls and lying on the floor, and a bunch of them that, just guessing, had fallen behind a desk or a filing cabinet and weren't worth retrieving. And it was, indeed, the biggest office in the place, so I'd guess you're right about whose notes these are."

He nodded. "Okay. After I'd gotten that far, I went through all the notes again, looking for any reference at all to BT."

"I take it you found something?"

"Yep. Read the next one."

"Different hand," I said. "Probably a man. Was it found in the same place?"

"Yes."

"Then it was written *to* her, not by her. Hmmm. Not as legible, but I think I can make it out. 'There are questions about dispersals to BT—I think we should tighten it up before it mirrors. Should we use the disc. fund?' And I can't read the signature at all—I imagine it's the scrawl someone uses informally."

"Yes, I suspect you're right. So what do you make of that one?"

"That's a curious little phrase, 'before it mirrors.' "

"Yeah, that's what I thought. Why not say, 'before it reflects?' And what would that mean, anyway? Do you have a guess?"

"Do you?"

"Yeah. Let's hear yours, though."

" 'Before it mirrors.' Hmmm."

"Give up?"

"Not yet; you're enjoying this too much." I pondered for a while and came up with nothing. "All right, I give up. What did you see that I didn't?"

Vlad smiled with one side of his face. "The next note."

"Heh. Okay." I looked at the fourth and last of the notes Vlad had found. This was the longest, and, as far as I could tell, the most innocuous. It said, *Lady—Lord Sustorr was in again—he now wants to secure his loan with his share of Northport Coal. I told him he had to talk to you, but it seems reasonable. I'm going to start running numbers on it. Some big shot from the Ministry of the Treasury was in today looking for you. He didn't leave his name, but says he'll be back tomorrow—it may be an Imperial Audit, but I don't think we have anything to worry about. I spoke with Nurtria about the complaint we received, and he promises to be more polite in the future. Lady Aise was in about the Club meeting. She left the flyer that's attached to this note. Firrna is still sick; we may have to replace him if this goes on—remind me to talk to you about it.* It was signed with the same illegible scrawl as the last one. I read it three times, then looked up at Vlad.

"Well?" he said. "Do you see it?"

"It's pretty thin," I said. "It fits, but it's pretty thin."

"It can't be that thin," said Vlad, "or you wouldn't have picked up on it."

I shrugged. "We think alike. That doesn't mean we're right."

"It explains the mirror line. What you see in a mirror is yourself, and if he was looking for what he must have been looking for—" Vlad punctuated the sentence with a shrug.

"No, I admit that. But still . . ."

"Yeah. It's something to go on when I talk to Her Ladyship the banker."

I stared at the letter again.

My, my, my.

9

VLAD HAD SAID SOMETHING about missing the people who once did his legwork for him, but I have my own ways of finding out what I need to know. Breaking into Fyres's house, when I had the house plans and all of the information ahead of time, was nice, and it had left me free to only look for certain things. This time, when I wasn't even going to break in, I had more leisure—I'd even had the leisure to return home and study up on the House of the Orca, so I wouldn't make any mistakes that I could avoid, although there could easily be pitfalls I wouldn't know about. But if you're trying to pull off a scam, the more information you have the better, so I went about collecting the information—my way.

I stood in a small wooded area, about two hundred meters from Lady Vonnith's front door, and studied her. That is, I studied her grounds and her house, which told me a great deal more about her than a similar study had told Vlad about Endra or Reega. But then, I have the advantage of age, and of spending a great deal of time learning about people only by seeing their houses (and especially trying to judge the inside by what I see of the outside), so maybe it isn't a fair comparison.

Vonnith's home was much older than Fyres's place, and, without doubt, had been built for an Orca. The gentle curves of roof and front were the trademark of the way they had liked their homes in the late Fifteenth and early Sixteenth Cycles—perhaps because it reminded them of their ships, but more likely because it reminded them of the sea. The late Fifteenth and early Sixteenth Cycles, incidentally, were also one of the periods when the richest of them made a point of living as far inland as duty and fortune would permit, which was a further indication, as we were several leagues from the shore and there wasn't even a river in sight.

There was a high, ivy-covered stone wall running along one side of the grounds. It was recent enough that it had to be Vonnith who had it put in. It certainly wasn't for security, or it would have gone around all the grounds, and it wasn't attractive enough to have been put in for aesthetic reasons, so it was probably done to hide whatever was on the other side of it, which a quick glance told me was more of the same gentle, grass-covered hill Vonnith's house was built on. Conclusion: she wanted to mark her boundaries. Second conclusion: she spent a great deal of time in that room on the second floor whose window looked out that way, with additional evidence provided by a not-unattractive stone monument midway between house and wall.

The monument was of a person, probably an ancestor, most likely the person who had had the house built, yet it seemed new enough that Vonnith had had it put up herself. This was starting to look like she had increased the family fortunes, in which case there should be signs of additions and improvements on the house. And, looking for them, there they were—a bit on the far side that, however well it blended in, had to have been added, and, yes, all the dormers, and even some stonework running up alongside the doors.

She seemed to have quite a fixation on stonework—maybe it had something to do with being an Orca and knowing that stone sinks, or maybe it had to do with being rich and wanting to do something that lasted. At a guess, the latter seemed most likely.

Well, her bank hadn't lasted.

I wondered how she'd taken that. Was she one of those who would shrug it off and make excuses for it, even to herself? Would it destroy her? Would she mourn for a while, or would it inspire her to try again? Fyres was the last sort, I knew—every time his schemes had fallen apart, he'd started over again. I had to admire that.

There were four guards out in the open, and after a few minutes I found another four concealed—one of them close enough to make me uncomfortable, even though I was doing nothing illegal. I continued watching, noticing the glass on the windows, just like Fyres's place, and the inlay work on the stones around the front door, the carriage posts for guests' conveyances, and the glint that came off the door clapper. Yes. She, too, had her ostentatious side, although it was nothing like Vlad had described Endra's house.

Come to that, though, I hadn't seen what the inside looked like. Still, all this time, I was only barely aware that my subconscious was putting together a layout of the house. It wasn't that I expected to need one, it's just how my mind works. I am, quite frankly, very good at it, and maybe that's where the real pleasure comes in—just the joy of doing something you do well. There are worse reasons for doing things; maybe there aren't any better ones.

I was doing something I was good at now, too: I was wearing makeup, to which I was unaccustomed, but I was being a good enough Orca to fool an Orca. Or so I hoped.

I walked up to the front door and pulled the clapper. You know it's a well-built house when you pull the clapper and you don't even hear the faintest echoes of it from outside—that is, either it's a well-built house or else the clapper's broken.

Evidently the clapper was working. The man who opened the door was at once recognizable as an Issola, and a fine specimen he was—old, perhaps a shade tall, well groomed, graceful in movements, plainly delighted to see me even though he had no idea who I was or what I was doing there. He said, "Welcome to the home of my lady Side-Captain Vonnith, Countess of Licotta and Baroness of T'rae. My name is Hub. What may we do to please you?"

I said, "Good morning, Hub. I am Third-Chart-Master Areik, from Adrilankha, with a message for the Side-Captain. If you wish, Sir Hub, I will wait outside; please tell her I'm from her friend in the Ministry of the Treasury and there may be some small difficulty with the arrangements."

He said, "There is no need for you to wait outside, Third-Chart-Master; please follow me." I did so, and he left me in a parlor while he went to deliver the message.

Vonnith had gone for the big, roomy look: I had the impression, even in the entryway, of lots of space. I was prepared for it because I'd been able to see the dimensions and the height of the ceilings from the outside, but it was different actually feeling it. It occurred to me for the first time that there was something strange about an Orca wanting to live in a big, spacious, airy house—and a house, looking around, that had no hint or pieces of shipboard life anywhere. One explanation was that, if they're used to life on a ship, that's the last thing they want to be reminded of when they're ashore. But I suspect the real explanation is that, just as most Jhereg have nothing to do with criminal activity, most Orca live out their whole lives on land, channeling their mercantile instincts into other pursuits—running banks, for example.

Hub returned. "The Side-Captain awaits you in West Room."

There were no hallways on this floor—it just flowed from one room to another, which meant all of them were big and open. From the parlor, where I'd been waiting, we passed into a dining room with a very long lacquered table, and from there we entered a spacious room with dark paneling and traces of something tangy-sweet—maybe incense, maybe something else. The chairs in this room were all stuffed and comfortable-looking, and set in clumps of three or four, as if to turn the one large room into several smaller ones without the benefit of walls. There was very little that seemed worth stealing, except some of the contents of the buffet, and I dislike stealing things that break easily.

I bowed to the woman before me and said, "Side-Captain Vonnith?"

She nodded and pointed to a chair. I sat. She looked at Hub and nodded, and he poured me a glass of wine. She already had one. I said, "Thank you." We both drank some. It was the sort of wine that Vlad calls *brandy,* and it was quite good. She nodded to Hub again. He bowed and left the room.

She said, "I wasn't aware that I had a friend in the Ministry of the Treasury. In fact, I don't believe I know anyone at all who works there."

I drank some more wine to give me time to think. She had invited me in, and she had given me wine, and now she was denying knowing what I was talking about. So, okay, she was playing a game, but was I supposed to play along with it, or convince her it was unnecessary?

"I understand," I said. "But if you did . . ."

"Yes? If I did?"

Okay, sometimes luck will out.

"You would probably be interested in knowing that the fire is getting hotter."

"I beg your pardon?"

"Questions are being asked."

"And are the answers forthcoming?"

"No." And I added, "Not yet."

Her lips tightened. "Some," she said, "might interpret that as a threat."

"No, no," I said. "Not a threat. But you know Lord Shortisle."

"Do I?" she said. "What makes you think so?"

"I mean, you know how he works."

"I thought I did," she said. "But now you say he's not threatening me, and yet—"

Well, well. All the way to the top. I said, "He's not. What I mean is, he's getting pressure from, well, you can guess where the pressure's coming from."

She frowned. "Actually, I can't. The Phoenix is off cavorting with her lover, as I understand it, so it can't be her, and there isn't anyone else who is in a position to threaten us, or has the desire to."

Now, that was extremely interesting. I said, "Because Her Majesty is gone doesn't mean she's out of touch."

For the first time, she looked worried. "It is her? Something has slipped?"

"Yes," I said.

"What?"

"I don't know; I'm just a messenger."

"How bad is it?"

"Not bad—yet. It's just a whisper. But Lord Sh—That is, certain parties thought you should be informed."

"Yes, yes. What does he say I should do?"

"Do you know Lord Loftis, who is running the—"

"Of course I do."

"That's where the pressure is coming down."

"Has he slipped?"

"Not badly, but enough so there's some danger. You should be prepared to move."

"Huh? What do you mean, move?"

"I mean run."

"Oh. Do you think it might come to that?"

"We hope not."

She nodded. "All right. Why didn't—uh—why wasn't I reached directly? Why send you?"

Hmmm. Good question. "Why do you think?"

For a moment I thought she wasn't going to be able to come up with anything, but her eyes got big. "The Empress? Using the Orb? She wouldn't! She's a *Phoenix*!"

I shrugged. "She hasn't yet, and she may not, but it would be the obvious next step, wouldn't it?"

"Impossible. Shortisle is getting paranoid."

"Maybe," I said. "Probably."

"Certainly. No one has done that since the seventh Jhereg Reign, and you know what happened then!"

"So is there any harm in being careful?"

"No, I suppose not." She shook her head. "We should have been more careful from the beginning—we should have arranged for methods of making contact, and signals." *That's right, you should have.* "But then, no one planned anything—it just happened, one thing led to another."

"Yes," I said. She looked like she was about to start asking questions, so I finished the wine and stood up. "There's a great deal to do, but nothing that should be impossible." That was general enough that I didn't think I could get into trouble with it.

"Of course," she said. "Tell him I'll await his word, but that I'll be ready to, as you put it, *move.*"

"Very good. I—or someone—will be in touch. For the future, whoever it is will say he's from the Adrilankha Eleemosynary Society."

"Adrilankha Eleemosynary Society," she said. "All right. Good luck."

"Yes," I said. "And you be careful."

I didn't realize how tense I was until I walked out the door. And even then I couldn't completely relax, because they might be watching me. I didn't think I gave myself away, but I couldn't be sure; Vonnith was the sort who could play the game on me that I thought I was playing on her.

I got up to the road and teleported to the Imperial Palace's Orca Wing just in case they decided to trace the teleport. It crossed my mind to visit the Ministry of the Treasury while I was there, but on reflection there was too much chance of my being recognized by the Jhereg who have business there from time to time, so I just waited for about ten or fifteen minutes, then teleported back to the cottage.

Vlad was talking to Hwdf'rjaanci, probably about Savn's condition, while Savn slept. When I came in, Vlad said, "Well?"

"I don't know," I told him. "I think it went well, but—"

"What did you learn?"

Buddy insinuated his nose into my person. I petted him and pushed him away. Loiosh, who was on Vlad's left shoulder, twitched his head in what was probably laughter. "It goes all the way to the top," I said.

"You mean Big Shot Treasury is Shortisle himself?"

"Not necessarily, but Shortisle is involved somewhere along the line." Vlad whistled softly. "Let's have the details," he said.

I gave him the conversation as well as I could remember it, and a few notes on architecture as well, after which he said, "Yeah, Shortisle's in it, all right. I suspect the Empress is not going to be happy about this, and I suspect that, if any of a number of people find out what we're doing, we could be in some very serious trouble."

"Right on both counts," I told him.

"Could Shortisle have enough pull to enlist the Tasks Group?"

"No chance," I said. "There has to be someone else."

"Okay." I could see him accept that. "The Tiassa? Lord Khaavren?"

"I know about him. I don't believe it. And you're the one who heard the way Loftis talked about him, and I threatened Loftis with telling him."

"The Empress?"

"Even less likely. I'd even risk 'impossible.' "

"Then who, dammit? Who else can order the Tasks Group to do something like this?"

"No one."

"Oh, good. Well, that's helpful." He frowned. "I remember I was at Dzur Mountain once—have you ever been there?"

I shrugged.

"Yeah. Well, I was there once, talking to Sethra Lavode, the Enchantress—"

"I know who she is."

"Right. She was telling me about the Dragon-Jhereg war."

"Yes."

"It was pretty ugly as I understand it. Were you involved in that?"

"Sure," I said. "On the side of the Dragons."

He gave me a polite smile. "The Dragons had the real power, but the Jhereg had one advantage—they always went for the top. While the Dragonlords were busily killing every Jhereg they came across—whether he worked for the Organization or not—the Jhereg were carefully wiping out all the military leaders in the House of the Dragon. It was a nasty little war, and, by the end, Sethra Lavode had to get involved. Do you know about that?"

"Go on."

"All she did was announce that she was in charge, and then, as she told me, she did nothing—she just sat in Dzur Mountain and waited for the Jhereg to try to assassinate her, and wiped them out as they did, which was pretty stupid on the part of the Jhereg, really. No one is going to assassinate the Enchantress of Dzur Mountain, unless maybe Mario reappears. But that's not the point. She also mentioned a time in Eighth Cycle when she was Warlord, and she had six hundred troops to defend this little hill against—"

"What's your point, Vlad?"

"That they're occupying the strong position—they don't have to do anything. We've been nipping at them here, and scouting them there, and we've learned a lot, but mostly what we've learned is that they're way tougher than we are, and they're in a secured position. All they have to do is dig in, and we can't touch them. If we tell the Empire what's going on, they'll go to ground and it'll take a hundred years to sort everything out. If we keep nibbling away at them, it'll take even longer."

"I see your point. So what do we do?"

"We need to get Sethra Lavode to leave Dzur Mountain—figuratively speaking."

I nodded slowly. "Yes, I see what you're getting at. How do you propose to do it?"

"They're scared as it is," he said. "That is, Loftis has been given the job of covering over Fyres's murder, and Vonnith is obviously up to something, and so is Shortisle. So I propose we give them something to chase—like me. Then we turn the chase around and nail them."

"Uh-huh. And, if they do chase you, how are you going to stay alive long enough to, as you put it, turn the chase around?"

He rubbed the spot above his lip where his facial hair was just starting to grow back. "I haven't worked that part out yet," he said.

"Yeah. Well, be sure and let me know when you do."

"Well, so what's *your* bright idea?"

"Let's go back to the beginning, Vlad. What do we know about Fyres?"

Vlad shrugged. "Not much. We have something to start with, but—"

"Yeah. I'd like to find out more."

"Kiera, that could take years. We have some of his private notes, okay. But between empty companies, and fake ships, and loans without backing, and reams of paper—most of which we *don't* have—we're never going to be able to track down what was really going on."

"Maybe," I said. "But remember Stony?"

"Your Jhereg friend? Sure."

"I'm thinking that if the Jhereg has been involved in this, then someone, somewhere, knows what's going on."

"And why would you think that?"

"Sheer number of Jhereg, Vlad. There are so many of us involved in financing this kind that at least one of them was bound to have been smart enough not to jump in, but to investigate the guy. All we have to do is find out who that is and get the information already collected."

He looked skeptical. "Do you think you can do that? That is, find just the right guy and get the information without giving the game away?"

"I can do it," I told him.

He shrugged. "Okay. Go to it."

"It may take a few days."

"All right."

"And there's something else I want to do, but we're going to have to think about whether it's a good idea."

"I'm not sure I like the sound of that."

"You're wise, Vlad. I'm not sure it's something we ought to do, but I'm thinking about it."

"Let's hear it, Kiera."

"You like honey in your klava, don't you?"

"Ah. So that's how it is?"

"You're very quick."

"Only because I've been stung. Let's hear what you have in mind."

I gave him the general outline, omitting details he didn't need and wouldn't have been happy knowing. He listened very intently, then he said, "Yes, indeed. And we don't even have gloves, much less whatever you're supposed to use to protect your face. The question is, how big is the swarm, and how nasty do they get when they're roused?"

"Yeah, that's the question. And can you think of a better way to find out?"

He sighed and shook his head. "Unfortunately, Kiera, I can't."

"So I should go ahead?"

He nodded briefly, like he didn't enjoy the prospect. Well, neither did I, come to that. I said, "What are you going to do while I'm off gathering sweets?"

A peculiar sort of smile came to his lips. "I'll think of something," he said.

ALL WE HAD TO do was keep our heads down and keep learning things, and eventually, maybe, we'd start to get an idea about what was going on; then, just maybe, we'd be able to figure out what to do about it. That, at least, was what I was thinking as I stepped out of the little cottage and repaired home to make myself annoying in a couple of different ways to several different people.

The next two days were no more fun than I'd thought they would be—most of those I spoke to I didn't like, and they didn't like me, and they couldn't or wouldn't tell me anything useful, anyway—but in the end I came up with some hard information. I noted it down carefully, and, psychic communication being impossible while Vlad wore the Phoenix Stones, I had to hold on to what I'd learned until I would see him next: tomorrow or the day after, depending on how things went tonight. When

I was done asking irritating questions of irritating people, which was in the afternoon of the second day, I picked up the tools I was going to need and prepared to do what I was good at.

Vlad and I, back in the old days, used to compare our respective crafts, and one of the things common to both was the need for preparation, and, in conjunction, how dangerous it was to try to do anything in a hurry. The trouble was, things were happening too fast, and I had the feeling they were going to happen even faster.

Well, I didn't like it, but there wasn't much I could do about it. After getting what I needed from home, I spent the rest of the afternoon going from place to place in Adrilankha, trying to get the information I needed to have a chance to pull this off.

I wished I had a familiar to grumble at while I did so. Vlad's told me about several times Loiosh has saved his life, or suggested the solution to a problem, or provided the necessary help to complete a witchcraft spell, but I have the feeling that the most important thing Loiosh does for Vlad is give him someone to grumble at. You feel stupid grumbling to yourself, so I didn't.

The day was waning when I had finally acquired everything I needed. I took about four hours to study the situation, curse about everything I didn't know, and come up with a tentative way in, a provisional agenda, and a possible way out, with maybe a couple of alternatives for the last, all of which I knew would likely be rendered useless if something went wrong. For the first time in more years than I could remember I actually thought about how humiliating it would be to get caught, because for the first time in more years than I could remember it seemed like a real possibility.

I cursed yet again and made my way to the Imperial Palace, Orca Wing.

The phrase "breaking into the Imperial Palace" has been used among people I know for a long time as an expression of the unthinkable: "Argue philosophy with an Athyra? Might as well break into the Imperial Palace," or, "Bet the round stones? Sure. And then we'll break into the Imperial Palace." That sort of thing. It's a fascinating little phrase, because it only makes sense if it goes back to the early days of the Empire, when all that existed was the old nucleus that became the Imperial Wing; breaking into the Imperial Palace is as easy in the execution as it is meaningless as a concept: most of the doors you can just walk into; *where* in the Imperial Palace do you want to break into?

And, of course, to do what?

In any case, I "broke into the Imperial Palace" by walking into the

Orca Wing. I wore a nice, full coat of Jhereg grey with natty black fringe, a hood in case it got cold, and one that was sufficiently voluminous to hide my tools. I nodded to the tired-looking Orca watchman as I went by.

So let's see. One, two, third corridor to the left, up the stairs, down the hall to the statue. A long way. There was no bloody statue of Sealord Cren; how old was that information, anyway? Well, it had to be either this passage or this one, and . . . yes, there were the marks where the statue used to be. Good. Now another stairway, and two more turnings, and it had been quite some time since I'd seen anyone. The Orca were forced to work long, irregular hours when at sea; they made up for it ashore by working no more than they had to.

There were supposed to be a couple more watchmen to circumvent right before I reached my destination, and I became worried when I didn't see them. But I waited in the corridor outside the doorway into the Ministry until at last I heard one walk by; the footsteps were measured and casual and went away after a while. Nine and a half minutes later I heard a different set. Eleven minutes later the first set returned. I spent another half hour there, just to make sure of the timing, then moved.

The door into the Ministry had only the most cursory lock, and the alarm was trivial. Once past it, I had to get into Shortisle's office, and I spent most of the seven minutes I'd given myself in checking for alarms; then I retreated once more to wait for another cycle of the watch. The next time I spent only five minutes more checking for alarms, about a minute disabling them, and maybe twenty seconds opening the door, slipping through, shutting it, and locking it again. Then I put the alarms back up in case the guards checked them. I put some cloth under the door so that no one would see light peeking out, then looked around.

There was a door in his office that had a nice little sign on it reading, "Records."

If Shortisle was engaged in anything shady—or, in fact, even if he wasn't—he wouldn't make it easy to get to the financial records of the Empire, so I intended to take this carefully and slowly, and make sure I'd found everything before I moved.

I studied the door, the floor, and the ceiling first, looking for anything obvious, and found nothing. Next I looked as closely as I could through and into the keyhole, but I didn't see anything that looked like an alarm.

The next step was to feel for the presence of sorcery in the area, and, yes indeed, it was all over the place; there was nothing subtle about it. Was it double-trapped? That is, would looking at it closely set off an alarm? Well, there are the tendrils of spells that hang in the real world like abandoned cobwebs; and one knows the feel of these strands if one has ever walked through a dark and gloomy place—so, too, were these bits of amorphia all around me in that place that was dark to the outer eye, but now filled with light to the inner. I can brush past cobwebs without making them fall, but what if the web is not abandoned, after all? Then the spider will know I am there; and if there is anyone watching the spider, then I cannot brush her or her threads aside without all the world being aware of me.

Ah, little spider, you have a bite, do you? And someone watching over you? Well, let him watch, little spider, and you—find me if you can, for I know cobwebs better even than you, and I will send up my own spider that will look like you, and act like you, and gobble you up, and then sit fat and happy in your place while the watcher watches, oblivious.

I took a few minutes to catch my breath before I proceeded. One becomes exhausted when using sorcery in proportion to the intricacy of the spell, not the amount of energy used; a fact that I think Vlad still doesn't understand since he still compares it to witchcraft—an art I've never begun to understand.

When I felt better, I used the same device I'd used at the bank to look into the room in preparation for teleporting. It was a fairly small room, but full to overflowing with cabinets, maybe forty-five or fifty of them, all of which were, no doubt, full to overflowing with the recent financial records of the Empire—whatever I was looking for was probably in there. I checked the room over carefully, fixed it in my mind, prepared to teleport, and stopped cold.

Something wasn't right.

I put the tube back against the wall, held it tight, relaxed, and looked again. The room was entirely dark, and I hadn't wanted to risk light until I could be sure they had nothing to detect it, so I'd used a spell that affected my sight rather than the room; this is tricky because it is very easy to miss things that are near other things—objects tend to blur and merge in the magical vision—but it seemed that there was something odd next to one of the cabinets against the wall.

I checked again, and there was no trace of sorcery except for those spells I had already found and circumvented, which meant, if this was an alarm, it wasn't a magical one. Of course, there was no reason to believe it was an alarm—it was just something that wasn't a filing cabinet or a pen, or an inkwell, or anything else I could readily identify. I almost talked myself into going in, but you don't get to be my age without developing

some instincts and learning to trust them, so I put a little more effort into
seeing it.

If the ceiling was as high as the ceiling of this room, then the filing
cabinets were about eight meters tall, in which case the object sitting on
the floor was about two meters tall (scale can be a problem when seeing
this way—try it yourself) and resembled, more than anything else, a small
gong, with some sort of round plate attached to a thin frame by a pair of
wires, and even what might be a diminutive beater positioned in front of
it, attached to the frame. I couldn't see how thick any of it was for sure,
which didn't help any. I doubted it was actually a gong but I couldn't
figure out what it was, or what it was doing there.

If it was magical, I'd lost all of my skills, and if it wasn't magical, what
was it? Could one use witchcraft to create an alarm? My guess was no,
but I couldn't reach Vlad to ask him, and I didn't want to ask Cawti
because she'd ask questions. No, I didn't think witchcraft could do something like that. And I really doubted that Shortisle would think to hire a
witch, anyway.

It was probably something completely harmless that had nothing to do
with anything, and when I looked at it I'd laugh. Except that I still had
this feeling.

Well, if it *was* an alarm, it had to be connected to a device to notify
someone, or a device to trigger a trap, or a device to make a noise, or
something. And if the connection wasn't magical, it had to be physical.
Well, was there a string or a wire running from it to somewhere else?

I looked, and focused, and . . .

Yes, there was.

A wire or a string ran from it up to the ceiling and disappeared above
the room.

Maybe it *was* an alarm.

If so, how did it work? What was it supposed to detect, and how would
it respond? How could it send a magical impulse through the string if
there was no magic around the device? And if it wasn't supposed to send
a magical impulse, what could it send? I had the sudden image of someone
creating an artifact that did nothing at all, but knowing that if there was
a strange device in the room, no competent thief would break in before
figuring out what it did. An effective deterrent to be sure, but I suspected
there was more to this object than that.

Well, what would have happened if I'd teleported into the room? Nothing. I'd have been there, maybe right by the device, maybe not, but it
couldn't sense me, anyway, so . . .

Slow down, Kiera.

What happens when someone teleports into a room?

The same thing, more or less, that happens when someone opens a door and *walks* into the room: air gets pushed around—just a little when the door is opened, more when you materialize from a teleport. And if that gonglike thing is thin, then just a little air movement would be enough to make it tap against the beater, and if that was a metal wire, it could carry the sound, or the vibration, through the Palace to a place where it could be amplified, and someone, somewhere, would know that the integrity of the room had been violated.

I'd have whistled to myself if I weren't being especially conscious of sound. It was a very clever device; just the sort of thing the Orca would come up with, and I was only surprised that no one had thought of it, or a variation on it, years and years ago: simple, elegant, and almost impossible to detect.

Almost impossible.

Thing is, I'm not just a good thief, I'm the best thief in the Empire. I reached the fingers of magic into the room and felt the thin metal plate. Careful now, Kiera. Don't get cocky with all those thoughts about how good you are: you're good because you're careful, and you're careful because you're patient. Take it slowly, and . . .

It was immobilized.

I sighed, took a breath, and teleported into the room. Nothing went off, nothing moved. I did yet another check for magic, then made a light and began looking through the Imperial financial records. These were, you understand, only the most recent and active sets: the rest were saved by some method known only to the sorcerers of the House of the Lyorn and the archivists of the House of the Orca, but it was the recent and active records I needed.

I imagine the organization of the packets in the cabinets, and, indeed, the arrangement of the cabinets, all of them marked with numbers or symbols or a combination, made sense to those who worked here, and I would even guess that somewhere was a key to the whole thing that would explain how to interpret everything else, but I had no clue how to make sense of any of it. Fortunately, I didn't need to. I opened a packet at random, saw nothing that meant anything to me, closed it, and put it back. Then I went to another cabinet and did the same. Then another, until I had opened at least one packet in each of them, and riffled through probably two hundred collections of notes, invoices, receipts, and other accounting arcana.

That done, I slipped out of the room, stopping long enough to erase any psychic traces of myself that I might have left. Then I locked the door behind me and very, very carefully released the spell that was holding the little wind-alarm. It didn't go off. As the last step, I got a metaphorical spider back and had it cough up the one it had euphemistically eaten.

I looked around the rest of the area until I found what had to be Shortisle's desk, judging from the size, the location, and his name appearing on plaques, markers, and papers all around it. Unlike the records, here there was a chance I could learn something if, indeed, Shortisle was the guilty party, and if he left evidence of his crimes lying around. Phrased that way, I didn't think much of my chances, but it wouldn't hurt to explore a little.

The alarms built into his desk were all sorcerous, and not terribly effective, which meant that he had nothing to hide—or he wasn't hiding it in his desk, at any rate. I dismantled the alarms, picked the locks, and looked through the contents. There were, in fact, no notes saying, "Today I accepted a large bribe from Vonnith in exchange for allowing her to close her bank and run with whatever money she could scrape together."

Oh, well.

The most irritating thing was that he had two small, hidden compartments in the desk, both of which required a great deal of time and effort to open, and both of which turned out to be entirely empty—not even a psiprint of his mistress. I took this as a personal affront.

When I finished with the desk, I realized just how exhausted I was. That's the most dangerous part: when you're all done, and you're tired, and everything has gone well, it becomes too easy to let your guard down and make some little mistake that will bring the watch running or allow you to be found after the fact. I made myself go slowly and carefully in removing all traces of my presence, both psychic and mundane, then I made sure of the timing of the watch (judging by the footsteps, they weren't the same pair who'd been there before) before I opened the last door between me and escape.

Even after I was past that, I was careful to avoid crowded places, and took little-known paths through the Palace, walking for almost two more hours until I could emerge from the Yendi Wing (just for the pleasure of giving the inhabitants something to wonder about) and teleported straight back home, where I poured myself a glass of the same kind of wine Vonnith had given me, drank it down at a single draught, and climbed into my bed, after which I slept soundly for several very pleasant hours that were only marred by a few dreams in which spiders were banging on gongs.

When at last I roused myself late the next morning, I took care of morning things, broke my fast with warmed nutbread, maizepie, and Eastern-style coffee (which Vlad claims is too bitter for him), and teleported back to Northport. I found a large and busy inn very close to City Hall, so I went in, found a table in the middle of the room, and began to drink klava, with the intention of continuing until something either happened or failed to happen.

I was, in effect, making myself a target. With any luck, I'd have stirred up Shortisle, or someone in his office, and it seemed likely that, with a little work, whoever it was would be able to figure out that the visitor had been Kiera the Thief (although, to be sure, no one would be able to prove it), and I expected to be able to learn something from who showed up and what he did when he got here—I'd be surprised if I had to sit here for more than two days.

This was a part of the plan Vlad knew nothing about, because he would have wanted to be involved. I have a great deal of confidence in my ability to get myself out of anything I get myself into, but if you add a hot-tempered assassin whose blade is often faster than his head, it might be that I'd save myself a few moments of worry and, in exchange, lose a lot of useful information.

Vlad, however, would not have liked the idea of my doing it.

By noon I was tired of klava, so I switched to a "seaman's ale," as they call it in Northport, or "storm brew," as it is called in Adrilankha, which is a very dark ale with traces of ginger; it was heavy, so I could pretend it was lunch. I felt very exposed at the table, and I hoped I wouldn't have to wait there too long. I finished the seaman's ale and ordered another, and considered asking for a bowl of whatever it was I could smell from the kitchen. People walked by the open window and often looked in, because that's what one does when walking by an inn, and I kept wondering if any of these were people who were spotting me. I rubbed my eyes. At one point, I thought I saw Devera go by, but if so she didn't recognize me, and it wasn't very likely, anyway. I drank some more seaman's ale. It was good. Two Jhereg came in, walked right up to my table, and sat down. They were Funnel-head and Mockman, both of whom had been in Stony's office when I'd visited him. This was something I hadn't expected at all.

Funnel-head said, "Stony wants to see you."

"All right," I said. "Now?"

"If you please."

I left the ale unfinished, which was a shame, and stood up. They flanked me as we stepped out of the inn. They each had a sword, and Funnel-head, on my right, had a long dagger concealed under his left arm, and no doubt they each had a few other things that would help them not at all if I decided not to accompany them, but they didn't know that.

Funnel-head said, "Shall we teleport?"

"I'd rather walk," I said, because I don't let strangers teleport me.

"It's a couple of miles," he said.

"It's a nice day."

"All right."

We exchanged no more words until we got there. We walked right up past where Dor was very careful not to be, then Funnel-head clapped outside Stony's door and said, "She's here, boss."

There was a muffled response, and Funnel-head opened the door and indicated I was to go in. I did so, stopping only long enough to hand him his dagger. "You dropped this," I said. He stared at it, then gave me a glare into which I smiled as I closed the door.

I sat down. "What is it, Stony? Why the summons?"

Stony, apparently, couldn't decide if he should be amused or annoyed by my interaction with his flunky; eventually he settled on ignoring it.

"I'm worried about you," he said.

"Worried about me?"

"About you, and for you."

I waited.

"Yeah," he said. "You've been looking into Fyres's death, and some people are getting itchy."

"People?" I said.

He shook his head. "You know I can't name names, Kiera."

"Then what are you saying?"

He shrugged. "I'm saying you should drop this, whatever it is, or else be very careful, that's all."

"What about you?"

"I'm not involved," he said. "I just heard that you lightened some files in some Orca's office at the Palace, and some Orca with connections to the Organization want you to go swimming. I thought you should know about it."

"You're not asking me to back off?"

He shook his head. "No. As I say, this isn't my game. I just thought you ought to be aware of it, you know?"

"Yes," I said. "Okay, thanks. Anything else?"

"No," he said.

"All right. See you around."

"Yeah. See you."

I got up and left. No one tried to stop me. I was glad Stony hadn't asked about Vlad again, because I hate lying to friends.

I hastened back to the Awful Blue Cottage to tell Vlad what I'd learned. It was late afternoon when I got there. Buddy ran out of the house, and I had to spend a moment getting reacquainted with him and allaying his suspicions before venturing inside.

Hwdf'rjaanci was seated at the table next to Vlad. Savn was sitting up in the chair facing the hearth, and he turned and looked at me as I came in, which caught me up short. I said, "Hello, Savn." He didn't say anything, but returned to staring at the fire.

"Good evening," I said. I gestured toward the boy. "I see some improvement."

"Some," agreed Vlad.

Hwdf'rjaanci nodded a greeting to me and asked if I wanted some tea, which I didn't.

I was pleased, and even a bit surprised, to note that Vlad didn't have any fresh wounds. He was drinking klava, and by the lack of sleep in his eyes I suspect he was on at least his second cup. Loiosh, on the other hand, was sound asleep next to Rocza, which was unusual for a jhereg in the middle of the day. "I have some information," I said.

"Me, too," said Vlad.

"Should I go first, or do you want to?"

"You might as well," said Vlad.

I sat down next to him. Hwdf'rjaanci got up and sat over by Savn—I had the impression she didn't want to know about any of this. I decided I couldn't really blame her.

"Did you do it?" he said.

"You mean enrage the bees? Yeah."

"Tell me about it."

"All right." This time I just gave him the brief version of my activities, especially the break-in, because the long version would have required telling him things I'd rather he didn't know, then I gave him all the details on the rest of it. I sort of brushed over the part about making myself a target, but I saw him press his lips together, so I quickly went on to discuss the conversation with Stony, and, before he could ask about that, I started in on the results of my inquiries the first couple of days.

I said, "I found a couple of them, Vlad. Three, really, but one had refused him a loan just because he didn't like Fyres's smell, so that didn't help us any. But there were two of them who actually did the checking."

"How many that didn't?"

"A lot. He was very good at making people trust him."

Vlad nodded. "Okay. Those who did check up on him—what did they find out?"

"That he was very good at making people trust him."

Vlad's smile came and went. "Yeah. What else?"

"Vlad, he didn't have *anything*. He had a great deal on paper, but all of his enterprises, worth maybe sixty million imperials—"

Vlad looked shocked. "That's right," I said. "Sixty million imperials. Sixty million imperials' worth of loans, that went for office space, marketing, buying up other companies that, in point of fact, he didn't know how to run so they went into surrender of debts inside of ten or twenty years—all of this was based on a contract, and a contract never fulfilled, by the way, for five men-o'-war for the Imperial Navy."

"House of the Orca, of course," said Vlad.

"Sure, Imperial Navy."

"I wonder," said Vlad.

"Yes?"

"I wonder why legitimate banks were loaning him money at all. I mean, I can see the Jhereg, but—"

"Are you sure they were? We know about Vonnith, but do we know there were any others?"

"Yes," he said. "I'll tell you about it."

"Okay. I don't know the answer, though. But it makes sense. It explains why the loans were at bank rates, not Jhereg rates."

"They were?"

"Yes. All of them."

"Interesting. Maybe the Jhereg loans went through the banks." He spread his palms. "Or the other way around, for all we know."

I nodded.

He said, "But all right. The Jhereg is in it deep, then?"

"Lots of us, Vlad. All the way up to the Council."

"Did either of your friends try to spread the word about the guy?"

"One of them tried to let a few friends know, but no one would listen.

The other, apparently, doesn't have any friends, and figured he could eliminate a great deal of competition. He was right, by the way—some very heavy people will be going down over this."

Hwdf'rjaanci got up and went outside, I suppose because she could still hear us. Buddy looked at her, thumped his tail once, but decided he wanted to stay and listen.

Vlad considered my remark and said, "That ties Fyres into the Jhereg without any question, but . . . how did he land that contract with the Imperial Navy, after having proved what he was twice before?"

"Ah," I said. "Very good. That *is* the question, isn't it? Because that brings the Empire into this. The answer is, I don't know. Somewhere along the line, he talked someone into something."

"Yep," said Vlad. He was quiet for quite a while then—maybe a minute. Then he said, "And that someone screwed up and then tried to cover himself. And I think . . . yeah, it all fits, I'm afraid."

"What does?"

"Here's what I think happened—no, on second thought, I'll tell you what I've been up to for the last couple of days, and see if you can put it together."

"All right," I said. "Go to it."

10

LET ME THINK NOW. When did you leave? A lot has happened since then. It was early afternoon, right? Okay, I'll just take it as it happened.

After you left, I made an effort to get Savn talking again, and he went off on knives some more. I decided that it probably wasn't healthy to keep him fixated like that, and the old woman told me the same thing a few minutes later, so that was about it. I couldn't think of anything else to do with him, and eventually I realized that half the reason I wanted to was to avoid having to do something I was a bit afraid of. Let me explain.

I kept thinking about that banker, and what you'd said about the Jhereg connections, and what I couldn't get away from was the idea that, if the Jhereg was connected to Fyres, and Fyres was connected to the Empire, then the Jhereg was connected to the Empire. If that was true, what was the connection, and how did it work, and like that? Now Side-Captain Vonnith—what's a side-captain, by the way?—must have been tied into Fyres because she'd jumped ship, so to speak, within a week of Fyres's death, and you'd proven that she was connected to the Empire, so I couldn't help wondering if she was connected to the Jhereg, too.

The trouble was, I couldn't go waltzing into Stony's office and ask about it, because he'd kill me on the spot and because you'd be annoyed with me, which meant I'd have to work through either Vonnith or Loftis.

From what you said, I had the impression that Vonnith would bolt if she got any more jumpy, and that might be inconvenient, so that left Loftis.

Loftis.

I have to tell you, Kiera: I wasn't all that excited about going up against him straight, and I wasn't very happy about trying to put anything past him again. You've met him, too, and you know what I'm talking about—I think we were both lucky the first time we ran into him.

The only thing I could think of was to keep him off balance long enough for me to learn what I needed to learn, and, with him alerted, I didn't think much of my chances of shoving another barrel of lies at him. To the left, however, telling him the truth wouldn't get me anywhere. So that left giving him some of the truth, and either feeding it to him a bit at a time—trading information, in other words—or hitting him with enough of the truth to make him stumble, and hoping to get something while he was recovering his balance, if you follow my metaphor. As for which of those I'd do, I didn't know—I was just going to approach him, talk to him, keep my ideas in mind, and see how it went.

That, at any rate, was the plan—if you can so dignify vague intentions with the word. After arriving at this magnificent conclusion, I had to make some food, and then clean up, and then try to talk to Savn about something other than knives, which produced no response at all. Unfortunately, after all of that, there was still time to visit Loftis, and I couldn't find any more reasons for putting it off, and Loiosh was making fun of me, so I got myself dressed up as myself—that is, an Easterner, although not a Jhereg—and headed into town.

I liked your method of finding a quiet place to talk, so I used it myself. When I'd located a suitable establishment, I paid for two rooms, across the hall from each other. The host probably wondered exactly what sort of bizarre activity I was going to engage in, but she didn't ask and I didn't volunteer the information. I found a kid to act as messenger and gave him a note to pass on to Loftis. The note said where I was, including the room number, and I signed it Margaret—I hope you don't mind. Then I went into the room across the hall from the one I'd given him, and amused myself by talking to Loiosh, who was, by the way, waiting outside the building—I didn't want to introduce that complication into things at this point, and I admit I was worried, because Loftis was potentially in touch with the Jhereg, and the Jhereg was looking for an Easterner with a pair of jhereg, so why take chances? The two-room bit, by the way, proved unnecessary. The idea was that if he decided to show up with a couple of additional blades, it would give me an edge to be behind him, but he had no such plans.

It took him about an hour and a half to get there, but eventually I heard him—that is, I heard one set of footsteps, and someone clapped outside the door. I moved the curtain back, and he turned quickly, and he saw me. Then he looked at me again, more closely, and I could see him start to put things together—Kaldor to the Easterner, the Easterner to Margaret, Margaret to the Empire, the Empire to Kaldor—and I took a certain pleasure in shocking him. I said, "I don't like this place for conversations. Let's walk. You lead." Then, in spite of my words, I stepped in front of him and led the way out of the place. He followed.

"*Anything?*"

"*All clear, boss.*"

"*Stay out of sight. I don't know where we're going, so—*"

"*I've done this before, boss. Honest.*"

When we reached the street, I indicated that he should take us somewhere, and he set off in a direction where there would be less traffic. I didn't want to give him too much time to think, so I said, "Margaret sends her regrets, but she was detained by the need to look into the Jhereg end of this—I assume you know about that?"

"Who are you?"

"Padraic," I said.

"And you're working with Margaret, is that it?"

I shrugged. "Things are happening faster than we'd thought they would, especially on the Jhereg side."

"What is the Jhereg side?"

"Don't play stupid, we don't have time for it. Vonnith is ready to bolt, and Shortisle is getting jumpy."

"*Getting* jumpy?"

"All right, getting even more jumpy. How soon can you close up shop?"

"We can finish tomorrow, if you don't care about everyone figuring out that we didn't run a real investigation. Now, I want to know—"

"I don't care what you want to know," I said. "What did Timmer say? Has she put it together?"

He fumed for a moment, then said, "If she has, she isn't saying anything."

"Huh," I said. "That's probably wise."

"How is it," he said grimly, "that you, that an Easterner, came to be involved in the security of the Empire?"

"Perhaps," I said, giving him a smile that was almost a leer, "Her

Majesty doesn't have the same feelings about Easterners that you do." He scowled. He's heard the rumors about Her Majesty's lover, too, but perhaps hadn't believed them. But then, I'm not sure if I believe them, either. Before he could come up with an answer, I said, "Are you aware how high this goes?"

"Yeah," he said.

I wished I knew. "All right, then. No, don't make it obvious, but hurry it up. Get your work done as fast as you can and get out."

He held up his hand in a signal to stop, and he began looking around. I did, too, and didn't see anything. The area we were walking through was almost empty of traffic and anything else—there were a couple of closed shops, a couple of houses with boards across the door, and a scattering of places that looked lived in. I said, "What is it?"

"Nothing special."

I looked around again, but still saw nothing except a desolate neighborhood, of which I'd seen plenty in South Adrilankha. I said, "Where are we?"

"I just wanted you to see this."

"What?"

"This area."

"What about it?"

"Look."

I'd been looking, but now I looked closer, and realized that the paint was new on most of the buildings and houses, and, furthermore, the houses, though small, looked like they'd been built for one family, and they were still in good condition. In fact, very good condition for how few people were here. I gave him a puzzled look.

He nodded. "When I got to town, just a couple of weeks ago, that place was open, and that place was open, and there were people living there, there, and there."

"Where are they now?"

"Gone," he said. "Maybe on the street, maybe moved to another town, maybe out in the woods hunting and living in tents. I don't know."

"Two weeks?" I said.

"Yeah."

"Fyres?"

"Yeah. The bank closings, and the closing of the three shipbuilders—"

"Three shipbuilders?"

"Yeah. He had a stake in about six or seven, and in three cases it was enough to shut them down. This area was developed about three hundred years ago by Sorenet and Family, Shipwrights, and pretty much everyone who lived around here worked for them. Some Orca, some Chreotha, mostly Teckla just in from your favorite village a generation ago. Now Sorenet is gone, and so is everyone who worked there."

"I've never seen a neighborhood die so quickly," I said.

"Nor have I."

We started walking again. "You've surprised me in another way," I said. "I hadn't been convinced that Fyres was ever involved in anything real at all."

He shrugged. "I wasn't, either. I still don't know how involved he was, or why, or what the mechanics are. That's the sort of thing we'd be finding out, if we were really doing what we're supposed to be doing."

This neighborhood seemed about the same as where we'd stopped. It was making me nervous. Loiosh, who was staying out of sight behind me, reported that nothing terrible was about to happen. I said, "Do you really think you can keep the Tiassa from finding out what you're up to?"

"Probably," he said. "He won't check on us—he trusts us." There was enough bitterness in that remark to ruin a hundred gallons of ale.

I said, "It isn't like you had a choice."

"I could have resigned."

"And done what? And what would you have told the Tiassa when he asked you why? And on top of it, you'd have known someone else was doing it, and probably bungling it—frankly, I don't trust your man Domm."

"The lieutenant's all right," he said quickly. "He has a bit of Waitman in him, but that just means he'll lose a few times before the Stand at Spinning Lake, which is nothing to be ashamed of. Waitman got an Imperial title for that, which isn't bad for someone with that sort of disposition."

"Maybe," I said. "And please don't explain. The point is, they knew just how to put the screws in."

"Sure," he said. "And who to put them to."

In case you've missed it, Kiera, I was now the one who was off balance; while showing me around the neighborhood, he'd had a chance to do some thinking, and now it was me who wanted some time to sort things out.

We had apparently sold Loftis on our story far more completely than I'd expected to, and that puzzled me. But more than that, I just couldn't reconcile everything he was saying with the idea that he was the sort of guy who'd go in for this kind of action. There was a piece of this—a *big* piece of this—that didn't make sense, and I was no longer at all sure how to proceed. I had this awful urge to just flat out ask him everything I needed to know, like, for example, who *was* behind this, and how exactly had the pressure been brought; but someone like Loftis is going to figure out more from the questions you ask than you will from the answers he gives, and if he figured out too much, he'd stop answering the questions at all. A damned tricky business, that made me long for the days when all I had to do was kill someone and not worry about it.

I needed a distraction.

I said, "There's another thing that's puzzling me."

"There's a lot that's puzzling me."

"Some of the smaller companies in Fyres's little Empire—"

"Not so little, Padraic."

"Yeah. Some of them hold land."

"Sure."

"And they're selling the land."

He nodded.

"And they're going under."

"Right."

"So they're not able to sell it."

"I guess. What's your point? If it's the legalities of it—"

"No, no. We have more advocates than the Orb has facets. I'm trying to figure out what sort of business sense that makes, or what kind of other sense it makes that overrides business sense."

"You think they have any choice?"

"Maybe."

He shook his head. "If you're going somewhere, I can't see it. As far as I can tell, they're bailing out as they go, and if that means they lose some property, they'll let the property courts and the advocates worry about it later. I don't think there's any plan involved."

This was all news to me. I said, "I'm not convinced."

"You have a devious mind."

"It goes with the job."

"Do you have any evidence? Any reason to think so?"

"Just a feeling. That's why I wanted to find out if you'd had any ideas about it."

"No."

"Okay," I said.

We were heading back in the general direction from which we'd come.

He said, "So, all right, what is it you wanted? You had me make contact with you for some reason, and so far all we've done is chat, along with a warning so general there's no point in giving it, and a question you could have had a messenger ask. What are you after?"

Damn. I had certainly given him too much time to think. I said, "There's someone who knows too much about what you're doing, and I can't find him."

"What do you mean?"

"I mean that something's slipped, and I'm pretty sure it's at the top, or near the top at any rate. I'm running into opposition, and I can't pin it down."

He shook his head. "I haven't run into it yet. The only suspicious action I've seen so far has been you and your friend Margaret."

Damn again. That wasn't the sort of thing I wanted him thinking about.

"Look," I said, "I'm going to have to trust you."

"Trust all you want," he said. "I haven't shut you down, but I'm not under your orders."

He was ahead of me again.

"And now I want a few answers."

And gaining.

"Your friend Margaret claimed to have a certain hold on me."

"The letters. Yes. They're real."

"I told her then they wouldn't go very far, and this is as far as they go. Exactly who do you work for, and what is your job?"

"I know *your* job, friend Loftis; but if you want to put everything out in front, then let's hear you say who *you* work for." As I said that, I was desperately trying to remember the names of the different groups you'd mentioned, and figure out which one I could most reasonably claim to be part of.

"Heh. I am a lieutenant in the Imperial Army, Corps of the Phoenix Guards, Special Tasks Group."

"And you know bloody well that wasn't my question."

"Are all Easterners psychically invisible, or just you? And is that why you were hired, or is it just a bonus?"

"It helps," I said.

"Exactly what are you after?"

"I've told you that."

"Yes, you have, haven't you? You've told me just about everything my heart could desire, haven't you?"

I shook my head. "Play all the games you want, Loftis, but I don't have time to muck around, not if I'm going to do what I was sent here to do."

"Shall we get something to eat?" he said.

Add another damn or two. He was pulling all of my tricks, and he was better at them than I was—which I suppose only made sense. I said, "I've been told that Undauntra always wanted her troops to fight hungry, whereas Sethra Lavode always wanted hers to fight with a full meal in them."

"I've heard that, too," he said. "But it isn't true. About Sethra, that is."

"I'll take your word for it. I'm also told that when a Jhereg boss hires an assassin, the deal is usually made during a meal."

"I can believe that."

"And I happen to know that there is a curious custom in parts of the East of making a big ceremony out of the last meal someone eats before he's executed. He's given pretty much anything he wants, and it's prepared and served quite carefully, and then they kill him. Isn't that odd?"

"I suppose, but I think it's rather nice, actually."

I shook my head. "If I were about to be executed, I either wouldn't be able to eat, or I'd lose the meal on the way to the Executioner's Star, or the gallows, or the Pilgrim's Block, or wherever they were to lead me."

"I see your point," he said. "But I think I'd like the meal, anyway."

"Well, perhaps I would, too."

"There's got to be someplace around here."

We stopped at the first place we came to, which meant nothing since he'd been leading the way. It was marked by a sign that was so faded I couldn't make it out, and reached from the street by walking down three steps below a hostel. It had probably been on the street level a few hundred years earlier—it seemed old enough, at any rate.

"*What do you think, Loiosh?*"

"*I don't like it, boss. There's no one hanging around outside, but he had plenty of time to set something up before we got here.*"

"Good point."

"*If you want to make a break, I can keep him busy.*"

"No. I'm going to run with it."

"*Boss—*"

"Stay alert."

The ceiling was low, the stone walls were damp, and the place was dark enough to be irritating—I suspected that, except for sinking, it hadn't changed much in quite some time. There was a big table with two long benches, about half of which were occupied by tradesmen, and a few isolated tables scattered about the room. We sat at one of those. It was toward the back, and Loftis could watch the front door while I watched the curtained-off doorway that presumably led to a private room of some sort. I could have made an issue about this—in fact, I was almost tempted to since I didn't have Loiosh with me—but I still had some faint hopes of convincing him that the story we'd given was true.

"What do you recommend?" I asked.

"I don't know; I've never been here before."

After too long, we realized that no one was going to bring us anything, so we went up to the bar and acquired a bottle of wine, a loaf of bread, two bowls of fish stew, glasses, spoons, a wooden platter to carry them all on. I did the paying, he did the carrying. We brought the stuff back to the table, sat down, poured, and sampled.

"The stew is too salty," suggested Loftis.

"The bread's all right."

"Better than the stew," he agreed.

"Or the wine," I added.

"I was thinking about bringing you in," he said.

"Do you have better wine than this?"

"A little better. Not enough to get excited about. The trouble is, we can't find your friend."

"You just haven't looked hard enough."

"Oh?"

"I know some excellent Eastern wines."

"Make a list of them for me. And while you're filling it out, maybe you can write down an address where I can find dear Margaret."

"I'll be sure to do that. But I don't feel too bad for you. You can't have been looking for more than half an hour. What do you expect? Searches and wines take time to mature."

"Wines do, certainly. But searches can be helped. And I'd take it as a personal favor."

"How about if I just pay for the next bottle of wine, instead?"

"That's a thought. You don't seem worried, Padraic. Is that your real name, by the way?"

"I don't remember anymore."

"Too much wine can do that to one's memory." He poured me some more. "You probably should be worried, though. Because, when I say that I might have to bring you in—"

"Please," I said. "Don't ruin the surprise. Or the meal, for that matter."

"You know, I can't even eat this stew. I wonder if they have anything else."

"I wouldn't risk it if they did. We got what they recommended; what do you suppose the inferior stuff is like?"

"Good point. Who did you say you're working for?"

"An unnamed Imperial group, devoted to the interests of the State."

"Excellent. I believe you, too. Only, I will require some form of identification, or a contact in the Imperial Palace, or a Signet."

I poured him some wine. "That could be problematical," I said.

"Yes. What exactly are you trying to do?"

"There's an old lady whose land is being taken away from her. We're trying to find out who owns the land so we can buy it for her, but the company is out of business. She's being evicted, you see—"

He held up his hand. "Say no more," he said. "Just give me her name, and I'll see that it's taken care of."

The worst of it was that he might be able to, and perhaps he even would; but I couldn't count on it, and I certainly couldn't give him any help in tracking you down, Kiera; especially after all the work I'd just gone through to destroy all the work you'd done in setting this up. I said, "I can't seem to remember, just at the moment. It must be the wine."

"Probably."

"*Boss, there are a couple of blades I don't recognize outside the door.*"

"*Outside the door? What are they doing?*"

"*If I didn't know better, I'd say they were getting ready to go charging in.*"

"*Oh.*"

Loftis sighed and pushed the food away. "Execrable," he said. "What am I going to do with you?"

Under the table, I let a dagger fall into my left hand, and made sure my sword was loose in its sheath. "You could paint me blue and trade me for bagpipes."

"Yes, that would be an option. But I'm afraid, as much as I've enjoyed sharing a meal with you, I'm going to have to insist on your accompanying me back to a place where I'm better equipped to get answers to questions."

"Damn," I said. "I just remembered. My niece is getting married this evening, and I have to pick out some new clothes, so I'm afraid I won't be able to make it today."

"Oh, I'm sure your niece will understand. Just what was her name, and where might I find her?" He smiled, then the smile went away and he looked at me very hard. "There are really only a couple of questions I need answered, but I *do* need them answered. Do you understand?"

I matched his stare.

He said, "Who do you work for, and what are you trying to accomplish? If you give me those answers, maybe we can work something out. If you don't, I'm going to have to start squeezing you."

"It isn't going to happen," I said.

"Boss, they're coming in!"

I rose to my feet, and I had my weapon halfway out when two men came through the curtain I was facing. I stepped to the side so Loftis couldn't get an easy shot at me and flipped my dagger at one of them; when he flinched, I lunged for the other one, knocking his weapon out of line and nailing him in the throat. I risked a quick glance toward the door, and then saw the other two, who were looking a little startled to see me noticing them and smiling; Loftis was now on his feet, too, and he had a weapon out, but he was looking at the pair who'd come through the door. He was facing away from me, so I couldn't see his expression, nor did I have time for a close look, because there was still the one I'd thrown my knife at. But Loftis did take the time to look at me, and there was no particular expression in that look. He said, "He didn't break the stick," which was just damned informative, but I didn't have the time to ask for an explanation.

As I turned back to the one I'd distracted, he made a break to get past me; that was fine, they could all run away as far as I was concerned.

Only he didn't run away.

He got past me, then he buried his sword in Loftis's skull, then he kept running out the door. The other two followed behind; they were gone before I realized it.

"Boss?"

"Don't worry, Loiosh. They weren't after me."

"They weren't?"

"Right. On the other hand, I suppose that means you can go ahead and worry."

Everyone in the room was staring at Loftis, and there was no sound, until the Dragonlord dropped his weapon, which made an appalling clamor as it hit the floor.

He turned very slowly and looked at me; there was an expression of surprise on his face. He opened his mouth, then closed it. I could see the muscles of his neck straining, and realized that it was hard work for him to keep his head straight with the weight of a sword attached to it.

Loftis sank to his knees, then he fell forward onto his face, looking absurd and pitiful with the sword still sticking out of the back of his head.

11

I GOT OUT OF there in a hurry, before anyone in the place could think to stop me.

Loiosh said, *"Should I follow them? Oh, never mind; they've just teleported. I can show you where they teleported from if you want."*

"I have no intention of tracing anyone's teleport, Loiosh; I just want to get out of here. Keep watching."

"Okay, boss."

I crossed the street and turned right at the first corner I came to, then right again, then left, then left again, and then right, then I went straight for a while, then I stopped and looked around, having gotten myself lost enough to have a chance of confusing anyone else."

"Well?"

"All clear, boss."

"Okay, back home, then."

"I'll keep watching."

We made it back to the cottage, both of us looking around fairly often. Buddy seemed happy to see me, Rocza seemed happy to see Loiosh, the old woman didn't seem happy about anything, and Savn didn't seem to care one way or another. I sat down at the table, closed my eyes, and took my first deep breath in what seemed like a year or so.

The old woman looked at me and didn't ask any questions, wherefore

I gave her no answers. I really wished you were here, Kiera, because I felt the need to confess and to have some help sorting out what had just happened. It had all made sense—Loftis figuring it out, sitting me down where he could give me one chance to come clean, and then having his people arrest me—up to the point where they'd killed him.

They'd killed *him*.

Had he been surprised by who came through the door? Or that anyone showed up? Or only by what they did?

He didn't break the stick.

That was a good one; I'd love to have found out what it meant, but there was no one around to ask. If I'd understood it, no doubt it would turn out to be the code phrase that made everything clear, and indicated exactly what I should do next. More probably, it went back to his childhood and had something to do with being hurt—at least, that's the sort of thing that went through my head when I decided I was about to become damaged, or maybe dead.

I regretted him. He was an honest son of a bitch, in spite of what he was doing, and he'd struck me as good at his job, although the only trace of evidence for that was that he'd hit you the same way, Kiera, so maybe he was really just a fool who knew how to impress people like us.

I wished his last meal had been better, though.

I said, "How's the boy, Mother?"

"No change," she said.

I said, "Savn?" He didn't seem to hear me. He was staring into the hearth as if it was the only thing in the world. At least there weren't any knives in it. I said, "Do you have any great ideas?"

She glared at me, then stood up, which took her quite a while. She came over and sat beside me, saying in a low voice, "I don't think I'm going to attempt the dreamwalk; at least, not for a while. He is responding, in a way, so that's some improvement. I want to know how far we'll get. I want to know if we can get him talking about something other than knives."

"How are you going to do that?"

"I've been talking to him. You could try it too."

"Just talking to him?"

"Yes."

"Even though he doesn't respond?"

"Yes."

"All right," I said.

She nodded, and I went over and sat down next to him. "So how are

you, boy?" I said. He didn't respond. "I hope you're feeling well physically, at least." I felt like an idiot. The old woman got up and went outside, taking Buddy with her.

"It's been about a year now, Savn." I said. "Look, I hope you know
that I'm sorry about what happened. You were never supposed to get
involved in it."

He stared at the hearth and didn't move.

"You saved my life, you know. Twice. First, when I was injured, and
then again. That isn't something I forget. And all those things you said to
me, they were hard to hear, but it was probably good for me." I laughed
a little. "Most things that are good for you hurt, maybe. To the left,
though, most things that hurt aren't good for you. There's a nice riddle,
if you want one. Do you like riddles? Do you like puzzles? I'm working
on a puzzle now, Savn, and it has me pretty thoroughly stumped. I'd like
to talk it over with you. You're a pretty sharp kid, you know.

"Why was Loftis killed? That's a puzzler, isn't it? He was working for
someone in the Empire who was trying to hide the fact that Fyres was
murdered, because if Fyres was murdered, they'd have to look into who
killed him, and they'd probably never find out, but they *would* find out
who wanted him dead, and that was a lot of people with a lot of connections to some of the people who keep our Empire chugging along. So
maybe someone didn't want the information hidden. I can imagine that,
Savn. But that's no reason to kill Loftis—it would be much easier, and
probably cheaper, just to let someone, say the Warlord, or Lord Khaavren,
or even Her Majesty, know what was going on. Killing Loftis doesn't
make any sense.

"And it couldn't be to help hide what he was doing, because now
they're going to have to investigate *that,* and that will almost certainly
lead them to find out everything. But if that was the goal, it was going
about it the hard way, and the dangerous way, and people don't do that
when there's a safe way and an easy way to do things—except maybe
Dzurlords, and they don't get into the sort of subtle thinking that goes
along with it. I just can't make it fit, Savn. What do you think?"

Evidently he thought the hearth was fascinating.

"There's got to be a piece of this I'm not seeing—a piece of information
I don't have. I wish I had more sources, like I used to. It used to be I
could just snap my fingers and people would go scurrying to discover
everything I needed to know. Now all I've got is what I can learn myself
(with the help of Loiosh and Rocza, and a few minstrels). Should I go
find a minstrel and talk to him, Savn? You were there the last time I did

that, and I got some useful information, too. Remember her? She was quite something, wasn't she? I remember thinking you were getting a crush on her, and I couldn't blame you. I was, too, if truth be known, but she's Dragaeran, and I'm an Easterner, and there you have it. Besides, I imagine she doesn't think much of me now, with what I've done to you. I suspect she blames me, and she's right to. I blame me, too."

I sat next to him and stared at the hearth. It was getting a bit chilly; maybe I should get a fire started. Back where Savn had come from, they were harvesting flax about now. They probably missed him.

"All right," I told him. "I'll go find a minstrel, and I'll see what the word is about Fyres, and about the investigation, and about the banks. Maybe I'll learn something. At least it'll keep me busy."

I stood up. "I'll talk to you later, all right?" He didn't object, so I headed out the door. The old woman was sitting on a wicker chair in front of the house, Buddy curled up beside her. I had the uncomfortable feeling she'd heard everything I said. I wondered if her whole reason for having me talk to him was so she could listen in, but I dismissed the thought; if there was one person in the whole mess who wasn't devious, it was her. But this affair was enough to make anyone paranoid, so I acquitted myself of paranoia and wrapped my cloak a little tighter around myself, because it was getting cold. Why is it you notice the weather more when you're out of town? I don't remember paying much attention to the weather when I lived in Adrilankha, even though I spent a lot of time walking around outside.

Minstrels, I've found, are rather like boot hooks—you keep running into them every time you go into your closet to find something else, but the minute you realize you need one they vanish without a trace. After walking all the way into Northport, I must have spent three hours going from one inn to another, and nowhere was there anyone singing for his supper, or telling stories in exchange for a room, or even sitting passed-out in the corner with a reed-pipe on his lap.

But diligence is sometimes rewarded. Seven times I asked locals where I might find some music. One didn't know, three didn't bother talking to me, and two were rude enough that I felt obligated to give them some minor damage as a lesson in courtesy. The seventh, however, was a pleasant young Teckla woman with flowing skirts and amazing black eyes who directed me to a public house about half a mile away, with feathers on its sign. I found it with no trouble (which surprised me just a little, as I'd become pessimistic about the whole adventure by that point) and I made my way into the small, smoke-filled little inn, in amongst a large crowd of mostly Teckla, with a couple of Orca and Chreotha surrounded by the entourage the minor nobility invariably attracts in such places, and, at the far end, a middle-aged Teckla playing a fretted gordstring as softly as such a twangy instrument can be played, and actually fairly well.

One part of a bench in the middle of the room was open, and I took it. Loiosh was with me, which may have accounted for some of the looks I got, but more likely they just weren't used to Easterners in there. The singer's voice was high and probably would have been unpleasant, but he picked songs that fit it—I suppose that's part of being a minstrel, just like part of being an assassin is knowing which jobs to take and which ones to leave alone. Eventually someone came by and brought me some wine, which I drank quickly because it wasn't very good, and some time later the minstrel stopped playing.

He stayed where he was and drank, and after a while I approached him. He looked at me, looked at Loiosh, and seemed uncomfortable, which was only natural. I said quietly, "My name is Vlad," and watched his face very closely for any sign of recognition.

"Yes?" he said. No, he didn't seem to recognize the name, which was good news. The first time a minstrel recognizes my name is the last time I can pull this stunt.

"Can we talk for a few minutes?"

"About what?"

I showed him the ring, then quickly put it away. The ring, by the way, represented one of the last things I arranged before I left Adrilankha; its design is a recognition symbol for the Minstrels' Guild, so when I showed it to him, he just said, "I see" and "Yes."

"I'm going to walk outside and cross the street. Meet me in twenty minutes, all right?"

"All right. Yes. How much—?"

"Ten imperials, or maybe more if you can help me."

"All right."

I nodded and left the place, walking around for a little while and eventually circling back. Loiosh flew around to look for signs of someone setting something up, but I didn't expect anything like that, and there wasn't.

After twenty minutes, he left the inn and crossed the street, and I stepped up next to him. "Let's walk together," I said, handing him ten coins. I'd said that to someone earlier that day, too.

We strolled together through the dark and quiet streets. This part of the city was far from the docks, and very narrow, and looked nothing at all like anywhere in Adrilankha, which I rather liked. I said, "What have you heard about Fyres?"

"The Orca?"

"Yes."

"Well, I mean, you know that he's dead."

"Yes. How did he die?"

"An accident on his yacht."

"Are you certain?"

We walked a little further. He said, "I've heard rumors, whispers. You know."

"No," I said. "I don't. Tell me."

"Who are you?"

"A friend of the Guild."

"Is there going—? That is, am I—?"

"In danger? No, as long we aren't seen together, and probably not even if we are."

"Probably not?"

"That's why we aren't talking inside, and why we're staying to areas without much light. Now, you were saying?"

"There's been talk that he was murdered."

"By whom?"

"People."

"What sort of people?"

"Just people."

"Why do they think so?"

"I don't know. But I'll tell you something: every time someone famous dies, however he dies, people say he was murdered."

"You think that's all it is?"

"Yeah. Am I wrong?"

"I don't know. I'm trying to find out. I'm asking you questions to find out. And I'm paying you. You have no reason to suspect—uh—foul play?"

"Not really, no."

"All right. What about all these bank closings?"

"It's the Empire."

"The Empire closed the banks?"

"No, but they allowed it."

"What do you mean?"

"I mean they aren't supposed to do that—let banks just close, anytime they want to; they're supposed to protect people."

"Why didn't they?"

"Because the bankers paid them."

"Are you sure about that?"

"Yeah."

"How do you know?"

"I know."

"How?"

He didn't answer. I said, "How much did you lose?"

"Almost eight hundred imperials."

"I see. Is that how you know?"

He didn't answer. I sighed. I wasn't getting a whole lot that I could use. I said, "What about the Jhereg?"

"What about them?"

"Are they involved?"

"With the banks? I don't know. I hadn't thought of that."

Oh, good. I was supposed to be tracking down rumors, and instead I was starting them. What I wanted to say was, "Can you tell me anything useful?" but that wasn't likely to produce results. I said, "What can you tell me about the people being kicked off their land?"

"Just what everyone knows," he said. "It's happening a lot, and no one knows why."

"What do you mean, no one knows why?"

He shrugged. "Well, it doesn't make any sense, does it? You get a notice of eviction, and then you go see if you can buy the place, and the owners have gone out of business."

"That's been happening a lot?"

"Sure. All over the place. I'm one of the lucky ones: we're still on Lord Sevaana's land, and he's still all right, as far as anyone knows. But I have friends and relatives who don't know what's going on, or what to do about it, or anything."

I don't know why I'd assumed the old woman's case was unique, but apparently I was wrong. That was certainly interesting. Who could stand to gain by forcing people to leave their land so it could be sold and then not selling it? And why force them to move before offering *them* the chance to buy it themselves? And how could Fyres's death have set all this off? And who wanted Loftis dead, and why? And—

No, wait a minute.

"Has anyone actually been made to move off his land yet?"

"Huh? Not this soon. No one could move that quickly, even if they made us."

"Yeah, I suppose you're right." But still . . .

"Is there anything else?" said the minstrel.

"Huh? What? On, no. Here. Vanish." I gave him another ten imperials. He vanished.

"*What is it, boss?*"

"*The inkling of the germ of a thread that might lead to the beginning of an idea.*"

"*Sure, boss. Whatever you say.*"

"*I think I might have a piece of something, anyway. Let me think for a minute.*"

He was polite enough not to make any of the obvious rejoinders, so I thought as I strolled. It isn't all that easy to just think, keeping your mind concentrated on the subject, unless you're talking to someone or writing things down, which is one reason I like to talk to Loiosh as I'm putting things together, but what I had right then wouldn't fit itself into words because it wasn't precise enough—it was just the vague, unformed notion that I'd, well, not exactly *missed* something, but that I'd been putting the wrong slant on things.

After a while I said, "*The trouble is, Loiosh, that the way Kiera and I got involved in this was through whatever oddity is involved in this business of putting what's-her-name's land on the market and then making it hard to track down, followed by impossible to track down. Just because that's where we started doesn't make that an important piece of whatever it is that's going on.*"

"*You knew that already, boss.*"

"*Sure. But knowing it is one thing; being aware of it as you work and taking it into account whenever you look at new information—*"

"*What are you saying?*"

"*Heh. That I've been looking at this thing skewed by what I knew about it. I have to look at it straight on. And I have a theory.*"

"*Oh, good. Only that was missing. All right, then, where to now?*"

"*I don't know.*" And, in my mind, Loiosh spoke the words as I did. "*You're funny, Loiosh,*" I told him. "*Do you have any great ideas?*"

"*Yeah. Let's get out of here.*"

I looked around, but didn't see anything.

"*No,*" he said. "*This city. This area. It isn't good, boss. They're still looking for you, and when you're in a city like this, you're too easy to find. I don't like it.*"

Neither did I, come to that. "*Soon,*" I told him. "*As soon as we get this settled.*"

"You can't do Savn any good with a Morganti knife between your shoulder blades."

"True."

"If I'd known we were going to be here this long, and that we'd be going around stirring up—"

"Okay, okay. I get the point." I'd thought about it, of course. Loiosh was right: a city, even one as small as Northport, was not a good place for me to hide when the whole Organization was looking for me. And, if what I'd just figured out was true, then I'd pretty much done what I'd agreed to do—the old woman would be able to stay on her land, and everything was fine.

"Where would we go instead?"

"The East."

"We've been there, remember?"

"It's big, there are lots of places. And no one would find us."

"Good point." There really wasn't any reason to stay here, if I could be certain that what I'd just figured out was true, and I could probably find that out.

Except that someone had cut Loftis down right in front of me, and there were neighborhoods full of people who had to leave because they no longer had any work, and I didn't understand why any of it was happening.

I said, *"The old woman is doing so well with Savn, it would be a shame to take him away so soon."*

"Boss—"

"Let's just take a few more days, all right?"

"You're the boss."

I wondered what you were finding out, Kiera; what would we learn about Fyres from the Jhereg? And, come to that, how heavily were the Jhereg involved? And if he'd gotten the Jhereg into it, why did he need the banks?

Did he need the banks at all?

There was only one banker we knew for certain was involved with Fyres, and that was Vonnith, and we knew she was bribing Imperial officials, which almost made her a Jhereg, too. Did I know of any legitimate banks that had made loans to Fyres? Did I even have any reason to suspect there were any?

How could I find out? Walking around pretending to be someone else has its uses, and we'd gotten some information that way, but there's a time for just being who you are. Had we reached it yet? Who was I, anyway?

Hmmm.

"Could work, boss."

"It's worth a shot."

"And even if it doesn't work, I'll enjoy it."

"Yeah, you probably will."

"And you won't?"

It wasn't easy finding a tailor's shop that was open at this hour—in fact, there were none. But after disturbing the tailor, it was easy enough to get what I wanted just by setting an appropriately large number of coins in front of him. My reserves of cash had been getting a bit low lately, and I wasn't excited about going to any of the places I'd need to in order to retrieve more of my wealth—for one thing, I'd have to remove the gold Phoenix Stone in order to teleport—but I could do it if I had to.

However, I was able to put in the order and he promised that he'd have what I needed early in the morning. That done, I wandered for a while, thinking over the plan and refining it in conversation with Loiosh.

I discovered that my feet were taking me back toward the cottage, and I decided to let them have their way, now that I had a plan for tomorrow. I walked, and I thought, and Loiosh flew above me, or sometimes sat on my shoulder, but kept watching so that I had the freedom to let ideas roll around in my head and turn into conclusions. I thought about stopping and performing a quick spell to make my feet hurt less, but I'd have to remove one of the Phoenix Stones or the other, and Loiosh gave me the benefit of his opinion on the wisdom of that, so by the time I reached the cottage I'd come to the conclusion that I was very tired of walking. I explained this to Buddy when he came out to greet me. He wagged his tail and sneezed in sympathy. Good dog.

Savn was sitting next to the hearth this time, not facing it. The old woman was next to him, talking to him softly. As I came in I waited to see if he would acknowledge my presence, but it was as if I didn't exist, as if nothing existed, even the old woman who was talking to him.

I walked over. "Hello, Savn," I said.

He didn't look at me, but he said, "Do you have a knife?"

I said, "Do you know my name?"

"You have a knife, don't you?"

"You know who I am, don't you Savn?"

"I . . . I lost Paener's knife, you know. I let it—"

"It's all right, Savn. No one is angry about that. Do you know who I am?"

"It was a good knife. It was very sharp."

"Let's talk about something else, Savn."

"I used it to cut—to cut things."

The old woman said, "Savn, your sister is all right."

He didn't seem to hear her any more than he'd heard me, but his hands started opening and closing. We sat there, but he didn't say anything else.

I looked at the old woman, who shrugged and stood up. She pulled me over to a corner and spoke in a low voice, saying, "I'm beginning to understand what's going on with him."

"His sister?"

She nodded. "She's the key. He thinks he killed her, or something. I'm not sure. He isn't really rational, you know. He doesn't know when he's dreaming and when he's really experiencing things."

"I could bring him back and show her to him."

She shook her head. "Not yet. He'd just think it was a dream."

"Then what do we do?"

"Just what we've been doing. We keep talking to him, even though he only wants to talk about knives and cutting, and we try to get him to talk about other things."

"Will that work?"

She shrugged. "If I'm right about what's going on in his head, then it should help, eventually. But I don't know what you mean by work. There's no way to know how much he'll recover, or what he'll be like. But we might be able to get him to the point where he responds to us, and then maybe we can teach him to look after himself."

"That would be good," I said.

"How about my problem?"

"You mean, about the cottage?"

"Yes."

"I'm not sure. I think I've figured out some of it. If my theories are right, you don't have anything to worry about. But you ought to worry about the possibility that my theories are wrong."

"All right," she said. "What if you're wrong?"

"Don't worry about it," I said.

12

I WAS UP EARLY, and, after almost enough klava, I stopped by the tailor's to retrieve the items that I'd ordered. The tailor had, evidently, been thinking, which can be unhealthy, but it had only frightened him, which is a natural survival reaction. I reassured him with words and coins, got the items, and left him reasonably content. Then I went by a weaponsmith and picked up a few things. Then I found an inn that was serving breakfast, stepped into the privy, and, amid odors that I will not bother describing, I spent some time getting dressed and set—it took me a while to remember how to conceal knives about my person without them showing, which surprised me a little. I covered everything, including the cloak, with my regular, nondescript brown cloak, which was far too hot for inside the privy, but would be only slightly too warm for the walk out to Vonnith's place.

I left the tavern a bit more bulky than I went in and made my plodding way out of Northport toward the home of our dear friend, Side-Captain Vonnith, and what *is* a side-captain, anyway?

There's no need to tell you about the trip out there—you did it yourself. And my compliments, Kiera, on the accuracy of the report, which gave me an excellent idea of what to expect, and when to expect it. About half a mile away, then, I took off the extra cloak, and appeared before some nameless birds and small animals as me, the old me, Vlad Taltos, Jhereg,

assassin, and friend to old ladies. I continued after stashing the brown
cloak in a thicket at the side of the road, and Loiosh grudgingly agreed
to wait outside after making a few remarks about who got to have all the
fun. I guess his idea of fun is different than mine.

Or maybe not.

Vonnith's guards got to me as I was walking up to the front door. Two
of them, flanking me as neat as you please. They made no hostile moves,
so I kept walking. They said, "My lord, may we be of some service to
you?"

"If you wish," I said. "You may tell the Side-Captain that a friend is
here to see her."

"A friend, my lord?"

"That's right. Don't I look friendly?" I smiled at them, but they didn't
answer. We reached the door. I said, "If you wish, you may tell her that
I represent the Adrilankha Eleemosynary Society."

"The—?"

"Adrilankha Eleemosynary Society."

"Uh, wait just a moment," he said. He was quiet for a time, I assume
making psychic contact with someone, then he looked over at his companion and nodded once. The companion hadn't opened his mouth the
entire time, but he was standing the right distance away from me, so I
assume he knew his business. In any case, they both inclined their heads
to me slightly and went back to their stations. I shrugged, gave a last
adjustment to my brand-new clothing, and pulled the clapper.

Hub appeared, looking just as you'd described him, and gave me a
greeting that made me miss Teldra. Have you met Teldra? Never mind.
He showed me in and brought me to the same room she met you in, and
there was Vonnith, just where she was supposed to be.

She stood up and gave me a slight bow—I don't think she knew how
polite she was supposed to be to me—and started to speak. I sat down
and said, "Give me the names of all the banks Fyres was involved in. I
don't need yours, we know about those. Which other ones?"

She frowned. "Why do you need to know that? And who are you,
anyway?"

"I'm not going to tell you my real name; you should know that.
And I don't have the energy to invent a good one. You know who I work
for—"

"You're a Jhereg!"

"Yes. And an Easterner. What's your point? We need to know what other banks Fyres was involved with, and we need to know before they go under."

"But how can you not know? How can—?" She seemed very puzzled, but I had no interest in letting her work things out; I'd made that mistake yesterday.

"Maybe we do know," I said, and let her put it together herself—wrong, of course. It's disgustingly easy to let people lie to themselves, and they do it so much better than you can. But as she was coming to the conclusion that this was all a test, and deciding how she ought to react to that, she wasn't considering the possibility that I wasn't involved with anyone except an old hedge-wizard and a notorious thief.

She said, "I don't know them all. I know the big ones, of course."

"Size isn't important; I mean the ones with heavy enough investments that they're at risk, or at any rate they've been seriously hurt."

"Oh," she said, and somehow that made things all right—perhaps she decided that she wasn't really being tested, we just didn't know who was heavily committed to Fyres. Or maybe she came up with some other explanation, I don't know. But I got what I was after. She said, "Well, the Bank of the Empire, of course."

Cracks and shards! "Yes. Go on."

"And the Turmoli Trust, and Havinger's."

"Quite."

"Should I include the House treasuries?"

House treasuries?

"Yes."

"Well, the only ones I know about are the Dragon and the Jhegaala. And the Orca, naturally."

"Naturally," I echoed, trying to keep my eyes from bulging too obviously. The Orca Treasury! The *Dragon* Treasury!

"I think those are the only Houses, or at least the only ones with potentially dangerous investments."

"Not the Jhereg?" I said.

"No," she said. "As far as I know, you—they are only in for small change. I think that was the deal to convince the Dragons to invest."

"That would make sense," I said. *Besides, what does the Jhereg Treasury matter if all the Jhereg in Northport and half the Jhereg in Adrilankha had already gotten involved? But then, maybe they hadn't—I still didn't know what you were going to uncover in Adrilankha, I was just guessing based on what your friend Stony had said.*

She kept talking, and I kept listening, but the details aren't important. She named about twenty or thirty banks, trusts, and moneylenders who were either going under or were in danger of going under, and, as I said, the Bank of the Empire, which embodies the Imperial Treasury, was at the very top of the list.

What happens if the Empire has to file surrender of debts, Kiera? Who can it surrender its debts *to*? It occurs to me that there are probably scholars of the House of the Orca who sit around and discuss things like this, or write long books about it, but nothing like it had ever crossed my mind before. When she finally ran down, I said, "Good. That's what we needed."

"But you knew all that."

"Maybe," I said. "That isn't your concern, is it?"

"I suppose not," she said, and looked at me with maybe just the hint of suspicion.

As if it were just an afterthought to the conversation, I said, "Loftis was killed yesterday."

"So I heard," she said coolly. "Poor fellow. Do the authorities know who did it?"

"Nope," I said.

She studied her fingernails. "I heard he was eating lunch with an Easterner at the time."

She heard that? Well, maybe that explained why she was so ready to believe I was who I claimed to be. That was almost funny. "It's possible," I said.

"It seemed like a professional job."

I looked at her and alarm bells went off inside my head. She knew as much about professionalism in assassination as I knew about professionalism in finance. And, in fact, it *hadn't* been a professional job; at least, not the way the Jhereg would have done it. Too many people involved, and too much left to chance, including a target who had the opportunity to draw his blade and a witness left alive. Whoever killed Loftis, it wasn't the Jhereg.

So who was it?

I tried to remember enough about the assassins to guess their House, but I couldn't really. They weren't Dzurlords, and they weren't Dragonlords. Orca? Maybe. Probably.

But, above all, why was she pretending it was a Jhereg job? Did she think I was pretending it was a Jhereg job, and she was just going along with it, even though she knew better? I looked at her, and my instincts answered *yes*.

"What is it?" she said. I'd been looking at her, even though I hadn't been aware of it, and apparently this was making her nervous. Good.

"What do you know?" I said.

"What do you mean?"

"You know something."

"About what?"

"You tell me."

"I don't—"

"I know we didn't do Loftis, and you know we didn't do Loftis. You've been scared, and you're getting ready to jump. You know something you shouldn't know, and that's scaring you, and well it should. What is it?"

"I don't know what you're talking about."

"Don't you?"

She tried to scowl at me. I stared back at her. I was Vlad again, a Jhereg assassin, if only for a moment, and she was an Orca—rich and fat, at least metaphorically. I'd become an assassin in the first place just for the pleasure of killing people like her. So I glared and waited, and eventually she cracked. It wasn't obvious, but I could see her resistance break down, and she knew I could see.

I said, "Well? Who killed him?"

She shook her head.

I said, "Don't be stupid. You know who I represent. Whoever you're scared of, you should be more scared of me. Now, which one of them was it?"

I threw in the "which one of them was it" phrase because it makes it sound like you know what you're talking about even when you don't, and this time it paid off. She said, "Reega."

"Good," I said. "Congratulations, you've just saved your life. How deep into her are you?"

"Heh," she said. "I'm not into her, she's into me."

"Same thing, isn't it? If she goes down, you follow her."

She nodded.

"Very well, Side-Captain. You know that we're all a little shy these days about throwing money at someone to keep an operation from going under—especially that bloodline. But it is possible something can be worked out."

"Something *has* been worked out," she snapped. "And if you people would just leave us alone—"

"You mean the land swindle? I know about that. What makes you think it's going to work?"

"What do you mean?"

"It isn't like it's a secret, Side-Captain."

"Who knows?"

"Everyone."

"Everyone?"

"Except maybe the victims."

"Well, it doesn't matter, does it? As long as the v—as long as the tenants don't find out, it doesn't matter who else does."

"Sure. But how long will it be until they realize what's going on? And then what?"

"We'll be gone by then."

"Do you really think you can move that quickly?"

"We can be done this week."

I pretended to consider. "It might work," I said.

"It will work. The Empire won't prosecute, and I don't even know what law they'd prosecute under if they wanted to. Right now we've got twelve thousand tenants who will go into debt for life to buy land at three times its value. If that isn't worth a little short-term Jhereg investment—"

"The Jhereg," I said, "doesn't have much to invest. You know why as well as I do."

She shrugged. "But I also know that you can come up with the funds, if you want to."

"Yes," I agreed. "We can."

"Boss! Trouble!"

"Just a moment," I said. *"What is it, Loiosh?"*

"Someone's just teleported in. Male, Jhereg colors, two bodyguards."

"Oh, nuts."

I stood up. "You must excuse me; there's a problem back home. I'll talk to my bosses."

Hub came into the room and whispered in Vonnith's ear. She nodded to him, then looked at me. "No need," she said. "I think your boss is here already."

I started heading toward where the back door had to be. *"Boss, two more just appeared in back."*

I looked at her, and realized she was in psychic communication—no doubt with whoever the Jhereg was. She focused on me and said, "Who are you?"

"Now don't you feel stupid," I told her.

The back was out and the front was out. *"Anyone watching the side windows, Loiosh?"*

"*Two.*"

Damn.

"Who *are* you?"

"Did you tell him that there was one of his people here?" I asked. "And did you mention it was an Easterner?"

"*Who are you?*" she said, as I saw the affirmative in her eyes. She had no idea why he'd reacted as he had, but now I was trapped. If I teleported, they'd just trace it, and I'd have to remove the black Phoenix Stone. I looked around. Here was as good as anywhere, I decided. So the question was, stand, or attempt to break out? I drew my blade.

"*Are they Jhereg at the side window?*"

"*No, Orca.*"

So that was the best path. I came to this conclusion about ten seconds too late, however, as three of them walked into the room. The one in the middle I knew from your description had to be Stony.

"Vlad Taltos," he said. "A pleasure to meet you."

"You, too, dead man."

He smiled.

His two "associates" spread out on either side of me. Vonnith said, "Not here!"

I said, "This is pretty sloppy work, you know, dead man."

"I know," said Stony. "Inelegant. But it's the best we can do, under the circumstances." He was armed as well, with a short, heavy sword, but he didn't look like someone who'd be all that good with it, whereas the two who were flanking me seemed to know their business.

"*Boss?*"

"*I'm going to be busy in here in a minute, Loiosh. If anyone else shows up to join the party, let me know, and if any escape routes show up, let me know that, too.*"

"*Sure, boss,*" he said in the tone that indicated he had his own plan and to the Falls with mine, so I wasn't startled when there was the sound of breaking glass, although everyone else was.

I took two steps that lasted about ten years each, and I was very much aware that my back was to a pair of blades, but Stony was taking twenty years to stop looking at Loiosh, so he wasn't ready for me and I took him, neat and clean, right through the heart. Then I turned around, drew a knife, and threw it at the one Loiosh wasn't busy with. To my amazement it actually hit him point-first, sticking in a spot on the left side of his lower chest, where it would certainly give him something to think about, and gave me time to step away from Stony, who was still on his feet and therefore dangerous. I prepared another knife very carefully.

"Up!"

Loiosh flew straight up to the ceiling and I threw, and, wouldn't you know it, the one I'd had time to aim hit him sort of edge-on in the stomach and did no damage to speak of, but that was all right, because Loiosh had scratched his face up pretty good and had bit him as well, so he probably had enough to keep him occupied.

I turned back to Stony, who picked that moment to fall over.

"Good work, Loiosh."

"Let's go, boss."

Side-Captain Vonnith stared at us with her mouth hanging open. I said, "Sorry about your window," and we headed for the front door, walking right in front of Hub, who looked like he wanted to say something polite but just couldn't manage. Lady Teldra would have.

"Why don't we teleport?"

"Because if Stony had any sense, he let someone know what was going down, and they'll be looking for me with everything they've got, just in case. If I take off the Phoenix Stone, I'll last just long enough to wish I hadn't."

"Oh."

"Are you all right, Loiosh?"

"Pretty much, boss. I cut myself on the glass a bit, but it isn't too bad."

"Then why do you sound that way?"

"Well, okay, so I'm bleeding a bit."

"Come here."

I looked him over, and found a nasty gash just where his left wing joined his body, and another on the left side of his neck. Both of them were bleeding. He licked himself a bit and said, "It's not as bad as it looks."

He folded himself up and I tucked him under my cloak, trusting him to hold on, and I stepped out of the doorway, blade first.

There were two Jhereg in front of me, and a pair of Vonnith's personal guardsmen next to them, and they all looked ready to scuffle. They stood, almost motionless, waiting for me to move. Back in the old days I'd have had a handful of nasty little things to throw at them to keep them busy, but these days I only had a few throwing knives, and I'd already lost half of them. It didn't look good, especially with Loiosh clinging helplessly to the inside of my cloak; I was morally certain that if this came to a true melee, one of them would end up skewering my familiar by accident, and I would hate that.

I looked at how everyone was positioned, then I pointed to the two Orca, one at a time, with my blade. "You two," I said. "Five hundred gold each if you nail these two for me."

No, they weren't going to go for it, but the Jhereg couldn't know that. They each stepped back and took a look at the Orca, and that was just long enough for me to nail one in the throat. He went down and I faced the other one for a second, then said, "Okay, so maybe you don't want to attack them. I still think you're best off out of there. This isn't your fight, you know. And you won't get any of the reward in any case. Ask the Side-Captain if you don't believe me. I'll wait."

I'm afraid I lied to them, Kiera; while they were checking in, I took a step and a lunge, cutting the other Jhereg's wrist, then shoulder, then face. He went back and I went forward and he tried to counter and I parried, riposted, and got him lightly in the chest. He backed up some more and raised his blade to charge me; I gave him a very nice cut on his forearm, and his blade fell to the ground.

"Get out of here," I suggested. He turned and ran up toward the road without another word.

There's no question that the two Orca could have taken me then, but I had to hope they were a little intimidated by now, and that they weren't even sure this was their fight in the first place—aside from which, I really expected to see a good number of Jhereg showing up any minute, so I didn't have time for anything fancy. I looked at them; they shrugged and lowered their weapons.

"See you," I said, and made tracks, aware of the weight of Loiosh clinging to my cloak, and to the increasing wetness against my side.

It was a long, long way to the main road, Kiera, but nothing untoward happened before I reached it. I headed back toward Northport, ducking into the woods as soon as there was enough woods to duck into.

"*I think we might make it, Loiosh,*" I said.

Then, "*Loiosh?*"

I stopped where I was, and if every assassin in the Empire had shown up just then, I don't think I would have noticed. He was gripping the inside of my cloak, and the first thing I noticed was that his chest was still rising and falling, and there was still blood seeping from the two wounds. I took the cloak off and spread it on the ground, then I gently spread his wings so I could look at the injuries. They didn't seem very deep, but the one near his wing was jagged and ugly. I spent a great deal of time looking for slivers of glass, but I didn't find any, which was good.

I didn't know what to do, so I cut the Jhereg cloak into strips and bandaged him up as best I could, binding his left wing tight to his body. Then I looked at the other wound and scowled mightily. I'd made jokes before, especially with Kragar and Melestev, about how they should be prepared to put a tourniquet around my throat if anyone cut it, but now that I was faced with the absurd problem of trying to put a bandage around Loiosh's snakelike neck, there wasn't anything funny about it. In the end, I just used a great deal of cloth and kept the wrapping loose enough so it wouldn't stop his breathing, and then I pressed my hand against it and held it there.

"*Loiosh?*"

No response.

I picked him up and made my way through the woods, doing my best to keep track of where I was, but I've never been a good woodsman.

Some animals, I'm told, will fall into a deep sleep in order to heal themselves. I didn't know if jhereg did that. Isn't that funny? Loiosh and I had been together since I was a kid, and there were so many things I didn't know about him. I wondered what that said about me, and whether it was something I wanted to hear. No doubt Savn—the old Savn, before he went away—would have had a great deal to say about it. He was a sharp kid, was Savn. I hoped that Savn wasn't gone forever. I hoped Loiosh wasn't gone forever. Cawti, the old Cawti, the woman I'd married, was probably gone forever. How much of all of this was my fault?

These were my thoughts, Kiera, as I tried to make my way to North-port, moving as fast as I could with the bundle of my familiar in front of me and thicket all around me. Good thing it was still daylight or I'd have killed myself; too bad it was daylight, because the Jhereg would have an easier time finding me. Where were they now? Had they arrived in force, and were they combing the woods, or had they not yet learned that I had escaped? They must, by now, have realized that Stony was dead, and at least they'd be sending someone to investigate.

There was a flapping above me, and I looked up, and there was Rocza. She landed on my shoulder and looked at me. Okay. I can take a hint.

I stopped, spread out the cloak, and removed the bandages from Loiosh's wounds. Rocza waited patiently while I did so, then gave me a look of stern disapproval and began methodically licking the wounds clean. I don't know if there's something about jhereg saliva, or if she was using her poison and there's something about *that*, but the bleeding had stopped by the time she was done. I reached out to pick up Loiosh, but Rocza hissed at me and I stopped. She picked him up in her talons, flapped once, and took to the air, though it seemed with a bit of trouble.

"Okay," I said. "Have it your way."

She flew in a careful circle, just over my head.

"I hope," I said aloud, "that you can lead me back home. And that you want to, for that matter."

I don't know if she understood me, or if she thought of it on her own, but she began flying, and she did such a good job of letting me stay in sight that it can't have been accidental. From time to time she would carefully lay Loiosh down in a tree limb, rest for a moment, and then fly around as if to scope out the area—maybe that's what she was doing, in which case Loiosh had certainly taught her well, because we didn't run into anyone. Once, when she had deposited Loiosh, another jhereg came and sat near him. Rocza returned and spread her wings and hissed with great enthusiasm, and the other jhereg flew off. I applauded silently.

Eventually the woods gave way to grassland, and I felt rather naked and exposed walking through it, except that by then it was growing dark, so I delayed a little while to give the darkness more time to settle in and get comfortable. Rocza didn't like that, and hissed at me, but then she probably decided she needed the rest, too, so she set Loiosh down in the grass and licked him some more, and when the light had faded enough we started off again.

It took a long time, but eventually we found the road through the woods, and then we found the hideous blue cottage, and we were home. Buddy came out, looked at us, barked once, then followed us in. Rocza flew into the house, went straight to the table, and gently laid Loiosh on it. It was only when I noticed how pleasantly warm the place was that I realized I'd been cold.

The old woman stood up.

"It's a long story," I said, "and I don't think you want to hear it. But Loiosh has been hurt, and—wait a minute."

Rocza flew over to where Savn was staring off into space, landed on his shoulder, and hissed at him. Savn very slowly turned to face her. The old woman and I looked at each other, then turned back to them.

Rocza hissed again, then flew over to the table. Savn followed her with his eyes. She flew back to his shoulder, hissed, then flew back to Loiosh.

Savn rose unsteadily to his feet and walked over to the table, and looked down at Loiosh.

"I'll need some water," he said to no one in particular. "And a small needle, as sharp as you can find, and some stout thread, a candle, and clean cloth."

He worked on Loiosh far into the night.

Interlude

"YOU'RE LOOKING PUZZLED AGAIN, Cawti."

"Yes. Your conversation with Loftis."

"What about it?"

"How did you convince him that you were involved with the Empire?"

"Just what I said. I fed him a few details about things his group had been involved in."

"But *what* details? What activities of theirs did you know about?"

"You and Vlad."

"Huh?"

"I mean, he wanted to know that, too. He positively interrogated me about it."

"And you said?"

"That I didn't care to discuss it."

"Oh."

"Sorry."

"I understand. How is Loiosh?"

"You want me to get ahead of the story?"

"Yes."

"Loiosh is fine, as far as I know."

"Okay."

"Should I go on?"

"Please do."

"All right."

13

I SAT FOR A long time after Vlad had finished speaking, digesting his words slowly and carefully, the way one might digest a seventeen-course Lyorn High Feast on Kieron's Eve—a day I've never celebrated for personal reasons, though I've had the feast. I kept looking back and forth between Loiosh and Savn, who had perhaps gone a long way toward healing each other, although Loiosh showed no signs of injury save that he wasn't moving much, and Savn showed no signs of healing save that he'd moved a little bit.

"Well?" said Vlad when he'd judged I'd been silent long enough.

"Well what?"

"Have you put it together?"

"Oh. Sorry, I was thinking about"—I gestured toward Savn—"other things."

He nodded. "Do you want to try, or should I explain it?"

"Some of it, at least, is pretty obvious."

"You mean, the land deal?"

"Yes. It was just a subtheme to the concerto: a few of them need to come up with a lot of cash in a hurry, so they buy out Fyres's companies cheap, since they're going under, anyway, then threaten people like our good Hwdf'rjaanci with eviction to make them worried, then vanish so they don't know what's happening so they'll panic, and then, in a day or two, our heroes will come back with offers to sell them the land at outrageous prices, in cash."

He nodded. "With nice offers of loans at Jhereg-style interest rates to go with them."

"So our hostess isn't really in danger of losing her cottage, and, if she's careful, she can probably avoid being overcharged too much. In fact, if we can come up with some cash for her, she can even avoid the interest rates."

"I think we can do that," said Vlad.

"Between us," I said, "I have no doubt that we can."

"What about the rest of it?" he said. "Can you put it together?"

"Maybe. Do you know it all?"

"Almost," he said. "There's still a piece or two missing, but I have some theories; and there's also a lot of background stuff that you can probably explain."

"What's missing?"

"Loftis."

"You mean, why did Reega have him killed?"

"Yes. If it was Reega."

"You think Vonnith was lying?"

"Not lying. But we don't know yet if it was Reega's choice, or if she just arranged it."

"Why would she arrange it?"

"Because she was in a position to. She had a lot to gain, and she was in touch with Loftis."

"How do you know that?" I said.

"Because of the way she reacted when I told her the Empire was covering up something."

"Oh, right. I'd forgotten. Yeah, she might have just arranged it. But, if so, who did she arrange it for? And why?"

"Good questions. That's what I'm still missing." He shook his head. "I wish I knew what 'he didn't break the stick' means."

"I think I know," I said.

"Huh?"

"It goes back to the Fifth and Sixth Cycles, and even into the Seventh, before flashstones."

"Yes?"

"Some elite corps were given sorcery. Nothing fancy, just a couple of location spells, and usually one or two offensive weapons to be used over a distance. They weren't all that effective, by the way."

"Go on."

"Whoever was the brigade's sorcerer would bind the spells into a stick so that any idiot could release the spell. They used wood because binding them into stone took longer and was more difficult, although also more reliable." I shrugged. "You point the stick at someone, and you release the spell, which doesn't take a lot of skill, and you get a nasty scrape on your palm, and whoever you pointed the stick at has a much nastier burn. You can kill with it, and at a pretty good distance, if your hand is steady and your eye is good and, mostly, if the spell was put on right in the first place. Which it usually wasn't," I added, "according to the histories."

"But what does—"

"Right. The thing is, the sticks were smoothed a bit to take the spell, but otherwise they were just sticks. Once you got into battle, you might be looking around and see one on the ground, but you'd have no way of knowing if it was discharged or not—that is, unless you were fairly skilled, the only way to find out if it had been used already was to discharge it. You can imagine that it might be embarrassing to pick one up on the field and assume it had a charge when it didn't, or even the reverse."

"Yeah, I can see that."

"So the custom was to break it in half as soon as you'd discharged it."

"And you think that's what he was talking about?"

" 'Breaking the stick' became a handy way of referring to leaving a signal, especially a warning."

"How long since it's been used?"

"A long time."

"Then—"

"He was a military historian, Vlad. Remember how he kept making references to obscure—"

"Got it."

I shrugged. "Maybe it meant something else, but . . ."

"Well, that's all very interesting." He closed his eyes for a moment, and I could practically hear the tides of his thoughts break against the shore of facts as he put things together in new ways; I waited and wondered. "Hmmm. Yes, Kiera, it's *all* very interesting."

"What do you mean?"

"I mean, I think I have the rest of it. And then some."

"And then some?"

"Yeah, I got more than I wanted. But never mind that, it doesn't matter. Can you put it together?"

"Maybe," I said. "Well, let's see what we have. We have Fyres murdered, and someone desperate to hide that fact. We have companies he was into falling like Teckla at the Wall of Baritt's Tomb. We have someone, or someones, in the Empire desperate to hide the fact that Fyres was murdered. Am I doing all right so far?"

"Yep. Keep going."

"Okay. We have Jhereg involvement with Fyres, and Imperial involvement with the banks, and—wait a minute."

"Yes?"

"Fyres owed the Jhereg. Fyres owed the banks. The banks and the Jhereg were depending on Fyres. The Empire was protecting the banks, and the banks were supporting the Empire. Have I got it?"

"Right. Conclusion?"

"The Empire is working with the Jhereg."

"Exactly," said Vlad. "Supporting the Jhereg, borrowing from the Jhereg, and, probably, using the Jhereg."

"Just as you were saying."

"Yeah, I guess it all seemed to be heading that way. But push it a little further, Kiera: what would the empire do if word of the Jhereg's influence in the Empire was about to emerge into the public?"

I shrugged. "Everything it could to hide that fact."

"Everything?"

I nodded. "Yes. Or, if it's what you want, everything including covering up the Fyres murder, and even—yes, and even murdering their own investigator if they thought he was no longer reliable."

"Yep. That's what 'he didn't break the stick' meant. It bothered me that someone like Loftis would be that careless. It either meant we were wrong about him or there was something we didn't know, and now we've figured it out."

"Yes," I said. "He was set up by his own side."

Vlad nodded. "He wasn't given the warning he was supposed to get if there was any danger. They'd probably picked that spot out, and there was supposed to be some indication either that it was all right or that it wasn't. And so he thought he was safe, and that's why they could take him out so easily."

"Right. Domm?"

"His name popped into my head," said Vlad.

I nodded. "Domm would be a safe guess. Reega set it up, and Domm made sure Loftis wouldn't be ready to defend himself, and they used you—"

I stopped, and looked at Vlad. He said, "What?" Then, "Oh."

"They were *too* ready, and you were too convenient."

"I didn't give the game away," said Vlad. "I didn't slip up. They already knew about me when I walked in, which means they already knew about you."

I nodded. "And that explains something else: namely, why it's been so easy to fool these people. We haven't fooled anyone, except maybe Vonnith. They've been playing with us, and letting us think we were playing with them."

"Not Vonnith, either," said Vlad. "She was onto me from the moment I first showed up."

"Stony?"

"Yes. I figured that it was just bad timing, him being there right then. But she must have gotten hold of him when I got there, and then all she had to do was delay me until he was ready to move."

I nodded.

He said, "Well, aren't we a couple of idiots?"

I nodded again. "Stony," I said. "That son of a bitch."

"What now, then?"

"Now, Vlad? What is there to do? We've solved Hwdf'rjaanci's problem, which was all we intended, and we've figured out what's going on, and we've also figured out that they had our number from the beginning. We're done."

He stared at me. "You mean, let them get away with it?"

I grinned. "I will if you will."

"For a minute there," he said, "you had me worried." Then he frowned. "When do you think they caught onto us?"

"Early," I said. "Remember Stony asking if I'd seen you?"

"Sure. I just figured it was a sign of how bad they want me, and they know we know each other."

"That's what I thought, too. And, right then, that's probably all it was. But then they put it together. Fyres's place is broken into, right?"

"Right."

"Okay. You didn't tell me why you wanted me to do that. If you had, maybe I'd have been messier, or done something atypical, but, as it was, it was a usual Kiera job, and anyone who knows my work, which certainly includes Stony, would—" I held up my hand as he started to speak. "No, I'm not blaming you: you had no reason to think I'd be involved after doing what you wanted; neither did I, really, I just got interested. But think about it. What's the next thing that happens after I break into Fyres's old place and steal his private papers?"

"You start asking Stony questions about him."

"Right."

"And we didn't know that Stony was involved enough to be hearing everything that happened regarding Fyres, the banks, the investigations, and everything else."

"That's it," I said. "Stony knows, right then and there, that I'm looking into Fyres's death, though he probably doesn't know why. But he knows Kiera the Thief is sniffing around the death of this rich guy who's made so much trouble."

"And then what does he do?"

I said, "He starts asking himself where the next logical place to look is, if someone is interested in Fyres's death. And it is?"

"The Imperial investigation."

"Exactly. So there he is, alerting Loftis and his merry band that Kiera the Thief might appear out of nowhere, or maybe someone working for Kiera. And who shows up there, right on schedule, but to everyone's amazement?"

Vlad nodded. "I do," he said, with more than a touch of bitterness in his voice. "In my great disguise that fooled them so completely."

"Yes. Loftis is looking for people to show up asking questions, and he's looking carefully for anyone in disguise, and there you are. We had no way of knowing that Loftis and Stony were in touch—and maybe they weren't, directly. But, one way or another, Stony hears that Loftis had a visit from an Easterner trying to disguise himself as a Chreotha. 'Tell me about this Easterner,' he probably says. 'And what kind of questions did he ask?' "

Vlad nodded. "Yes. And, all of a sudden, you and I are tied together, looking into Fyres's death."

"Right. Now the Jhereg is hot for you. Somehow or other, Reega learns of it."

"Not somehow or other," said Vlad. "Because they went to her, the same way they went to Vonnith, and probably Endra as well. After all, they followed me. I let them. I thought I was being clever. Vonnith is so far into the Jhereg that she had no choice, and they probably offered her a good piece of change to help them. But Reega had her own ideas."

"You're right," I said. "That's probably how it worked. If we'd gone back to Reega, rather than to Vonnith, the same thing would have happened, most likely. But first, Reega either decided or, more likely, was told to get rid of Loftis."

"Yes. And Loftis was told to try to pump me. So Loftis tries to pump me, and he brings me to this place where the arrest is planned, and then, bang, no more Loftis. All without the Jhereg's knowledge, because the Jhereg wouldn't have let me out of there alive. Do I have it?"

"That's how I read it," I said.

"Kiera, we have been thoroughly taken."

"Yes."

"You don't like it any more than I do, do you?"

"Rather less, in fact, I would imagine."

"So, what are we going to do about it?"

"At the moment," I said, "I cannot say. But, no doubt, something will occur. Let us consider the matter."

"Right," said Vlad, who was looking at me a little funny.

I said, "What about the information from Vonnith? Can we trust it, if she knew you weren't who you claimed to be?"

"I think so," said Vlad. "She knew her job; she was supposed to keep me there long enough for them to kill me. Why bother to think up lies when the guy who's hearing the truth is about to become deceased?"

"Good point."

"So, what now?"

I said, "Lieutenant Domm?"

"Eh?" said Vlad. And, "Oh. You think he's the one who wanted Loftis out of the way? There was no love lost between them, but they were in the same corps."

"Were they?" I said.

"Eh?"

"Think back to that conversation you overheard—"

"You don't mean that was staged, do you? I don't believe—"

"Neither do I. No, at that point they didn't know who you were, and they weren't looking for witchcraft. I mean after that."

"My talk with Domm at the Riversend?"

"Yes. They probably hadn't had time to figure out who you were yet, so you might have even had them fooled. But maybe not. Think over that conversation. You made Domm slip and let what's-her-name, Timmer, know that something wasn't right."

"What about it?"

"I think that was legit. But what evidence is there that Domm was in the same corps as Loftis?"

"Then who—"

"Who would normally conduct such an investigation?"

"Uh . . . I don't remember. That group that reports to Indus?"

"Right. The Surveillance group. And there almost had to be someone from that group involved, just because it would look funny if there weren't."

"But now we're implicating Indus."

"So? As far as I can tell, Vlad, we're implicating everyone in the Empire with the possible exception of Her Majesty and Lord Khaavren."

"I—"

"I don't think you realize what we're dealing with here, Vlad."

"You mean it's that big?"

"No, I mean it's that—I don't know the word—*pervasive*. We've been looking for corrupt officials, and checking them off our list when we decided they weren't corruptible. But that isn't the point at all."

"Go on," he said, frowning.

"Corruption doesn't enter into it. Oh, maybe Shortisle, or someone on his staff, is lining his pocket. But that's trivial. What's happening here is everyone involved in the mechanism of the Empire is working together to do his job just the way he's supposed to."

"Come again?"

"The Empire is nothing more than a great big, overgrown, understaffed, and horribly inefficient system for keeping things working."

"Thank you," he said, "for the lesson in government. But—"

"Bear with me, please."

He sighed. "All right."

"By things," I said, "I mean, mostly, trade."

"I thought putting down rebellions was the big thing."

"Sure," I said. "Because it's hard to trade if there's a rebellion in progress." He smiled, and I shook my head. "No, I'm really not kidding. Whether a certain piece of ground is ruled by Baron Wasteland or Count Backward doesn't make a difference to much of anyone, except maybe our hypothetical aristocrats. But if the trees from that piece of ground don't reach the shipwrights here in Northport, then, eventually, we're going to run out of that particular lime they have in Elde, which we use as an agent mixed with our lime to make mortar to keep our buildings from falling down."

"Reminds me of the couple who didn't know the difference between—"

"Hush. I'm being grandiloquent."

"Sorry."

"And we'd also, by the way, run out of that lovely Phoenix Stone from Greenaere that I think you know something about. That's one of the simplest examples. Do you want to hear about how a dearth of wheat from the Northwest shuts down all the coal mines in the Kanefthali Mountains? I didn't think so.

"The point," I continued, "is trade. If it weren't for the Empire, which controls it, everyone would make up his own rules, and change them as occasion warrants, and create tariffs that would send prices through the overcast, and everyone would suffer. If you need proof, look to your homeland, and consider how they live, and think about why."

"Life span has something to do with that," he said. "As does the tendency of the Empire to invade whenever it doesn't have anything better to do."

"Trade has more to do with it."

"Maybe." He shrugged. "I suppose. But how does all of this relate to corruption among the great and wonderful leaders of our great and wonderful—"

"That's what I'm saying, Vlad. It isn't corruption. It's worse—it's incompetence. And, worse than that, it's inevitable incompetence."

"I'm listening, Kiera."

"Why does a banker go into business?"

"I thought we were talking about the Empire?"

"Trust me."

"All right. A banker goes into business because he's an Orca and he doesn't like the sea."

"Stop being difficult."

"What do you want?"

"Obvious answers to stupid questions. Why does a banker go into business?"

"To make money."

"How does he make money."

"He steals it."

"Vlad."

"All right. The same way a Jhereg moneylender does, only he doesn't make as much because his interest rate is lower and he has to pay taxes—though he does save some in bribes."

"Spell it out for me, Vlad. How does a banker make money?"

He sighed. "He makes loans to people and charges them for it, so they pay him more than he loaned them. In the Jhereg, interest is calculated so that—"

"Right. Okay. Here's another easy one: what determines how much profit a banker makes?"

"How much money he loans, and at what interest rate. What do I win?"

"So what keeps him from running up the interest rates?"

"All the other bankers."

"And what keeps them from getting together and agreeing to raise the rates?"

"Competition from the Jhereg."

"Wrong."

"Really? Damn. And I was doing so well. Why is that wrong?"

"I'll put it another way: what keeps them from getting together, *including* the Jhereg, and fixing interest rates that way?"

"Uh . . . hmm. The Empire?"

"Congratulations. The Empire sets limits on the rates, because the Empire has to take loans out, too, and if the Empire got rates that were *too* much better than everyone else's, the Great Houses would object, and the Empire has to always play the Houses off against each other, because, really, the Empire is just the sum of the Great Houses, and if they all combined against the Empire . . ."

"Got it. No more Empire."

"Exactly."

"Okay, so the Empire fixes the maximum loan rate."

"Rates. There are several, having to do with, well, all sorts of complicated things. That's Shortisle's job."

"Got it. Okay, go on. So, in effect, the maximum profit a banker can get is set by law."

"Nope."

"Uh . . . okay, why not?"

"Because there's another way to maximize profits."

"Oh, right. Loan more money. But you can't make loans if people don't need the money."

"Sure you can. You can create the need."

"You mean the land swindle?"

"No. That's trivial. Oh, I'm sure that's why it's being done, but it isn't happening on anywhere near the scale that would pull the Empire into it."

"All right. Go on, then. How?"

"Undercut the Jhereg."

He shrugged. "They always do that. But the Jhereg moneylenders stay in business, anyway."

"Why?"

"Because we aren't as fussy about making sure the customer can pay us back, because we have our own ways of making sure we get paid back."

It was interesting that Vlad still thought of the Organization as "we," but I didn't choose to comment on that. I said, "Exactly. And so . . . ?"

He frowned. "You mean they start making it easier to get loans?"

"Precisely."

"But then, what if the loans aren't paid back?"

"Vlad, I'm not talking about small stuff, like someone wanting to buy a house. I'm talking about big finance, like someone wanting to start a major shipping firm."

He smiled. "Just to pick an example by random? Well, all right. So then what happens?" He answered his own question. "Then the banks go under. That's stupid business."

"Maybe. But what if you don't have any choice?"

"What do you mean?"

"If you had a pile of cash—"

He smiled. I'd forgotten how much money he had.

"Let me rephrase. If you had a pile of cash that you wanted to put into a bank—"

"Ah!"

"Which bank would you choose?"

"I wouldn't. I'd give it to an Organization moneylender."

"Work with me, Vlad."

"All right. I don't know. I guess the one that had the best rates."

"What if they were all the same?"

"Then the one that seemed the most reliable."

"Right. What makes a bank reliable? Or, more precisely, what would make you *think* a bank was reliable?"

"I don't know. How long it's been around, I suppose, and its reputation, how much money it has."

"How do you know how much money it has?"

"The Empire publishes lists of that sort of thing, doesn't it?"

"Yes. Another of Shortisle's jobs."

"You mean he's been lying?"

"Not exactly. Don't get ahead of me. What determines how much money the bank has, or, rather, how much money the Empire reports the bank as having? I mean, do you think they go in and count it?"

"Well, sort of. Don't they do audits?"

"Yes. And do you know how the audits work?"

"Not exactly."

"They look at how much gold they claim to have on hand and compare it with what they find in the vaults, and then—here's the fun part—they look at their paperwork and add the amount they have, as we'd put it, on the street. And the more money they have on the street, the richer they are. Or, rather, the richer they *look*."

He frowned. "So, you mean, if they start making risky loans, it looks like they're doing really well, when in fact they may be—"

"Tottering on the edge of ruin. Yes."

He didn't speak for a moment. Savn was snoring in a corner, Buddy curled up on one side of him, Rocza on the other, with Loiosh next to her. There were occasional sounds from the predators outside, but nothing else. I gave Vlad some time to think over what I'd told him.

Eventually he said, "The Empire—"

"Yes, Vlad. Exactly. The Empire."

"Aren't they supposed to check on things like that?"

"They do their best, sure. But how many banks are there making how many loans? Do you really think Shortisle has the means to inspect every loan from every bank to make sure it isn't too risky? And, even if it is, it has to be pretty extreme before the Empire has the right to step in."

"But—"

"Yes, but. But if several banks fail all at once, then what happens to trade?"

"It falls apart. And they can't allow that."

"So what do they do?"

"You tell me," said Vlad.

"All right. First of all, they curse themselves soundly for having allowed things to get into that sort of mess in the first place."

"Good move. Then what?"

"Then they try to cover for the banks as much as they can."

"Ah ha."

"Right. If word get out that Fyres was murdered, then they'll have to find out why, and then—"

"Right," said Vlad. "Then word will get out that lots of big banks, starting with the Verra-be-damned bank of the Verra-be-damned Empire, are very rich on paper and, in fact, are on the edge of taking that big tumble into oblivion. And if that happens—"

"Panic, bank runs, and—"

"Trade goes overboard in a big way."

I nodded. "That's what I didn't see right away. This isn't a few slime-bags in the Empire lining their pockets, this is the Empire doing what it's supposed to do—protecting trade."

He shook his head. "And all of this starting off just because somebody knocked a big-time scam artist in the head."

"A big-time, extremely wealthy scam artist."

"Yes. Only one thing."

"Yes, Vlad?"

"Why?"

"Why what?"

"Well, this sort of mess isn't good for anyone, right?"

"Right."

"So if all this was set off by Fyres's death, why was he killed?"

I stared off into space for a moment, then I said, "You know, Vlad, that is a very, very good question."

"Yeah, I thought so. So what's the answer?"

"I don't know."

"And here's another question: with Stony dead, is the Jhereg still onto me? I mean, are they still breathing down my neck, or do I have a little time to find the answer to the first question?"

I nodded. "That one I think I can find the answer to."

"I'd appreciate it. What about the other one?"

"We'll see," I said. "I'll be back."

"I'll wait here," he said.

14

I LEFT THE COTTAGE and was instantly in Northport; a quicker teleport than was my custom, but I realized after I performed it that there was a feeling of urgency within me that was still growing.

So I deliberately teleported to a place more than a mile away and made myself walk the rest of the distance so I could calm down. I strolled casually—at least, I did my best to stroll casually—through the narrow, winding streets, where the second-floor balconies almost touched each other and the roofs all but hid the sky, until I arrived at a place I knew. This time Dor was in.

He looked up when I came in, and he seemed afraid. That made me sad. The last thing I want is to inspire fear. I said, "What's wrong, Dor?"

His brow furrowed, and he said, "You don't know?"

"No, I don't, unless it's about Stony's death. But I had nothing to do with that."

"That Easterner did."

"Perhaps."

"No perhaps about it. We were able to revivify Raafla, and he told us."

"I imagine Stony hasn't been saying much."

He glared at me. "That isn't funny. I liked him."

Liked.

Past tense.

"What do you mean?" I said. "Hasn't he been revivified?"

"You know damned well—"

"Dor, I know very little 'damned well'; even less than I'd thought. What are you telling me?"

"He wasn't revivifiable."

"He wasn't? What happened?"

He stared. "You really don't know?"

"Please tell me, Dor. What happened?"

"The kind of spells assassins always use, that's what."

If Vlad had ever used those sorts of spells, I sure didn't know about it. And he hadn't said anything. . . .

"You'd better tell me all about it," I said.

"Why?"

"Because I'm curious, and because I need to know."

"If you're looking for your friend," he said bitterly, "he'll be long gone by now."

"Tell me, please," I said.

He did so.

His story shook me up enough that I had trouble believing it, so after leaving him there, I used some of my other contacts in Northport to verify it. The details aren't important, but the story stayed the same. I was convinced, and also confused, but I'd at least answered Vlad's second question, about whether the Jhereg thought he was still in town.

About Vlad's first question, why was Fyres killed, I still had no clue, but I returned at once to tell Vlad what I'd learned. When I arrived at the blue cottage, and had said hello to Buddy, I found Vlad sitting near the hearth having a one-sided conversation with Savn.

Vlad looked at me, blinked, and stood up. We moved over to the table in the kitchen and I sat down. Vlad brought me some klava. "The honey is almost gone," he said. "And we haven't been stung too badly."

"Yet," I said.

He raised his eyebrows.

I said, "Well, Vlad, it goes like this."

He poured himself a cup, sweetened it, and said, "Not here."

"All right," I said.

Vlad and I stepped outside. Loiosh rode on his shoulder and seemed better, but I hadn't seen him flying yet. Vlad leaned against a tree and said, "Uh-huh?"

"The first item is that, while everyone knows you shined Stony, no one has any idea of the circumstances. They figure he somehow found you and wanted to be there personally for the kill, and you were too quick, or too tough, or too nasty for him. Which means, I suppose, that next time they'll be even more careful."

"Next time," said Vlad, smiling wryly. "I can hardly wait."

"Yes."

"Are you sure they told you the truth? I mean, we're known to be friends, and—"

"Vlad, I didn't come right out and ask, you know. Trust me."

"All right."

"There's more. Everyone is pretty sure you've left town."

"Really?"

"Yeah. It's what any of them would do."

"So, for the moment, I'm safe."

"Yes. Until you do something stupid."

"Right. So I'm safe for another five minutes, anyway. All right. Anything else?"

"Yes," I said. "One more thing: there's also some speculation that you had it in for Stony personally, and no one knows why."

He shrugged. "They're wrong. So what?" Then he looked at me again and said, "All right, let's have it. Why do they think so?"

"Because otherwise why, in the middle of a fight, would you have taken the time to put the spells on him that make him unrevivifiable?"

"Huh? Oh."

"Right."

"Well, now, isn't *that* interesting."

"I thought so."

"I take it you didn't disabuse them of the notion?"

"How could I?"

"Good point. Not that it matters; they don't like me, anyway. What about his associates?"

"All four were extremely dead, as were three of Vonnith's personal guards who, as they suppose, got in your way. And so was her servant."

"Shards! All unrevivifiable?"

"Not all, but there's another interesting point."

"Go on."

"Stony was unrevivifiable, and so were all three of the Orca guardsmen, but the Jhereg weren't, and there were another three of Vonnith's private guards who weren't even touched."

"Did they see what happened?"

"No. It was all inside. Some of the guards were summoned in, and then . . ." I let the sentence trail off with a shrug.

"My word," said Vlad. "What a bloodbath! Jhereg don't kill like that, Kiera, at least not since prehistory. Only Dragons kill like that, and Dzur, I suppose."

"You're right," I said. "Dragons and Dzur. And also Orca, if there's a profit in it."

"Good point," he said. "Orca. Yes."

"What are you thinking now?" I said.

"Thinking? I'm not thinking; I'm being angry. I'll get over it."

"Vlad—"

"I've been hanging around Orca quite a bit lately. Usually, when I get to know people I begin to be more sympathetic with them. You'd have thought that, now that I've gotten a chance to know these Orca, I'd have a little more understanding of them. But I don't. I hate them, Kiera. I hated them when I was a kid, and I hate them now, and I think I always will hate them."

I started to defend them, then shrugged and said, "So you don't invite Shortisle to dinner. We still need to—what is it?"

"Shortisle to dinner," said Vlad. "That's what's odd about it—to *dinner*."

"Huh?"

"Those notes you stole from Fyres. Here, just a minute."

He walked into the cottage and emerged with Buddy and the sheaf of notes I'd stolen from Fyres's place. He looked through them for a while, then held one up triumphantly. "It says, 'Shortisle to dinner.' "

"What's your point?"

He waved the papers in front of my face. "My point, Kiera, is that it was included in his financial notes, not his personal notes."

"I'm sure it was a business meeting, Vlad. What does that tell you?"

"Everything," he said.

"Huh?"

Vlad shook his head and was quiet for several minutes, and, once more, I could almost watch him working things out. It was like seeing someone assemble a puzzle, but not being able to see the puzzle itself; it was a trifle annoying. Eventually he said, "One question."

"Yes?"

"When Stony told you he wasn't in debt to Fyres, did you believe him?"

"Well, at the time I did, but—"

"That's good enough for me."

Then he frowned, and Rocza flew out of the house, landing on his other shoulder. "I'll see you in a bit, Kiera," he said abruptly, and started walking away from the cottage.

"Wait a minute—"

"No time," he said.

"What about your sword?"

"It'll just get in the way."

"Where are you going?"

"To town."

"But—"

"Keep an eye on Savn," he added over his shoulder as he headed down the road toward Northport.

I watched him go, hoping he wasn't going to do anything stupid. I had the sudden realization that we hadn't talked about my decision to let myself be a target in hopes of flushing out whoever was behind it—back when we'd thought there was someone behind it. This mattered because, although he would come up with some reason for justifying it, especially to himself, Vlad might well feel it necessary to go and do something equally dangerous, and if I let him get himself killed, I'd never be able to explain it to Cawti.

On the other hand, I couldn't insult him by following him. Nothing to do but worry, I suppose. Savn was awake, and looking at me.

"Hello," I said. "My name is Kiera."

He looked away, then closed his eyes as if he were going back to sleep. On impulse, I stood up and said, "Come on, Savn. We're going for a walk."

He dutifully stood, and I led the way out the door, into air that was crisp with that indefinable smell of snow that hasn't arrived yet, but is coming, coming; and all overlaid with the ocean, fainter than it smelled in my Adrilankha, but still there.

Buddy got up and padded along after us, a few paces behind. It was odd, not having Rocza there—I'd begun to associate her with Savn even more than with Vlad; I kept expecting to see her on Savn's shoulder. I wondered if he had a future as a witch. Odd how the jhereg seemed to be so protective of the boy. I wondered if there was a story in it.

What now, Kiera? I'd gotten him moving; should I try to get him talking? I didn't particularly want to talk about knives.

"The jhereg, Rocza, seems very attached to you," I said. "She spends a lot of time watching over you. I wonder why that is?" Buddy came up beside us, then suddenly lunged ahead to chase something or other through the leafless trees. After a while he came back. He'd missed whatever it was, but didn't seem to mind, having enjoyed the chase.

"Although I suppose it's reasonable to wonder why anyone watches over anyone. Vlad still doesn't know why I watch over him, you know." Savn kept walking along, oblivious to me and everything else, but at least not tripping over tree roots. "Come to that," I added, "I'm not altogether certain myself." The ground dropped a bit, not like a hill, but more like a small depression, and the trees here were a little more sparse. There are many things that can cause this sort of land formation; even the ground has its story to tell. Not all stories are worth listening to, however.

"Guilt, I suppose," I said. "At least, that's part of it." We rose up again and were back in a part of the forest that was thicker; we splashed through a tiny brook, perhaps four meters across and two or three centimeters deep, running back past us toward the depression. "Though I doubt that Rocza has anything to feel guilty about. And I shouldn't still feel guilty toward Vlad. It was a long time ago, and, well, we all do what we have to.

"Vlad, too," I added. "He's a good person, you know. In spite of many things, including his own opinion, he's a good person. Maybe a bit conceited, overbearing, and arrogant, but then, people without a trace of these diseases aren't usually worth one's time." I heard myself chuckling. "Or maybe I'm talking about myself, there.

"It's odd, Savn, addressing someone who doesn't respond. It's uncomfortable, but it also frees you up in a way: you can say things and pretend it doesn't matter, that no one is really hearing them, but, at the same time, you've said them, and you don't really know what you think until you've found a way to get your thoughts outside of you, in words, or some other way. And so, my friend Savn, while it may seem that I am speaking for your benefit, to help you overcome whatever it is that pulls you away from us and from the world outside of your head, in fact, I should be thanking you. And I do.

"But enough self-indulgence. We have a problem, Vlad and I, and I'm not certain what to do about it." We had been moving in a large circle because I didn't want to get too far away from the cottage; now I caught a glimpse of it, blue and ugly, through the trees. Savn didn't look at it, he just kept walking, one foot in front of the other, careful not to trip. He was doing fine, I suppose. If there was nothing more to life than walking without tripping, I'd pronounce him cured on the spot.

I headed us away from the place, though not quite so far this time. I wondered what Vlad was doing. Buddy bounded about here and there, energetic for as old as he was. A good dog, probably a good companion for a woman like Hwdf'rjaanci, just as Loiosh was a good companion for an assassin. Or an ex-assassin, or whatever he was now.

Game, that's what he was. Hunted game. The target of the Organization he'd worked for and been a part of, but, in my opinion, never really belonged in. It's not his fault, but he's not human, and he doesn't have whatever it is within the genes of a human being that makes a Jhereg.

But whether he had ever belonged or not, now they were hunting him, and he was off doing something improbable that might make it easier for them. What? "What do you think he's up to, Savn? I doubt he'd go after Vonnith again, after how close it was last time. Endra? Reega? I just don't know. And there's nothing I can do about it, anyway, except wait and see what he comes up with. I don't like being responsible for other people, Savn; present company excepted. I don't like having to rely on them. I think that's the big difference between me and Vlad: he's always liked people, and I've always liked being by myself. So, of course, the way things worked out, he's the one who has to take off and spend his short lifetime away from everyone he cares about. Feh. No sense complaining about fate, though, Savn; it never listens. When there's nothing you can do except worry, that's a good time to worry. I don't remember who said that. Maybe me."

We made our way back to the house, Buddy preceding us through the door. Hwdf'rjaanci was washing some sort of tuber that would probably feed us later. Savn sat down near the hearth, facing out, rather than looking at it. Buddy poked his nose at Hwdf'rjaanci's leg, was petted, wagged his tail, and sat down by Savn. I said to Savn, "Are you hungry?"

He shook his head.

I nodded, pretending that having him respond to a question was the most natural thing in the world, but I realized that my heart was pounding. There was no question, we'd made progress. On the other hand, we deserved to, because we had paid for it. Or, more precisely, others had paid for it.

Fyres was dead.

Stony was dead.

Loftis was dead.

I looked at the boy, who had closed his eyes and was resting easily. At least Vlad wasn't dead. But there was still too much death. Death follows Vlad around like another familiar, and sometimes I wondered if he even noticed, much less cared. I knew what that felt like, and what it could do to you, but it wasn't supposed to happen to Kiera the Thief, who had never killed anyone, and who didn't enjoy being around when things like that were going on, and who especially hated it when she couldn't do anything about it. But this was too big for Kiera the Thief. Much too big for Kiera. And much, much too big for Vlad.

On the other hand, it was clear he had figured something out, there at the end. What? And why hadn't he told me? I hate it when he does that. If he managed to return in one piece, though, I'd be able to tell him that there was progress—that the boy had responded to a question that had nothing to do with knives, and that there was probably hope for him. Vlad would think it worth whatever trouble he'd been through; oddly enough, I thought so, too.

Buddy's head came up, and he padded out the door, his tail giving a couple of perfunctory wags. I heard the sound of a familiar walk, and something in me relaxed, and I was able to look entirely normal an instant later when Vlad walked in, looking smug.

"What?" I said.

"It's done," he said.

"What, everything?"

He glanced quickly at Savn and said, "Almost everything. Everything we can take care of, at least."

"I have good news on that front, too," I said.

"Tell me," he said, almost snapping out the words.

"You first."

"No, you."

"I—all right." So I told him about Savn not wanting to eat, and Vlad was every bit as pleased about it as I was. Then Hwdf'rjaanci came in, and I had to tell her, too, and she grew a smile, too.

When I'd waited as long as I could, I said, "All right, Vlad. Your turn."

"Sure," he said. "Let's go outside."

Hwdf'rjaanci sniffed, and Vlad winked at her. Then we went outside and he told me about his day.

15

I HID AS BEST I could, which was pretty well, in a doorway across the street from City Hall—maybe the same place you hid, Kiera—and I waited for the day to fade. I didn't feel especially safe. Loiosh wasn't fit to fly, so Rocza was doing the watching, and I was getting the information from her through Loiosh, which is too indirect for my taste, and Rocza wasn't trained for this kind of work. Loiosh attempted to reassure me, without much success.

Eventually Domm left the building. I gritted my teeth and watched him go by. He took a few steps away from the door and teleported. I kept waiting. Things were shutting down and people were going home from work. Had I missed her? Had she gone out a back way, or not been there at all, or teleported from inside the building? These are the questions that inevitably go through your head when you're doing what I was doing, and you don't have a partner. When I was with the Jhereg, I made sure people doing this sort of thing always worked in pairs, at least one of whom was a competent sorcerer. I was a competent sorcerer, but as long as I wore the gold Phoenix Stone, it didn't help a bit, and whenever I removed it, even for an instant, I was risking rather more than my life— the Jhereg are tenacious, I know because I was one, and I was as tenacious as any of them, damn them to Verra's coldest hell.

Timmer came out, walked a few steps down the street, paused, no doubt to teleport, then stopped as Rocza flew down, almost into her face, then away. She reached for a weapon, frowning, and looked for her; then she saw me walking toward her, hands in front of me and open.

Rocza landed on my shoulder. Timmer waited, her hand still on her blade. "Let's talk," I said.

"We have nothing to talk about."

"Oh, no, my lady. We have a lot to talk about. If you try to arrest me, which I know you're thinking about, you'll get nothing. If you don't, you'll find out who killed your associate, and why."

She looked like she was starting to get angry, so I added, "I didn't do it. I had no reason to do it. I suspect you don't know who did. I do. Give me a chance and I'll prove it, and what I want in return is something I don't think you'll mind giving me at all."

"Who are you this time?"

"Someone who's all done playing games, Ensign. I'm not asking you to trust me, you know. Just to listen. Can you afford not to?"

Her face twitched, and she said, "Inside, then."

"No, not there. Anywhere else, as long as it's public."

"All right. This way, then."

We walked about a quarter of a mile, past two or three public houses, and then we entered one; she was being careful, which I approved of. The place was just starting to fill up, but we found a corner, anyway. She didn't drink anything, or offer to buy me anything, either. She took out a dagger, set it on the table. She said, "All right, let's have it. All of it."

"That's my intention," I said.

She waited. Loiosh and Rocza sat on my shoulders like statues, drawing stares from everyone in the place except her. That was all right. I said, "I'm betting a great deal on a single glance, Ensign."

She waited.

I said, "The Surveillance Corps and the Tasks Group. I'm betting that you're with the latter and that Lieutenant Domm is in the former, and I'm basing this guess just on the way you looked at him that time at the Riversend. Care to tell me if I'm right?"

"You talk," she said. "I'll listen."

"Okay." I was beginning to think she didn't like me. "My name is Vladimir Taltos. I used to work for the Jhereg, now I'm being hunted by the Jhereg." I stopped to give her a chance to respond, if she cared to.

"Keep talking," she said.

"There's a boy, a Teckla boy. He has brain fever—"

"Stay on the subject."

"If you want to know what's happening, Ensign, don't interrupt. He has brain fever. I've arranged for him to be cured. The woman who's working on him is a victim of a very minor land swindle that you may or may not know about, but it's what led me into this. I believe I need some wine."

She got the attention of the host, who had a servant bring a bottle and two glasses. I poured some for myself, Timmer declined. I drank and my throat felt better. "The land swindle isn't really important," I said, "but it is, as I said, the piece of the whole thing that got me involved. And it isn't even a swindle, really—I'm not certain it's illegal. It's just a means of putting some pressure on a few people and raising prices a little—inducing panic. In an atmosphere of general panic, where everyone is wondering how bad he's going to be hit, everyone is susceptible to—"

"Go on, please."

"You know how the land thing works?"

"Go on."

"I don't think she likes you, boss."

"What was your first clue, Loiosh?"

I collected my thoughts. Someday I hope to have them all. I said, "Let's start with Fyres, then. I assume you've heard of him."

"Don't be sarcastic with me, Easterner."

Her hand was casually near her dagger. I nodded. "Lord Fyres," I said, "duke of—of whatever it is. Sixty million imperials' worth of fraud, left to a not-grieving widow, a son who probably doesn't even notice, a daughter who intends to continue the tradition, and another daughter who—but we'll get to her. Fyres was worth about sixty million, as I said, and almost none of it was real, except for a bit that he'd put into legitimate shipbuilding and shipping companies, most of whom have now gone belly-up, as the Orca say.

"Now, Ensign, allow me to do some speculating. Most of what I have is based on fact, but some of it is guesswork based on the rest. Feel free to correct me if I say something you know is wrong."

"Go ahead."

"All right. Fyres was getting fatter and fatter, and more and more large banks were involved, and many of them—many of the biggest—were so heavily involved that, when he came to them and said he'd need another fifty dots—excuse me, fifty thousand imperials—or he'd go under, they had no choice but to give it to him, because if he defaulted on his loans, the banks would go under, too, or at least be pretty seriously crippled. This included the Bank of the Empire, the Orca Treasury, and the Dragon

Treasury, as well as some very large banks and some extremely powerful Jhereg about whom I suspect you don't care but you ought to."

"Stony?"

"No, oddly enough. As far as I know, he wasn't directly in debt to Fyres at all. But, yeah, he's in this—mostly because he wasn't in debt."

"How is that?"

"Wait. I'll get to it."

She nodded. I tried to read her expression, to see how she was taking this, but she wasn't giving me anything. So be it, then.

"Eventually Lord Shortisle realized what was going on. One of his accountants found out first, but agreed not to say anything about the bank he knew was in jeopardy. He did this, you understand, in fine old Orca tradition, in exchange for having his pocket lined." I considered, then said, "Maybe several of them did this, but I only know about one. And that poor bastard had no idea what scale this was on, or he wouldn't have tried it. For all I know, this was happening all through Shortisle's department, but it doesn't matter, because eventually Shortisle found out about it."

"How?"

"I don't know, frankly. I suspect he has ways of knowing when his accountants are spending more money than they ought to; it was probably something like that."

She shrugged. "All right. Go on, then."

I nodded. "So Shortisle spoke to this mysterious accountant. I'm speculating now, I don't know the accountant's name, but I'm sure he was important in Shortisle's organization because Vonnith always referred to him as a 'big shot.' At a guess, then, the conversation went something like this: Shortisle bitched him out, and informed him he was dismissed from the Ministry and was probably going to face criminal charges. The accountant said that if he was dismissed, the news would come out about why he was dismissed and the bank would fail. Shortisle asked why he should care about one bank. The accountant, who by now had at least a glimmer of what was going on, pointed out that, once that bank failed, others might, and maybe Shortisle should find how big the problem was before creating a scandal that would result in a general loss of confidence. Shortisle was forced to agree that this was a good idea.

"So our man from the Ministry of the Treasury starts looking into things, and finds Vonnith, or maybe someone like her, and discovers that every bank she owns or runs is in danger of collapse because everything she has—on paper—is tied into someone named Fyres. So he checks on

Fyres to see who else is into him, and discovers that everyone and his partner is in the same position, and that it's getting worse." I paused. "The only reason I know about Vonnith is that she happens to own the bank that the old woman I'm trying to help saved at. There are probably scores of bankers in the same position she's in, and she only gained importance because of me."

"I don't follow you," she said.

"Never mind. You'll see."

"Continue, then." Her hand was still resting near the dagger, but she seemed interested now.

I nodded and said, "So Shortisle pays Fyres a visit—"

"How much of this do you know?" she said. "Are you still speculating?"

"Yes. This is almost all speculation. But it holds up with what's happened. Bear with me and I'll try to draw all the connections."

"All right. Go on, then."

"He pays Fyres a visit to find out what can be done. Fyres is intractable. He tries to bribe Shortisle, he tries to dazzle him, he tries to sell him. He doesn't get away with it, because, by now, Shortisle knows Fyres's history, and he also knows, or is starting to know, how big this is. So he threatens to have Fyres brought down. Now, this is a bluff, Ensign. Shortisle *can't* bring Fyres down, because it would bring down too many others and create chaos in the finances of the Empire, and it's Shortisle's job to prevent exactly that. What Shortisle wants is for Fyres to work with him in trying to ease out of this with as little damage as possible, and the threat is just to get Fyres's attention so they can start negotiating. But the threat backfires—"

"Still speculation? It almost sounds as if you were listening to them."

"Just bear with me. I may have a lot of the details wrong, but I know that Shortisle paid Fyres a visit. Chances are the conversation didn't go like that, but the results are the same as if it had, so I'm trying to show you how it might have ended up the way it did. And, by the way, with what I know about Shortisle and Fyres, I might not be all that wrong."

She shrugged. "Okay."

I nodded. "Fyres gets scared by the idea of losing everything, because he's done that twice before. If he, Fyres, is going to help Shortisle, he wants guarantees that he's going to come out of this rich and powerful. Shortisle makes a counteroffer, saying Fyres will come out of this a free man, instead of spending the rest of his life in the Imperial prisons. That's not good enough for our man Fyres—he's on top now, and he sees no reason why he shouldn't stay there. So he does something stupid: he threatens Shortisle. He tells him that he has contacts in the Jhereg—which he does—and that he, Shortisle, had better leave him alone.

"But Shortisle has a friend in the Jhereg, too; a fellow named Stony. Remember him? I promised we'd come back to him. Now, our dear friend Stony is extremely powerful in the Jhereg, and, just as important, he's not directly in debt to Fyres, and, most important of all, he's always, always, *always* willing to help out the Empire, because the Jhereg can't function without help from the Empire."

Timmer opened her mouth then, but I said, "No. I know what I'm talking about here. When I was a Jhereg, I regularly bribed the Phoenix Guards to overlook small illegalities. Nothing big, and nothing violent, you understand, but the little stuff that keeps the Jhereg earning, and keeps the Phoenix Guards in pocket change. It didn't occur to me that the same thing was happening on a much larger scale all the way to the top until I messed with the official Jhereg contact to the Empire and I saw the heat that came down on me for it—that's the main reason I'm on the run right now."

She didn't like it, but she said, "All right. Go on, then."

"So one week later—"

"A week? What is this, a hard date, or more guessing?"

"A hard date. One week after Shortisle and Fyres have dinner together, Fyres goes out on his private boat to have a nice, relaxing sail with some business associates—how many of those aboard the boat were Jhereg, by the way?"

"Three," she said.

"Okay. So he goes out sailing, and, late at night, he slips on the deck and—"

"Yes. I know that part."

"Right. Okay, so Fyres is dead. Shortisle goes into action right away. Or, in fact, he's probably ready to go into action before it even happens. He talks to Indus, explains the problem, and says they have to minimize the damage or everything falls apart, and there's major chaos, and, just incidentally, Shortisle loses his job, because the Empress is a reborn Phoenix and doesn't take people's heads for incompetence.

"So someone—probably Indus—tells Domm, who works for her, that he has to just go through the motions of investigating Fyres's death and conclude that it was an accident. Domm comes in, and, a week later, announces that everything is fine. The Empress hears about this, and the Warlord, and probably Khaavren, and they all immediately smell something funny, because there's no way you could conclude something like that in a week. So, what do they do when there's something fishy from one of the special Imperial groups? They send in the Tasks Group—yours, isn't it?" I stopped and looked at her. "That's what I'm betting my life on, you know. And I'm betting on it based on that one look you gave Domm. I don't think you're from Surveillance."

She nodded once, quickly.

"Okay," I said. I relaxed. "Good."

"Keep talking," she said.

I nodded. "So Khaavren tells Loftis to get a group together and find out what's going on. Shortisle, who always knows what's going on with the Empire, finds out about this and, instead of panicking, does something smart—he tells Indus about it."

"Do you know that? I mean, couldn't it have been Indus who found out about it in the first place, and she told Shortisle and it went from there?"

"Actually, yes," I said. "I was just enjoying putting the story together my way. But it could well have happened the other way, and probably did, because the Minister of the Houses hears even more than the Minister of the Treasury."

"It doesn't matter, anyway," she said. "Go on with your story."

"Okay. However it worked, Indus knows about the problem, and she knows how much trouble there will be, for her, too, now, if word gets out about what's going on. I'm pretty sure that the Warlord or the Empress or both were involved in sending your group in, because if it was just Khaavren, Shortisle would probably have had him killed."

Timmer looked shocked at that, and opened her mouth, but then she closed it again and nodded for me to continue.

I said, "Now, Indus, as we know, is very persuasive; she's an Issola, after all. She finds Loftis, whom she knows somehow or other—"

"They worked together when our group was called in to find a security leak in Division Six during the Elde Island war."

"Okay," I said. I still wanted to wince every time someone mentioned the Elde Island war, but that wasn't important now. "She persuades him to help behind Khaavren's back, because they both know Khaavren wouldn't go for anything like this, and they both know that, however much they dislike it, it's the only way to keep the financial roof of the Empire from collapsing and to save both of their metaphorical heads.

"So you and Loftis show up in Northport, just the two of you, with three others in reserve. Is that right?"

"Why?"

"It doesn't matter. Loftis told me there were six of you and three in reserve, and I think he was telling me a half-truth by including Domm and his people, just to test me."

"Yes," she said. "It was he and I, with some others on call if we needed them."

"Okay," I said. "Anyway, Domm is already here with Daythiefnest and three others, and they've bungled things up nicely. You and Loftis know the score, and Domm knows what's going on, but no one else does. You and Loftis have probably done a lot of things you didn't enjoy, but this has to be one of the worst—when Loftis and I were pumping each other for information, I got that out of him and I think he meant it. Your job was to cover up a murder, and, at the same time, cover up for the fact that the guy whose job it was to do the cover-up—Domm—had bungled it horribly by being impatient. That meant tracing every little indication that people thought the investigation wasn't real, while, at the same time, keeping up the appearances of making the investigation, and still coming up with enough to convince, among others, the Empress, the Warlord, and your own chief that, no, really, Fyres's death was an accident. Have I got that right?"

"Go on," she said.

I wetted my throat again. "Just about this time, Loftis learns that Fyres's home has been burglarized and his private notes taken. I'm sure he had words about that. Why didn't Domm take those notes in the first place? And why wasn't the house better protected against burglary? Answer: because Domm didn't care. Maybe—I'm speculating again—maybe it was then that Loftis realized he only had one way to go: he had to throw Domm to the dzur. That is, he was going to have to make it look like Domm was just plain incompetent—which he is—and then do the investigation himself and come up, with a greater appearance of honesty, with the same results Domm got.

"The trouble was, Domm, whatever else he is, isn't stupid. He figured that out, too."

Timmer's eyes got wide.

"You mean *Domm*—"

"Wait for it, Ensign. I'm not going anywhere, and neither is Domm."

Her eyes narrowed then, but she said, "All right." Then she said, "About Fyres's death—"

"Yes?"

"How was it arranged?"

"It was a Jhereg assassination."

"I know that. But how?"

"Huh? You should know that. Making it look like an accident—"

"No, not that. I mean, how could a Jhereg assassin get close to Fyres on his private boat, especially when he knew—when he must have known—that he was messing with dangerous matters and dangerous people?"

"Ah," I said. "I'm glad you asked. Stony set it up, and he had Shortisle's cooperation. Between the two of them, they were able to get inside help. Again, I'm guessing, but it does all fit."

"Inside help?"

"Yep. Someone Fyres trusted, or, at any rate, was willing to let onto the boat, along with a friend. Who was on the boat, Ensign? That's something you know but I don't. I think I can guess, though."

"Go ahead," she said. "Guess."

"I'd say that at least one of his daughters was there, and had a date with her. In particular, I think it has to be Reega, judging by the way she reacted when I suggested to her that the investigation wasn't entirely honest."

I waited.

"Yes," she said, after a moment. "Reega. We know she brought a date, and the guy she was with . . . yes, he could have been a Jhereg. We can still find him—"

"Three pennies that you can't."

She shrugged. "All right, then: why would she go along with that?"

"Remember the land swindle I mentioned?"

"Yes."

"That was the price. Shortisle put her in touch with Vonnith and some others, or maybe they all knew each other, anyway; they probably did. They cooked it up among themselves, with Shortisle's help, in exchange for Papa's life. That way, however things went, they each knew they'd still have enough wealth for what they wanted: Vonnith to keep her lovely house and Reega to be able to live alone and do nothing, which seems to be her goal. Of course, it could have been the wife, the son, or the other daughter; as far as I can tell they all had reasons."

"Nice family."

"Yeah."

"All right. Go on."

I nodded. "Then my friend and I enter the arena. First, there's the burglary."

"Yes. Loftis was, uh, not happy about that."

"Right. Okay, but Loftis finds himself having to work with the Jhereg, right? So he tells Stony about it, and then my friend—"

"Who?"

I shook my head. "You don't get that."

She started to object, then shrugged. "All right."

"My friend starts asking Stony questions, which information he passes on to Loftis, and then I show up, and Loftis passes that information to Stony, and then I go leading you and Domm all around the countryside, and, at about the point my feet are getting ready to fall off, we wind up at the Riversend, and Loftis gets hold of you or Domm, probably you—"

"Me."

"With orders to question me."

"No, with orders to bring you in."

"But—"

"Domm wanted to question you first. I objected, but he outranked me." Her face twitched and contorted just a bit as she said that.

"I see." I nodded. "He was nervous about what Loftis intended, and wanted to know where I fit in, and if I could be used."

"Yes. What was your game?"

"Trying to learn what was going on. Remember, all I really knew about was that our hostess was having problems with her land; I didn't even know that the investigation into Fyres's death was phony."

"And that's what you were trying to find out?"

"Yes. And I did, both from Domm's reaction and from yours, although I misread a look you gave him as indicating that you didn't know what was going on, when in fact the look was just one of contempt for him being such an idiot as to let me pump him like that. That was the last thing I got, and what made me decide to come to you now."

She nodded. "Then what?"

"Then we come back to Reega. If it *was* her who set up Fyres, and, from what you say, I'm sure it was, then it fits even better. When I showed up at her door, she panicked. She thought it was all going to come out, and someone—namely Loftis—would *really* investigate dear Papa's death, and she'd get caught. So she—"

"Arranged with Domm to kill Loftis," said Timmer, very slowly and distinctly.

I nodded. "That's how I read it."

"So why did you kill Stony and all those others?"

I smiled. "Well, actually, I didn't."

She frowned.

I shook my head. "I did kill Stony, but I put no spell on him to prevent revivification. I had no reason to, and, even when I did that sort of thing, I didn't use spells because I'm not fast enough with them. And I certainly had no time then."

"But who—"

"Think it through," I said. "Domm has killed Loftis. Stony and Loftis know each other, and Stony is in touch with powerful people in the Empire."

"Does Domm know that?"

"He has to at least be pretty sure about it. So Domm uses me to set up Stony, knowing that, eventually, I'll be sure to go blundering into Vonnith's place, or Endra's, or Reega's."

"Wait. He used *you* to set up *Stony*?"

"Yeah. That's how I read it. He probably thought I'd be killed, too, which would have been fine, but he had some of his people there to make sure Stony didn't get out alive in any case."

"Did you spot them?"

"No. But I got away."

"I don't understand."

"I shouldn't have been able to escape. My familiar here"—I gestured to Loiosh—"was injured, and that slowed me down. And, for various reasons, I can't teleport. And the Jhereg wants me *bad*. So how could I go tromping away from there through the woods and escape without even having to draw my blade? Answer: because Domm arranged for a teleport block around the house and grounds to seal Stony and his people in, then—"

"Did you feel a teleport block?"

"No, but I wouldn't, for the same reason that I don't teleport myself." She looked a question at me. I said, "I, uh, I have a device that prevents anyone from finding me with sorcery, and it has the side effect of preventing me from detecting it. Loiosh here usually lets me know if there's sorcery happening around me, but, as I said, he wasn't in any shape to do that then."

"Sorry about that, boss."

"Don't sweat it, chum."

"When did you work all this out?"

"Just a little while ago, when my friend informed me that Stony was unrevivifiable and that there'd been a mass slaughter in the house. My first thought was that it was being done so I'd be blamed, but that didn't make sense. The Jhereg were after me already, and they, frankly, have better resources for that sort of thing than the Empire, so what was the point? The point, of course, was Domm."

"Yes."

"And now, Ensign, can you figure out why it was not only Stony whose death was made permanent but also three of those Orca who are Vonnith's private guards?"

She nodded. "Three of the four who killed Loftis." She frowned. "What about the fourth?"

"I would imagine," I said, "that he died of the wounds I gave him, and was given to Deathgate Falls. And, as far as I'm concerned, you now know everything."

She nodded slowly. Then she said, "Why did you tell me all of this?"

I shrugged. "A number of reasons. For one thing, I rather liked Loftis." She frowned, but didn't speak. "For another, it annoys me to see these people tromping over lives like that—Loftis, Stony, all of those people whose lives have been messed up by the shipwrights closing and by the banks closing. And, for another, I want something in exchange."

Her eyes narrowed. "I believe that, Jhereg. What do you want?"

I said, "There are not witnesses who can implicate Domm, you know."

"Except Vonnith."

"Yes. Except Vonnith and Reega. Will you be going after Vonnith?"

"Maybe. I don't know if I can touch her. I'll have to check with—" She got a look of distaste on her features. "With Shortisle and Indus."

"Reega?"

"Not a chance. She gets away with it."

"I thought so. Well, that's fine. I don't care. Everyone involved in killing Fyres deserves an Imperial Title, as far as I'm concerned. But I do care about Vonnith."

"As I say, I don't know if I can—"

I held up my hand. "You can put pressure on her, and a little pressure is all it should take."

"For what?"

"To get her to cough up the deed to a small piece of property on the north side of town. A very small piece, a couple of acres, with a hideously ugly blue cottage on it. There's an old woman living there. I can't pronounce her name, but here it is." I passed it to her and enjoyed watching her lips move as she tried to figure out how to say it.

Then she said, "That's all you want?"

"What do *you* want, Ensign?"

She glared at me. "I want . . ." She stopped glaring, but continued staring, if you know what I mean.

"What do you want?" I repeated. "What would please you right now?"

"I . . ."

"Yes?" I said.

"Are you—?"

I looked away and waited.

Presently she said, "You used to be in the Jhereg?"

"Yes," I said.

"And what, exactly, did you do?"

I turned back to her. "You know what I did."

She nodded slowly. "The deed to the land for the old woman—that's what you're getting out of this?"

"Yes."

"That's all?"

"That's all."

"What about Fyres's personal notes?"

I extracted them from inside my cloak and put them on the table. She looked at them, riffled through them, nodded, and put them in her pouch.

She said, "Are you, uh, going to be somewhere for a while?"

I remembered the area and said, "This is as good a place as any, I think."

"Yes," she said. "I suppose it is."

She looked at me for a long time, and then she picked up her dagger and sheathed it. She reached for the wine, poured herself a glass, held it up to me, and drank. She held out her hand to Loiosh. He hesitated a moment, then hopped over to her wrist. She studied him for a moment, looking closely into his eyes and showing no sign of fear at all.

"I've never been this close to one of these before. It looks very intelligent."

"More intelligent than me sometimes," I said. *"That's just banter, Loiosh. Forget I said it."*

"No chance, boss. You're stuck with that forever."

She held her hand out and Loiosh hopped back over to my shoulder. She took out a handkerchief and wiped her wrist, then folded the handkerchief and put it away.

Then she looked at me and nodded.

"You got it, Easterner," she said.

16

AND THEN, KIERA, I waited. And, as I waited, I was just a bit nervous. I mean, you speak Jhereg—You know what we were talking about, or, rather, *not* talking about; and of course I knew, but I wasn't sure if Timmer knew. I thought she did, I hoped she did, but I didn't know, and so I sat there and waited and was nervous, in spite of Loiosh's comments designed to irritate me into relaxing.

No, don't ask me to explain that.

By this time I had blended into the background of the public house, and no one was really looking at me, so at least I didn't have that to worry about. In fact, Kiera, while I was nervous about Timmer, I wasn't really *worried* about anything; it seemed that the time for worrying was well past; besides, I had plans to make, and the time to worry is when you don't have anything else to do. I'm not sure who said that; I think it was you.

An hour later she came back and sat down. She looked at me. There was no expression on her face.

I said, "Well?"

She said, "I've asked the local magistrate for a seizure card. Just temporary, of course; until the investigation is over."

"For me?"

"Yes, for you. Of course," she added, "I don't know your real name, so I had to mark it 'name unknown,' but I know that you have information about Fyres's death, and that's what we're investigating."

"I understand. When will it go into effect?"

"In about fifteen minutes."

"Fifteen minutes," I repeated. "All right."

"Until that time," she said carefully, "I cannot legally stop you from leaving the city, or even this public house; but I would ask, from one loyal citizen to another, that you consider your duty to the Empire and remain here, as a gesture of cooperation."

"Here?"

"Yes. The card will be served here."

"Will you be remaining here as well, to serve the card?"

"I'm afraid that's impossible; I have to act on the information that you've given me. But, ah, someone will be by to serve it as soon as it's ready."

"About twenty minutes, then."

"Or less." She stared off at nothing. "Someone will be arriving with it, directly from the magistrate."

"And where is the magistrate?"

"A quarter of a mile away. To the east."

I nodded. "All right," I said.

I started to drink some more wine, then thought better of it. Wine sometimes affects me very quickly. "I'm afraid," I said slowly, "that I'm going to have to decline. I'll be running from the seizure, so you will have to send someone after me to serve it."

"I thought you might," she said. "Unfortunately, I cannot, at this time, detain you."

"I'm already being hunted," I pointed out.

"Not by the Empire."

"No," I said. "That's true. Not by the Empire."

"With some crimes, the Empire looks for the fugitive harder than with other crimes. And there are even some crimes, some very serious crimes, that never get properly handled, and where descriptions are lost or mixed up."

"I understand," I said.

She rose to her feet. "Too bad I can't stay to serve the card," she said. "But duty calls."

"In a very clear voice," I said.

"I'll see you again," she said.

"Why, yes. If I'm arrested—"

"Detained."

"Detained. Right. If I'm detained, then, no doubt, I'll be at City Hall tomorrow, being interrogated."

"And if you're not?"

"Who knows?" I said. "You know, I rather like this place. It's especially nice at this time of the evening."

"Yes," she said. She opened her mouth as if she had something else to say, but closed it again, leaving whatever it was unsaid. Then she stood and left without any ceremony whatsoever.

I waited a decent interval—say, about a minute—then I settled the score, got up, and went outside. It was a lovely, crisp day, with the winter not yet arrived. The street was almost empty of people. I looked around carefully, as did Loiosh, and we consulted.

There were about a hundred places to choose from in an area like this, but I settled on a doorway right next to the public house—it was deep, and quiet, and didn't look like it got much use. I slumped against it and sent Rocza into the air.

I stood there for perhaps twenty minutes. A few people walked by but none of them noticed me. One elderly Teckla walked past me to go into the building whose doorway I was occupying, but even he didn't appear to notice me as I stepped out of his way. You taught me how to do that, Kiera; you said it's more attitude than anything else. Maybe you're right.

"Rocza says he's coming, boss."

"The right way, or the wrong way?"

"The right way. From the east."

"Can't ask for better than that."

I let a dagger fall into my hand. It was one of the new ones. I wiped the hilt on my cloak, as much for luck as for any other reason, then took my position.

Domm walked right past me. There was a rolled-up piece of paper in his hand, no doubt the seizure card, naming some nameless person who happened to be me as a witness wanted for questioning in an Imperial investigation.

Pretty serious stuff.

I fell into step behind him, and I left nothing to chance, nor did I speak. Afterward, I continued past, walking easily, as if nothing had happened. I turned a corner, and then another, and Rocza informed Loiosh, who informed me, that no one was following me.

Interlude

"Did it seem to bother him?"

"Killing Domm? I don't think so. Should it have?"

"I'm not sure. I suppose I would have been happier if it had, but—"

"You've changed, Cawti."

"So has he."

"Not as much as you have."

"From what you've told me, I'm not sure that's true."

"Come to think of it, neither am I. But . . ."

"Yes?"

"There's so *much* you're leaving out. I can see the gaps in your story."

"I told you—"

"I know, I know."

"In any case, that was about it."

"And there's another gap."

"Cawti—"

"Sorry. You mean, you just left after that?"

"Pretty much, yes. There was a bit of excitement that proved to be nothing, and we got some reassurances, and then Vlad took Savn and went away for parts unknown, and I came back home where I found your letter waiting for me."

"Tell me about the excitement that proved to be nothing, and about the reassurances."

"All right. What is it?"

"I don't know, Kiera. It's good to hear this, but it just makes me want to find out more."

"Are you going to try to?"

"Not if you don't want me to."

"I don't want you to."

"All right."

"Should we have more tea?"

"I think something stronger."

"Good idea."

"And then some food. I'll buy."

"Thank you."

"It's the least I can do."

"Is there a hint of irony there, Cawti?"

"No, actually, I don't think there is."

17

"And then I came back here," he concluded.

"What next?"

"As I said, we arranged that I'd meet her tomorrow evening at that same place, and she'll give me the deed to this chunk of land. And that is the story of my latest triumph."

"Triumph," I repeated. "Will it still be a triumph tomorrow, when you walk into that public house to find yourself arrested, if you're lucky, or surrounded by Jhereg if you're not?"

"She promised," said Vlad smugly.

"And what," I said, "makes you think you can trust her?"

"Instinct," he said.

I bit back a nasty reply. As much as we'd both bungled these last few days, I still trusted my own instincts, so I could hardly blame him for trusting his. The thing is, I didn't trust his.

He said, "Okay, maybe that was one more screwup. But, Kiera, it felt right. Loftis was her friend, and her superior officer, and an associate. I don't know, maybe she hated his guts. But—"

I shook my head. "No, you're probably right, only—" I stopped.

"What is it?" he said.

"I don't know. A spell of some kind, centered around here."

"Aw nuts," said Vlad.

"Perhaps," I said slowly, "we had best gather up Savn and Hwdf'rjaanci and head into the woods while we can."

"I don't believe it," he said.

"I think," I said carefully, "that it was a location spell."

He gave me an odd look and said, "The Jhereg?"

"Maybe."

"Where can we go?"

I cursed softly and didn't answer.

He said, "You take the old woman and the boy and make tracks. It's only me they want."

"Wrong answer, Vlad."

"Heh."

He walked into the house, emerging a minute later with his sword belt. He wore no cloak at all and had several knives strapped to his body. He said, "Go, Kiera."

"Not a chance."

He indicated the house. "What about them? Can't you stash them someplace and then retrieve them later, if there is a later?"

Well, in point of fact, I could. Then something else happened. "Someone has just teleported into the area," I said. "About a quarter of a mile away."

"How many?"

"One."

"One?"

"That's right."

He shook his head. "If it's Mario, there's no point in trying to run, and if it isn't, well, there isn't any other one person I'm particularly afraid of."

I nodded. I felt the same way, except that I didn't have his superstitious dread of Mario.

He drew his blade and waited. "May I borrow a knife?" I said.

"You don't want to use your own?"

"I'm not armed," I told him.

"Oh, yes. I forgot." He handed me a weapon. I tested the feel, the balance, and the edge, and then we stood back-to-back and waited. Loiosh and Rocza sat on Vlad's shoulders. Buddy came out of the house, sniffed curiously, then sat down next to us; it was somehow comforting that he was there, though I didn't know if he'd be useful.

Vlad saw her first. He said, "There she is."

I turned. She was walking through the woods toward us, a sword at her side, but her hands were empty. Buddy stood up and started growling, and a glance told me that his teeth were bared. Well, well.

The woman ignored Buddy, and ignored the fact that Vlad and I were holding weapons, but nodded hello to each of us as she stopped about five feet away and looked at the cottage.

"It *is* blue," she said.

"You thought I lied?" said Vlad.

She shrugged. "It was a possibility. But you told the truth about everything else, so—"

"How did you find me?"

"In the public house," she said. "With the help of your uh, familiar, is that the right word?"

Vlad used a word he wouldn't have wanted Hwdf'rjaanci to hear. "A bit of Loiosh's skin on the handkerchief," he said. "And then you went to a sorcerer with it, and located him, because you knew you couldn't locate me."

She nodded. "Shall we go inside?"

"Let's settle it out here," said Vlad.

"Settle what?" said Timmer.

"Aren't you here to arrest me?"

"No."

"But—"

"I wanted to meet the rest of this little troupe that's caused so much trouble, and I thought you'd want to hear how everything came out."

For a moment no one spoke. Then Vlad said, "Oh."

He put his sword away, then the knife I handed him. Then he petted Buddy, who took that as a clue that everything was all right, and introduced himself to Timmer. The old woman came out as this was going on.

"Who are you?" she snapped. "And what are you doing here?"

"Ensign Timmer," said Vlad, "this is the woman we call Mother, because her name sounds rather like a sneeze and no one but Kiera here can say it. Oh, and this is Kiera—I don't think you two have been introduced yet. And this is Buddy, who I think is, really, the intelligent one of the bunch—at least, he's the one who hasn't made any mistakes yet."

Rocza hissed. Vlad laughed and said, "One of the two, then."

"A pleasure, my lady," said Timmer. "I have something for you." I heard a quick intake of breath from Vlad.

"You got it?" he said.

She smiled. "Of course. I said I would."

"That was quick. What's it been, three, four hours at the most?"

"Yes. Shall we go inside?"

"By all means," said Vlad. "After you."

We trooped into the cottage, Hwdf'rjaanci leading and Buddy bringing up the rear. Once inside, Timmer looked around the place, then licked her lips, probably because biting them would have been too obvious. We introduced her to Savn, who almost, maybe, just a little bit, might have given a flicker of acknowledgment. Or maybe not.

"Brain fever, you said?" asked Timmer.

"There is no such thing as brain fever," said Hwdf'rjaanci.

Vlad shrugged. Hwdf'rjaanci sat next to Savn, Vlad and I sat at the table. Timmer declined a chair, preferring to lean against the wall. Buddy curled up near Savn and Hwdf'rjaanci and tried to insinuate himself between them. Savn absently stroked Buddy's head. That was, as far as I knew, another first. I caught Vlad's eye and saw that he had seen it, too.

"Where shall I begin?" said Timmer. "Does everyone know what has been going on?"

"Kiera knows everything up through our conversation today. The old woman doesn't know much of anything about the affair," said Vlad.

"That's because I don't want to," she snapped. "And I won't thank you for telling me."

Timmer nodded. "All right," she said. "Do you want us to go somewhere else, then?"

"No. Say what you want, and I'll listen, but don't bother explaining it."

"Very well," said Timmer.

She turned to us. "There isn't all that much to tell, truly. Domm was found murdered, just a few hours ago. A dagger was driven into his head."

"Oh?" said Vlad with that assumed casualness he does so badly. "Any idea who did it?"

"A fugitive. Someone we wanted in connection with our ongoing investigation into the death of Lord Fyres. We think he was a Chreotha," she added.

"I see," said Vlad. "What else is new?"

"I spoke to, uh, to certain persons in the Empire, and was told to leave well enough alone." She looked like she'd just eaten a jimmberry thinking it was a rednut.

"So Vonnith goes free?" said Vlad.

"Free? Yes. Free and clear. And still rich. And still the owner, or manager, of three or four banks. We can't touch her."

"And Reega?"

"The same." She shrugged, as if Reega didn't much matter to her, which was probably true; Reega hadn't been involved in Loftis's death.

Vlad shook his head. "Not the way I'd have preferred them to end up."

"Nor I," said Timmer. "But then"—she spread her hands—"it isn't my choice."

"And?" said Vlad. "In exchange?"

She nodded. "Cooperation. They're both going to do what they can to minimize the damage to the Empire. That, after all, is what's important." In her voice was a trace of the same bitterness that Vlad had described in Loftis's voice when he spoke about having betrayed his chief.

"What else?" said Vlad.

She nodded, and, from a pouch at her side, pulled a rolled-up piece of parchment, which she handed to Hwdf'rjaanci. She took it hesitantly, looked at Timmer, then at the document. Her hands trembled a bit as she undid the ribbon with which it was tied and broke the wax with which it was sealed and unrolled it. She read it slowly and carefully, her lips moving, and I saw that there was a tear in her eye.

Vlad loudly cleared his throat, stood up, and said, "Does anyone want klava?"

No one did. Vlad sat down again.

I said, "Timmer."

"Yes?"

"Vonnith and Reega now know, or can easily learn, who it was who—"

"No," she said. "Don't worry about it. This old woman's continued health is now my business."

Hwdf'rjaanci looked up and said, "What was that? My health?"

"Never mind," I said.

She looked at the three of us one at a time, harrumphed softly, and went back to reading the deed to her land.

"Okay," I said. "I trust you."

"So do I," said Vlad. "Only . . ."

"Yes?"

"Do me a favor, and don't tell anyone how you found me. I don't think the Jhereg would figure it out on their own in a million years, but—"

"Right," she said. "Don't worry." She stood up. "I think that's it, then."

"Yes," said Vlad. "Good luck."

"And to you," she said. She looked at me and we nodded to each other, then she turned and left and it was over.

"It's over," said Vlad.

"Not quite," I said.

"Oh?"

"Care to take a walk with me?"

He frowned, then he shrugged and stood up. We stepped outside. Buddy followed us, and Loiosh was on Vlad's shoulder, but there was no one else there. We walked into the woods near the house. "What is it, Kiera?" he said.

"How long have you known?"

"Known what?"

"I'm not stupid, Vlad, and I don't think you are, either."

"I—"

"Vlad, how long have you known?"

"I hadn't been planning on talking about it," he said. "What gave me away?"

"That's *my* question."

He laughed. "I suppose it is. But you go first. When did you know that I knew?"

I shrugged. "Just now, a few minutes ago. You're sometimes very careless with your life, Vlad—especially when you're annoyed. But you're never careless with other people's. Even when you were in the Jhereg—"

"Who's life was I careless with?"

"No one's. That's the point."

"I don't understand."

"Don't you? Think about it."

He did, and I could see him going back over the last hour in his mind; then he nodded. "I see."

"Yes. You told me to get the boy and the woman somewhere safe. You asked me to, uh, *stash* them somewhere. Where could Kiera the Thief stash anyone that would be safe? It didn't occur to you to ask if there was a teleport block up, you just assumed there was, because the Jhereg, or the Empire, was coming to get you, and you can't tell if there is one or not with the Phoenix Stone you wear. So how could Kiera the Thief break through a teleport block?"

"Right," he said. "I was scared—"

"Sure. For Savn and Hwdf'rjaanci. And then there was the remark about the knife, which is what really convinced me."

"Yeah. I was panicking, I guess."

"I guess. So, your turn. How did you find out, when did you find out, and who have you told?"

"I haven't told anyone, Kiera."

"You may as well call me by my real name."

"All right, Sethra. I haven't told anyone. You should know that."

I nodded. "Yes, I guess I know that. When did you figure it out?"

He shrugged. "I've known you in both guises, you know—I mean, known you well. And there can't be many of us who have."

"No one. Only you."

He bowed his head as if he felt he had been honored; which he had been, of course.

"How long have you known?"

"Not long. Since yesterday. No, today, I guess. I don't know."

"What did I do yesterday?"

He shrugged. "It was an accumulation of little things."

"What? I'm curious. You know, I never cheat. I mean, when I'm Kiera, I only do Kiera things—"

"You almost cheated tonight."

"Oh, you noticed that?"

"I sort of guessed, at any rate—just before we realized there was only one person coming, I was expecting to see Iceflame in your hand."

I nodded. "And you almost did, especially since I knew that you knew. Which brings us back to the question: how did you know? What were these little things that accumulated?"

He spread his hands. "I'm not sure if I can even identify them all, Kie—Sethra."

"No, call me Kiera. It'll make it easier."

"Are you trying to confuse me? Don't answer that. Kiera. Yes. As I say, it was a lot of little things. This is the first time we've worked this closely together, but we've known each other for a long time, and I've always wondered why you gave a damn for a little Easterner kid. Now I know, of course."

"Of course."

"And I'm still grateful. Only . . ."

"Yes?"

"I don't know. I keep thinking of things, like the way you recruited me to find Aliera."

"There was no other way, Vlad."

"I understand that, but still. And what was that whole business with the blood of the goddess? Not that I haven't figured out who the goddess is."

"I can't tell you that, Vlad. She said it was important for you to have that vial, and that she, herself, didn't know why."

"The ways of the gods are mysterious."

"Don't be sarcastic."

"Why not?"

I shrugged. "I want to know what gave me away, Vlad."

"It was simple, really. You see, I've known you and Sethra for a long time, but I've never seen you at the same time or in the same—"

"Cut it out. I'm serious. This matters to me. I want to know."

He nodded. "All right." He got his considering look on his face and said, "Well, for one thing, you got upset once, when you were talking about how we'd been fooled, and your speech patterns changed. Come to think of it, that happened more than once. I remember when I first told you things that implied that the Empire was involved, you, uh, you talked different."

"My speech patterns slipped," I said, shaking my head.

He nodded. "Not very often, or for very long, but it was one of the things that got me thinking."

"I suppose it would be. Damn. After two thousand years, you'd think . . . never mind. What else?"

"What else? Oh, how little you ate was probably part of it, though by itself it didn't mean anything. But I know that Sethra is undead, and lives on, well, on other things, so she doesn't eat much. And, by the same token, there was the way the dog reacted to you, and—how did you fool Loiosh, by the way? He can usually tell the undead with one sniff."

"He's not as good at it as Buddy, apparently," Loiosh hissed and I heard myself chuckle and I suspected that Vlad was never going to let Loiosh forget that. "But," I continued, "there are ways to conceal the fact that one is undead. It's difficult, but—"

"But you're Sethra Lavode. Right. I keep forgetting that."

"How else did I give myself away?"

"I heard you muttering something about battle shock when you first saw Savn, and I thought it was odd that Kiera would recognize battle shock."

"Cracks and shards. I'm an idiot."

"No, I just know you well."

"Okay, keep going."

"Well, you knew stuff that I couldn't see how Kiera knew."

"Like what?"

"Like what 'he didn't break the stick' meant, and, more than that, what it feels like to have a spell-stick discharge in your hand. And you knew more about Imperial Signets and secret Imperial organizations than seemed reasonable for your basic thief. Or even your extraordinary thief."

"Oh." I shook my head. "It's starting to sound like a miracle that no one else has figured it out. That must have been what you meant when you said you got more than you wanted."

"Did I say that?" He shrugged. "But remember: no one else knows both of you. And you *are* a very effective Jhereg—I've known you since I was a child, and I never suspected that you were anything but what you seemed to be. But then, as I said, we've never worked together before. You, Kiera, have never worked closely with anyone, have you? And that's the reason, isn't it?"

I nodded. "Continue, then."

"Okay." He was getting warmed up now. "When you first met with Loftis, there was something odd in the way you reported the encounter."

"Odd? How?"

"Like you left something out—like you didn't tell me everything that happened."

"What didn't I tell you?"

"The part where you were first bluffing him, you talked about mentioning a few details about some activities the Tasks Group had done, but you wouldn't tell me what the activities were. Later, when I was putting things together, it occurred to me that maybe that was because they were things that would make you seem knowledgeable to him, but would connect Kiera with someone else for me—like something Kiera couldn't know about, but Sethra could. Am I right? Or maybe just things Kiera couldn't know about. I don't know. I think it was one of the things that first made me think there was something funny going on, although I didn't really pay too much attention at the time. But it was a hole in your report and it only made sense later."

The Jenoine at Dzur Mountain. I nodded, while trying not to think too much about the experience itself; it was one I hadn't enjoyed, and I'd been damn glad to have the help of the Tasks Group at the time. And, of course, I'd had to leave out all the other incidents that Sethra knew about from having been Warlord, but Kiera couldn't. Damn.

"All right," he continued. "What else gave you away? It's hard to think back on it this way, because I wasn't really trying to put it together; it just happened. Oh, well, I remember one thing. You—that is, Sethra—once told me that you were originally from the Northwest."

"So what's your point?"

"How easy you found it to say the old woman's name."

"Hwdf'rjaanci? That's a Kanefthali name. There are lots of people who can pronounce Kanefthali names."

"Maybe," he said. "But there are even more who can't; you'll notice that Timmer didn't try." I started to speak, but he held up his hand. "Okay, maybe it didn't mean anything by itself, but it was another piece, all right?"

I scowled at him.

"And you were too sensitive to magic—you kept reminding me of Aliera, the way you'd pick up on spells. In fact, I wasn't really convinced until you detected that teleport just now, and knew right away how many there were."

"That was stupid, too," I said, or, I suppose, growled.

He said, "Tell me something."

"What?"

"Why, Kiera? Or, rather: Sethra, why Kiera?"

"You mean why the name? In the old form of the language there are female endings of—"

"No, not the name. Although, now that I think of it, that should have tipped me off, too—a very, very old feminine version of 'Kieron.' But, no. I mean, why does she exist at all?"

"Oh, why did I invent her?" I shrugged. "At first, to keep in touch with the Underworld—it was part of the job of the Lavodes to keep track of what the Jhereg and various others were up to. After that, well, I got to like it. It was different, it was a challenge, it was scary at a time when it was hard for anything to frighten me—"

"Yes," said Vlad, his face twisting into part of a smile. "You'd hate never being frightened, wouldn't you?"

I smiled back. "As I say, I never cheated when I was being Kiera. I never used, well, anything that Kiera didn't come by herself, or any skill that wasn't Kiera's own. I've gotten to like her."

"And no one knows?"

"Only you."

He licked his lips. "Uh, Sethra—"

"Don't worry about it."

"Okay."

I smiled. "I still like you, you know."

"That's a relief."

"Kiera has never killed anyone, and I decided long ago that keeping that secret wasn't worth a life."

He shook his head. "Sethra doesn't value life as much as Kiera does, I think."

"I don't think you know Sethra as well as you know Kiera," I said.

"Maybe not, maybe not."

He didn't say anything for a while. Trying to keep my voice casual, I asked, "What now?"

He pointed to his upper lip.

I said, "Right. In addition to growing your facial hair back."

He shrugged. "I don't know. I think I'm going to bring Savn back home."

"Teleport?"

He shook his head. "It'll take a long time to get back there, and, with any luck, by the time we make it he'll be better. Some better, anyway. Better enough that he can see his family again."

"How will they react to you?"

He smiled. "I don't think I'll want to settle down there. Although, come to think of it, there is an Issola minstrel in the area I could stand to see again."

I shook my head. "I wish . . ."

"Yeah. Me, too. Wait here," he said. He went back into the cottage and returned a few minutes later with his backpack, Savn trailing along behind.

"That was a short goodbye," I said.

"I don't think the old woman likes me," he said. "But don't tell her I know. I think it would hurt her feelings."

"Vlad—"

"And, look, give my regards to, uh, to people, all right? And look in on Noish-pa when you can."

"I will," I said.

"Then that's all," he said.

"I doubt it very much," I told him.

He smiled, nodded, and began walking down the road, Savn keeping pace. Buddy and I watched them. I petted Buddy, who didn't seem to mind.

Being Vlad, and thus needing to get in the last word, he turned around just before reaching the road, and called back, "We all need work on our disguises, don't we?"

They were gone before I could think up a good answer.

Epilogue

My Dear Cawti:

It was delightful, as always, seeing you, although perhaps you don't feel the same way. If not, I can certainly understand. Maybe you were upset by what I didn't tell you, yet you know there are things that I had to leave out, both on Vlad's behalf and on my own. I had hoped I told you enough for your peace of mind. On the other hand, perhaps it bothers you not to tell Vlad those things you have chosen to keep from him, and perhaps it should bother you; I am hardly one to judge what another person's secrets ought to be.

You seemed concerned about the boy. I know no more than I told you, but do not be discouraged. You cannot expect such a complex ailment to be cured at once in its entirety. There has been clear progress, and I feel confident that, in time, his cure will be effected. As for what will become of Vlad—that is a more difficult matter to judge.

And yet, as I said yesterday, he is well, and in this matter he emerged unscathed. You cannot reach him, and I cannot reach him, and we accept this because we also know that the Jhereg cannot reach him. Of course, he always takes chances, yet he is being very careful and that is a consolation to us; and Loiosh is watching over him, and that is another consolation to us; and now I believe there may be another, of whom I cannot *speak, who has found a way to watch over him. No, you must not ask what I mean, Cawti, you must simply trust me. That is what trust is, you know: if we never. had secrets from our friends and loved ones, there would never be any need for them to trust us.*

There is little more I can say, my dear, except that I'm sorry to have caused you any distress, and I hope you can understand that I have done my best in a very difficult situation.

Let us give it some time, and then we'll meet again, and if you have any more questions you may ask them, and if you feel the need to berate me, well, I will listen and take it like a trooper. In the meantime, you know that you can always call on me if you are in trouble, and I will repeat that it was a joy to me to see you and Vlad Norathar, who seems to already have the good looks of his father and the iron will of his mother.

Faithfully,
Kiera